JON GEORGE

ZOOTSUIT BLACK

TOR

First published 2006 by Tor

This edition published 2007 by Tor
an imprint of Pan Macmillan Ltd
Pan Macmillan, 20 New Wharf Road, London N1 9RR
Basingstoke and Oxford
Associated companies throughout the world
www.panmacmillan.com

ISBN 978-0-330-41985-7

1 3 5 7 9 8 6 4 2

A CIP catalogue record for this book is available from
the British Library.

Typeset by Intype Libra Ltd
Printed and bound in Great Britain by
Mackays of Chatham plc, Chatham, Kent

ZOOTSUIT BLACK

Jon George lives in Ipswich, Suffolk. He vaguely remembers acquiring a degree in electronics, but now it's his wife who programmes the video. Supposedly gainful employment has included: telecommunications research, pizza delivery, graphic design, and driving very quickly when ferrying doctors to emergency calls.

He currently rides his motorbike when the sun is out, drinks beer when the pub is open, and is generally of a cheerful disposition.

Jon's initial publishing success was with a succession of short stories in the independent press, which was followed by the 2004 publication of his first novel, *Faces of Mist and Flame*.

Video programming notwithstanding, Jon George can still change a plug.

If you ask nicely.

Read more at
lost-in-blogspace.blogspot.com
www.jongeorge.co.uk

Also by Jon George

Faces of Mist and Flame

For Lynda

Acknowledgements

Thanks must go to Callum MacDonald for his excellent book *The Killing of SS Obergruppenführer REINHARD HEYDRICH*. I heartily recommend it, and the author, to anyone interested in this particular episode of the war. Any factual discrepancies are deliberate on my part.

Grateful thanks to the men and women who maintain the WWII museums at the various disused airfields around East Anglia, in particular the ones recording the fate of the aircraft that gave this book its name. We must never forget.

To Mark Vaughan – war historian and drinking buddy – cheers, mate!

Thanks also to John Jarrold for his editorial guidance.

To Peter Lavery and all those who make up the Team (their contribution put this book where it is now – in your hands), your help is truly appreciated.

In Germany, the Nazis first came for the communists, and I did not speak up, for I was not a communist. Then they came for the Jews, and I did not speak up, for I was not a Jew. Then they came for the trade unionists, and I did not speak up, for I was not a trade unionist. Then they came for the Catholics, and I did not speak up, for I was a Protestant. And then they came for me . . . and by that time, no one was left to speak up.

Martin Niemoller,
WWI U-boat captain and initially a supporter of Hitler;
his later denouncements of Nazism resulted in
imprisonment at Sachsenhausen and Dachau.

Chapter One

My escalating déjà vu scares me. What's worse, these freakish incidents are becoming coupled with my dreams and daytime hallucinations, the ones where I become unnerved by the possibility of somehow having manipulated the past. It's a rare complaint this: to believe that you can alter reality. And to think you may have done so already.

Consequently, I detest nightmares.

Have I changed the past?

I try to breathe. And I fail miserably.

Such a trial, such a terrible thing.

Even as it starts, the rational part of me screams that, however real the sensations I experience, it is not actually happening – the images are simply one of the many recurring nightmares and visitations from the past I have suffered during these last seven years.

But this time there is a reality like nothing experienced before.

A faint, and different, childlike, subconscious voice tells me that, yes, once again, this is all being prompted by recollection of the deaths of both my two hero grandfathers, the American Roy and the Englishman Eric – events I have never come to terms with – and particularly the strange and peculiar premonition Roy experienced all those years ago. It was his violent death, as a consequence of his clairvoyant insight during wartime, that caused me to consider forsaking athletics at sixteen, sent me on this mission to pursue a fascist, and consequently forces me to suffer glances from people when I tell them about the ghosts I see.

And now it has led me to suffer *this*. A nightmare assisted by Roy's historically significant photographs.

The striped-pyjama uniforms immediately indicate my location with stupefying realism. But those old photographs, depicting the desperate inhabitants of the camps, missed out the other sensations that I now experience. Yes, each slow-moving figure inspects me with shadowed eyes peering out from skeletal hollows, as each ghost, one by one, tries to give a puzzled smile in my direction. Each face is indeed living mummification, each body so delicate, fragile and wasted that just to be touched would hurt it, yet they clasp me to their chests nevertheless. But the photographs cannot relay the frightening silence – this mass of humanity and not a word spoken – nor do they portray the stench.

I start to giggle, they look so comical – these clown-dolls are clearly not human. I laugh and point at these caricatures, while moving among them.

In the part of my brain that knows I am sleeping, I begin fervently to hope that this nightmare will soon change. I *will* it to change. This is *too* real, this nightmare that makes me believe I am actually here in the compound.

I begin to run, slowly, through this bleak crowd, as though my energy is drained, all used up. The shadowed eyes watch my passage along rows of low huts, me still laughing loud and brash – so comical, so comical. Along past the now-silent wire fences that used to hum, still decorated with the dead flotsam of those who chose electrocution rather than continue with something less than existence. Past more huts, past a haystack of broken sticks that is not really a haystack of broken sticks; I am laughing louder . . . laughing hysterically now. Into a brick building furnished with tall chimney stacks, through corridors from whence I can imagine echoing screams being cut short, and where I spy hooks lining the ceiling. Into a room where hell itself was kept warm, where the living waifs of humanity stoked ovens with the dead from the broken stacks of human hay outside. But the reality of this nightmare is nothing like the photographic images I inspected during my studies, for the air has a taste and I want to keep my mouth shut.

My manic outburst is finally forced to abate. In a warm room with rows of thick metal doors, my laughter splutters to a halt. I begin to cry instead. In seconds, as I falter and stoop, a hand to my mouth, it becomes a lament of such strong and passionate pity, a despair from such depths that the world is rarely aware of, or acknowledges. And its echoes within the dust-filled room only help feed itself.

I shuffle on over to the crematorium, peering through the open doors with unblinking eyes, to see the still-smouldering fire and the half-burnt bodies. My sobbing is caught short in a gasp, my knees weaken, my stomach and bowels give up the fight, until finally my soul cries out and leaves me. It escapes. It flees by racing up and out of the chimney.

Up and out, and then drifting on the wind, all the time feeling the heat and yet not burning, until I am back on my feet again, dressed in my customary jeans, boots and pseudo-military jerkin. But this time the nightmare doesn't end . . . I am now standing at a street junction at one o'clock in the morning. And I realize instantly – as one does in dreams exhibiting such terrible clarity and logic – that I am just about to experience what it was like in the Hammerbrook district of Hamburg, on 28 July 1943, as nearly eight hundred RAF planes – Lancasters, Halifaxes, Stirlings and Wellingtons – began their bombing runs during Operation Gomorrah.

This part of my nightmare is totally new.

I try to draw breath, try to contradict myself about where I am. But I am not mistaken. I have researched Operation Gomorrah – initiated four days earlier, mainly against the Hamburg dockyard – and I already know the consequences of this fateful night.

This raid, I know, will be different, for it will actually *achieve* Gomorrah in a way never envisaged.

I try to draw a breath. I know I'll need it.

This impending raid will last only forty-three minutes, but each minute will kill about a thousand people – more victims than achieved by the entire Blitz on London.

I wonder if the nightmare will allow me time to escape.

But, as in all bad dreams, I discover that it is I alone who is forced to move with invisible weights attached to my arms and legs. The few people out on the streets push past me easily in their belated flight to the shelters. I, too, feel compelled to escape, yet I cannot – there is something I need to do.

But what?

Instead of running, I scrutinize the urban area around me. The junction I stand at is broad: there are many roads off it to inspect. One such avenue leads down to the river Bille. I should head for there, or maybe to the Elbe itself, but I can't stop myself from studying the neighbourhood. My English grandfather, Eric, himself flew on this same raid. And I feel this new extension of the nightmare demands careful attention. I blink and try to take it all in with a historian's eye. The four-storey houses exude a noble presence – almost as if they possess second sight and are defiantly bracing themselves for the inevitable. Nearby a siren calls out a warning in the dry, hot night air.

Dry and hot – even the weather is colluding.

I brace myself in readiness – if I cannot escape to the river, I may as well brazen it out here. For some reason it seems I *need* to be here.

Stepping over to a slender lamp post, I grip it with both hands and try to shake it. As expected, it remains immobile. Grunting with satisfaction, I undo my belt and slip it off, wrap it around the lamp post and also my right leg. I tighten the belt, and then clasp my hands together behind the post itself in a sailor's grip: the fingers of both hands hooked into each other.

It feels like I am performing some weird lover's embrace.

My breathing quickens. I already know why.

I look up, recognizing that particular engine noise – remembered from memorial flights at Duxford aerodrome and elsewhere, but here multiplied many times over.

So this is what it sounded like.

The lamp post I am holding so tightly vibrates.

Gomorrah begins.

The air pulses with that sound – one continuous throb and beat, now rumbling in my stomach and heart.

Then the bombs descend.

There comes first that insane whistle that builds to impossible intensity before it suddenly stops. A pause. Then the rabbit-punch of a brutal shock wave – a fast-moving wall of momentum and energy that shakes the ground in its thunderous passage. It is soon repeated – and multiplied. There becomes no distinction, no beginning, no end to the cacophony of violence. Yet, even as I lose track, finding I cannot distinguish one explosion from another, I know that they are only unified in their actions and are in fact individual bombs. And I somehow survive each one of them.

The damage to the nearby houses is extensive. The concussion of successive heavy high-explosive bombs destroys windows and doors; blasts holes in walls. In the adjoining streets, I can see other houses in the near-vicinity of each bomb, with every window smashed in by the fists of the shock waves. Wherever bombs have exploded inside the buildings, glass and debris have been propelled out onto the road surface like some kind of surreal snow. I myself am soon covered in scratches from flying fragments.

More screaming whistles sound as another plane passes overhead, letting loose its load of high explosives. Hamburg is being well prepared for something hideous – the terrible obliteration that is the object of Operation Gomorrah.

The subsequent stage follows quickly as sticks of incendiaries, dropped by the next wave of aircraft, flutter out of the night sky towards recently exposed attics and smashed-in windows. Larger phosphorous firebombs crash deep into cellars, to ignite with a horrible whooping noise. The individual cries of the stricken inhabitants start to increase in their frequency – I am shocked at the alien sound of a man screaming. As more planes pass overhead, further incendiaries flutter down or crash deep before exploding. Numerous fires are thus started in a city sleeping off days of summer sun, in tinder-dry buildings that have first been splintered into kindling.

People run from their hiding places, as the bomb shelters become potential death traps. But where to go? The streets fill quickly. Some head instinctively for the canals and the river. Others stand still, their faces blank as they wait quietly to go mad. As I feel my own panic growing, I never realized that there is a taste associated with fear. Yet more incendiaries tumble down, more heavy firebombs joining them. Buildings begin to explode with increased violence, masonry shrapnel clattering and whizzing about. Out on the streets it is now fatally dangerous. But where to hide?

I grip the lamp post tighter with both arms. The metal of it trembles to the engines' roar.

The scattered fires have meanwhile been linking flames, and they now begin to murmur together as one. A faint breeze on my back tells me they are all sucking in breath from the surrounding atmosphere, getting ready to sing their mutual chorus of death.

The fires are becoming one – and it grows in size.

So quickly, the wind picks up speed – sucking in further oxygen to help the swelling inferno sing even louder, and the intense heat from the fire forces the air upwards in a matter of simple physics. And still the aircraft drop their loads, so that within a few minutes the conflagration has become a single beast of mythical proportions, and it is *ravenous*.

The blast wind increases . . . and increases further. I somehow keep on my feet as I cling to the now hot lamp post – instead of rolling and tumbling along with the rest of the Hammerbrook population that has ventured out on to the streets in its panic.

Some of these frightened citizens reach out to me. I try to help them, risking my tenuous grip, but time after time I feel my fingers slip from theirs. Even though they pass too quickly to allow any chance of catching them, I persist in trying. They disappear, one by one, into the surrounding flames. I finally manage to take hold of the elbow of a woman carrying a child and I pull them close to me, both wide-eyed with fear.

The firestorm continues to scream its ululation, like a grotesque mutation of a cathedral's organ music. It belches and sighs as the devil feeds it anything that it can consume – including its human victims. Everything not firmly secured becomes airborne. Literally *everything*. Even trees become uprooted, and those that survive bend under the hurricane winds to lie parallel to the ground. A plank of wood cleaves the light surmounting the lamp post, and the horror then tries its best to surpass itself.

Opposite us, a man is thrown against a wall and, falling, is bounced along the road himself, perversely slowing in the fierce wind, while the baby he was clutching to his chest is snatched away. I cannot even hear his screams of torment above the roar of the flames. And then the reason he was slowed down becomes apparent: he is stuck to the road surface by melting tar. As he desperately struggles to escape, his clothes begin to smoke, then ignite in a sharp burst. I clasp the woman and child tighter to me. I try to call out to reassure them somehow, but can hardly breathe. Flames lick the heavens, as the inferno climbs a mile into the sky. Torrents of flame roll like giant barrels down roads and alleys – a tsunami of heat. Flames leap out from buildings, turning passers-by into stumbling torches of incandescent blue. Fragments of broken glass, pinned into the road surface by the force of the initial explosions, finally melt and run in rivulets along with the tar and human fat.

But still, I clasp the woman and her child tightly to me, the heat searing my throat.

With multiplying strength, the firestorm rises to a long final scream that seems to last for hours. Those not already dead in the cellars are suffocating because there is no more oxygen, and cannot even have the dignity of hearing their own last cries as they perish. They die recumbent, silent. The flames tower so high they now threaten the bombers *still* unloading their cargo. One plane explodes and catches fire, its crew desperately trying to escape. And still the inferno races upwards and outwards, shooting along the ground faster than any man can run. In every searing corner of this cauldron, this frenzy of hell's dancing cohorts, the living become the dead and the dead become ash.

Yet, along with the woman and child I have saved, I live through it all – just as some few actually did. But, after all, that's what nightmares are all about: to *remember* terror . . . and to still taste it.

I awake so shocked I cannot even scream.

I sit upright in bed so quickly that my back issues a painful protest.

I lunge out of bed with a desperate desire for fresh air.

Opening wider the bedroom window of my Oxford temporary first-floor bedsit, I lean out into the dawn to let the June air cool my blood. I try to force myself to inhale slowly, which causes me to suffer a brief coughing fit, but gradually the ferocity of my breathing loses some of its intensity. I grit my teeth till I am able to see properly again.

As the sweat on my naked torso begins to evaporate, a chill streaks down my back. Fresh air has never tasted so good, yet been so strange to me.

Off in the distance, somewhere near Brewer Street and Pembroke College, sounds another plaintive cry – the fourth I have heard since getting myself to the window – while nearby I hear a girl's stuttering sobs from two windows away. Just to my left, the motor of an automatic CCTV whines as it hunts out the source of these sudden noises. With a muffled bell tone a church clock announces four o'clock, but there is no town crier to declare 'All's well'.

Because it so obviously isn't.

From my vantage point, I can see bedroom lights still coming on all over Oxford, even though the sun is rising. Everyone, it appears, has been waking up at the same time. Perhaps some bleak devil has been abroad tonight, casting seeds of disharmony among the sleeping inhabitants, causing them to sweat and shiver under his deadly touch and black suggestions. The nearby CCTV seems as much affected as those people it is monitoring – its frenetic responses to these unexpected disturbances indicate that it cannot settle on one specific source. There are just too many points of interest for its normal settings to cope with.

Gripping the window sill, I lean out further. The feeling of relief after my nightmare would be complete, inspirational even, if it weren't for the mournful sounds emerging from the previously sleeping city.

I utter a long sigh almost wishing never to dream again – never to suffer again the pain of my own subconscious being laid bare in such a frightening fashion. It was so much worse tonight than the other nightmares I have experienced over the last few years.

Visiting the death camp has been a recurring motif for me in bad dreams ever since my grandfather Roy's funeral. But tonight's hideous sequel involving Hamburg is some new dimension of terror never visited before.

Yet I have actually been to that city – as a child. I recall playing with my older brother and sister in a park there. It was a simple game of tag, but they were unable to catch me – early evidence of how I would later excel at athletics. Their adult lives would take them in very different directions from myself, along paths *they* seemed destined to head down, as naturally as my own would be to me.

Michael has followed our father and grandfather

Roy into the army. As Second Lieutenant M. Anderson, he is currently on some sort of secondment in America where he is training with the Yanks. Susan has shown herself part of the same mould by enrolling as an army nurse. Stationed now in the Falklands, she has her eyes set on a civilian doctor who, knowing my sister, had better accept the inevitable and propose to her soon. After demonstrating a potential to excel at athletics – the decathlon was my chosen field since about the age of fourteen – I myself took the family mould and shattered it. At sixteen I finally told my father where he could stuff Sandhurst – that was *some* Christmas. At eighteen I went off to study history at some godforsaken little university to specialize in WWII, while still enthusiastically pursuing athletics – a decision that confused and angered my father even more.

It's now seven years since my discovery that grandfather Roy's prediction about the neo-fascist Pascal Toluene was coming true. Just before his death, resulting from injuries received at the hands of Toluene's thugs, he showed me what he'd forecast in his diary. He'd missed absolutely nothing; it was as if he'd visited the future. It is my anger at his needless death that motivates me now. It affected me traumatically. That is why I'm here in Oxford for discussions with a visiting American professor about doing further research in the States – which will mean getting closer to Toluene, who I realize, from my grandfather's guidance, must be stopped at all costs. I am also celebrating an offer made to me by an IT company, to partake in a promotional youth experiment they are hyping up as a competition. It entails a sort of reality Internet at a new level, and it will give me a useful public platform from which to express my passionate views about the dangers posed by Toluene and his growing followers. Athlete turned political prophet – that should attract the curious.

The path I've chosen could prove a dangerous gamble . . . but I consider time is running out to make people aware. I may just have to take the risk that nobody will believe me, but I owe it to my grandfather's memory.

This last week of selection for the IT experiment has been chaotic, but now it all appears to be falling into place. It seems I *will* get my chance to expose Pascal Toluene using worldwide publicity, so American academia and their sports facilities will probably have to wait.

I am convinced that Toluene is somehow entwined with the nightmares I have endured since my grandfather's murder. Roy always motivates me. I keep a picture of him in my wallet.

So, I stand here and remember running barefoot across the grass in that park in Hamburg, outpacing my older brother and sister, and loving the attention and smiles from my parents, while still blissfully unaware that somewhere in the earth below me – perhaps still in the breeze – was the ash of that dreadful night in July 1943.

As I move away from the window, the murmur of sobbing and shouting all around remains constant . . . is even increasing. A threatening disquiet steals through the night, as the local population seems to be suffering as I have just done and I wonder, incongruously, if it has anything to do with the recent unusually hot weather. Oh, to be by the sea.

Suddenly I am assailed with an incredible longing to be home with my family. I actually sense it calling me, like a living thing.

But I've never before had that nostalgia for home. *In fact I couldn't wait to get away from it.*

My early years were spent following my father's military postings around the world, but that hamlet on the Suffolk coast where he eventually settled was the place where I passed most of my youth. I have been intending to head back there over the next few days, to attend TC's mother's funeral. Toni Cartermann is someone I had grown up with in my teens and, being the daughter of an influential television producer, it was she who pointed me towards the IT opportunity I am about to embark on. Her mother, the producer, was recently killed in a horrific car accident, and I had not really been looking forward to seeing my old friend under such trying circumstances. But now there is this awful compunction to return there as soon as possible. It's as if I need to check that the place is safe, that nothing terrible has happened to it – that at least my *home* has been spared this same weird night all around me. I have never known such homesickness as now besets me.

The cries and shouting outside continue unabated.

As I head for the shower to wash the residue of sweat from my body, I again hesitate. I stand at the bedroom door, looking over my shoulder towards the open window. And I ask myself, what if *everyone* – not only in Oxford, but throughout Britain, the entire sleeping *world* – has suffered these appalling nightmares at the same time?

Is it something sweeping across the world as it turns?

For some further moments I cannot move. Then I look down and notice I am unwittingly cradling my genitals, as if subconsciously protecting myself from harm. And so instead I rapidly shadow-box – to loosen up and instil some bravado. But there is no one watching to convince.

Dr Jake Crux is one of a minority of people in Britain who has not been asleep – in fact the American scientist hasn't even noticed what time it is, so engrossed in confirming the latest scientific theory at the Eisencrick Institute. Jake believes his experiment is now approaching some sort of fundamental turning point, that something important is there and ready to be detected – if only he continues to study the evidence long enough. A professional assiduousness prevents any possibility of sleep for him – not to mention the huge quantities of extra-strong Java coffee consumed over the last eighteen hours.

Jake drains the remains of his mug and leaps up for a refill. In the cramped room he skilfully avoids banging his elbow against a nearby monitor – the world not being built for men of his stature. He glances up at the mini-camera positioned in one corner of the ceiling, and wonders if his balletic reaction has been recorded for posterity. As he taps another monitor with a finger, Jake momentarily catches sight of his reflection in the long window separating his office from one area of his experiment beyond. He continues to track his own image as he moves to the far end of the room, realizing that he does not resemble the archetypal scientist. Rather, Jake looks like a brutish bald-headed NFL Running-Back caught moonlighting as a night-watchman in some high-tech china shop. And he is contradictory in other ways.

Ever since taking up chess at the age of ten, Jake has been making himself fantasy dragon chess pieces out of plastic, or carving them from wood and stone, even using – with such large hands – fine sable brushes to paint their miniature faces. So he is not inherently clumsy, then; it's just that around his equipment, he appears to be so . . . *big*, so out of place. And instead of the mandatory lab coat, he wears faded black jeans, a lightly starched white shirt and an embroidered waistcoat. He suspects his superiors tolerate his casual attitude to the clothing rules only because he may be on to 'something good'.

In contrast to him are the clean, white surfaces and straight lines of the room he works in. Besides twelve flat-screen monitors, whose screens are each sectioned into dozens of separate cam-shots of individual mice, it contains two chairs and another, tidier desk complete with its own PC for general office use. The secondary chair is standard office furniture, but the one Jake mainly occupies is a large, leather, company-executive swivel model purloined from a manager's office, with gaffer-tape patches covering the parts that have split through constant use.

The wall facing the window sports a large poster of Buzz Aldrin standing on the moon, and right beside it is a postcard of a UFO with the stencilled legend: 'JOE'S ICES – STOP ME AND BUY ONE'. Elsewhere on the same wall are about a dozen images of various dragons cut from books and magazines.

The coffee percolator sits at one end of the bench supporting the row of monitors. Four different brands of coffee beans are arranged alongside it, together with the grinder but no milk or sugar. Six old mugs hang on a rail above, each labelled with one of the days of the week and each one a different colour of the rainbow. The gap in this collection is for the one Jake is currently using: Yellow Monday.

Armed with a fresh caffeine supply, Jake resumes his position before the bank of monitors. He settles back into his chair and starts to raise the mug to his lips, then pauses – his mouth half-open – and glances from one screen to another, then back again. Jake slowly puts down his mug and pushes it to one side of the desk, sliding a keyboard closer to him. As he quickly taps in commands with a touch-typist's skills, each of the screens begins to flicker as one collection of images is replaced with another, but similar, set.

Within seconds, Jake manages to scan through hundreds upon hundreds of pictures of individual, but identical-looking, white lab mice. What arouses his professional curiosity, what made him pause in the first place, is the huge number of cam-shots momentarily highlighted in a border of red – a software response indicating that the vast majority of mice are performing the completely identical action of cleaning their whiskers. It is as though some malfunction has caused the very same image to appear on multiple screens. Even as he watches, the red borders begin to switch off – their synchronicity breaking down as the animals turn to other activities.

Jake pushes his chair away from the bench, its casters protesting, and stares through the viewing window into the larger area beyond. He minutely scans the entire laboratory that contains the cloned mice – his gaze moving from cage to cage – and ignores the thrill of suddenly discovering that the rules of a game have been changed.

There have been previous small hints that his experiment was about to yield its potential. That is why he decided to stay here on watch tonight, even though everything is being constantly recorded.

And then suddenly, before he can contemplate further a surprising sense of apprehension, even as he begins to suspect that it might be coincidental, something materializes before him.

The adjacent room seems unexpectedly ablaze with a tremendous fire – its flames a fierce red and yellow – till billowing smoke clouds the partition window and obscures the cages. Perplexed that he didn't hear any explosion that might have caused it, and before he can leap to his feet to hit the fire alarm, a gap appears through the flames and smoke, and a large green eye blinks in at him from the other side of the window. He recoils as, unbelievably, the smoke rolls away further to reveal an entire head that might belong to some giant species of lizard. A Komodo dragon or some sort of medieval demon brought to life? It just stares at him – alien, reptilian. Jake also senses that behind it, deeper in the flames, there are other things, other creatures – imps and grotesque goblins?

The blaze intensifies, as if some sort of Armageddon has erupted before him. He imagines he can hear the low moaning of the damned as they burn in a heat that he, strangely, cannot feel. Their faint screaming seems worse because he cannot quite discern what it is they are yelling. Jake has a twinge of frustration, since he is convinced their utterance is of serious import.

Though his mind is piqued at the discovery, he also realizes that somehow he physically feels weak and nauseous. The sudden empty feeling in his gut makes him perversely think of black holes – huge gaping chasms in space where everything, including light, gravity and time itself, is swallowed and removed from existence. To flirt with such an entity, to fly too close to it, would be to risk everything. Jake now thinks he is being shown what it would be like to feel the fear of the damned dangling above the chasm of Hell, and he is able to envisage those very souls, which he imagines he can now hear, stretching out their hands, begging him to help.

Goddam it, what a hallucination!

Then, with a flash of intense white light, the dragon is gone – taking with it the fire.

For ten seconds, Jake seems to have witnessed a terrible conflagration – he still, stubbornly dispassionate, feels correct in equating it to a twisting distortion of the universe that has somehow affected him in its physical presence – and now, just as suddenly, everything is as it was before. There is no visible damage.

He feels as though the universe is sliding back into its normal course.

If it was somehow real, then what could it have meant? The universe itself changing . . . somehow shifting?

Jake struggles to think rationally, but the only thought, the only notion that shouts within his brain, is of an acute, deep-set foreboding.

There was genuine evil there. There was malevolence in those creatures.

It has been a long time since Jake Crux has been genuinely startled, and he finds that experience an affront to his senses. As he begins to recover, he shakes his head in disbelief.

Then Jake discovers something else regarding himself that disturbs him bizarrely. He may have recently formed an embryonic relationship with a certain young woman named Toni Cartermann, but at the moment he still has no one to go home to. He now considers TC the only possible escape route out of solitude to have been presented to him in years. This realization makes him feel as though someone has held up a mirror to his soul – and he has never liked that sort of close inspection.

While still staring around at the monitors, he grudgingly considers his present feelings of loneliness more frightening even than any hellish hallucination perceived through some shift in the universe.

He feels it to be *ominous*.

And so the whole universe was completed. By the seventh day God finished what He had been doing and stopped working. He blessed the seventh day and set it apart as a special day, because by that day He had completed His creation and stopped working. And that was how the universe was created.

Tuesday
Day 7

Chapter Two

Jake doesn't simply walk as he heads down the connecting corridors – it's more akin to a big cat on the prowl, apparently ignoring the whirr of the company aerial-security CAMIC – a miniature airborne camera fitted with a microphone – following his progress. The silence of his footfall never gives colleagues ample warning of his approach, so he often surprises them.

One wall of the long passage is lined with floor-to-ceiling windows, the other is solid white brick, devoid of any decoration. Maybe the architects – more probably, the managers of the Institute – thought that unnecessary, as the expanse of windows opposite provides ample visual stimulation. Giving a panoramic view of the river Deben, upstream is the red-roofed country town of Woodbridge, Victorian, quaint and a now polished middle-class commuter retreat, and, beyond it, the ancient Saxon burial ground of Sutton Hoo – also visible if you open a window wide enough to look out of. Downriver is the small marina of Waldringfield, in which an unusually large flotilla of yachts currently sits at anchor. That would be picture-postcard pretty and reassuring, if it weren't for the fact that the navigable waters of the world have become particularly unpredictable recently – the nearby North Sea into which the river Deben runs being no exception. Days of intermittent, immensely thick sea fog have kept all pleasure boats at harbour, though the weather has been clear now for the last week. With unseasonable and savage typhoons in the Pacific and hurricanes in the Atlantic disrupting container and oil-tanker traffic, nobody is currently keen to be out on the open seas.

The view in front of him also includes the research complex gatehouse, under siege by about thirty noisy demonstrators.

During recent weeks, scientific institutions like the Eisencrick, all around the world, have been plagued by increasingly vocal protesters. They are furious, apparently, with the direction science has been taking the world, and now intend to do something about it. This unease has been prompted by a growing suspicion that the nightmare hallucinations, experienced globally just three weeks earlier, were caused by some rogue government experiment gone wrong. A mind-control satellite is the latest conspiracy theory, and the fact that every individual apparently suffered quite distinct visions supports their argument, they are claiming.

Jake knows that their irrational reactions follow classic terror-management theory – whereby those persons forced to consider their mortality are more prone to harshly impose their world view on others around them. But those accusations and the subsequent denials by governments and scientists just seem to intensify a general belief that something somehow has gone terribly wrong, and science is to blame. The whole world has been scared witless and is seeking an answer, however obtuse. Yet, as Jake realizes, *something* must have caused it.

The phenomenon was established to have begun at approximately two-forty-seven GMT in a longitudinal line extending from the North Pole, through Sweden, down through Libya, South Africa and thence to the Antarctic, and then swept westwards around the world in less than six minutes. To all intents and purposes, it seemed solely confined to humans. Asleep or awake, young or old, idiots and geniuses, astronauts in space, submariners under the Arctic ice cap, presidents and undertakers . . . *everyone* suffered, succumbing to terrible visions that lasted from just a few seconds to a quarter of an hour. And they were completely personal: as if some probe had deliberately plucked out an individual's innermost fears for closer examination.

Biologists to astronomers strove for instant explanations. Psychiatrists and psychoanalysts found themselves overwhelmed with new patients. But the only scientific physical evidence came from electromagnetic sensors detecting a momentary spike during the rapid worldwide transit of the event, and from seismographs picking up minute tremors extending many miles deep into the Earth's crust.

Jake has joined in many dispassionate discussions with his senior colleagues about the traumatic incident. But whatever rational or scientific theories they provided between them, the grim reality was that – apart from the devastating tragedy that all foetuses up to the age of eight weeks spontaneously aborted – hundreds of people had died in accidents occurring on Earth's dayside. Thousands more were seriously injured. And though the event – or The Night, as most of the Western hemisphere now referred to it – might have eventually faded into being considered just another quirk of nature, the freak weather evident since then has sustained a fear of what might happen next.

The short blast of a two-tone siren stops Jake in mid-pace. The aerial CAMIC tracking him nearly overshoots, and whines as it turns around to compensate for his sudden change in pace. Jake snaps his head round, looking back over his shoulder towards the gatehouse, where a police car is pulling up, its blue lights flashing. The driver switches off the siren, then the engine, but not the pulsing lights. He and his colleague get out of their air-conditioned vehicle and, even though in shirtsleeves, appear to wince under the intense heat outside. They adjust their caps, and head towards the noisy group of protesters. Jake surveys the crowd, opens one of the windows, and decides to wait for the outcome.

The majority of the dissidents seem to be in their late twenties, like Jake himself, and mostly dressed in the turquoise-and-white camouflage, pseudo-army gear, currently popular with students. Without exception they wear the scarlet ribbon that has become the symbol of anti-science protests worldwide – some encircling their heads, others their upper arms. The sole elderly couple among them is holding hands, attached to each other by a ribbon around their wrists. To Jake's experienced eye, these protesters exude purpose – there definitely seems a common power to their cause.

A mob indeed.

If it wasn't for his own position here, Jake feels he might enjoy researching them. Their group purpose would be interesting to get amongst, to monitor and study. As they might equally wish to study their opposition.

Jake Crux reckons he went bald at puberty because his hair took fright at the large amounts of testosterone starting to course through his body. He is tall and broad, with an old face on a bodybuilder's shoulders, and would look equally at home on a faded poster for bare-knuckle fighting: The Pennsylvania Puncher. At twenty-eight, he could easily be mistaken for someone in his early twenties, yet at other times he can appear like a man in his late forties. It is the baldness that will forever place him in a limbo of ageing – until finally he withers away at ninety.

As a kid, he imagined his small home town near Scranton, Pennsylvania, as some place lost and forgotten in time. It seemed a remote purgatory to someone of his burgeoning intellect. He even used to fantasize that he lived somewhere in the Chinese hinterland, where fabulous dragons still roamed. His parents thought him peculiar and he did little to change their opinion.

Along with the other local teenagers, Jake would take the bus daily from his imagined mystical China into a suburb of Scranton to get to school. There he excelled and the others in his year were inclined to bully him for his scholastic success, but he'd at least been taught by his father how bullies like victims, rather than kids who stand up for themselves, and he soon found he could punch hard and with a scientific precision. Yet, for all his solitary status, Jake was fascinated by how the other children would be calling each other degrading names one second, and then cutting their thumbs in blood-brotherhood the next. He particularly observed how readily the other kids formed themselves into gangs and alliances.

And then, in the midst of this silent purgatory to which he had been condemned by the other pupils, an angel appeared. When a newly qualified teacher became his year tutor, Jake quickly became her personal project. In the years following, achieving grades far in excess of anybody else at his school, he ended up in university, in this case Harvard. His scholarship there made the news – local boy done good – though reporters had trouble finding anyone legitimately claiming to be his friend. At Harvard, he studied evolutionary anthropology and biology, and acquired a taste for strong coffee. He subsequently exploded onto the scientific scene with the publication of his research paper entitled *Group Culpability*. With that he became one of the first scientists postulating that mankind's desire for knowledge is due to an inherited desire to copy the best. *Because that's what has made humans successful*, he explained, *the ability to copy*. His new theories caused a seismic stir, and soon became incredibly fashionable.

So Jake found himself snapped up by the prestigious Eisencrick Research Institute and shipped over to Britain to work in their extensive labs in Suffolk. They had made the proverbial offer he couldn't refuse. They now pay large amounts of money monthly into his bank account and, apart from their intrusive on-site security system, just leave him to get on with it. Having bought himself an old house – big gables, huge windows – near Dunwich, he allocated one room to his chessboards and a workbench for the construction of his fantasy chess pieces; and purchased little other furniture except for a huge bed for his room overlooking both the heath and the sea. Every few months, he heads up to London to stock up on his quota of small, black, expensive cigars at a specialist tobacconist, and to maybe also buy another waistcoat of the kind he favours or again visit the anthropological section of the Natural History Museum. He also has additional interests now.

One evening he had been sitting smoking one of his favoured cigars outside a local pub, when a young woman came out to ask him for a light. They formed an instant bond. Unfortunately, his subsequent tentative relationship with TC had been only two dates old when she had to deal with the trauma of her mother's death. He has not yet found an opportunity to see her again, but deeply wants to because he suspects she has intuitively guessed what he hides behind his professionally aloof exterior. For when Jake manages to take a rare day off, he likes to get on his 1200cc Harley Davidson Sportster motorcycle – shipped over from home and stripped of all its accessories down to its mean core – and make a lot of noise roaring along the country roads, exhibiting an exuberance that few people suspect he possesses – except maybe TC.

For some reason, the thought of her makes him feel satisfyingly happy. He gets so taken in with euphoria that he is totally unprepared for how his universe is just about to shift.

The change in reality is effected more violently than on The Night itself.

Glancing at his watch, Jake is about to turn away from the window and head on to his laboratory, when several warning flashes of a vivid hallucination assail him, more potent and far beyond anything he could previously imagine. Stumbling, he puts out a hand to stop himself from falling over. The clarity of the new sensation is incredible, and in the same instant, Jake *knows* for sure he is not just undergoing some mirage of the mind. Instead, he is increasingly aware of being physically transported: flashing images of alien surroundings growing more frequent, till the corridor around him begins to flicker and finally disappear.

Click, click . . . *click*!

It is done.

Jake has been removed from one reality to another: he is in an alternate universe – a real, bona-fide other place where the rules of perception are different. He tries to engage the scientific part of his brain, to monitor every sensation, even though aware that he's momentarily stopped breathing.

It is literally another world – perhaps another time – astounding in its clarity and totality of sensation. There is none of the distortion and indistinct image blurring that occurs when a mere idea takes shape in the mind's eye. He can feel the light, warm breeze on his cheeks; he can smell the country air, the grass of the flood meadow, the slight rank nip from the mud of the riverbank, the musk from the tall reeds. And he has to narrow his eyes against the glare of the sun.

He finally manages to inhale a few quick breaths, as he brings his horse to a stop.

Jake looks down, astonished to find himself dressed in armour *astride* a horse, then he glances back up again, and, fascinated, begins to study his location, looking for some sort of answer. All the while, he has a strange feeling that he is being observed.

The water meadow is all thick-bladed grass and dog-daisies, with a number of huge oaks looming round its borders. A river meanders through, its course indicated by bulrushes and willows. The scene is classic pastoral England, but Jake senses that it is an England of long ago; there is no haze of pollution in the distance, only the clean blue horizon and the hint of forest adjoining forest. Jake looks back to the river, where mayflies rise from the water's surface to swirl by the banks, and the only distraction of sound is the trout sucking down any emerging insects with a *slurp!* The swarms of insects continue their dance, swallows and martins joining in with their own song, as they flit in amongst the mayflies, taking their toll.

An alternate reality? Some parallel universe?

And yet, tranquil though it all seems, he cannot dispel the feeling of something ominous, that sensation of being watched.

Then the birds suddenly shriek away, and even the trout stop rising. Jake turns around in his saddle and gasps at what he sees.

What kind of world is this? This is *a fantasy – isn't it?*

Over there, through the trees, he can see a fully grown wyvern – a two-legged dragon-dinosaur with no forelimbs, but with wings sprouting from its back instead. Standing twice the height of a man, it seems the embodiment of gargoyle evil. Gone are the soft emerald scales of its infancy, now replaced with razor-edged plates of aquamarine possessing a metallic sheen; while its youthful transparent fairy wings have thickened into bat-leather, so that now, even loosely folded, they arc high above the beast's snake-like head, sweeping downwards to the ground near its ebony blood-smeared talons. The monster has the air of having just returned from battle.

Jake immediately feels that he recognizes this place: recalling a picture cut from a magazine, which he has stuck on his laboratory wall. It illustrated the old children's story about a girl called Maud and the dragon she had looked after from its infancy. Jake also develops a horrible feeling that he is in a world, and a time, which is actually a metaphor – a premonition in which the ending is not obvious. That realization removes his sense of being an impartial observer and makes him suddenly nauseous.

The wyvern is not a clean creature. From the end of its barbed tail, extending up past its muscular legs to its spiralled horns, there is a coated layer of dirt and filth amid strands of decaying flesh. The smell of it, drifting on the breeze towards him, makes Jake choke. It has a fetid marshy tang.

He can imagine its habitat: some blackened dell resembling a charnel house. Broken, charred, skeletal corpses of sheep and cattle strewn everywhere, stripped of most of their meat – and what remains is putrid and flyblown. In several places the more recent remnants of humans – a skull missing its jaw, the crown of it cracked open, the edges of the eye sockets scored with teeth marks.

How involved with this universe will I get? the objective part of him asks. *Am I supposed to kill this beast?*

The wyvern pricks up its ears.

It raises its head a little higher and snorts, beating its wings a number of times. Then the wyvern contracts its neck and crouches down, beginning to ease its bulk through the bushes, its ears now flattened down below the horns.

What now?

It seems Jake does indeed have to get involved.

He dismounts from the horse, his armour grinding against the chain mail undergarment. He lets the reins fall from his hand, instinctively takes up a lance and shield, pushes the horse away from him and takes a few steps forward. Tightening his grip on the weapons, Jake gradually steadies himself for action.

He then glances down at himself, as best he can. His armour seems a collection of various styles – but from the ease with which he moves, it clearly has become customized with years of use. He eyes it appreciatively.

Though helmetless, he is covered by a sleeved shirt of mail extending down as far as his hips, over which he wears a brigandine of flexible torso armour – plates of metal encased in leather – which resembles a long waistcoat made of two back sections sewn together. It is where the leather has worn that the metal plates rub against the mail, creating a faint, grinding squeal. He squints further down, at his feet, and then he checks the rest of his body. Over his calfskin boots, he has a pair of scratched and rusty greaves to protect his lower legs; his shoulders are covered with oversized cup-shaped spaulders that make him feel wider across the shoulders than he already is. On his hands he wears gauntlets that have had the finger protection removed – so he is better able to grip his lightweight lance and his kite-shaped shield which he suspects some Norman soldier must have discarded a couple of centuries before. Hanging from the thick belt is a long sword in a scabbard. He is clearly a man who has fought before. Jake flexes on the balls of his feet a number of times to ease his tension. There is an economy – a sort of natural hunter stealth – in his instinctive actions. For all his strange garb, there is a feeling of the totally practical about his armour. Jake stops stretching. He feels ready.

Okay, let's do this, and sort out the logic later.

Jake adjusts his grip on the shield and readies his lance. He licks his lips – he has never known having such a dry mouth before. He rolls his shoulders under the spaulders. The horse whinnies and shies away to his right. Jake glances briefly at the animal, then turns to brace himself.

He feels a kind of fist tighten in his chest. Then the moment passes, and the silence breaks.

There is a splintering of branches, a wild screech, and the wyvern bursts out of the undergrowth. Jake takes a step back. This should be a moment of intense terror, but he is somehow aware that . . . no, he *knows* that his destiny is tied up in this moment. He has a profound knowledge that this *has* to be done, that he *has* to kill the monster – it should never have been allowed to grow this big.

The wyvern stops in its charge, just out of reach of the lance. Jake senses that the animal is calculating the danger he represents.

The wyvern steps sideways, then backwards, extends its wings and flaps them a number of times, as if testing the air. It snorts out smoke and tries to fix Jake with its reptilian eyes, as if to distract him in their mutual deadly intrigue.

Jake lowers his shield, leans forward so that the point of his shield digs into the ground, and suddenly jabs out with his lance.

'Come on, you mother! What are you made of?'

The wyvern emits a gust of flame, then its wings begin beating in powerful strokes and it takes to the air. Higher and higher it rises into the sky, then hovers for an instant before swooping down on Jake. It screams at him with a howl of flame. As the blast-wave rushes in on him, Jake thrusts up his shield and crouches behind it.

Flames envelop his narrow defence, and Jake is pushed backwards by the pressure, but still keeps on his feet. The creature's two wing tips meet to strike him about the head, slicing through the intense heat to crash about his ears. Jake curses as the heat of the flame buckles the metal of his shield, smoke billowing on either side of him. The wyvern then flies off quickly to Jake's right.

He takes a step to his left and turns the shield again, keeping its slender protection between himself and the dragon. It screeches again with another explosion of flame. Jake feels his forehead singe, but not too severely.

Damn it!

As the latest assault subsides, Jake risks a look at his adversary. The wyvern's throat is now so bloated from its expulsion of fire that the scales there have lifted to expose the flesh below. As this bulge contracts, the wyvern rises into the air. Now directly above Jake, the down-thrust from its wings throws up dust, so he is blinded.

Think!

Instead of taking time to wipe his eyes, Jake throws himself to the ground, clutching the hot metal of his shield above him. With a further scream of combustion, he is immersed in heat again, the flames licking around the shield towards him. There is a heavy thump on the ground as the wyvern lands near his head. As the blast of flame continues, Jake is aware that the wyvern is moving in closer. He can now see its talons – could even *touch* them if he wished. But before the latest fiery maelstrom has time to die away, Jake throws his shield to one side, rises up into a crouch and thrusts his lance at the exposed area just below the monster's jaw. As he pushes up towards his target, Jake knows he will not get a second chance.

The lance makes contact where the wyvern's throat has again distended. With a grunt, Jake uses both hands to drive the lance in deeper. Spurting blood scalds his fingers, and the wyvern's scream sounds like a cry from the devil himself. It is only cut short as blood gushes into the beast's lungs. With the gurgle becoming obscene, the wyvern rips its head away, opening the wound further as the lance is worked free. Giving three powerful flaps of its wings, it rises above Jake's head, then suddenly falters, and the next beat of its wings possesses no strength. After another feeble effort, it tumbles to the ground. The bones of one wing crack with a snap, the other wing whips Jake across his face.

The wyvern calls out mournfully. Then it calls again.

Jake finally drops the lance and unsheathes his sword. He hoists it aloft in both hands and begins to swing it back around and over one shoulder, then again and again, to gather as great a momentum as possible before delivering the coup de grâce.

A high-pitched shriek suddenly causes him to pause. A young girl runs out from the copse, straight over to the wyvern. Jake had forgotten about her – the other character associated with this story, this fable that he is now being forced to re-enact in another universe. This clearly is Maud, who raised the wyvern from birth. The story is really about her. Maud has never been able to see the wyvern for what it is – to her it is just a sweet little pet. With blood still pumping from the gash in the monster's throat, Maud bends over and pushes her hands to the wound, desperately trying to stem the flow. But her small hands cannot span the massive rip. She frantically scrabbles amidst the worst of the gushing blood, but nothing she can do is of any good, and gradually the spouting of blood diminishes. The little girl turns for a moment to stare at Jake with tears in her eyes.

He sheathes his sword, then bends down to pick up the bloody lance and blackened shield. Walking away to collect his horse, he doesn't look back.

Just as he reaches his mount and goes to take the reins, the universe shifts again in a series of crossovers and flashing images. Though it is again so sudden, Jake is better prepared this time.

Click, click . . . *click*!

He blinks rapidly. Through the corridor windows, he can see an animated discussion still going on between a couple of women protesters and a police sergeant. The blue light continues to flash on the roof of the police car.

Jake shakes his head. *Amazing!*

He stares down at his watch. It seems that the whole fifteen-minute encounter with the wyvern has been compressed into an instant in Jake's normal universe. No time at all has passed. Again he shakes his head – he can't understand it. He just can't fathom this contraction of time.

Reality can't be bent like that.

But as he inhales, there still lingers in his nostrils the stench of the wyvern, the acrid smell of burning.

Confirmation that it all happened? Or simply a delusional reinforcement of a hallucination?

He turns and prowls back almost automatically to his office. There he pauses in the doorway, staring off into space. He ignores the aerial CAMIC that is taking up its position again in one corner of the ceiling. Jake then realizes that he has been unconsciously staring at his UFO postcard, but can no longer make out the words printed on the side of the spacecraft.

Aware of a dull headache, he blinks and screws up his eyes.

'JOE'S ICES – STOP ME AND BUY ONE.'

Jake rubs his forehead and winces, then gingerly touches his forehead. He goes over to study his reflection in the windowpane and sees a bright red mark on his bald skull, looking rather like a burn.

Jake slumps into his seat. Maud's wyvern had burnt his forehead.

He sits very still for a couple of minutes, as various possible explanations rapidly run through his mind. Just before he lets it all sink away into his subconscious, he feels a slight buzz of anticipation that, while the protesters at the gate seemed currently unaffected, maybe this is something that everyone else can expect to go through – like on The Night.

Another thought quickly follows. *What if I'd lost the battle? What would have happened to me, then?*

And then he remembers a strange awareness of something else being there, as though he were fighting not just the dragon itself. It is some minutes more before Jake can force himself up to get some coffee. All he can think about is the wild idea of satellites raining mind-altering beams onto the planet Earth. He's not even inclined to discover if his colleagues have experienced anything similar.

He suddenly feels very tired.

'Hey, Scott, listen to this: "And so the whole universe was completed. By the seventh day God finished what He had been doing and stopped working." What do you think?'

'That was left on the message board, Gareth – specifically for me?'

'Uh-huh.'

'It's probably from one of the born-again converts, someone who's been reading too much of the Bible.'

'I'd worked *that* one out, sweetie. I meant, what do you think they're talking about here?'

'Ah, come on, the same as everyone else who's taking part in this show, the same as *everyone* . . . They believe something big is going to happen in approximately a week's time and it's frightening them and they've got a handy quote.'

'Oh, really?'

'Don't be so disappointed, Gareth. I mean, what did you expect? You were telling me only last week that there've been hoards of complaints because various religious nuts didn't make the cut in the first few days and were voted off. It's not my fault the born-againers didn't pick up on this competition quick enough to give their standard bearers a push up the ladder. And anyhow, that message is probably from those bastard neo-fascist weirdos in Sonat, who want to let *everyone* know that they've got God on their side.'

'I suppose. Now, don't forget today's task – some sort of practical joke, please.'

'That'll be fun. I've elicited some help.'

'Good work.'

'As long as Unit-C are making money, Gareth.'

'We are, dear boy, we are. And you could be, too.'

'Whoopee.'

It is so hot, approaching noon, that even the gulls have given up patrolling the surf. They bob on the surface of the sea, without moving, as if the heat has stolen their enthusiasm. The beach, though, has that fresh gritty feel of sand and pebbles beneath my boots that makes me want to run along it, even in this sweltering temperature – as if I could thus escape what I have to continue with in the next few days. It adds to the stomach-churning sense of disquiet I've experienced for the last hour.

A little further inland, and above the cliffs, is the syrupy summer aroma of ferns that sickened me when we passed through them earlier; and, in the dense and ancient woods beyond, there was the scuttling and chirping of unseen animals hinting at bad spirits ready to be awakened. When we were walking along that path, I felt the same shiver you get as a child when you look up a flight of dark, unlit stairs, to the door standing slightly ajar at the top of them . . . and imagine what might be waiting behind it.

It makes me feel out of sorts and pensive, as if I've reverted to being a nervy impatient kid. It would be a relief if I were just allowed to be frightened.

The gannet-eye blue sky is big and empty, and reflects on the surface of the water like a tropical sea. Here the waves usually roll onto the beach with a pebble-laden grey-brown thump, half a metre high, but today they do not seem to have the energy to break, gliding onto the beach as mere ripples, slop, slop, slop. The water is so calm and languid that if you were to skip a flat pebble on its surface, you could imagine it would travel forever. My own effort, however, makes one big splash and disappears from view.

'Hey, Scott!' a female voice calls from near the low cliff. 'Over here? I want at least one picture of us that we don't have to pay for.'

As I glance back over my shoulder at TC, I feel a pang of sympathy for how hard she's trying to return to some sort of normality after her mother's death, then reach down to the shingle to select another flat stone. I fondle this until it sits in my hand just right, then bend my knees slightly, bring back my arm, and launch the pebble low and fast out towards the horizon. This one skims beautifully. Seven, eight, nine . . . *eleven* times it bounces off the water. I stand up slowly, resisting the temptation to adjust my portable personal CAMIC, which I have been wearing plugged -

into my ear these last three weeks, and I turn at the sound of slow hand-clapping. Standing with TC now is Benjamin, theatrically applauding me as slowly as he can. I jog up the beach to join my friends. By the time I reach them, sweat has broken out on my brow.

TC places her digital camera carefully on a concrete post, then bends down to check that she has the required image captured in the viewfinder. She stands up, pushes a button on the camera, then runs over to join Benjamin who is now standing beside an old WWII pillbox.

'What are you waiting for?' he yells at me.

I reluctantly scramble to join them, making it just in time.

The camera clicks as we try to compose ourselves: three friends together.

I visualize the result. Innocent gallows victim Benjamin Archer – a vulpine red-headed stick – will look just like he is waiting for the firing-squad bullets. Toni Cartermann, in her mirror sunglasses, stares up at the sun from under a Pre-Raphaelite mane – trying to look confident but instead looking more vulnerable than ever. I myself run a hand through my own short-cropped black hair. It has been commented on the Internet that, with my designer stubble and moody look, I could make a living acting in dark French thrillers. As if.

TC is intently studying the small display screen on her camera, checking the image before she transmits it to her home PC.

I then notice how Benjamin seems to be forcing himself to smile.

I don't know what is troubling him, but *I* myself

am struggling to think of anything other than the sudden intense feelings of déjà vu brought on just by standing next to the pillbox. What I fear is going to happen is some spectral vision drifting into view – a phenomenon that has been happening to me for seven years now. People say that it's just my imagination working overtime due to my chronic lack of sleep, or even to the physical effort involved in reaching top athletic performance. It's tolerated as a sport-celebrity quirk. And yet, even as I try not to begin trembling too visibly – *that's* something new – I find myself supposing that if I were ever to see an apparition just here, it would be one of my grandfather Eric finally managing to jettison the remainder of his bomb-load from his Stirling bomber, along this same coast, before heading on for a crash-landing at Woodbridge airfield.

For a brief instant, I clearly visualize myself at the controls as I have done before. I feel the trembling of the aircraft travel up from my feet to my thighs. I hear the engines. I smell the fear from the crew.

They fade, but I find I can't stop the shivers running like cold knives down my back.

With a shaking hand, I feel for my CAMIC, wondering if, bizarrely, my imaginings have been caught on camera. I quickly look to both left and right, checking for any evidence that the people involved with Unit-C are somehow setting me up. But I know, deep down, it is all coming from me.

I flex my fists, then dare myself to touch the pill-box.

I feel nothing, and give a little snort as I regain my

composure. I touch the pillbox yet again – just to be sure that I still can do it. I don't like being ruffled.

I first met TC and Benjamin when we became day pupils at Springgreen Open School – an institution whose founder believed passionately in the principle of freedom. There are more of this type of college than most people think – one of the first of them was established not too far from here. Our own school got closed down after only a few years. While there, we could choose if we wanted to attend lessons, all had an equal vote on deciding about rules, and could do pretty much what we wanted as long as it didn't compromise another's freedom. That was the mantra and practically everyone educated there left its confines better set up for adult life than other school kids. We were given an inner strength. So I am curious about my friends' motivations: they are both at the beginning of challenging careers, so should be out there 'doing the business' and yet they've taken time off because they felt a need to return home. Just like myself, my coach, and seemingly a large proportion of the country, retreating from the outside world to hunker down at home, and looking for diversions, serious or frivolous. The economy is nose-diving through excessive absenteeism.

I look at TC. My main excuse for returning here now was to attend her mother's funeral. That explains TC's consumption of cigarettes, I suppose, breaking all the current government regulations.

Her family home is situated on a bend after a long straight, and her mother approached at speed and crashed into her own house. TC isn't staying there currently, since the repairs are still in progress. From what I hear, Sally Cartermann was driving back from an evening at the Bell and Fox, doing between sixty and seventy miles an hour down the straight, but unaccountably didn't slow down for the familiar corner. There were no signs of skid marks where she crashed through the wooden fence and straight into a corner of the house itself.

'It wasn't pretty,' my mother had said sadly. 'The crash itself hadn't killed her, but the car burst into flames.'

'Was she still conscious?' I couldn't stop myself from asking.

'The post-mortem indicated that she'd torn several fingernails trying to undo the seatbelt. The damn thing had got stuck.'

INTERNET NEWS UPDATE by Janice Maclean

Total Cover is now entering its final week, and is already down to its last seven celebrity contestants. Tiffany Young, the nineteen-year-old big lottery winner from Lyme Regis, is still favourite – the web watchers are voting her well into the lead. And as for the rest: it's ex-girl-band member Natalie Brooks, followed by footballer Adi Coniston, skateboard hero Mickey Smote, ex-soap star Jo Kingwaverly, the decathlete Scott Anderson, and currently in last place is children's TV presenter Tricia McAllen.

Unit-C representatives were yesterday quoted as saying: 'This experiment continues to demonstrate how it is possible to enjoy using a personal CAMIC without any sense of intrusion. The number of hits to our website is increasing dramatically as the remaining contestants become more vocal in expressing their views on current global problems.'

Considered a bit of an outsider, the decathlon athlete Scott Anderson continues to entertain us with his particularly forceful views. He could even stand a chance of winning, but can he beat off Tiffany? We'll have to wait and see.

I find my father is still not talking to me much . . . which is just fine by me, I have to admit.

Col. Kevin Anderson, honourably discharged after receiving a serious wound on a supposed peace-keeping tour in West Africa, is himself the fourth son of an American soldier who served in Britain during World War II. When the arguments between us reached their zenith – or nadir depending on how you see it – I once commented that if the doctors ever decided to amputate my father's dodgy leg, they'd find the inscription 'Leg, Right, One-Off, Army Issue' circling inside the stump like in a stick of rock. My father snarled back that there would be nothing wrong with that either.

All because of my ducking out of Sandhurst. And perhaps, in its own little way, because he suspected my mother's ambition for me to go to Springgreen Open School may have sparked my waywardness – my standing up to him, in other words – and refusal to get involved with the army or its rules and regulations, unaware that I had so long detested its way of life.

Ever since I was fourteen and we were finally settled, returning to any form of military establishment has given me a shiver of fear. It eventually turned into a major phobia, and I have never been able to rationalize that. Perhaps it was triggered by seeing, on the news report, an army medical team hastily carrying the stretcher with my father on it, a sergeant holding the plasma high, the blood splattering on the road; perhaps it was the horror stories my grandfather Roy told me later that same night of his time during WWII, as the old man sat drinking large malt whiskies, one after the other, while his daughter-in-law sat with her husband in the hospital; perhaps it was just a sudden discovery of a fear of commitment. Perhaps any of those, but what military buildings represent to me now is something I can't describe.

As if to compensate for the disappointment I knew I would cause my father, I turned increasingly to sport. I ran harder and faster than anyone else in my school. I added the long-jump as something extra to distract me; I discovered I had a knack for the javelin; and I loved the fierce pleasure I got from spinning in a circle to launch the discus, skimming it through the air in a perfect arc.

Eventually I united these skills, took up the decathlon, and became strong and fit. As my father noticed my prowess, he began making noises about Sandhurst, about the leading of men.

How on earth could I ever explain to him that even the mere *thought* of spending ten months training at that place turned my bowels to water, particularly after so long being used to making my own rules at school? By that stage all things military repelled me and I would never even willingly go near any of the decaying WWII concrete structures littered around my home. They are now seemingly filled with ghosts, dedicated to depriving me of sleep, and I intuitively know that soon one will manifest itself to me here today. I have never been wrong.

And yet the same period in history they derive from continues to fascinate me. I feel I *understand* it – completely, deeply and intuitively.

I was extremely close to my American-born grandfather, Roy – my father's father – who stayed on in Britain after the war and married a girl he'd met during the weeks building up to D-Day. He nearly lost his life while parachuting into Normandy near Utah beach; was later wounded in Holland; saw several of his close friends killed at Bastogne; and eventually helped liberate a concentration camp. My British-born grandfather, Eric, was an RAF pilot who flew Stirling bombers in a dramatic fashion. On one occasion nearly having to make a crash-landing with a third of his bomb-load still on board, he eventually managed to ditch them in the sea near where I stand right now. That must have been some scary flight for him and his crew.

After all that action, both men settled down locally and raised their families.

My father, Kevin, is now fifty-two, square-faced with cropped grey hair. He listens habitually to vinyl jazz records, and smells of the orchids he specializes in growing. My mother Margaret is three years younger. Her hair is cropped short as well, but in her case is still raven black, and she rushes around singing old R & B songs in a voice tarnished by forty Gauloises a day. She smuggles them into the country when on her frequent shopping runs to France.

Both grandmothers died while I was still very

young, but the deaths of my two grandfathers affected me more than I could ever confide to anyone. There was a closeness with them because, as I reached my teens, they both realized that I understood *something* that their own offspring had not been able to grasp: and that was what it was like to have actually been in combat.

All their many war stories quickened my interest, and prompted me to study history as a suitable counterpoint to my athletics: I realized that to know who you are, you need to know your origins. As Truman once said, 'The only thing new in the world is the history you don't know.' And if I discover that, I reckon I might eventually lay the ghosts that for years have oppressed me. Yes, I need to find *their* origins.

So that's partially the reason why academia calls me these days. And now I have also found a convenient means of hitting back at the neo-right-wing reactionaries who were responsible for Roy's early death. In my one-man crusade against Pascal Toluene, I hope my grandfather Roy would be proud of what I'm doing.

As a participant in the current promotional campaign for the IT company Unit-C, I volunteered in order to gain a public platform by which to warn people of the real dangers building up with Toluene and his fanatical followers. In a way, it has become an obsession, this urge to avenge my grandfather – I have even temporarily withdrawn from international competition. But with such public exposure, I suspect I'll provoke him to assign one of his thugs to come after me soon. That's where my omnipresent, shockproof, waterproof, all singing and dancing tiny CAMIC can provide invaluable evidence of whatever may happen to me.

Like all the contestants I need to wear a camera, no wider or longer than a matchstick, protruding from one side of my head beside my right eye, with a small but very powerful microphone fixed alongside an integral loudspeaker. Looking like a miniature bright blue hearing-aid, the CAMIC is linked to a modified mobile phone which I carry around to relay any information back to my own PC. At the tip of the camera stalk, right near the lens, are also three optical fibres transmitting interlaced low-intensity lasers – red, green and blue – able to form images onto my eye when required, or when the home system wishes to alert me to something important.

The resulting pale-coloured transparent Webvis picture duplicates what then appears on my PC screen, and I can scroll through it by using the mouse controls on my mobile. It took me surprisingly little time to adjust to what appears to me like cinema-sized projections of web pages, and they're available at a click of a button whenever I want to see them. Extra goodies include the facility to project a low-grade full-colour image onto any flat surface using the mobile itself and a wafer-thin touch-sensitive keyboard capable of being rolled up and stuffed into my back pocket – but I don't use these much. Though both the CAMIC and mobile units are actually very small and discreet, I still have to charge them both each night, alternating them with another pair for the following day. But that's about as far as I need to go on the technical side.

Before going online, I had to fill out a detailed questionnaire about my interests, which were then used as the initial parameters for the program installed by Unit-C on my PC. Certain portions of my hard drive are now accessible full-time to the public, and the program does a constant update of my day – it's a sort of software-driven Blog. It automatically edits what has happened to me during any given period of time, for compilations of various activities, allows for constant live coverage, and keeps *me* up to date by monitoring other PCs for information it thinks I'll be interested in, like music and news, and how events local and global could affect me. (I avoided a huge traffic jam a fortnight ago when the software alerted me that several CAMIC users were caught up in it.) It also constantly analyses my actions, using software initially designed to track individual animals in group experiments, comparing these to the records of the others to check if they've ever done anything similar, and then goes on to suggest the best approach to solving any problem.

As more people link up, the more diverse will become the experiences of the participants the program has access to, and ever more refined will be this electronic advice gleaned from their accumulated monitored activities. I can access any of this information via the mobile, my Webvis retina cam-screen or through an audible rendition. Unit-C obviously aims to make their profit through the sales of these CAMICs and software, and also by selling advertising via my hard drive. By launching this promotional campaign, they also get to advertise their security equipment – which forms another hefty part of their business. I meanwhile have, in effect, a tailor-made automatic search engine that constantly updates its search patterns – answering questions before I've barely composed them, and, more important to me, I also get to make my opinions widely available. It is next-generation Internet – the accessible brain for the future. So goes the sales pitch: Maxnet, they call it. Current sales of CAMICs are astronomical.

To spark initial interest, Unit-C sought to establish a sort of platform for naked greed: you convince everyone who is following the contest via the Internet to vote for you, and for your particular motive for wanting the prize money – however eccentric, however contentious – and at the close of the promotion, due a week from now, the last surviving contestant will receive a cash sum in direct relation to the number of votes he or she has acquired. It is doubtful it will go to charity. To increase the ongoing tension, at the end of each day the participant receiving the least amount of votes is kicked off and their votes distributed equally among the remaining contestants.

To stimulate the greed factor, for every five seconds I keep my CAMIC switched off, I lose a vote . . . and therefore money. Some contestants are even leaving them on when they visit the toilet, but the world out there has yet to be treated to that delight from me – I recognize there are some personal activities that I might not want comment on.

To add to this close personal monitoring, at strategic places near each contestant's home is set up a number of base stations for the new brand of aerial, mobile CAMICs, but these flying versions do not yet possess sufficient range to follow me all the way out here into the countryside. City-dwellers, however, can have three or more of them following them around at

any one time, complementing the ubiquitous surveillance cameras on every lamp post that the company
has been granted a licence to use locally. I'm glad I'm
out here, because I've never got used to the idea of
CCTV with wings.

After the events of 'The Night', the Unit-C promotion was given a substantial, yet subtle, extra spin.
The company asked its Internet audience to vote not
only for the most deserving candidate, but now also
the one providing the most convincing prediction for
the immediate future, however weird.

That certainly increased the interest level. *Everybody*
seems to have their own opinion on the current crisis.
Many, of course, blame the institutions – scientific,
government, financial – that they think put us in this
position, significant numbers of others have turned to
religion for reassurance, while inevitably various political parties are trying to make capital from the general
unease and panic.

Which is where I come in.

I'm writing my biting comparison of a certain
Nazi by the name of Reinhard Heydrich with the
genuine heroes in WWII, partially out of sheer bloody-
mindedness, but also because I can equate his actions
to Toluene's and my fear of the dangers of neo-
fascism.

For most of the duration of the contest, I've been
swimming near the bottom feeders. Most votes seem
to be going to certain attractive young women who
think that little green men were responsible, and
who express their disgust at this by taking frequent
showers with their CAMICs still switched on. Somehow, they always seem to forget to close the shower

curtains properly – providing views from mirrors positioned judiciously. Benjamin has suggested I do the same, but I've told him I'm saving myself for this final week.

Integral to the CAMIC is the tiny loudspeaker that enables Gareth, my supervisor from Unit-C, to talk to me privately over any Maxnet web page commentary. It was unnerving at first to have this disembodied voice in my ear, as he offered suggestions or explained the tasks I had to complete, but gradually I've got used to it. He makes a fair amount of idiotic requests – most of which I ignore – but the viewing public is saved from overhearing these because his voice initiates an automatic mute button that also cuts out my replies to him. That means it's only me who is lucky enough to hear his high-pitched squeaking, except when he decides to make a webcast announcement.

Once a day, I am obligated to spend some time answering questions from the public. Gareth has also been obliged to start filtering these questions, since they've been getting personal to the point of threatening – which is exactly what I expected, and hoped for.

My e-writing stories about Sonat and Pascal Toluene were initially prompted by my personal anger, stoked by an increasing sense of déjà vu menace about what they represented. In some way, stupid as I may feel about vocalizing this gut instinct to a largely uncomprehending audience, I feel overwhelmed by the need to give expression to the sense of danger that *I* consider us all to be in. Exactly the remit from Unit-C. And by drawing comparison to the incidents I have studied – the camps, the Hamburg firestorm, the Butcher of Prague, though all dating back to World War II – I feel I can convey the malaise that oppresses me regarding our current situation.

And now, standing by this pillbox, I conceive the idea of bracing myself to visit all the old WWII sites I know locally, the very decaying objects that I fear, yet am fascinated by, just to see what ghosts they may have for me, just to see how I can test myself. My convictions invigorate me.

Toluene is on a roll now because of the disturbing events of last month, since when there has been a massive resurgence in right-wing politics trying to make capital of the crisis in public confidence. The Jacksonville demagogue and his Socialized Nationals Party has since been driving the Left into apoplexy, as they continue to spin out their inflammatory claims and pronouncements. It's as if they've been waiting all along for some catastrophe like this one to emerge, enabling them to rev up their obnoxious dogmas and thus attract frightened and impressionable people desperately looking for answers.

And now they *hate* me. Ever since I established my political credentials on the first day of Unit-C's promotion, I have had to face an escalating amount of abuse – even death threats.

The police are taking it seriously enough to increase the number of officers keeping a watch out for intrusive fans, stalkers or whatever, that have proliferated as the contest draws to a close. But, of course, I don't care, because it's what I'd hoped for.

I've been privately requested by Gareth not to antagonize them further, but I've told him that I will not bow to any threats from the right wing. At least, that's what I keep telling myself when I'm feeling brave. It doesn't seem so good a course at three in the morning as I lie in a sweat, worrying.

Jake sits at his desk studying his correlation data, as he attempts to refocus on the phenomenon his experiment discerned the previous month regarding the synchronicity of the mice. The system has again alerted him to the fact that a substantial number of his cloned mice have been performing identical actions.

He leans back in his chair, wishing briefly that he had an external window to look out of, something to indicate that the rest of the world is still out there.

Seen from the outside, the Institute resembles a self-replicating labyrinth. Not only do all the connecting corridors have one side constructed entirely of windows, but the central administrative buildings resemble an ultra-modern greenhouse from which these corridors lead off to the separate laboratories. Yet the laboratories themselves have no external windows at all – for security reasons, Jake has been informed. Apparently, the absence of any glass surfaces obviates the possibility of anyone bouncing a laser off a window pane in order to pick up the minute vibrations of human speech. This obsessive concern for security also explains why he is constantly tracked in his routine progress around the complex by an aerial CAMIC. Jake would be happier to have a view, even at the risk of people listening in to him talk non-sense to himself – to his mice – all day.

The complex is situated on what was once an upmarket golf course. A team of gardeners fanatically grooms its disused fairways and greens, so that the grass is all kept down to a uniform height – resembling one huge putting green. With its old giant copper beech trees and even older, low-branched yews, the place still retains an echo of the lunatic asylum that was situated here even before the golf course. For all its clinical appearance, Jake quite likes the place.

Jake seldom socializes with the other doctors and scientists working at the Institute apart from Edwina, a professor in her early fifties, who exudes the practical nature of someone who could run Ground Control all on her own and bring a dozen astronauts safely to land on Mars. Edwina is also relatively new to the Institute, arriving just after Jake's experiment was initiated. The only other people with whom he has regular contact are the Institute's Director, Oscar Brightwell, who's a fifty-two-year-old, square-jawed advertisement for aftershave, and a couple of scientists who work in the neighbouring labs. One of these is Dr Otis Meridian, a twenty-five-year-old anthropologist just down from Cambridge, who stutters and never manages to look Jake in the eye. To the other side of Jake's laboratory works Dr Mark Kristen – a thirty-four-year-old American behavioural scientist who compensates for his five-foot-four stature by speaking twice as slowly as everyone else.

As an evolutionary anthropologist Jake became fascinated by how the races evolved, and is currently preoccupied in the age-old topic of *nature versus nurture*, and how much of it is also applicable to mankind. Therefore he has devised an experiment to see how identical mice will react to identical environments – in effect, to calculate how much of their behaviour is learnt and how much is inherited. It is his contention that, even if he finds only a rough percentage, it will be possible to project the results onto similar behaviour patterns in humans. And there is now even a way of obtaining large numbers of identical mice for such an experiment.

Cloning was once a difficult process, but a recent experimental development by another scientist here at the Institute, using artificial placentas and a genetically modified enzyme to assist in the replication, means that the cloning can be achieved on a mass-production scale, without the associated high loss-rate of embryos, without the degradation of life-span (because the enzyme ensures the chromosome time-clock has been reset to zero), and without the ravages of mutations.

The Eisencrick Institute has, of course, patented this invention and is increasing its research finances considerably by renting it out under licence. (A large number of organizations have already professed their desire to try it out on humans, and three laboratories – in Mexico, Italy and Russia – have claimed they have achieved that with a number of embryos nearing their full term.) The Institute thus receives frequent visits from interested parties, with a consequent increase in the number of staff employed to produce the stock of cloned animals. Jake himself is using two thousand CM32 mice in his experiment. He could have used fruit flies or some other sort of insect, but he chose mammals because of their increased brain size – anticipating more independent action from them beyond instinct and conditioned response.

In another room is located the control group – in identical conditions, but made up of mice from a variety of sources, and none of them cloned. They too have displayed odd moments of synchronicity, involving just two or three mice at a time, but that he has decided to put down to coincidence. At the inception of his experiment, Jake reasoned that using two thousand cloned mice would reduce statistical error, incidentally noting it happened to be roughly how many mice it would take to provide the collective cerebellum cortex brain size – the thinking bit of the brain – equal to that possessed by two average humans.

He also gives sponsors to the Institute his speculations on genetics and on the controversial subject of eugenics, and shows them numerous interesting graphs that do not take into account the ethics involved, until their minds have been assailed with enough info-dump for Jake's boss to steer them away for lunch and further discussions about corporate sponsorship. Jake doesn't get involved in any of the moral arguments, since he is convinced he is on the verge of a spectacular discovery where the ends will justify the means of getting there.

The environmental conditions for this study have to be precise. Every single aspect of their mouse-lives has to be the same – they all have to experience the exact same stimuli at exactly the same time. (If a light above one cage were to blow, for instance, all the others go out too.) The mice are placed in a low-ceilinged air-conditioned room, their small cages lined in long rows. (The mesh-covered open front of one cage faces the solid back of the one in the next row along so that they cannot be influenced by observing each other's actions.) They are fed, watered, even have their cages cleaned, automatically and at the same time, so as to minimize any human contact. Individual miniature cameras record their actions and responses, then everything is carefully analysed. And now at last the experiment is producing results. Even as he watches, Jake sees cam-shots begin highlighting in red again, meaning numbers of mice are clearly performing identical actions. Jake leans forward in his seat.

Over the past three weeks, he has been removing a small number of mice from the cloned group in his experiment, and a similar number from the control group, to further observe their capacity for learning, before returning them to quarantine cages in their respective laboratories. (They no longer form part of the monitoring process, of course, because they have meanwhile experienced different stimuli from the rest.) He has tested them in a complex maze and observed how quickly they have improved the times they have taken to find their prize – which is food, as always. Out of curiosity, today he has removed additional mice from both groups, and exposed them to the same test.

The cam-shot boxes are frantically turning red because the new mice from the cloned group are running, at exactly the same speed as each other, down the same routes in their identical mazes, and the system is therefore alerting Jake to their synchronicity. And they all now complete the maze – which astounds him even more – in the same time, and just as quickly, as his initial batch of cloned mice eventually achieved only after three weeks.

'Awesome,' whispers Jake to himself. 'How the devil have they learnt that? *Where* did they learn that?'

He slowly stands up and goes to peer through the one-way observation window viewing the quarantine cages placed to one side. He places a hand on the glass and the thoughts he has right now are momentous. And incredible.

This lot appear to have passed on their knowledge of the maze to the others. But how?

He takes his hand away from the glass and then places it back again, one finger slowly tapping a soft rhythm on it. Jake suddenly ceases his quiet drumming.

They're communicating. They must *be.*

Jake frowns as he rechecks the logic of his thinking.

I can't be thinking straight.

He stands motionless for a while, furiously analysing, then darts back to his PC, where he stands over the keyboard and quickly taps in a few instructions. Within a moment, the recorded and dated sequences from the initial batches, their eventual speedy completion of the maze and the synchronicity of the final group are repeated on the screen. He has his proof. And he rubs his injured forehead again.

Two such major events occurring so close together in my life? Isn't that too much *coincidence?*

He nods to himself as, yet again, he watches the animals on the recording reach their prizes at the ends of the mazes. There can be no doubt: somehow, the cloned mice that completed the mazes initially have communicated the solution to their fellows.

Speech? Conversation?

And then another option.

Or perhaps even telepathy? A sort of group consciousness?

Jake knows this is a stupid conclusion, realizes he must be wrong; but it seems an answer in some ways no less amazing than his first conclusion.

Telepathy – some form of previously unrecognized communication system? Or can it be some sort of speech?

Jake stands very still, a finger to his lips.

And which would be more believable? Mice don't have the physical facility for complex language and even chimps can only just manage a basic version – unless, of course, the noises they do make represent something more sophisticated, something more intelligent than generally believed.

And if it was achieved through some sort of vocalization, he argues to himself, *then one of the great tenets of humanity – that we are the only animals capable of passing on knowledge through speech – would be finally shattered. Especially if witnessed in a mammal as small and insignificant as a mouse.*

Jake allows himself a brief smile, reminding himself how it seems that every time the human race appropriates characteristics it considers are unique to itself, someone eventually points out how another animal is doing exactly the same – though perhaps on a more primitive level. Jake's analytical mind quickly appraises the impact of releasing such startling information to the scientific community via the Institute, particularly with the whole world in its current state of nervousness. Momentous knowledge has a way of leaking out into the wider domain, and it spreads – twisted, manipulated, misrepresented – through the public networks within hours. He'll have to find some way of controlling its release.

He glances over his shoulder at the CAMIC, currently recharging itself in its wall socket. Even with such proliferation of these devices, Jake doubts whether his current observations have been registered – those things are supposedly programmed to pick up only specific security risks, like fires or unexpected physical disruptions. The Institute would need a whole panel of experts to track each individual scientist's progress. Unless, Jake now considers, they possess the computer capacity to run monitoring software on a permanent basis. He shakes his head and forces his mind back onto his discovery.

The knowledge that creatures as insignificant as mice can communicate using their own form of speech could prove too startling for many people. And that other telepathic interpretation would be too incredible, yet he keeps coming back to it. Jake turns back to the window.

If a group of mammals as small as mice can exhibit telepathy, what would that mean for us?

He remembers that he is using two thousand mice, two thousand identical mice with a total cerebellum cortex brain size equal to that of two humans.

What a brain that would make!

As Jake considers the implications further, the burn on his forehead begins to throb again, and he realizes he must be *absolutely* sure of his analysis and *so* careful about how it is announced. Just then the monitor screens begin to turn red again. Box after box, screen after screen. The cloned mice in the main room – the rest of the experiment – are acting in synchronicity again.

Except there are even more of them involved this time.

Many more.

Chapter Three

How about this then for a piece of sycophantic report-ing? It's taken from an 'interview' by Kirsty Newington conducted for USA South Today, a TV company indi-rectly owned by Toluene.

KN: I'm here now with the media magnate Mr Toluene. A very fit-looking fifty-eight, some years ago he left his Tallahassee birthplace to return to his ancestral roots in the city of Jacksonville, where he continues as chief executive of Media National USA (MNU). And now Mr Toluene is running for political office, as leader of the brand-new Socialized Nationals Party – or Sonat as it is better known. Mr Toluene, tell me, what do you hope to achieve eventually with Sonat?

PT: First off, we are not interested in such a tenuous con-cept as hope, Kirsty. The Socialized Nationals Party is all about intent, not about giving people empty platitudes, patting their hands and saying that everything is going to be all right. That approach is fine for dealing with small children, but no way to engage with responsible adults.

We are therefore offering people a solid platform on which to stand and shout about what matters to them. It is time we should be more united, more comfortable with pride in our heritage, and remember that a nation's flag is its people's statement of identity. A great many people realize how weak government has caused the chaos around us, exacerbated by the economic migration allowed to flood in from the Third World countries. We must start to respect our own borders, and forestall the dilution of our culture by outsiders. God in his wisdom gave us the brains to create the technology we need, so let's use it. Given a mandate, our Party will employ the new DNA database, and its genetic analysis of the whole population, as a means of defining our national identity, and thereby provide a method for tightening national security. Those displaying inherently unsuitable genetic personalities, or those with high susceptibility to danger-ous diseases, will have to be excluded from the developments we are intending. Regarding the much-discussed events of recent weeks, we have not come all this way over the centuries just to be frightened by a few bad dreams. That was not a time of nightmares, but a wake-up call to every right-thinking person. The world needs strength now, and Sonat possesses it. Both in depth and in breadth.

KN: What then do you have to say about your detrac-tors, Mr Toluene?

PT: It's the usual mindless background noise, Kirsty. Exceptional times demand exceptional people making exceptional decisions. I am the man to do that, and if weak-willed people do not like what I say, then I suggest they do not bother listening. We have important work to do and sanctimonious criticisms from the same idiots who got us into this current mess of indecision should be rightly ignored. I look forward therefore to a time, in the very near future, when we will be able to say welcome to a New World – a world of certainties.

Jake sits at a table in the Institute's cafeteria. The place being practically empty, the canteen staff chat amongst themselves, their whispers amplified by the lack of lunchers. The head chef shakes her head as she inspects the waiting meals, seemingly now going to waste. A joke shared amongst the others prompts some self-conscious laughter, but Jake glances across at them only momentarily. The burn on his forehead has suddenly and miraculously stopped hurting, and he is still asking himself what would have happened if he'd lost the contest with the wyvern. And what should he do if it happens again?

The excitement generated by his experiment has not helped either, since he is troubled by further thoughts concerning it. He knows he'll have to repeat the maze experiment, but this time with a different layout, and if the results of that secondary experiment duplicate what has occurred before, he will have to devise yet more puzzles to confirm that the mice have been using telepathy, however off the wall that might appear to everyone else.

If cloned mice can do this, why not humans, too? Millions of us must be similar enough in our thought processes to forge such a link.

He has tried to take his mind off things by proof-reading a scientific paper he prepared. But it remains uncorrected, even after fifteen minutes of staring at it over lunch. Jake has eaten only a few of the thick-sliced fries that the British call chips and taken a small bite from the Aberdeen Angus beefburger, distracted by the ideas that are beginning to crystallize. Just as he is about to push his plate away and head back to his lab, Edwina Byfoot sits down opposite him, unannounced, with her tray of lunch. She never exhibits any awe of him.

Edwina seems deliberately to ignore the burn mark on his brow, while she updates him on the latest Internet obsession, *Total Cover*; and finishes most of her lunch – half a chargrilled poussin in a garlic sauce, a warm salad in a honey and mustard dressing, and a huge wholegrain bap. She mops up the remains of the sauce with a chunk of buttered bread.

'I should have spoiled myself, Jakey,' she comments, 'and had a whole one.' She looks down at the bones of the poussin. 'It was delicious.'

Jake manages a smile. 'I'm sure it was.'

'Now that's out of the way,' she says, 'what can I do for you?'

Jake blinks at her rapidly. 'How do you know I want anything?'

'You're not eating, not even that tasty burger, and are showing no signs of itching to get stuck into your latest scientific paper.'

Jake merely treats her to a grunt of a laugh.

'And what have you been doing here?' She points at the burn mark on his forehead.

Jake now eyes Edwina, forcing himself not to

glance over his shoulder at the cameras lining the canteen walls.

'Ed . . .?' he begins.

'Ah-ha,' she says triumphantly, leaning forward conspiratorially. 'Tell me more.'

'Ed, I got an unusual result today in my experiment.' He lowers his voice. 'That, and . . . and some other things.'

He briefly touches his brow.

'I'm listening,' she says.

'I also . . . ' He clears his throat. 'I also *experienced* something strange. And however crazy this may seem to you, I can't help having a nagging feeling that they're somehow linked.'

Edwina leans in a bit closer and cups her chin in one hand. 'It's currently a common event.'

'What is?' says Jake, frowning.

'Odd moments? Noticed coincidence? Dreams? Visions? It's crowd instincts, Jake, shared response to a shared experience. The trauma of The Night has got everybody fixated – especially since they can't explain it. *You* should know that.'

Jake pushes himself back in his seat, frowning, then leans forward again.

'Crowd instincts?' He pauses. 'What is it you told me you do here again?'

Edwina smiles. 'I've *never* told you exactly, but I'm studying crowd responses to certain stimuli. It's considered a sort of Terror Management Theory – TMT. I'm building up a database of how the members of any mob drive themselves along, what their delusions are, their prejudices, their motivations. *And* I get to be in control, and appear as if I know what I'm doing.

I'm in my element after The Night. I've also been getting quite a lot of pressure over the last few weeks to formulate my conclusions more rapidly, so the other bright stars here can use it in their research. Like with you too. The powers that be are poking their noses in more than usual – haven't you been aware?'

Jake nods slowly. 'Yep, Oscar has definitely been a bit more frequent with his sorties into my lab. Been too busy myself to ask him why.'

'Of course,' says Edwina, 'they *would* be interested, wouldn't they?'

When she obviously notices his confusion, she leans even closer, until anyone watching them would conclude that they were lovers about to kiss.

'This place is all about human behaviour,' she continues quietly. 'It's why *you* came here, isn't it? And me too. But why would an organization overtly concerned with commercial considerations, like the Eisencrick Institute, be so interested in behavioural sciences?' She changes direction abruptly. 'Tell me, Jake, do you know the best way to control a crowd?'

'Know what they're thinking?' he replies immediately.

'Good boy. If you know what they're thinking, you can predict what they will do. And then control it. Now how useful would that be – and to whom?'

He gives a quick snort and sits back in his seat, closing his eyes. He doesn't tell Edwina that he's only just realized the answer, because he now feels such a fool. He has been so absorbed in his work, and so pleased with the money he earns, that he never really considered or cared about the ultimate applications for others of what he is doing. For him, it is all about the work and doing the research. But if he himself is investigating behaviour patterns that apply to large groups of people, and Edwina is doing just the same, and if that is what the Eisencrick Institute is really about; then what are going to be the final applications of all that research? Finding out how and why humans react the way they do, in the name of behavioural science, ostensibly seems far enough removed from seeking out new ways of controlling crowds. Jake paranoidly wonders if his boss is, even now, checking his research progress while he is here at lunch.

He stands up. 'Got to go, Ed.'

She sits back, a big smile forming on her lips.

'It's new work we're doing here, Jakey. And they pay us well. I've no problem with that as I'm doing good research. Anyway, as you get older, you get a little more cynical. So, bye for now, okay? Oh . . . I *still* want a ride on that awesome bike of yours.'

'Next week, next week.'

'Bless.'

And he snatches up the burger and begins to munch it as he strides back to his lab. It takes him just four minutes to get there.

Jake stands quietly in the large room where the cloned mice are kept. Fortunately, there is no sign of his manager – or anyone else from the company's hierarchy. He glances along the rows of cages, careful not to let himself be seen by any of the tiny animals inside them. As always, because of the sheer numbers of mice, there is a continuous background noise of scratches, squeaking and scuffling. There is also that faint smell of pet shops that the air conditioning constantly attempts to disperse. Just as Jake swallows the last of his burger, the sounds the mice are making fades away. Finally there is total quiet, the mice making no sound whatsoever.

Seconds pass – long and empty ones. The silence continues.

Jake takes a slow, silent step forward, and pauses. He then takes a step back, more quickly this time. And another. And another. Reaching the door stops him from retreating any further. He rapidly looks around him; a chilling sensation of there being some other entity in the room with him raising the hairs on the back of his neck. But there is no one else with him. Only the mice. Only the mice are with him in the room. The mice, himself and . . . and something else?

The silence is now overwhelming.

And it possesses form.

It is like the silent awareness occurring when an audience is enthralled by a performance: they are all holding their breath, all thinking the same . . . they all have the same thought. And if you are paying attention, you can sense what that is. Whatever anyone might say about it, you *know* what they're thinking. And what Jake senses now is the product of group consciousness – of a newly formed mind, a common mind, expressing interest in an intriguing smell.

The mice have smelt my burger.

The mind then moves on as the aroma disperses and is circulated away.

The multiple sounds begin again and, after the brief silence, the effect is like an explosion. Jake presses back against the door, his hand gently fumbling for the handle. He is now filled with a mixture of curiosity and excitement.

The mice are a single entity. And it is possible to physically sense their mind.

This is beyond his wildest dreams.

What was it that Edwina said: *Noticed coincidence?*

As this idea grows and takes further form, he again begins to consider that it may be all *too* much of a coincidence – that today's major events may indeed be actually related. And indeed with The Night? Jake realizes he needs to decide quickly how to reveal what is now happening with his experiment. Because there is a remote and frightening chance that some of the protesters out there may be right in what they are claiming – specifically, they have a premonition that in seven days' time an event even worse than The Night itself will occur. If that turns out to be correct, then these coincidences may just be indicating that humanity itself is already unconsciously beginning to communicate paranormally, trying to prepare as it approaches some great transformation in self-knowledge, some great evolutionary catastrophe, and may urgently *need* awareness of a group telepathy to help itself cope. And if he is correct in his hypothesis that mankind possesses such ability, then not only must the Eisencrick Institute be prevented from slowing everything down – demanding months of retesting, and a *total* security clamp-down – he'll also need to get it known to the world scientific forum as soon as possible. But he will need to demonstrate it as convincingly and as expeditiously as possible. Jake immediately thinks about the new systems available to the Internet, and asks himself two questions: *Who do I know with immediate and constant contact?* And: *Who controls the greatest instant access to the greatest number of people?*

He quickly and quietly exits the room full of mice, and grabs his coat.

He has just remembered his new acquaintance, TC, briefly mentioning that one of the numerous participants in the new Unit-C Internet promotion, *Total Cover*, is a local minor celebrity who has recently returned to the area. Jake doesn't even consider if he should ask Eisencrick for permission, he has decided to accost Scott Anderson directly.

As the office door laboriously swings shut after him, the CAMIC just managing to flit through in time, he tries to ignore a bleep from the PC alerting him that, yet again, the mice are turning the screens red with their synchronicity. This only adds to his haste.

Jake lets out the clutch of his open-topped Landrover and jabs at the accelerator. He's still not quite used to driving a vehicle with its gear-shift on his left-hand side, and the slight confusion, combined with his haste, causes him to forget to strap on the seat belt. It's difficult to get a Landrover's tyres squealing, especially one as old as this battered one, but he manages it, hurtling out of his parking spot, gaining speed. As he changes gear into second, and then third, he spares no thoughts to how he is mistreating his vehicle. It is obvious to anyone watching from the administrative building that Dr Jake Crux is in one hell of a hurry.

Overtaking a car that is also leaving the Institute grounds – a hatchback the guards have already raised the barrier for – he is suddenly confronted with three stark choices. He can brake hard to miss the female protester who is standing right in front of him, thereby probably spearing himself on the steering wheel and flipping her onto the bonnet; or he can swerve into the gatehouse and be thrown out against the brickwork; or he can aim to the left of the surprised female obstacle and just pray.

Jake does the last of these and aims to the left.

The woman herself tries to strike him with her placard as Jake speeds past, but, realizing he has successfully avoided her, Jake needs to forget her instantly and concentrate on a new challenge.

As he careers up the high verge bordering the far side of the road, beginning to brake to prevent himself from crashing into the hedge, reality stutters and jumps and flickers, and again he is suddenly transported into another dimension.

As quickly as blinking. Click, click . . . *click*!

Not now!

This time, Jake instantly knows who he has become, even before he can adjust his eyes to what he finds before him. He has received the sudden intuition that this is simply another aspect of his personality, but one clothed in another universe, one that is being inspected by others, who are about to judge him.

And what he sees before him should be terrifying, for there, in an open field by a fast-moving river, is a Worm – just as depicted in another of his wall pictures. It is at least ten metres long, its girth thicker than his hands could enclose, and is covered in a protective mail of black scales, which in turn are immersed in thick slime. The creature before him writhes slow and sure, a muscular ripple running down its entire length. Its head resembles the skull of a giant dead hound that has been left to putrefy out in the open for several weeks. Its dozens of teeth are like grey-white needles – row upon row adorning both upper and lower jaws – and its pig-like eyes are a foul green and seem to shimmer with an inner fire. Nine sets of gills open and close constantly below the slits that are its ears. And he also suspects – recalling the legend – that even if he were to slice it apart, its flesh would magically re-form and heal itself.

It smells of plague midden and, gagging at the stench, Jake tries to adjust his thinking and get ready for battle.

He finds he is wearing something radically different this time – a complete suit of armour which must have taken many hours of work by a master blacksmith. Welded to its surface – on the breastplate, on the cuisses that cover his thighs, on the greaves for the lower leg, on the cylindrical helm with only a narrow slit to see through – are a hundred spearheads, carefully sharpened and resharpened, pointing in every direction. Though these points glitter themselves like silver sword blades, the blacksmith has not bothered to clean or polish the rest of his work – there is still a forge blue visible where the spearheads are attached.

Jake wades out into the shallow river to take up a position for battle. He already knows the story, and he knows the trick involved.

He does not have to wait long for the beast's onslaught. The Worm roars and hisses, and slithers into attack while Jake is buffeted by the force of the river's current swirling around his knees. This monster generates the same detached fortitude in him as the wyvern did.

He raises his sword in one hand, and holds it aloft. With his other hand, Jake tests a number of the spear-head points to reassure himself, then yells out, 'Yoh! What y'all waiting for, boy?'

The Worm slides into the water and sweeps, snake-like, towards him. Jake braces himself and allows it to get in close. Suddenly wary, it begins to circle him. Jake adjusts his position, and footing, so that he con-tinues to face it. And, with that, the Worm suddenly submerges. With his sword still aloft, Jake tries to follow its shadow moving under the rippling surface of the water. There is a sudden movement to his right – a flash of dark green, and he stumbles round to keep it in view. It happens again . . .

But it is only a huge pike. Jake quickly looks around. Nothing else is visible . . .

The water erupts on his left side, and the Worm lunges at him before he can finally face it. The force of its attack nearly knocks him off his feet. Jake still resists the temptation to strike out with his sword. He knows that such an attack would render him vulner-able, lose him his advantage. As the Worm bites at his face-plate, its teeth scratching on the eye and mouth slits, it quickly coils as much of itself around his body as it can, obviously intent on crushing him to death. Jake cannot believe he is taking such a risk. He feels as though he is being smothered, as though the Worm will crush him before the extensions to his armour can work.

But as the Worm, its head still snapping and slob-bering at his helm, tightens its coils, the spearheads on

Jake's armour begin to find their way through the scales and pierce its flesh. The pain only enrages the Worm, which squeezes even harder so that its flesh begins to tear. The wounds begin to gape and, as the Worm howls and spits, parts of it begin to fall away and splash into the river. Enraged further, it contracts itself even tighter. More pieces of it slice off and are swept down the river. Jake's armour begins to buckle, as the spearheads penetrate deeper. The Worm hisses with a hellish squeal, and raises its head above Jake's own for one last attempt at crunching through his armour. Then Jake assists it in its journey to Hell, as finally, with a downward sweep of his sword, he slices off its head.

The last segments of the Worm spill into the river, and are swept away before they have any chance of regrouping themselves.

Click, click . . . *click*!

He is back in the Landrover. And he is still braking desperately while swerving to avoid the hedge.

No, no . . . NO!

The Landrover finally skids to a stop, a hawthorn branch painfully jabbing into Jake's arm. He sits very still, vaguely aware of the number of people quickly surrounding his vehicle and yelling at him. All he can think of now is that his feet are wet. He wriggles his toes inside his boots: his feet are most definitely wet.

Where are all these thoughts coming from? Dragons? Worms? And where is the place I keep being dragged off to?

The answer may have something to do with the insight revealed to him as the shift was initiated: that it concerns some aspect of his personality that needs to be resolved. Most likely, an element of himself that he doesn't talk about much.

And he was being assessed, he realizes.

I wasn't fighting just *the Worm: there was something else there guiding its actions. I could so easily have lost, and then what?*

Dr Jake Crux convinces himself that it was all about who he *is*.

When he was twelve, he first read *The Lord of the Rings* and never looked back. Jake found in fantasy novels' alternate worlds there were beautiful places to lose himself in, and he loved completely the allusions and imagery they evoked. Around the age of fifteen, he discovered those plastic model-making kits with their fantasy characters, and combining this interest with chess, he displayed a natural talent for making the fantastic pieces that he likes to use.

He currently has numerous games in progress with various academics scattered around the world. Acquiring several of those little cameras used to oversee his experiment at the Institute, he has positioned them at home above several different chessboards, and is currently waging Internet matches using goblins, riders of the dark side, light-warriors, and inherent skill, tactics and strategy, to defeat his adversaries.

He also regularly constructs fabulous evil dragons as pieces, aware of how early Christians gave them religious significance – the antithesis of everything a knight must strive for: honour, purity and salvation. That must explain, in part, the focus of his experiences.

Jake notes that he is feeling a great sense of foreboding. The sun may be out, and the sky is clear, but he still shivers, and rubs at his arms to dispel the goose pimples. There is a significance to what is happening to him that he has yet to discern fully. But he knows he'll be obliged to do something about it. Definitely.

The shouts of the protesters get louder in his ears, and someone starts shaking him by the arm. Jake unaccountably recalls the occasion as a child on vacation, paddling in the Atlantic Ocean off Long Island, while shrieking in delight as the waves broke over his ankles. It conjures a profound longing for happy memories of the past.

He again glances down and wriggles his toes inside his boots.

Yes, definitely wet!

He puts the Landrover into gear suddenly and accelerates away, ignoring the shouts of police officers, and the headache throbbing in the side of his head.

He has to get his message across as soon as possible. For he is now fully convinced that humanity has a huge problem on its hands. And though Jake hates to agree with the protesters, he has an awful premonition that mankind *will* indeed have to confront it in less than seven days' time.

But not in any form that the protesters themselves would recognize.

Following my two companions as they begin to creep into the pillbox, I am assailed with memories of panic attacks involving similar places during my teenage years, but I rebuke myself; I need to be focused, without such a legacy hanging over me. I ignore the sudden surge of agitation that this whole damned roller coaster is about to go over the top.

'Careful,' says Benjamin, who is the first to enter, doing his best not to brush against the moss-stained concrete.

TC, following behind him, takes off her sunglasses.

I have decided she is on a war footing against her grief today: wearing new tangerine-and-white camouflage trousers, Yank combat boots with rainbow laces, and a black T-shirt so loose on her that I get to see deep cleavage whenever she bends over.

Once all three of us are inside it, the pillbox seems cramped, and we lurch around feeling awkward because we've forgotten how much we've grown since we last entered it.

'I have to get out of here,' says TC, suddenly. She squeezes back past me, jamming the mirror shades back on again. A minute later we see her camouflaged legs dangling from above the observation slit. She has climbed up onto the roof and is sitting swinging her booted heels. I can hear the wheel of her Zippo lighter flick a couple of times and wonder where she gets all the smuggled cigarettes from – the official government limit is now only five per day per person, regulated by chip-link card and an automatic health warning by post.

Benjamin looks down, seemingly disappointed, at the rubbish-strewn floor.

'The kids of today, hey, Ben?' I say.

He shakes his head. 'No respect,' he replies.

A mobile phone suddenly trills, echoing loudly inside the confined space. I'm surprised all the concrete hasn't cut off the signal.

Benjamin reaches into a pocket and produces a tiny phone. He flips it open and looks at the screen. A rare expression of anger flashes in his eyes.

'I *told* him I'm here and not there – no matter!'

He then flips the phone shut, pauses, and then throws it as hard as he can against the inside wall of the pillbox. It explodes into fragments.

'I'm busy,' he says to the bits that fall onto the floor.

He must be getting immense pressure to return to running his company personally, rather than continue doing so long-distance from home.

I suddenly discover I *really* don't like being here inside the pillbox after all, and that I, too, have to get outside, *now*. It comes over me with a fierce rush and I lurch towards the doorway.

Then I'm in the open again, and I stare out at the sea, mustering as much dignity as I can.

Benjamin, emerging from the pillbox, stumbles into me.

'What's the matter?' I ask when I notice his hand trembling.

'Nothing. Just so many ants I thought they'd start crawling all over me.'

He appears to shrug it off, but I have a frightening insight into what particular demons afflicted Benjamin during *his* nightmare three weeks earlier.

Fuck.

'Hey, what are you reading?' I'm intent on changing the conversation, and I reach over to snatch a paperback out of the back pocket of his jeans. I flick through the pages, then hold it up for TC to inspect.

I read out the title, '*Do Dolphins Drink Water?*'

'Chillwood Davies?' she suggests.

'Who else?'

We both smile at each other. Benjamin, IT expert and self-confessed computer geek, has a formidable library of science fiction, which contains every published work by some American writer based in England whose name no one has really heard of.

'Chillwood Davies provides a very good explanation for what happened last month,' he begins to explain. 'He describes there the zeitgeist situation that occurs when different people entertain the same ideas at the same time – very much like the Borg Collective.'

TC abruptly jumps down from the pillbox. 'Can we go?' she asks. 'Let's move on down to The Level and get Scott's next task done for him.' She turns around and heads off before either of us can disagree.

Benjamin follows her, without continuing his monologue.

I watch them both go. I decide I still like TC, though I'm surprised her renewed chain-smoking hasn't been picked up by Maxnet and reported – like my mother's has before now. (She just throws the warning letters in the bin.) TC still obviously misses her own mother terribly.

I scratch at the faint stubble on my chin as I struggle to remember how close TC had been to her father, but as I endeavour to recall him, I begin to panic that I can't.

I hear TC call out to me. 'Scott?'

I start to answer, then suddenly have to stop. I literally feel my heart falter. It starts properly up again a moment later, with a surge.

It is as quick as that.

I step back, confused, one hand brushing the pillbox's exterior. As I do so, an anxiety envelops me the like of which I have never known. Not even on The Night itself. It seems as though my feeling of apprehension has increased by several orders of magnitude. *And then I see him.*

I see a man standing, unmoving, some distance away down on the beach. He is staring right back at me, and wears the classic sheepskin coat of a WWII RAF fighter pilot, complete with Mae West, gauntlet leather gloves, a parachute slung around his backside and an oxygen mask dangling from his neck. I cannot quite discern his youthful features, but he appears so impassive – just watching me, *staring*.

So, yet again, I am witnessing one of the ghosts – the ones practically no one else believes I can see. What do they mean?

There is noisy movement off to one side and I force myself to look away from him and shudder in surprise as the semi-transparent spectre of an RAF Hurricane fighter suddenly appears just out to sea. It is chasing a Junkers Ju 87 – a 'Stuka' – flying parallel to the beach, and now nearly overhead. At seeing this incredible vision, I am frightened, but unexpectedly in awe. The ghost of the British fighter plane flicks its wings, wiggles to position itself behind the tail of its rival, then drops towards the waves, accelerates, and rises with a roar of Merlin engine to come up underneath it. The Hurricane fires its guns, just as the Stuka responds in kind.

Tat-tat-tat. Tat-tat-tat.

Pieces fly off the Stuka's fuselage, smoke plumes from the Hurricane's engine, and the German aircraft rolls into a spin. Within seconds, it is plunging into the sea, its rear-gunner catapulting out through the canopy and into an explosion of spray. The Hurricane does a slow banking turn, the smoke billowing from it now melting into flames, then comes back over the body lying prone in the eddies left by the sinking enemy.

Tat-tat-tat. Tat-tat-tat-tat-tat.

The gunner's body disintegrates.

Then the Hurricane heads inland, smoke and flames increasing.

It dissolves in a shimmer.

The man on the beach is now gone.

Thankfully I didn't look at him too closely.

Shivering, I stand away from the pillbox. And then I sense something else happening. More of the same?

But this time, instead of ghosts – . . .

Click, click . . . *click*!

My surroundings are juddering, stuttering and jerking into another image – as if watching a film that has been spliced too crudely. In the next instant I feel I am being forced into another existence.

For the first time in my life, at least since I was a child, I am so startled that I nearly urinate. I glance to my right, then a quick look to my left. It is all so confusing, all so frightening. I cannot understand how I have come to be where I am now, nor yet why it seems somehow so familiar. It must surely be some mental aberration on my part, a startlingly realistic delusion, and maybe it is evidence that I have surely gone mad. There is such clarity to it, such a perfect assault on my senses – it possesses such an absolute veracity.

This is beyond a vision. Can it be another nightmare instead?

I am standing close to a long dining table, as several young male staff, dressed in white shirts and black trousers, hurry to finish laying out a sumptuous buffet meal. The young men – teenagers really – make no noise and appear to be concentrating totally. Because of the two years of my childhood when my father was based in Germany, I recognize that all this is German food. It is arranged on fine white china, accompanied by elaborately engraved silver cutlery. An older man is fussing about the arrangements and suddenly stoops to pick up and polish a fork. Although there are various salad dishes – *Kartoffelsalat*, *Gurkensalat*, *Karottensalat* and thinly sliced *Roggenbrot* or rye bread – the table is predominantly laden with a wide variety of meats. There is a *Wiener Schnitzel* cut thin almost to transparency, and thicker slices of salami festooned with heart-seizing white chunks of fat, several versions of a meat pasty called *Frikadellen* heaped in miniature golden piles, and inevitably a myriad of *Wurst*. The smell reminds me of a little delicatessen in Hamburg – filled with a pervading aroma of smoked delicacies – where my mother used to take me as a child.

The number of servants begins to dissipate as they finish off their preparations, but they still ignore me.

I discover, as I concentrate, that I can breathe normally, but the utter *realness* of everything around me still makes me want to gulp and gasp. I dare myself to look around, to risk drawing attention to myself. I fervently wish I could be invisible.

The room itself appears to be some sort of plush anteroom in a large mansion. Two huge landscapes hang on the opposite wall – forests and mountains, and men striking heroic poses on cliff edges. From behind a closed door of polished oak at one end of the room comes the murmur of voices, and at this end, another door opens onto a spacious hall. I crane my neck to get a better view, and what I see amazes me. Beyond the open door, men in the black uniform of the *Schutzstaffeln* stand guard. I do a double take and blink rapidly. No, I am not mistaken: there are men dressed in SS uniform standing guard out in the hall. I close my eyes for a moment, but when I reopen them, the soldiers are still there.

I slowly drop my eyes to study my own clothes. I too am dressed in the same uniform and am standing to attention, an StG.44 assault rifle at my side, the butt resting against my left boot. As my concentration breaks, I splutter briefly in disbelief. The last remaining servant pauses to arrange another plate of *Frikadellen* on the table. He looks at me, then at the closed door, then glances back at me. He gives me a brief smile, reaches down and picks up two of the pasties. Popping one into his mouth, he hands the other to me with a wink.

He hisses, 'Take it,' when I don't accept it.

Though the man is speaking German, I understand his words as if they were my native tongue, as if I am German myself.

'Take it,' he repeats.

When I still don't respond, he moves nearer to me, reaching up to shove the small pasty into my half-open mouth. I have to chew it to stop myself from choking. To my surprise, the food tastes divine – the meat so tender and full of flavour – bringing back a flood of memories of that Hamburg deli. The servant then smiles, and he hurries from the room.

Just as I begin to relax a little, my panic builds again as I hear chairs scraping against the floor in the room behind the closed door. I *know* that I am not going to like what is going to happen next. The far door opens.

When I see who is standing there, gesturing to others gathered in the room beyond, I cannot believe it. The man is Adolf Eichmann, I am convinced of it. I know my history and the people who took part and the man at the far door is Adolf Eichmann. He looks much younger and fitter than the used-up old Nazi the Israelis put on trial in the Sixties, but it is definitely him. I nearly vomit with fear.

This is all happening too fast. What's going on?

Other men in uniform – black of the SS, brown of the Nazi Party – together with a few in business suits begin to wander out towards the buffet. Some rub their hands at the sight of the meal laid out in front of them, others gesture animatedly as they continue some conversation. I then recognize another of them: it is Reinhard Heydrich, the Butcher of Prague.

When I see *him*, I suddenly realize where I am, and a tremor causes me to shiver uncontrollably, retriggering that urgent need to urinate.

I know where I am.

It is the 20th January 1942 and I am standing guard near the buffet table of Wannsee Haus – the private house in the lakeside district of Berlin used by the SS and where the Third Reich's implementation of the 'Final Solution' was worked out. That is why the room seemed familiar – this event itself and the man now striding out of the other room are all wrapped up in the accounts I am writing and purveying to the e-viewers. I am shocked into immobility and I can't even blink.

SS Obergruppenführer Reinhard Heydrich was Himmler's right-hand man, and many people were of the opinion that the race to succeed Hitler would be between Himmler, Heydrich and Martin Bormann. All were shrewd manipulators of the system, but Heydrich was the most calculating and ruthless of them. No one who ever encountered this man forgot him – that is if they survived. I notice how the other men in the room shy away from him, yet always try to ensure he is kept in their line of sight. Heydrich resembles a great white shark gliding menacingly through a pack of dogfish.

At first glance he appears to be the archetypal Aryan – tall, broad-shouldered, blond – but with his noticeably large forehead, androgynous hips and a rather high-pitched voice for so big a man – turning shrill as he shares a joke with a delegate in brown uni-form – there is a suggestion of the sinister, of the soulless, of something dangerous.

And this man is assuredly someone to be feared. Bormann or Himmler would never have won the con-test.

As Reichsprotektor, Heydrich has already made his presence known in Czechoslovakia, where an unsubtle combination of firing squads and an increase in rations for the armaments workers is used as a crude means of 'encouragement' or 'inducement'. The political intelligentsia has been rounded up and many hundreds of them have been summarily executed –

thus removing any potential leader that might rise from their ranks. He has already arranged for all the Jews in his domain to be transported east – less than one in thirty of them would survive the war. He is keen to demonstrate to Hitler how a province should be run – a blueprint for controlling the rest of Europe that he will have a hand in shaping. No dissent is tolerated, by the application of terror and death.

As the last man exits the conference room, Eichmann leaves his position at the door and begins to circulate – ensuring his visitors are taking advantage of the hospitality available. He need not have bothered, since the guests are now all eating something or are reaching for it.

I glance beyond them into the room they have just vacated – the same room where the Wannsee Protocol was formulated. A stenographer is putting away his equipment. I can see a long table surrounded by chairs, can see the scattered paperwork, but however hard I look, I cannot see the Devil. Surely *he* must be lurking there somewhere.

Postponed due to the Japanese attack on Pearl Harbor, this meeting was called at the behest of Heydrich, but arranged by Eichmann. It was a one-and-a-half-hour session where Heydrich instructed the mandarins of the Third Reich that they had further administrative duties to perform for the Fatherland, ones involving the removal of eleven million European Jews to places that could cope with such an influx of humanity. The Fatherland had now given up on enforced emigration, so they were going to deal with the problem in other ways.

I know for sure that everyone who has attended

this meeting is aware, as they stand around chatting and eating, how certain camps are already operational and that others – on a bigger scale – are near completion. The mass extermination of a whole population is set to increase in magnitude and pace, and with considerably less cost. It has all just been clinically explained to these men who are hesitating as to which delicacy to try next.

As I survey the men assembled, all I can see is simply corporate farmers, viewing the human race as so much livestock that needs to be selectively bred. And any animal on their farm that cannot assist in the advance of eugenics will be taken away and slaughtered ruthlessly. Over the last few years, such animals as were shown to be deficient in any way have already been removed – the so-called feeble-minded, or deformed. The freaks. Gone too are those whose temperament was perceived likely to cause distress to the majority, even including other 'farmers' who stood up to ask questions about the agricultural methodology here. The farmers now in control have this dream of a herd of prime cattle they can take pride in – offering no protest, no contradictory opinion, no rebellion – and they will do *anything* to achieve this.

Apart from Heydrich himself, that is what frightens me most: the men gathered here, like so many men anywhere in positions of power, are just petty middle-management personalities who have risen to the top of a hierarchy that fosters vicious political infighting. They have used intelligence above morals, for the simple reason that they possess none or choose to ignore them. Yet they could equally be your boss, your neighbour, your brother. They are just *ordinary* men, corrupted and perverted by a lust for the power that they have ended up obtaining.

It doesn't occur to them that they are about to assist in one of the most monstrous deeds of human history. What is wrong with a noble cause and basic common sense? The world will be henceforth pure – and what the man who convened this meeting wants, he gets. Only a fool would stand in his way, or he has a death wish. Heydrich may seem an ordinary man, in having a wife and children; as an urbane man coming from a family of musicians and playing the violin; as the brave fighter-pilot adventurer shot down in 1941 in Russia, and who also seems reckless in shunning the personal security which he insists everyone else maintains. But, as I know in retrospect, the numerous prostitutes he abuses are all too well aware of his sexual sadism. And he may not be personally present in the death chambers when they gas and burn his victims, but he still issues the orders. So while there may indeed appear to be part of him that corresponds to ordinary men, significantly he is cold and monstrous: a psychopath.

I finger the barrel of the rifle standing at my side as I gaze at Heydrich.

This gun has to be loaded, what use would it be to me as a guard if it were otherwise? Can I really alter the outcome? Or is it a delusion?

Maybe if I do shoot Heydrich, there will surely be no escape for me. I too will be gunned down instantly – or worse. These men regularly use torture. I grip the barrel again, gently, raising it slightly. I feel the weight of it, and wish I could make a move, wish I could face down this demon now in the same room with me.

Like a shark sensing a rhythm change to the water, Heydrich pauses in mid-conversation, and looks around the room. His gaze settles on me and for a moment he frowns, as if he seems to recognize me. I know I am partaking in some extraordinary illusion. No one made an attempt on Heydrich's life that day – but my being here gives me an opportunity to *do* something, surely.

My tremors intensify and I realize I am sweating profusely. As Heydrich begins to move towards me, I find I am lost in total confusion, by the crushing feeling of being trapped in a dilemma, one that I can extricate myself from only by making a decision quickly. At last I understand that the Devil has been there all along. The Devil is SS Obergruppenführer Reinhard Heydrich, who is now standing directly in front of me and reaching for his pistol. As I fumble with my own StG.44 rifle, it is a race between us.

He is suddenly replaced with an image of the pill-box.

But then he is back, closer to me.

Next, he judders and flickers away again.

Click, click . . . *click*!

With a relief that makes me cry out, I feel the vision dissolving into nothing. I clutch the side of my head, now throbbing like I've been physically hit.

I am back.

I knock the CAMIC partially off, then readjust it, my hands shaking. I have *no* idea what has just happened.

Did I win?

I adjust the CAMIC again.

They'll be glad they didn't see that.

The pillbox blurs and I'm hyperventilating. Forcing myself to steady my breathing, I look down at Benjamin's paperback I'm still holding.

Do what drink what?

I frown – the difficulty of reading the words is a welcome curiosity.

Do Dolphins Drink Water?

I feel again like a little boy, frightened by my father's scolding over some misdemeanour. I look down along the beach towards my friends, but they are in the exact same positions as I remember them last – TC half-turning towards me as she calls out.

Where have the last ten minutes gone?

Panic begins to build again as I suddenly realize that I still retain the taste of the *Frikadellen* in my mouth . . . together with fragments of meat caught in my teeth.

Oh, shit.

Chapter Four

I run to catch up with the others as they head for The Level in Cobbsmere Nature Reserve, taking the coastal path.

It's cooler in the shade available here. The path alternates between a tunnel of greenery, running via lofty nettles and tracking through small copses. The nettles catch me as I hasten past, but I ignore their little flicks of pain. Stumps of trees and the broken walls of forgotten buildings submerged in rampant ivy are littered everywhere; stunted trees creak in the mildest of breezes and the path itself is bounded by a newly erected pine fence to stop tourists falling over the crumbling cliffs beyond. I run harder.

I've heard some say recently that this pathway seems odd to them: disturbing, unsettling. I tend to agree with them, half expecting a multitude of silent ghosts to step into my way as I run.

I try meanwhile to deal with my pillbox experience, terrified at imagining myself in the same room as Heydrich, terrified that it seemed so necessary for me to kill him.

But what did it all mean?

I think again of those last moments: *pull the trigger*

or not? If in my imagination I could shoot Heydrich, then maybe I could kill Toluene?

Just as I catch up with him, Benjamin stumbles on some chicken wire covering a stile that is supposedly there to stop people slipping when the wood is wet.

Collecting my thoughts, I slow to a walk and I choke out a sort of laugh at my accident-prone friend. Benjamin has been a sort of vortex for such absurd mischief ever since I've known him.

Then, as it is programmed to, my CAMIC mobile softly bleeps and I pause to check it. When I touch a button, a huge distorted pale-coloured image flashes in front of me in mid-air. It jerks, disappears, then reappears, stable and focused, tracking the movement of my right eye. Illuminated before me now is a Webvis report announcing that there are just over five thousand Maxnet users getting ready to watch. I turn the image off.

We emerge from the wood and in front of us lies the open plain of Dunwich Heath. It slopes away into a mile-wide bowl of undulating and uncultivated sandy soil, bounded by woodland on three sides and on its fourth by the west-facing bay, which itself has been carved out by centuries of tide. My nostrils twitch at the thick smell of lilac-coloured heather spreading over the thin layer of sand sustaining the heath, like some huge moth-eaten blanket trying to engulf it all, converting it into more of the same.

'Look at all those people,' says Benjamin.

We stand on the rise, above the path leading down to The Level, and look along the coast to the Large-water nuclear power station. The mere sight of it causes a little skip of the heart.

Join the technophobes' club.

The place below me seems so completely and absolutely foreign. Dominating the skyline near the beach is a giant white football of a building – I suppose it houses the reactor – but against the greens and browns and lilacs of the shoreline, against the shimmer of the sea, it appears *too* white, *too* clean. As if to add contrast to this blinding starkness, there is a dirty, grey-and-blue box of a windowless building right beside it – resembling an enormous battery-charger for a mobile phone, so squat and solidly built that it appears to be plugged into the ground. A number of auxiliary buildings surround it, with pipes running from it in haphazard directions, and beyond it strange narrow towers stand out in the sea. The whole complex is enclosed by a high fence topped with razor wire, which is currently surrounded by large numbers of people.

'Good God,' says TC. 'There's even *more* down there than yesterday.'

At a rough guess, I'd estimate about five hundred of them encamped around the perimeter – giving the appearance of a music festival, with all the tents and camper vans, but without the jovial atmosphere. Most of the people are milling around waving placards, and the red ribbons tied to the fence make it look as if a wall of poppies surrounds Largewater. As we look on, impressed by the increase in numbers of protesters, another big group arrives, on foot. Though there are several police cars, the cops themselves don't seem particularly busy. The protesters, though vocal, appear peaceful for the moment. An underlying tension exists though – I can sense it. The occasional shout of real anger exacerbates it.

My CAMIC mobile softly bleeps again but I decide not to check it out.

'I never realized how ugly that place is,' observes TC.

'I think it's kind of pretty,' argues Benjamin.

She frowns at him and hesitates, as if wary of getting into an argument.

'Don't you ever think those people down there may have a point,' she eventually says. 'Don't you *feel* it?' She wraps her arms around herself comfortingly.

'No way.' Benjamin shakes his head. 'No way are they right. Where do you think we'd be now if it wasn't for science?'

'Freer and happier?' suggests TC.

I laugh as Benjamin sticks his hands into his pockets and frowns, apparently searching for inspiration. For a moment, he seems preoccupied in studying the huge white dome of the reactor, then quickly finds his answer.

'Galileo,' he says, taking a hand from his pocket and snapping his fingers. 'If it hadn't been for Galileo building a telescope and proving Copernicus right, we might still be thinking that the sun went around the Earth. That's the sort of reality you get through science, that's the usefulness of science.'

'I don't know any more,' TC says, 'and that's exactly what those people down there are asking. What's the use of science if its consequences are worse than whatever it is it's supposed to be improving?' She takes out her chip-link card and waves it at Benjamin. 'We have CCTV recording people's every move, with fancy software spotting any abnormal behaviour and face recognition for deterring criminals. There's the National DNA Authority offering us perfect partners, but charging higher insurance premiums if you possess a slight genetic flaw or are prone to illness. They're monitoring our shopping to prevent us buying too many cigarettes or too much alcohol. And now public buildings and company offices are being equipped with toilets that analyse your pee and pass on positive results of any over-indulgence to the police so that they can disable your car. How much do *they* need to know to protect us?' She returns her chip-link card to her back pocket. 'Those people down there, they think those terrible nightmares we all suffered, and all those fatal accidents in consequence, were the result of a technology gone wrong. I even think I agree with them.'

I'm tempted to access my mobile and see what other Maxnet users think, but stop myself.

Perhaps we're all starting to experience similar things happening to us: all our lives being spliced into another reality – a sort of universe-shift. Mention it openly so the e-viewers pick it up?

I glance at Benjamin. He's probably the likeliest person I know when it comes to understanding if there was a scientific reason behind what occurred to us all last month. He knows what is and what isn't possible in the world of science; he knows what is on its way in, on its way out, what benefits will possibly derive – or their downside. To him, technology will always be vital – he even signed up for a chip-link card before they became compulsory.

'Being caught up in a crowd,' he is saying, 'that's my recurring version of last month's nightmare.'

Oh shit, Benjamin is experiencing them as well.

'What happened, Ben?' TC says, with a sudden panic in her eyes.

I think of the death camps, and the Hamburg blitz, and now Heydrich. *I* am *right. We're* all *beginning to have our own separate nightmares.*

Benjamin slumps to the ground, as if he's a surly teenager. 'I know it sounds daft,' he says, 'but in my nightmare – which I've had many times over the last week – I'm always being pursued by some sort of group who appear to have the same sort of mentality as the Borg in *Star Trek.*'

We stare at each other and it is Benjamin himself who tries to laugh it off.

'Okay, okay,' he says, 'I'm a *Star Trek* nut, and the Borg are just fictional cyborgs with a group collective mind, but these people in my dreams . . . no, it's not a dream, it seems so *real* . . . Anyway, these people pursuing me, they seem to all know exactly what the others are thinking. It's rather like the Maxnet system, except there's no individual choice about one's actions – you have to do what the rest want you to do and you don't have a choice about switching them off. And, the thing is, they want me to join them. It's the way they *insist* on that that makes it so frightening. It scares me shitless. Imagine losing your will and being submerged, assimilated into something like *that.*'

With the current jagged nature of my mind – exacerbated by my continual lack of sleep – I suddenly decide I have to do this now, or I never will.

'I experienced something similar,' I say, 'just a few minutes ago.'

They both stare at me.

'It seemed so real, just like Ben's experience.' I explain about Reinhard Heydrich, and then I quickly glance at Benjamin. 'I think I was meant to try to kill him – as some sort of test.'

I notice TC looking confused, and the fear in her eyes builds until she catches me watching her. She immediately looks to the ground.

'Come on,' she says suddenly, and starts walking away, 'let's get Scott's task done now. Let's go see Jenny.'

Her abruptness startles me. She's changed her mind and just *doesn't* want to talk about it.

Ben stands up and we both meekly follow TC.

Benjamin's sister Jenny has been working at the nature reserve for the past year after finishing university. She is nearly twenty-two, and the red curls of her childhood have straightened out and been cut short; the baggy sportswear has been swapped for jeans and sleeveless windcheater, and she now possesses the shape of an athlete. She has more vibrant life in one little finger than many people have in their entire bodies.

Jenny too went to Springgreen Open School, and is still heavily into New Age culture – as she says I should be with my pronouncements on my youthful supernatural experiences – and seems to have settled on a belief system part-way between Buddhism and the Baha'i faith. It sounds like some sort of paganism-white-witchery-Druidism. Her delightful artlessness has spawned several National DNA Authority suitors but she has turned them all down – I think she may even still be a virgin.

My thoughts about her are interrupted as TC suddenly stops in her tracks – she apparently wants to re-ignite the discussion, even as we head down to The Level.

Her face flushes. 'What's next?' she asks, shakily lighting a cigarette. 'What comes *next*?'

I have a sudden strong urge to kiss TC, and I instantly find myself wondering what it would be like to have sex with her – to roll around naked and sweat up some passion. The sheer guttural desire makes my mouth go suddenly dry.

Where did that *come from?*

What's happening to me?

INTERNET NEWS UPDATE by Janice Maclean
Hornchurch, Kent

The annual open day at Middleton Manor gardens had to be abandoned today due to a plague of insects. Crowds at the famous gardens were surprised when large swarms of small black flies appeared at about eleven o'clock in the morning, and were soon covering their clothes, and even their faces.

'It was when they started getting into my eyes that I began to worry,' said Ashford resident Sue Tennerbacker, twenty-five and mother of three. 'When my little one started to choke on the things, that's when I headed back to the safety of our car.'

Mr David Stufinder, owner of Middleton Manor, said, 'We had just opened up the picnic area when these enormous clouds of insects descended upon us. The staff and I were able to get many of the visitors safely inside our house, which is not normally open to the public, while the rest were fortunately able to reach their cars. Luckily, we were not as busy today as we have been recently. The whole incident must have lasted about half an hour.'

Bernard Allcross, a local gardener, explained, 'These insects – I've known of them since a child as storm flies – are fairly common at this time of year. Though not normally in such huge numbers, that's quite rare.'

'I just don't want to go through that experience again,' confessed Mrs Tennerbacker.

The reed beds in Cobbsmere Nature Reserve are growing exceptionally high this year – even Benjamin barely needs to lower his head to disappear from view. Up there in the distance is the hide that the bird-watchers use to observe the marshes. Earlier, as we passed the car park they use, there seemed far fewer vehicles than usual.

TC glances at both of us in turn. 'We ready?' she checks.

'Get on with it,' I urge her, nervously.

She nods and turns back towards the bird-hide up on the rise.

As a child, TC learnt the knack of bird imitations from the best pheasant poacher in these parts. She now cups both hands about her mouth and emits a kind of strangled bark. The sound bounces out into the marsh – in a sort of boom like a bittern calling. Since it's July and you mostly hear their particularly deep call only in spring, when they're being territorial, that should cause quite a stir amongst today's few birdwatchers.

Oh, the delights of getting involved in company promotions.

TC repeats the sound.

In the distance, we can just see the door to the hide open, as someone emerges and takes a few steps in our direction.

It is Ben's sister Jenny.

And even as I see her, something she said yesterday evening becomes invested with relevance after my experience earlier today.

As I stood in their kitchen while Benjamin went to fetch the homemade cider from under the stairs, Jenny was busying herself preparing a snack of cheese sandwiches, explaining that she was retreating to her garden-shed studio to finish some glasswork.

She suddenly paused at what she was doing, losing, for an instant, all the colour in her cheeks.

'What's up?' I asked, alarmed.

She shook her head and composed herself. 'Oh, oh nothing – it's just something I've been getting these last couple of days.'

'What do you mean?' I was both concerned and fascinated.

She shook her head again, then her whole body shivered – as though she had just been touched by something cold and unpleasant.

Before I could enquire further, Benjamin burst into the kitchen with two small flagons.

'You want to come too, Jen?' he asked her.

'I'd love to, but I've got work to finish.'

And so I followed Benjamin to the beach, without discovering any more about what had happened to her. If I had done, it might have prepared me a bit better for today's events.

Now, Jenny waves towards the spot where we are half hidden among the reeds.

'Go on,' TC urges me. 'Give her a wave back.'

I sigh and raise an arm reluctantly. Benjamin bursts out laughing.

Our good humour lasts but two or three seconds, till I suddenly realize that TC is wiping away tears – but not of laughter.

'Hey, what's up?' I ask her.

Benjamin, practical as always, quickly susses that she is thinking of her mother.

She blinks away her tears. 'Look,' she says, rather quietly.

'We are,' replies Benjamin soothingly.

'No,' says TC, 'look, up *there*.'

And she points, back in the direction we have just come from, back towards the low cliff that rises above the beach. Benjamin turns with me, and I spot the man who is standing there in the distance. I feel a sudden chill – reminding me of that ghostly WWII pilot who was standing on the beach, watching me.

'It's Jake,' says TC. 'Dr Jake Crux.'

'Who?' says Benjamin, shading his eyes with a hand. 'Oh, yeah, that American scientist who made the news.'

It's a real person, since the other two recognize him.

I breathe out, at last.

So do I, now.

The man seems like a giant waiting to hurl a thunderbolt at us from his elevated position on the rise, and the sight of him immediately provokes a range of conflicting emotions in me. If anyone could be said to be spooky, just by the way that they stand, this man's posture says it all. He seems to be standing immovable, yet wary at the same time, as if preparing to confront some huge invisible object heading towards him. And he is watching us still, in that spectral manner I don't like.

'He gives me the creeps,' mutters Benjamin.

So I'm not the only one.

TC just frowns.

I don't say anything, for all I can think about is how the weird premonition that has been building in me for the last hour or so – the one I assumed was to do with Reinhard Heydrich – has now been given form in the shape of Dr Jake Crux.

A distant yell from the hide distracts us for a moment. A woman dressed in typical birdwatcher gear is standing beside Jenny and furiously gesturing at us. We all decide it would be better if we get out of here. As we hurry off, I notice how we all keep glancing over at Jake, who remains motionless on the rise, staring after us.

I try to laugh it off.

We, a motley crew of practical jokers, in my case hiccuping, fall over ourselves like hyped-up teenagers as we hasten back into the ruins of the friary – Benjamin and TC colliding with each other in an effort to squeeze down a narrow, roofless passageway, while I leap through the single-arched window. There is really not much left of the medieval building – just a few flint-and-red-brick walls increasingly obscured by the mass of vigorous ivy that has sprung up over the last four years. I think about switching off the CAMIC, and therefore the Maxnet users, so we can get ourselves some privacy here – but I quickly dismiss the idea because I need all the votes I can get. I *must* keep focused on winning the contest even though it's difficult with the echoes of Wannsee still echoing in my mind.

Sitting down with the others, I turn this way and that, giving my viewers a good look around the place. Barely more extensive than the average modern house, the remains of the friary sit in a field of grass and thistle which is currently used as pasture for a couple of horses. Its perimeter is still enclosed by an ancient flint wall, and the irregular humps and hillocks all around it presumably cover the rest of Henry VIII's destruction of the monasteries. There are three, randomly positioned, rust-covered, corrugated-iron shacks-cum-stables, and corralling the horses themselves is an electrified fence. The old friary used to be a comforting source of escape to us when we were children, but now I find I don't quite feel comfortable with the way the sunlight glints off sharp edges of flint.

We all simultaneously become aware of a silhouette suddenly looming.

All three of us stiffen, and wait expectantly.

Jake is standing just on the other side of the arched window, looking at us with his hands casually in his pockets. He looks so pale I suppress a sudden dread that he'll melt through the low wall of the window like a ghost or shimmer away to nothing.

TC slaps a hand to her cheek, and glances at each

of us in turn. I find this delayed reaction curious, as if done just to draw attention to herself.

Jake takes his hands from his pockets. 'Do you mind if I join you?' Without waiting for an answer, he vaults through the window with unexpected elegance. As he squats cross-legged amongst us, he grins broadly, if momentarily.

'Hello, strangers,' he says, in his broad American accent, as he eyes each of us in turn.

I flinch, wondering if it is my imagination or a reaction to just how dangerous this man could be.

I see TC give him a brief flicker of a smile as she releases her hair from the scrunchie and rubs her forehead with the back of one hand. Gradually the tension flashing around in muscular spasms on his face disappears as he watches her. Incredible as I find it, I recognize at once that there's a sort of connection between them. Or even an attraction?

I'm startled at TC's transparent reaction: it's obvious that they've both perceived something potentially engrossing in each other. It's even as though they have already met before. I look at TC holding Jake's stare as she flicks a long strand of unbound hair from her eyes, then I glance at Benjamin. He winks at me, and I smile in return, and then slowly turn back to watch TC and Jake with apprehension.

I wonder what exactly has brought this man here to seek us out.

And what our e-viewers must be making of this new development.

Jake Crux is something of an imported celebrity. He seems to have popped up fully formed as a genius from America just to impress on the rest of us that anything is possible. It made quite a local stir when he arrived from the States to head up some research project at the nearby Eisencrick Institute.

If anyone could remain unaffected by that traumatic night of three weeks ago, I would imagine Dr Jake Crux would be one of the very few. But from his current twitchy demeanour, it looks like he must be suffering the after-effects just like the rest of us. It is so unexpected to see such an authoritative presence so obviously on edge . . . even though he is trying desperately to appear relaxed now that he has finally joined us.

Since no security bods from Unit-C have shot onto the scene to escort him away, I assume Gareth is waiting to see what happens first.

Or else he knew Crux was going to turn up anyway?

There is a long moment of silence, then TC holds out her hand to him.

'Hi,' she says. 'Nice to see you again.'

He takes her hand without shaking it – it looks petite in his grasp – but it appears as if TC is gripping his hand as hard as she can.

'Hello, again. Yes, I remember you,' he says, still involved in that intense staring contest. Then he abruptly glances around at the rest of us, first at Benjamin, then at me. 'I remember all three of you. You were all there together when that local news team was interviewing me when I first arrived from America.'

I'm stunned at such recall. We had bumped into him and the news crew momentarily at the railway station while passing through.

Incredible that he can remember noticing us standing watching for just a couple of minutes.

TC tries to conceal a pleased smile.

Crux cocks his head to one side, as if deciding what to say next. Meanwhile I take a long look at him. Over the last few days, stooges whose sole intent seems to be stirring up additional controversy have accosted several of the other Unit-C contestants. I resent this cheap ploy, and at least he doesn't look happy about it either. I've seen this same agitation manifest in athletes about to go up against stiffer competition for the first time. That same expression of concern and uncertainty is exactly what I notice in Crux's eyes right now. It makes me wary – he is after all a total stranger to us.

He gives me a momentary smile.

'It's nothing unusual for me to remember people,' he says. 'Human behaviour is what I primarily study. But I have to confess that some people think my skill at recollection has to be a sort of telepathy.'

He's so obviously been set up for this encounter by Gareth and the PR reps for Unit-C.

But the other two seem prepared to tolerate him – especially TC. I decide to postpone asking him why he is here.

Jake Crux gets out a silver cigarette case and extracts a small, black cigar. He slips it in his mouth and then offers the case around. Only TC accepts one and then they both light up.

'Human behaviour?' says Benjamin. 'So that's what you're investigating at Eisencrick?'

'Yep, that's about right,' Jake nods. Once again, he treats us to a microsecond smile. 'Some of my subjects

say the way I come to know things about them so inti-
mately has to be a sort of ESP – Extrasensory
Perception. But it's actually about being acutely aware
of how we all do things and react to things on a subconscious level.'

He steeples his fingers, the cigar still sticking out
between two of them. 'You know how people rarely
think about how their bodies give them away once
they become interested in someone else?'

We all swap glances with each other, then TC turns
back to him. 'Yeah, we've read about that stuff often
enough, but remind us how it's relevant.'

Jake holds her stare intently as he continues. 'If
you're attracted to someone, your pupils will dilate.
Women are far better at reading this particular signal
than men are. Now I'm primarily interested in how
those simple mechanics of behaviour evolved. That's
what I find fascinating, not the behaviour itself.'

'How's that anything to do with ESP?' Benjamin
interrupts.

Jake turns and focuses his full attention, as if our
friend is being evaluated under a microscope. I
instinctively dislike it.

'The ability to second-guess someone, by assessing
their subliminal body movements, their micro-
reactions, can appear to others as possessing psychic
capabilities, which in turn can prove *unsettling*. And
that's primarily because the idea of ESP frightens
people – it just doesn't fit in with how they view the
world.'

He spreads his arms wide to indicate the friary.
'For instance, take this place. Whatever they may
claim, they wouldn't like the idea that history could

have left a paranormal legacy here – in the form of ghosts, I mean. And that's considered a form of ESP too . . . you know, seeing them?'

'Do you *really* believe in that sort of thing?' asks TC.

'ESP?' says Jake. 'Ghosts?'

'Yes,' she says, 'the unexplained.'

'It's a big universe,' Benjamin again interrupts them, 'who says we've found all the secrets?'

Jake inhales deeply on his cigar.

The people at Unit-C are good. This man is getting all of us really hooked on what he has to say. Ghosts? ESP? He must have been given personal information about me. I can feel an excitement rising, but I still don't trust him.

'You're right,' Jake finally replies, 'it's an infinite universe . . . depending on whose theory you currently believe. Why shouldn't there be intriguing possibilities out there that we don't understand yet, scary stuff that we suspect *might* just exist? I mean, a worldwide, mass-hallucination-nightmare is definitely something from the Twilight Zone, isn't it?'

He's not only talking about The Night, I bet.

I sit up a little straighter – still wary, but now really curious.

'They could have been prompted by some rogue satellite,' suggests TC, looking a little upset.

'No,' insists Jake, 'they couldn't. And they weren't.'

There is a momentary silence, then Benjamin slowly claps; one, two, three.

'Brilliant,' he says. 'At last, someone who's on *my* side.'

'So, if it didn't frighten *you*, too,' TC asks Jake, 'tell us what happened that night?'

'I didn't *say* that. But no man-made satellite possesses the power or capacity to influence so many. That's just a blind alley trotted out to soothe frightened people. And why isn't the possibility being considered that it was caused by some totally natural phenomenon: some freakish paranormal twist in the cosmos, a universe-shift of some sort beyond our current understanding? Something *real*, I mean, in the sense that it wasn't artificial . . . Something *provably* authentic.'

I lean forward.

He's hooked me now . . . I myself called it a 'universe-shift'. How can he be using precisely the same words as me? Ones that I have not expressed out loud?

Crux gazes around again at the remains of the friary.

'I bet this place does have memories of the kind I've been talking about, preserved here in our immediate vicinity to be released by the right person. That's been mooted as a concept for decades.'

I think about when I touched the wartime pillbox earlier.

'Haven't we *all* had some experience at one time or the other that we couldn't explain?' he continues. 'An occurrence beyond coincidence? If so, could you tell me about it? I'd really like to know. Ghost? Sixth-sense? Anything? Especially if it was recent.'

Ben and TC look at me.

Can I trust him enough?

To test Jake's response, I decide to tell him first about the phantom aircraft at the pillbox – my other recent experience can wait. Maybe I can at least find out if Gareth set him up.

'I only just had something really strange happen to me, today,' I blurt out.

He is immediately curious, and I suddenly feel vulnerable and stupid. Benjamin and TC probably think I'm going to start on Heydrich.

'It was back there at the pillbox, just before we moved down onto The Level,' I begin. 'I saw this – . . . this *apparition* from the Second World War. It involved a dogfight between a Hurricane and a Stuka. And there was something else – there was a pilot just standing watching me.'

'That's not what you told us,' TC says. 'Couldn't that have just been your imagination?' She obviously thinks I'm trying to wind Crux up.

On top of my feeling a bit stupid, I now feel frustrated.

'Yes, yes, I know it *could* be,' I say. 'But seeing that man *standing* there, I'm certain it wasn't *just* imagination. This sort of thing has been happening to me for years, as I've always told you, but it's been getting much worse since . . . since The Night.'

I turn towards Jake. 'I think I triggered it,' I say to him.

I then glance around at the others, who are watching me silently. 'You're right, this old friary is exactly the sort of place you'd see phantoms. So why not other spots where traumatic events have occurred?'

Jake nods understandingly.

'This whole part of the country is littered with sites of wartime incidents,' I continue. 'Wouldn't they all be likely to have their own sort of ghosts, like the one I witnessed over near the pillbox?'

'You know,' Jake says at last, 'I don't doubt you saw *something*. But perhaps it was something that needs a clearer explanation.'

I now notice how close he and TC are sitting together, and I suddenly want to get up and separate them forcibly. Is that what Gareth counted on – that TC and Jake would hit it off instantly? I'm fighting to hold on to any sense of continuity in my life, and yet I'm assailed by further changes even as I attempt to add some extra purpose to my direction.

But then . . . I have other thoughts.

I suddenly sense – perhaps we all did, which would explain why we've accepted him so quickly – that Jake is the holder, the guardian, of some great new secret. I also decide that he knows this and is acutely aware of his responsibility.

It's become impossible. I can't believe my world is changing so much.

Where has my initial caution about this man gone? Why do I now think he is someone who can help?

He's a scientist, hell! And how much credence do they possess at the moment?

I become suddenly aware of the CAMIC mobile phone digging into my side, and I feel a slight disgust at its proximity so near to my skin.

INTERNET NEWS UPDATE by Janice Maclean
It seems Unit-C is having fun and the person(s) responsible for *Total Cover* should take a bow. Introducing agents provocateurs has been pure inspiration. Tiffany is

clearly not best pleased to have the man who broke her heart suddenly back in her life. Her ratings, however, are expected to increase rapidly – along with Maxnet shares as more viewers join up to partake of the experience. Unit-C are at pains to insist that any Internet user can follow the progress of the remaining contestants, but of course don't deny that using Maxnet is the better option. I must admit to having been using one for the last few days, that the provision of instant information it enables is excellent and well recommended. It apparently works in much the same way as the Internet, but Maxnet includes user-experience along with simple user-knowledge. It's like an organic library housing knowledgeable people instead of books.

As for stirring up the others in the promotion, Scott now seems to face a bit of competition for TC's affections. It appears Dr Jake Crux is really going to mix it up.

I catch Jake looking at me and I hold his stare. For a moment I imagine I'm back on the field again, competing against a top-class decathlon athlete who has decided to psyche me out. I become very conscious of the CAMIC again: Jake probably knows how they work and considers them nothing out of the ordinary. He blinks rapidly, then closes his eyes for several seconds. When he opens them again he continues to stare at me. The other two begin to notice, and their conversation becomes hesitant, then stops completely.

'I have an idea,' Jake says directly to me, as he grinds his cigar out on the nearby wall. 'I want to show you something.' His voice has a rasp to it, as if his throat is extremely dry. Not for the first time do I wonder if he's talking to me or to Maxnet. 'It's a kind of guessing game. I say "kind of" because, as it progresses, you'll swear there's *more* to it. Are you willing?'

I nod, curious to know what he is intending, or what I need to watch out for.

He eyes his cigar butt, before flicking it to one side, then takes out his cigarette case again and removes a fresh cigar. After putting the case back into his pocket, he carefully takes the new cigar and breaks off one end of it.

Jake tosses away all but the stub, then puts both hands behind his back.

'Scott, when I reveal my hands in a moment, I want you to guess which closed fist that bit of cigar is in. It'll be easy, no tricks – as my hands will never leave my arms.'

An instant memory: a picnic in that park in Hamburg. We are sitting in a circle – my father, my mother, my brother Michael, my sister Susan and I. It is a beautiful day and the park is crowded. In front of us is a large plate containing ham and cheese sandwiches, and another with smoked chicken wings and a small tub of mayonnaise in which to dip them. The delicious smells of food mingle with that of newly mown grass. We already know what is coming, because my father has just uttered the words, 'No tricks, my hands will never leave my arms,' and produced a pack of cards from his jacket pocket. Magic time! Every time we come here, our father demonstrates to us yet another card trick. For a boy of my young age, they are wonderful and somewhat scary. When he picks Susan as his 'volunteer' this time, I feel a little envious. As he shuffles the pack, then fans the cards out face-down in front of her, we know the ritual.

'Take one,' my father says, 'look at it carefully, but don't tell me what it is. Then show it to everyone else, and put it back into the pack.'

He turns his head away as Susan picks her card. Michael and I watch excitedly as she shows us the card with much ceremony – this time the seven of diamonds – and she then replaces it in the pack. On her cue, my father turns back, retrieves the deck and shuffles it. He gives the cards a final riffle with what he calls 'the waterfall', then deals them out face-down into four piles.

'Now,' he says, 'I'll need some help here.'

I must have looked very eager, because he turns to me and shakes his head. 'Sorry, Scott, this time I'll be needing some extra help. This is a *royal* problem.'

He lets me feel glum only for a couple of seconds. 'But you can give them a call for me,' he continues. 'Why don't you knock on their doors?'

My mother laughs as I reach over and solemnly tap on each pile of cards with my knuckles.

'Hey,' says my father, with that big magician's grin all over his face. 'You must have a powerful knock – they've come to the door straightaway.'

And, with that, he proceeds to flip over the top card of each pile . . . revealing in turn each one of the four kings. My father times it perfectly. As we all gasp in wonder, he scoops up the cards, again gives them his 'waterfall' shuffle, but letting it slip out of control so that the cards fly in all directions, and he snatches one out of the air . . .

It is the seven of diamonds.

I find it mind-boggling. So does everyone else. We all clap and cheer, though I notice Michael seems less enthusiastic.

'Hey, Dad,' he says, 'I can top that.'

We clap and cheer again.

'Oh, yes?' says my father, uncertainly.

My brother reaches over to the plate and picks up a sandwich.

'What sort of sandwich is this?' asks Michael. He hands it to my father.

My father begins to lift the upper slice of bread. He stops and frowns, every trace of his earlier smile disappearing as he reaches two fingers in to extract something from the inside. Smeared in butter is a playing card – and I know what it is before he shows us. It is a seven of diamonds from the spare pack we always bring along.

While my mother smiles, my sister and I stand up and jump about, and cheer and clap. My father just sits there, shaking his head. To this day, I don't know if Michael had been in on some greater trick that my father himself had organized, but the look on my father's face suggested not. Michael had genuinely outwitted him.

As Jake stares at me still, I feel lost in the time and place of this moment. All I can feel is a slight breeze filtering into the dank heat amid the ruins. All I can hear is the distant waves of the sea, the cry of a gull and a whinny from one of the nearby horses. All I can smell is the dryness of long grass. All I can see is Jake looking at me intently. There is even a vague recall of how the *Frikadellen* tasted in my mouth.

As Jake presents his closed fists, I know immediately which one I want to point to.

'Guess,' he says.

I point to his right hand. He rotates his fist, opens it up, and there is the cigar end.

'That's only a fifty–fifty guess,' remarks Benjamin.

'You're a genius, Benjamin,' I mutter.

'I know,' Benjamin says. 'It troubles me sometimes.'

We both grin at each other.

'Again,' Jake says. It is not a question, but a demand.

His hands disappear behind him again and then re-emerge. I take a deep breath and point to the fist I believe it is in this time. He opens that hand, and then the other right under Benjamin's nose, to prove both that I am right and that the other hand is empty.

'Again?' Jake says.

'Okay.' I glance around at the others.

TC is sitting there wide-eyed.

Twelve times Jake does it in all. Ten times I successfully identify the correct hand.

Then he moves on to Benjamin, who gets five out of twelve correct and claims that balances things out.

Then it is TC's turn herself. She gets it right all twelve times.

I feel like I am back in the Hamburg park again, sitting in the sun. That seven of diamonds is dancing before my eyes again.

'She got a hundred per cent,' breathes Benjamin.

'Yeah,' I say quietly, but it seems none of us knows what to make of this little trick of Jake's.

'And again,' Jake insists.

He slides the cigar end behind his back. As he produces both fists, TC points to the correct one once more.

'And again,' he says.

TC gets it right another time.

Even Benjamin says nothing now. What is there to say?

Jake continues the ritual repeatedly. Finally, TC gets it wrong on the thirty-fifth go.

I suspect both my friends are feeling as stunned as I am. I find I am mentally drained with just trying to work out the odds for this achievement.

'Well,' says Jake glancing from TC to myself, 'any ideas how you two just managed that?'

Neither of us is prepared to vocalize a guess. We just look at each other silently. The breeze on my cheeks feels suddenly cold. I figure it must be some trick on Jake's part, but I can't get over that feeling of myself *knowing* in advance which hand the cigar fragment would appear in. And I'm damned sure TC too had been guessing correctly while Benjamin and I made our various attempts. Usually this trick works with the magician guessing which hand a member of the audience is concealing an object in – but Jake has somehow reversed this routine.

Can he be that *brilliant at working out how we'll react?*

I shake my head. I myself felt so positive each time about which hand he had the cigar in. I was *positive*.

I look from Jake to TC – hoping they might have an answer for me. TC and Jake.

Huh?

TC and Jake . . .

For a moment, I feel as though something is

different, as though there is a gap of silence and a space that needs filling with a lost moan. It is an awareness of some oblique presence, just out of recognizable vision, one that cannot be defined – a memory that cannot be recalled. Cold feathery touches on my face, and running down my neck, make me shiver. I don't know what prompts them.

Jake, TC.

TC, Jake.

I notice the two other people here with me seem as perplexed as I am.

And I stare down at some flattened grass that looks as if it's been recently scorched by vandals setting an illegal camp fire, and I smell a pungent odour similar to that of electrical sparks.

It seems meaningless.

Somewhere in my head is the beginning of a slight pain, while in my ears begins the dull whisper of a crowd that ebbs and flows, rises and falls, a huge crowd of people talking to themselves a long, long way from me. They could be chanting, singing, they could be arguing – I can't tell. There could be thousands upon thousands involved, there could be millions. I want to reach out and catch what they're saying. Instead, I catch a whiff from the ash of the Hamburg firestorm. And then . . . and then I smell the dry grass surrounding the friary, and I hear the sea and the gulls as the voices fade away. I feel a slight warm breeze on my flushed face.

All I can see is the person I came here with, TC, and our new acquaintance, Jake.

He wears the same confused expression as my father did when my brother surprised him with that seven of diamonds hidden in the sandwich. TC herself is frowning and we all still seem to be lost in our own thoughts. It is as though something really bad has happened and we've somehow forgotten what.

I cannot work out why I feel so perturbed. My thinking must be all out of kilter after that tremendous guessing feat TC has just performed.

How did she do that? How did Jake know . . .?

I can't complete the thought.

I look around yet again.

It is as if I have misplaced something.

Or someone.

Then God commanded, 'Let the Earth produce all kinds of animal life: domestic and wild, large and small' – and it was done. So God made them all and He was pleased with what He saw. Evening passed and morning came – that was the sixth day.

Wednesday
Day 6

Chapter Five

Josh Candy – English, sixteen-year-old grunge-garage-rock devotee in sloth and clothes, curious that he's remembered how to smile and, moments ago, revelling in that giddy feeling that everything is actually all right with the world and that he does indeed have a place in it – stands on the spit of shingle at Bawdsey estuary on the Suffolk coast at five-fifteen in the morning after an all-night party, scratches his nose, adjusts his brand-new CAMIC, and wonders what the hell the skipper of Sea Thrush *thinks he is doing. Out to sea there is a good twelve miles' visibility, the tide is nearly as low as it will get (the slack oil-sheen water hardly ripples), and here is the* Sea Thrush *– all white and go-faster blue stripes – heading straight for him.*

Josh has lived all his life in Felixstowe Ferry, across the mouth of the river Deben from Bawdsey, and, even at his age, believes he's seen it all, and that every possible excitement the hamlet of Felixstowe Ferry can offer has been used up in the four years that he's really begun to notice the tourist girls in their swimsuits.

He sticks both hands in the back pockets of his jeans. Even at high tide, a yacht the size of the Thrush should never attempt to cross the shingle bar – the water is just too shallow there. When Josh and his friends race the surge in

*their Laser dinghies, they have to raise their daggerboards
when they ride the bar, yet the* Sea Thrush *has its throttle
wide open and is making at least five knots, moving straight
towards the exposed shingle. Towards Josh himself. He
steps back as the* Sea Thrush *lurches big at him. The keel
hits the beach, and it sounds like a giant is crunching and
slicing equally outsize crab shells. There is a last squeal, a
shriek, a loud crack, and the bow pushes a huge fore-wave
up onto the spit, which splashes over Josh's feet, then the
yacht jars to a dead stop.*

*Josh swears, and then starts wading out into the water
to see if he can help. He feels slightly nervous, acting alone
here, but he's been raised to deal with coastal emergencies.
Josh leans on the hull and calls aft.*

'Are you all right?' *he shouts.*

No one answers.

Shit, I wonder if the skipper's had a heart attack?

*Josh wades further and deeper into the water, heads
around to the transom, reaches up and pulls himself onto
the deck of the yacht. He stands up and yells again.*

'Hello? Anyone aboard?'

You prat – what a stupid question if they're out
cold.

*Josh edges forward. There is nobody slumped at the
wheel. The only oddity is a faint smell of burnt varnish, and
a scorch mark on the deck nearby. Josh ducks down into the
cabin. No one there either. He comes up to the wheel again,
cups his eyes and peers up-river. Then downstream. All
that can be seen in the distance is the diminishing wake that
the* Sea Thrush *generated.*

If the skipper's fallen overboard, he must be
underwater now.

Josh reaches for the radio and summons the coastguard, while scanning the length of river again.

Shit, where the fuck did the owner get to?

INTERNET NEWS UPDATE by Janice Maclean
They're now down to the last six contenders in *Total Cover*. This is certainly promising to be an exciting final few days. Since yesterday, we've lost Tricia, while Scott has been catapulted right up into third place. The interest generated by the mysterious Dr Jake Crux perhaps? The ratings for today mean that Tiffany is still ahead, but is now closely followed by Natalie, and then comes Scott. After that, Adi has Mickey Smote, the baby of the contest at eighteen, snapping at his heels, and finally comes Jo.

The contest is getting close, and it's proving a totally fascinating method to introduce Maxnet to the nation. As Unit-C proclaims: it's next-generation Internet – the accessible brain for the future.

Though just after five-thirty in the morning, Jake is already downing his fourth cup of coffee. It is Kenyan Mountain today, in his Green Wednesday mug. He has been working steadily since four o'clock, busy checking all his results, then backing them up by burning them onto CD. Jake still has niggles concerning yesterday's unplanned experiment at the friary, and meanwhile, the more telepathic connections he uncovers in his research with the mice, the more he is realizing the magnitude of the implications. If they have any connections to The Night, then time is fast running out for everyone. For an extrapolation of the amount of synchronicity in the uncloned mice, compared to the cloned group, suggests that – given its usual rate of growth – in about six days the human population itself will self-generate a synchronized group-mind.

Yesterday's encounter has certainly left its psychological mark on him in other ways. It is one thing to produce a hypothesis, it is entirely another to have it confirmed experimentally. Time after time those two young people guessed successfully which hand the cigar fragment was concealed in. It was what he expected would happen – though the experience still left him perplexed, as if he'd missed something.

Returning his attention to the maze, he has simplified it so that it now consists of just two adjoining tracks, separated by a narrow three-metre-long partition, which are accessible to each other by an opening at the far end. Jake now releases a cloned mouse into the left-hand track, while depositing a small amount of food at the near end of the right-hand track simultaneously. By wrapping it in cling film he has ensured the food emits no aroma. The mouse scurries up the left-hand track, locates the opening, heads back down the right-hand track and discovers the little parcel. The creature breaks into it with its teeth and starts chewing the contents.

By its fourth go, the mouse is scampering with definite purpose up one side and down the other. Thereupon, Jake places it back into a quarantine cage, waiting patiently for a full ten minutes, then he selects a second mouse.

This one shoots straight up and straight down the two long tracks to reach its goal. On its second attempt, it makes the interesting decision to see if it can simply climb over the barrier to get near the food even sooner.

Its ploy is successful.

And each of the mice that Jake releases subsequently behaves exactly the same. As soon as he places them on the left-hand track, they pause briefly, then scramble over the partition into the right-hand track. And each time Jake returns one to the cage, there is a moment of silence among all the other mice in the room. The changeover from general background mouse-noises to mute awareness occurs with increasing rapidity each time this happens. He feels the hairs on his arms stand up. This is clearly group consciousness at work, as if each individual mouse's brain is just a separate part of some greater whole. Like the way CAMIC connects to the *Total Cover* Maxnet system.

This being the case, what else might it be possible to teach the creatures?

Or the group consciousness?

And what is therefore the potential of Maxnet? They're similar.

Studying the control group of mice more closely, Jake notes the vague and minute cohesion of their group-mind. Having been made aware of this phenomenon – greatly exaggerated – by the cloned animals, he believes he can detect the same with the control group. Not nearly as powerful an entity, and certainly not as sophisticated, but Jake is able to discern a group consciousness there, too.

This from only an hour of experimentation, so what results could I achieve after a week? And what if this is fundamental to everything else that's living on this planet? Maybe, as I conjectured yesterday, something is changing in the universe, altering reality, and enabling me for one – and probably everyone else – consciously to detect things that have gone unnoticed to us for years.

The sheer strength of the combined purpose of the cloned group still makes him cautious – like a lurking presence ready to pounce at some unexpected moment – but he is determined to adjust his thinking to it.

As Jake goes over to his percolator to refill his mug, he studies this morning's addition to his picture collection. It is a download from the *Total Cover* website and he now runs a finger over a printed image of TC's full lips. As a different image suddenly springs into view, he realizes too late that he should have prepared himself better for such a reoccurrence.

Within an instant, reality takes a juddering step elsewhere . . . and he is again in another place, another universe, in another reality.

Click, click . . . *click!*

Jake is astride a horse, riding hard across sand and scrub, toeing the beast again and again to make it gallop faster. He sees only a narrow strip of the surrounding world through the eye-slit in his helm – an azure sky extending above a parched landscape of coastal desert. He adjusts quickly to this reality shift, and can smell and taste the dryness all around him. His armour chafes his shoulders, and his thighs feel raw where they squeeze his mount, but he ignores the discomfort in a sudden realization that he is filled with a terrible rage, and woe betide anybody who stands in his path. It is an amazing feeling of sheer murderous aggression.

His left hand grips the reins tighter as he adjusts the lance that he cradles in his right arm. Ahead of him, on the dusty plains, a young woman is bound to a sacrificial post, cowering in front of a huge snarling winged creature. The dragon turns its head as it hears the pounding hooves.

'I'm coming,' Jake bellows, unsure which of the two he is addressing.

As the dragon turns fully to face him, Jake kicks the snorting horse viciously one last time, and then he is upon the beast just as it begins to react. It rises up on its rear legs, fearsome mouth agape, its forelegs ready for combat. But at the last second, Jake tilts his lance towards the beast's chest, and leans heavily into the thrust. The point of the weapon plunges into the dragon's heart, the shudder of impact transferring to both horse and rider. The tip of the lance snaps off, and the horse stumbles, but Jake manages to remain in the saddle. As the dragon's shrieks of pain rip through the air, it falls, writhing, to the ground.

After Jake brings the horse to a halt, he throws the broken lance away, dismounts and pulls a long sword from the scabbard that hangs from the saddle. Striding over to his still-screaming victim, with one swift blow he decapitates the monster. For a long moment he stares down at the swift violence he has wrought, before turning to the captive woman. And is startled when he recognizes her.

'Thank you,' says TC.

And, just as comprehension envelops him, her face suddenly stiffens, freezes, goes out of focus, comes back again . . . and becomes just a downloaded photograph pinned to the wall in front of him.

Click, click . . . *click*!

Jake staggers backwards, reaching out to the workbench to stop himself from falling over. He gradually forces himself to regain control.

Frowning with a sudden headache, Jake looks around him. As his eye catches the UFO postcard, he again has trouble reading the words on the spacecraft.

His dyslexia quickly evaporates till he can again read: 'STOP ME AND BUY ONE'. Just as suddenly, his headache has gone.

Jake slumps into his chair and takes a gulp of coffee that he doesn't remember pouring. He thinks about the altered reality, where such violent anger broke surface. This time TC had been transported with him – or, at least, some version of her was.

Does it mean she is in danger?

He seems more certain now that they've definitely established a bond of some kind, other than just natural attraction.

Jake decides to head outside for an early morning smoke. And maybe give himself time to think.

Three minutes later and he is standing in his favoured smoking corner. Rolling up his shirtsleeves, he rests his back against the wall. In front of him stretches a wide expanse of lawn dotted with old trees – a peaceful landscape, with the morning mist already burning away. Even the fact that his personal Institute CAMIC is still hovering just above his shoulder doesn't worry him, and not many other people are around at this early hour. Just as he starts to reach for a cigar, a security guard happens to pass by, with a vicious-looking mongrel dog – Alsatian mixed with something else angry – trotting beside him on a lead.

'Hi, Dr Crux,' the man calls out.

'Hi, Gary.' Jake turns his attention to the dog.

Wearing a fur coat in this extreme heat, poor mutt.

Though its fur looks like it has recently been given a major trim, the dog pants with its tongue hanging out.

'You should find some shade for that hound before the day really heats up,' Jake calls after the guard.

Gary glances over his shoulder. 'I'll just let him lick the sweat off those idiots camped outside the gate-house.'

As Jake smiles, he looks down at his own bare arms, and realizes he is already sweating profusely in the short duration he has been standing outside. Even here in the shade, the stickiness of the air drains any enjoyment of the moment. The days are heating up quicker than ever.

Slowly and purposefully he extracts the cigar, lights it, then takes pleasure in blowing smoke into the growing swarm of flies hovering around him. His thoughts turn again to TC.

Yesterday afternoon he had given her a lift in his Landrover to her temporary lodgings.

'How fast can it go?' she had asked, sitting back in the passenger seat and folding her arms expectantly.

'I'll show you. Luckily, this thing's old enough not to have a speed inhibitor or need GPS tracking.' Warning her to brace herself, he started up the engine. She jammed herself firmly into place, with her boots pressed hard against the dashboard.

Soon they were heading down the Bestleton

straight. But the road undulates steeply so the Land-rover kept pitching up, then bouncing in all directions as it landed. Jake cast her a quick glance and was pleased to see her grinning broadly, her hair stream-ing out behind her.

As he overtook another car while ascending a blind hill, the other driver swerved aside, blaring his horn continuously.

'Yes!' TC cried out. '*Yes!!*'

As Jake glanced at her again, he noticed tears in her eyes. At first he thought this was due to the wind, and then he realized it was something else. There was a grim passion to her pleasure, and he sensed she didn't want him to slow down.

As she turned to hold his gaze, he found it hard to take his eyes off her.

Now, as Jake stands there in the open air, enjoying his cigar, he can't wait to see that look again.

And they both knew that they had proved some-thing astounding back at the friary.

The universe is changing. So are we.

He finally stubs out his cigar and heads back to his research.

I have completed about three miles of my regular six-mile morning run. I have decided to put my other decathlon training on hold – resting a week will be good. Earlier, out on the road, two teenage girls – six-teen or seventeen – accosted me and demanded my autograph, and one of them even kissed me. Their humour could not have prepared me less.

I may bounce with measured steps along the sandy soil of the bridleway through Dunwich woods and feel my lungs fill with the fresh new-day smell of the early morning; there may be an easy energy to my running as I try to take some enjoyment out of the experience; but I notice there are no rabbits out feeding as there normally would be, no woodland birds inspecting the soil for worms – usually a robin flutters behind me, to see what grubs I may kick up – and the sun is positioned at such an angle that it lights up the surrounding trees in eerie haloes. It doesn't bode well.

During these morning runs, I usually feel empowered to take on the world. Now all I can think about is Crux being together with TC, and this after my restless night of insomnia spent thinking about their uncanny performance at the friary and the other experiences. It seems like I don't even know whether I'm awake or still part of some fretful nightmare, unable to rouse myself.

I grit my teeth and endeavour to concentrate on something more positive.

I've drawn up a mental list of places I want to visit in the perverse hope of triggering a manifestation of any ghosts that may still haunt them. Apart from a couple of local spots – Bawdsey and Orford Ness – the areas that I think will have most significance for me personally are the old airfields scattered around practically every once-available flat open space in East Anglia. The main site to investigate – for a number of reasons – would be Fersfield, just outside of Diss in Norfolk, because that is from where Joseph Kennedy Jnr took off, in an aircraft nicknamed *Zootsuit Black*.

Among all the wartime heroes, Joe Jnr is the one who stands out particularly in my mind, for he had so much to lose. Joe was destined to become a president of the United States of America, except he undertook one flight too many. I'm sure there's some significant ghosts at the old airfield he was based in.

I can, I will, I must.

I am focused again. Yesterday's demons are mostly dismissed.

As I jog on – still no rabbits scattering before me, no robin following at my heels – my CAMIC bleeps to indicate that it has new information for me.

I push the download button on the mobile so that a semitransparent pale-coloured Webvis web page appears and a disembodied voice in my ear begins reeling off salient points. The information is just what I want – a compilation of stuff I've suspected for a long time.

UNITED STATES DEPARTMENT OF JUSTICE
FEDERAL BUREAU OF INVESTIGATION
Florida Office
RE: PASCAL TOLUENE

PASCAL TOLUENE, contrary to frequent assertions of a long family connection with the USA, is the son of a German immigrant who adopted the surname TOLUENE upon arriving in JACKSONVILLE following a period of internment in a Canadian prison during the last stages of World War II. PASCAL TOLUENE himself completed High School in TALLAHASSEE, but never went to college. He served for two terms in VIETNAM and was given an honorable discharge in 1970, leaving with the rank of Staff Sergeant.

TOLUENE first came to the attention of the FEDERAL BUREAU OF INVESTIGATION shortly after leaving the army, when he set up a business providing guard dogs for the Military Police. According to sources (RE: Memo 65–4837–82673), TOLUENE used contacts developed at that stage to establish himself as an arms dealer.

During the eighties he was indicted on fourteen counts of illegal arms trading, but these charges were subsequently dropped when three essential witnesses suffered fatal accidents. There are strong suspicions that TOLUENE engineered the fatalities.

In 1984 TOLUENE set up MEDIA NATIONAL USA as a front for his swelling coterie of far-right political thinkers. Meanwhile his astute evaluation of the future potential in electronics, telecommunications and computers ensured that he eventually became a multimillionaire.

Though direct evidence against him is sparse, he is suspected of being involved in the planning of five military coups recently attempted around the world, including three in AFRICA.

The subject has long entertained political ambitions and frequently uses his USA SOUTH TODAY media corporation to issue controversial statements via his mouthpiece reporter KIRSTY NEWINGTON. It is widely believed he set up the SOCIALIZED NATIONALS PARTY (SONAT) as a means of ultimately fulfilling his presidential ambitions.

It is our opinion, given his political aspirations, that he should be placed under even stricter surveillance during the current period of social and political crisis.

I spent the rest of my morning run glancing over my shoulder as I know these neo-Nazis are serious about their threats against me. If I don't stop making negative comments publicly about them, and more so, if I actually *win* this silly promotional gimmick, then they'll do their utmost to eliminate me. I may be deliberately tempting them into attacking me in full view of millions of potential witnesses, but it is chilling nevertheless to have your own mortality emphasized to you so starkly.

I'm meeting TC for lunch today. I saw Jake offer her a lift home yesterday afternoon, and I still don't know how I feel about that intimacy. Depressed mostly . . . scared in a way, too. They managed to demonstrate some sort of bond with each other that excludes me. Thoughts about them being together begin to obsess me.

I close a file on my PC and push myself away sharply from my desk, the wheels of the chair rattling across polished oak floorboards. I gaze around my room and find myself thinking about how different I feel in contrast to only three or four weeks ago. This is evidenced by the current state of my bedroom, for all the medals and cups won for my decathlons are now stored downstairs, though I've kept one good photograph of me launching myself on a long jump. The image is striking because of the concentration of utter effort on my face. And the anger?

Instead, book upon book upon book about the Second World War is now ranged on specially constructed shelves. I've gradually built up quite a collection of them from sources on the Internet or second-hand bookshops. There's also the usual bloke stuff, of course: a big bed, a couple of childhood plastic aeroplanes suspended from the ceiling, forever chasing one another in a dogfight, two posters of a female lead singer, and a set of weights. At the moment I just use the latter to work off my tension. There's been lots of it recently.

'Your brother rang earlier from America,' my father had announced last night.

'Oh?' I answered, as I fiddled with my CAMIC, which I'd taken out to inspect halfway through dinner.

'Yes, Michael says that Unit-C have started up an American version of that blasted PR job over there, like the one you're taking part in . . . Is that thing still switched *on*?'

When I confessed yes, he immediately got up and left the room. My mother just smiled at me nervously, before standing up to light herself a cigarette.

After that, she eyed me for a few seconds in silence, then turned to follow my father out of the room.

I now stare out of my bedroom window, losing myself in the view. On a good day like today, I can see the distant shimmer of the sea. Today it ripples like green-blue tinsel. Inland, the countryside looks glorious: with such hot weather and cloudless blue skies, it has turned into the classic English summer that everyone fantasizes about. I suddenly find it extremely easy to imagine what it must have felt like here at the beginning of World War II, realizing there was a good chance of the country being invaded at anytime – and comprehending that someone might actually try to take all this away from you, unless you did something about it.

And it makes me feel good to know that I, too, am trying to take control and change things.

Even as I think that, a pain sparks up in the side of my head. Reality flickers – and I see different images. In the first instant of panic, I take several quick, deep, calming breaths in instinctive preparation.

It's happening again.

Once more, what I am seeing alternates between where I am and someplace else. Life for me still continues – but in another dimension, another place.

Click, click . . . *click*!

I am running fast across a frost-covered field, along a track many have used before me. The sky is autumn-clear, cold and clean. The ground is hard. It is early morning and my breath expels in clouds before me. But I cannot adjust quickly enough to this sudden change in reality and I falter, stumble . . . and a hand reaches out to steady me.

'Butter-feet . . . are you getting old?' gasps the man holding my elbow. 'Or just too cold?'

Once again, the language is foreign – something mid-European – yet I understand it. He has a mass of black hair confined under a woollen cap, a big smile and dark eyes hidden in the wrinkles of the laugh that he manages even while catching his breath.

'Yeah,' I pant. 'Yeah.' I look around while I pace my breathing.

Just get your bearings, Scott. Work out what you are meant to do next.

We are clearly on some sort of assault course – with ropes hanging over pits and climbing-nets slung over large obstacles looming just ahead of us. Both of us are dressed in brown serge fatigues, and we are festooned with British Army 'light-raiding order' WWII military paraphernalia. We wear plimsolls instead of boots, have a multitude of bulging pouches hanging from our webbing, and each of us carries an American Thompson machine gun. I notice a slight steam of sweat rising from the other man's open collar. Then, with a start, I recognize the flash sewn on his shoulder above his sergeant's chevrons: it is that of the WWII Czech Brigade. I too wear the same badge and stripes, so I am now – I realize – a Free Czech soldier on training in this different world where I find myself.

My companion slaps me on the back and we start running again.

Immediately ahead, a set of wooden steps leads up towards a couple of ropes dangling over a pit. I do as my companion does. With him still right beside me, we charge towards the ropes, after sliding our weapons around on their straps to hang over our shoulders, thus freeing our hands as we pump our arms and we gather speed to make the jump.

We hit the bottom-most step simultaneously.

As I reach the top and begin to launch myself towards the rope directly in front of me, I feel someone grip my ankle. I am instantly pulled off-balance. Just before I tumble into the pit, I manage to twist my body enough to see another soldier who has been hiding right behind the steps. I crash into the frozen mud at the bottom of the hole, jarring my shoulder, but in a moment – without thinking, just using some instinct I've always known I possessed – I spring to my feet and begin tackling my assailant who has also plummeted to the floor of the pit. The fellow compatriot I have been running with is also engaged in a similar contest.

My attacker whips back his left hand, preparing to

deliver a karate-chop to my neck, but I deflect the blow with my right forearm, grip his left wrist with my own left hand, then pull his arm out straight, duck underneath it, and jerk it up behind its owner into an arm-lock. These actions are all automatic: the martial arts lessons learnt in childhood rushing back into my consciousness. I wrap my right arm around my opponent's throat for good measure, then drive my right knee straight into his right thigh. The assailant cries out, becoming suddenly heavy in my arms as he crumples to the ground. I release him, let him fall, then raise my foot ready to kick him hard in the face.

A whistle note blares out. I hesitate.

'Okay, okay,' orders an officer in English, as yet invisible as he runs towards us. 'Enough now, gentlemen, enough.'

Realizing what I was about to do, I stop and glance over at my companion on the course. He himself has a bloody nose, but his assailant now lies at his feet, curled into a ball, both hands clutching his genitals.

The officer stands above us, hands on hips at the edge of the pit.

'Well, as the Yanks would say, you Czechs sure play hardball.' He smiles. 'I reckon you'll both fit in perfectly well at SOE.'

I quickly bend over, hands clasping my knees. This may hopefully look as if I'm just catching my breath, whereas it is to hide my expression.

SOE meaning Special Operations Executive: the World War II behind-the-lines taskforce that specialized in sabotage and assisting internal resistance.

I sneak a look at my companion, who is holding out a helping hand to the man he himself has disabled. Since we both wear Czech uniform, I can even now make a shrewd guess as to what SOE will eventually ask us to do. We'll take part in Operation Anthropoid, whose purpose will be to send men covertly back into Czechoslovakia to assassinate SS Obergruppenführer Reinhard Heydrich, the Butcher of Prague.

The thought of that surprisingly makes me extremely happy.

But am I trapped here now, in this other reality?

I am suddenly aware of confronting something else, something invisible – something made up of a multitude of minds which recognizes my thoughts and intends to fight back, giving me no quarter. Though frightening, this realization enables me to make connections. I am somehow being giving a chance to confront my own inner fears. They are suddenly being forced upon me. It must surely be something to do with the trauma affecting us all last month.

It offers a simple choice of possibilities.

I could win.

Or lose.

As I begin to climb out of the pit, reality slows, stutters, changes.

Click, click . . . *click*!

And then all I can see is open countryside again, viewed from my bedroom window. My head aches – and so does my shoulder. Bothered by this pain, I roll it in its socket, then ease my shirt down off my shoulder. There's an ugly bruise forming, so I have a memento – like before with my Wannsee experience.

I pull up my shirt again and stare through the window with this awful conviction that I need to do something *now*, something really important. These jumps into another universe clearly herald some coming event that will affect me deeply.

But how long will they continue till it does?

Just after noon, I meet up with TC, as agreed, down on the shore. We're treating ourselves to lunch today at the upmarket café adjoining the car park, and are enthusiastic in that we overdo our anticipation of it.

The café looks like a cottage and a jumble of converted barns knocked through to each other. It is now all done up in black-and-white timber style, but it's still essentially a glorified fish and chip shop, providing a major attraction for the tourists each summer. In addition, the nearby Cobbsmere Nature Reserve usually attracts crowds of birdwatchers, though there are few in evidence here today. This self-styled café does the best fries for miles around, its fresh fish supplied by Joe Cope, who is also a purveyor of tall tales extraordinaire at no extra cost.

Joe Cope is a fisherman and local hero, whose real-life exploits outshine even his stories. Though now an old man, both weathered and withered, he still maintains a steady eye and a grip of iron. Joe was in bomb disposal during the war, yet will talk about his experiences only with a considerable deal of reluctance. I sense he gets embarrassed because to him it was nothing special and he was only doing his bit.

We spurn the popular patio area with its polished wood tables and brick-built benches, and instead head over towards one of the small wooden winching sheds that sit on concrete blocks, waiting for the fishing boats. Cod-and-chunks is what we've both chosen – the fish, straight from shoals that have put in an unusually massed appearance this summer, coated in crisp batter, together with thick-sliced chips. They are all crackly and golden, salty and vinegary, snappy on the tongue, hot on the fingers.

From where I sit, I can see over to the vast extent of Dingle Marsh with its isolated island humps of gorse and heather amongst the reed beds, and I pause eating as I again receive an overwhelming, frightening, humbling sense of the passage of time in this place – of the fate of the monks displaced by a king's wrath, of the innocent women pursued by Matthew Hopkins the 'Witchfinder General', of the whole unstoppable march of time hidden under the surface in this secluded region. It is the same poignant sensation I experienced in my bedroom earlier: a sudden feeling of the utter smallness and yet uniqueness of my own identity. This place is my home, that feeling says; and, deep down, I know it also contains an awareness of my mortality, an acknowledgement of my fear of dying, brought to the fore by the bizarre universe-shifts I've been recently experiencing.

It's suddenly difficult to swallow my food.

I glance at TC, who is licking tomato ketchup from her fingertips. I give a start, finding her action incredibly erotic.

Just then a voice breaks my concentration.

'Hi, you two,' says Jenny.

I turn to look at her, a subtle guilt overcoming me – it's as if she *knows* what I've just been thinking.

'Hi, Jenny,' TC greets her.

Jenny sits down between us, her back against the shed.

I notice that, as the sun catches her eyes, they sparkle with refractive colours like those you often see in the coating used on spectacles. It is as though her eyes have acquired a sort of sheen, and I've never seen the like of it before.

'So, how's work, Jenny?' asks TC suddenly.

Jenny shakes her head. 'Just before you performed your stunt yesterday, we spotted an entire *flock* of blue tits. You might occasionally get three or four together – a family, say – but I myself counted about sixty. And just a fortnight ago, I saw eight male robins all perching together in a row. Robins are incredibly territorial, so they'd usually be fighting one another off rather than sitting side by side. It's as if Nature has been given this huge great shove and it's all gone off-kilter.'

Thwack!

A loud crack on the shingle makes us all jump, and pebbles scatter everywhere. We whip around to where the sound came from, as TC stands up to investigate.

'Jesus,' I hear her whisper, and she bends down to pick something up. 'Will you look at that?' she then says aloud.

What she holds up between thumb and forefinger looks like a sizeable chunk of grey pumice stone. We look back towards the café to see if there's anyone there throwing rocks at us.

Thwack! Thwack!

We jump in surprise again.

'There's more!' yells TC.

Looking up into the utterly clear sky, I'm just in time to dodge one about to hit me in my face.

'They're nearly the size of my bloody fist!' I yell.

And more and more of them start to cascade from

the sky – a myriad of pumice stones showering us with chunks of volcanic rock. Covering her head for protection, TC starts to run for shelter. The sound of these rocks thumping onto the beach soon drowns out any other noises, but I manage to hear Jenny who cries out in pain as a large fragment strikes her on the head. The stones themselves may be light in weight, but they're descending at speed. As I go to her aid, one hits me on the shoulder, then another my head, then my back. Fighting to stay upright, Jenny is now trying to stagger to safety. Though she looks partly concussed, she is determined to save herself – but just can't move quickly enough. She falls to the ground. All the time the intensity of the pumice shower is increasing. I realize that if we don't do something drastic, we both might die under its onslaught.

I push Jenny to one side and violently kick in the small door to the winching shed she had been leaning against. Shattered wood flies in every direction. Quickly I bend down and push most of her upper body into the shed itself, squeezing myself in beside her and the winching machinery. We try to drag in as much of our protruding legs as we can. The downfall of pumice increases to a thunderous roar, smashing against the roof of the shed above us. It begins to splinter under such a continued onslaught.

Jenny grabs my arm, pulling herself close to me. I don't know if that's to comfort me, comfort herself, or emphasize her sudden mysterious calm amid this raging storm crashing around us.

And then, just as suddenly, it stops.

*

When eventually Jenny and I emerge from the winching shed, we find the beach littered with thousands of pumice stones of all sizes. I stare up at the sky which is still clear, blue, empty. I then turn to Jenny and register the ugly bruise on her forehead. But that's apparently all she has suffered. She's been very lucky.

'Scott,' she stares back at me, 'your head's bleeding.'

I put my hand up and feel dampness. Some of these missiles obviously had very sharp edges. I don't bother to study my wet fingers, just pull out my handkerchief. As I put it to my head, Jenny reaches up to reposition my hand.

'Press hard,' she says.

'Yes, nurse,' I oblige.

And we both turn together and glance up and down the beach. The entire shore is strewn with these stones, as if covered in a grey blanket.

'How?' asks Jenny.

I shrug. 'I run and jump, and I study history, Jenny. I don't major on the weather.'

I stare up into the sky again. And then that feeling of foreboding comes again.

As I look back towards her, I can see clearly over her shoulder towards the car park. People are now creeping out of the shelter of the café, and others climbing out of their vehicles to inspect smashed windscreens or dented roofs . . . and I know then with an absolute certainty that Jake is just about to arrive. I don't know how or where the thought comes from, but I *know* he'll be arriving soon.

Jenny and I begin to stumble towards the café,

both almost having to hold each other up. TC suddenly runs over towards us.

'You all right?' she asks, then falls silent, a hand to her mouth, as she spots the obvious answer to her question.

And then we all hear the throaty grumble of a revving engine and into the car park careers that familiar Landrover. Before I can congratulate myself on my premonition, I have a sudden vivid memory of my most recent visionary experience – running down that assault course, sensing that I have a mission to complete. I take a different spin on it now, as TC heads over towards Jake Crux, and I put him in another mental pigeonhole – as someone it would be wise to distrust.

Jenny suddenly puts her hand in mine and I don't pull away.

I'm fascinated. Mild static shocks prickle my arm, and hairs rise on the nape of my neck. As with Jake's arrival, I am convinced about something else: *Jenny here knows more than I do about what's happening.*

She squeezes my hand tighter, as though she heard my thought.

It is a little later, and we still stand around reassuring one another, when I notice that Jake is no longer examining shattered pumice remnants but staring out to sea. I forget whatever I'm saying to Jenny and follow his gaze. Hovering near the shoreline, just where the waves try to break, is a large flock of gulls. They swoop and dive, swoop and dive, and then, as one, fly further along down the surge-line – just as I've seen them do ever since I was a child. But when Jake notices them do this, he turns back to the car park. His face is pale and drawn, his forehead wrinkled in a deep frown.

His reaction makes me shiver. *What can make him seem so frightened?*

Chapter Six

Ike Chivers is American, forty-two, ex-Green Beret, ex-security consultant, ex-bodyguard. Now team leader for Blaze-Trail Adventure Holidays, he is big, bronzed and Houston, Texas, through to his little pinkie. He stands on the peak of Mount Huascaran on the Cordillera Blanca Range in Peru. It's ten degrees below, and the overnight fresh snow comes halfway up his calves. He has a touch of altitude sickness, and thinks he'll have to do something pretty soon to prevent his toes developing frostbite. Worse, he realizes it's going to be a three-day trek back down to base camp. But he's happy still: this early morning view before him has the authority of God.

Stretching away in front of him, amid the smoky clouds, is peak after snow-capped peak belonging to the massive mountain range of the Peruvian Andes. Each white-hatted, jagged thrust of rock, highlighted against the blue bowl of sky, seems to work together with its neighbours to provide something better than just the sum of its parts. As the sun catches them in turn, they shimmer into golden teeth – a combination of beauty, beast and dragon. Ike stretches one gloved hand up towards the sky, as if trying to reach for something even higher. For a moment, he imagines he can hear angels talking to him.

He laughs loud and long, places both hands on his hips, and continues to look around him.

By God, it's good to be alive.

Ike gazes along down the saddle of the mountain, towards the lower northern summit, and there sees a group of climbers about to claim that particular peak.

They're gonna love all this.

His attention drops to the snow covering his feet.

Ike Chivers has seen action in the Gulf Wars, Parts One and Two, and he did the Basra Road. He's followed Abraham M1 tanks in after they've shelled positions that were not defended by anything more potent than an ancient Russian mortar. He's seen vehicles incinerated that contained nothing more threatening than women and children. In fact, Sergeant Chivers has seen sights no human should ever witness. But what he notices at his feet now makes him catch his breath.

What the—?

Ike takes a quick step back.

There, in the new snow are his own tracks, the ones he has just made ascending to this summit. And there, alongside them, is another set – clear, distinct, but definitely not his.

And they lead nowhere – they just end in a pool of melted ice.

Ike stands there silently on the summit of Mount Huascaran, in Peru, staring down at two sets of footprints in the snow, and wonders if he is going mad.

He spins around – and around again. In the unbroken snow extending immediately all around, there is nothing else to see except for these two sets of tracks. Yet Ike Chivers is unmistakably alone here. He finally stops turning, and slowly looks back up to the sky.

Raising a gloved hand to the heavens again, Ike Chivers pleads, with as much passion as he can muster, for the Lord of Lost Soldiers to give him guidance. He only hopes someone up there is listening, because he reckons he'll need some sort of assistance to dispel this altitude-induced hallucination.

Those footprints look so goddam real!

SCOTT'S WEB-BOX COMMENTARY
Let's be upfront: this is just the sort of puerile nonsense you'd expect from this neo-Nazi cretin – so you have been warned.

UNITED STATES DEPARTMENT OF JUSTICE
FEDERAL BUREAU OF INVESTIGATION
Washington Office
RE: PASCAL TOLUENE
The following is an extract from a statement made by PASCAL TOLUENE, as recorded by a special agent of the FEDERAL BUREAU OF INVESTIGATION at a massed public meeting in WASHINGTON DC.

'What is the motivation of these many deluded individuals intent on tearing down our scientific faculties? Exactly what do they imagine will result from that? Do they really think they will be able to undo history? Do they think they have the right to tell *us* what to do? I say that the first thing they should have is the decency to admit that it's the very mark of the society they live in which enables them to question it at all. But, of course, they lack the common sense to see that.

'They are being naive and totally childish if they think they can halt scientific progress. An improved social order is what is demanded: it is necessary that we move forward, not backwards as they advocate. These same individuals must accept the benefit of strong leadership – and that leadership is now here – and here to stay.'

Jenny hurries back towards the nature reserve where she works, TC and Jake drive off together, while I return home, bruised and shaken, struggling to find a focus on the aims I must clarify on *Total Cover*.

'Good grief,' my mother says when I get home, 'you got caught outside in that downfall?'

The stink of Gauloises is even stronger than usual, and she has some R & B band turned up particularly loud on the CD player. She has obviously made her own decision on how to handle what she's witnessed this afternoon, though it looks like considerably fewer stones fell by our house than over at the beach.

I nod and promptly find myself seized by the hand and led towards the kitchen first-aid box. Since my injuries occurred at least half an hour ago, I think any remedy she finds is probably a little late.

My father comes in and turns down her music, and for a moment I feel some sympathy for him. Here is a man who's been trained to face the blood and guts of war, and he comes into his own kitchen to make a cup of tea and finds his son, the world-class athlete, being fussed over because of some minor cut that has already stopped bleeding.

'So,' he grumbles, 'this is how Springgreen School prepared its pupils for the rough and tumble of life?'

I say nothing, but go upstairs and think about the big and little extra intrusions that have affected my life recently: incredible shifts into seemingly other worlds, freak storms of pumice, my father's renewed contempt for me.

I distract myself from such dark thoughts by checking where I currently stand in the contest ratings.

Moving upwards?

That is grimly satisfying, if equally sobering, and I lean back in my seat to reflect. So far my apparent popularity is being tempered by the negative reaction of a small but vocal section of the public, and the hatred for me expressed by this minority is vitriolic. It is probably because of such outpourings of anger – in a world seemingly gone mad – that Unit-C's project is proving so unexpectedly popular. But there are even more people out there loving the way I contemptuously deal with this anger, so they are consequently voting to keep me in the contest.

But we're not alone in this animosity of debate. The worldwide unease about the negative consequences of science has generated the main topics for discussion on Maxnet. I only need to type the words 'The Night' on the Internet, and I can't believe how many hits I get as a result. It seems the world is increasingly abuzz with theories and counter-theories about what may be in store now for us little humans, sitting here on our water-covered lump of rock revolving in space. In fact, such is people's anxiety that the anti-science red-ribbon brigade is now racing ahead in terms of popular acceptability.

I come off-line after a few minutes and carry on writing.

The CAMIC bleeps at me. It feels heavy. And alien.

CENTRAL INTELLIGENCE AGENCY
TOP SECRET
Langley
RE: GEN-FORK

Evidence discovered by agents in EUROPE confirms that the adjustable genetic virus GEN-FORK has finally been perfected. GEN-FORK itself results from completion of a genome project specially designed to attack certain portions (programmed to any chosen ethnic standard) of the DNA strand and introduce a version of the smallpox gene. Easily transmissible by a proxy carrier, it will prove infectious only to those belonging to the ethnic group selected as its target. It is believed to be lethal and there is no known antidote.

As I read this report, I wonder why Maxnet considered it is relevant to me – unless such a repulsive development somehow ties in with Toluene's aspirations. After considering whether I should release the copy of this report on my web-box, thereby attracting Sonat's attention, I realize that it's more than likely they know about it anyway. So I post a comment suggesting they're such evil bastards they would dish it out to innocent children just for fun and immediately receive a torrent of abuse on the message board which gives me grim satisfaction.

It is about eight in the evening when I reach the Bell and Fox. I spent the rest of the afternoon sitting out in our garden in the shade, trying to ignore the unnatural stillness. My intention for tonight is to relax with my friends and have a few beers. Then have a few more, get drunk – another deliberate slip from my training schedule – and try to forget for a while that the world seems to be in a mess, and heading for much worse, and also overwhelm my building foreboding that some of the responsibility for preventing this somehow lies in my own hands. It's been a long time since I've got drunk, and I've brought enough cash with me to bypass the government alcohol limit programmed into my chip-link card. That way I'll pay a substantial premium for using real money, but I'll be able to get inebriated without my motor-vehicle-disabling remote lock being activated or risking any possibility of receiving an invite from the Health Authority to attend an alcohol-awareness course.

I push open the pub door, and my first reaction is that I've stumbled into a party – I have never seen the place so full, let alone on a Wednesday evening, so I brace myself quickly for some serious enjoyment. I've told Gareth not to bother me tonight – or else I'll switch off the CAMIC completely. He got a bit emotional at that threat, and called me a few names – but I thought my insults delivered in response were sharper.

A couple of local builders I know give me a cheer when they see me appear in the doorway. From their red faces and slightly swaying stance, it's pretty obvious that they must have run in here at lunchtime to escape the freak pumice-storm, and then decided to stay on. As I smile back at them, my sense of enjoyment lasts only a second for I suddenly have to reach

out and grasp the doorframe for support, as a feeling
of anxiety, even of timidity, overwhelms me. It's a bit
like the prospect of being dunked in a winter sea. With
a shiver, I glance over my shoulder, receiving a distinct
sense of déjà vu. It is as if I already have a distinct
memory of how this evening will unfold. And it's one
that reminds me there's going to be trouble.

*Four men? One with a knife? Sonat thugs? What are
these thoughts?*

I shiver again, and peer around in front of me,
through the multitude of heads packing the small
interior of the pub. I spot a space at the far end of the
bar, and I quickly move away from the door.

I edge my way through the crowd, the builders
thumping me heartily on the back while mugging for
the CAMIC, until I finally reach the spot I was aiming
for. Curtis the barman has already poured me out a
pint of cold lager. I lick my lips, eager to get down to
the evening's business.

There is an electric atmosphere in the pub this
evening: an amazing cocktail of hearty enjoyment and
tense anticipation. It makes a pleasant change from
the sense of emptiness elsewhere. Yet I also notice
how, for some reason, practically everyone in the place
is occasionally glancing nervously towards the door.
Some even seem to realize they are doing so, and compensate by laughing louder than is necessary.

Suddenly the door opens. I see it is TC – followed
by Jake.

The other customers relax momentarily.

I do my best not to consider that my evening is
now ruined.

As the new arrivals make their way over to me,

most of the men in the pub are following TC with their eyes. Her own, however, remain well hidden behind her sunglasses.

Jake has changed into yet another fancy waistcoat. TC has changed her clothes, too – the new T-shirt is skin-tight and she wears no bra. She also has a slight smile – and it's been some time since I've seen that.

'Two pints of Summer Thunder,' Jake Crux demands. Curtis looks him up and down questioningly, but springs into action.

Jake leaves some money on the bar. Curtis' profits will be good tonight.

'Hey, Jake,' I say a little harshly, 'do your scientific pals at the Institute have any idea what the hell happened today? You know, like how do bloody huge bits of volcano fall out of an empty sky?' I feel extremely belligerent. 'And also why it's so fucking *hot*?'

A group of people standing nearby halt their conversation and pointedly glance in my direction, and then at Jake. I now notice that some of them are wearing red ribbons, undoubtedly protesters from Largewater, so Jake will not be popular with any of them, representing as he does the face of modern science. They're probably not too impressed with me either, but then I notice a number of other younger people sporting their own personal Maxnet CAMICs. Perhaps Jake is the person everybody was subconsciously waiting for, the one that generated those apprehensive glances towards the door.

I catch TC exchanging a look with Jake – one that instantly has me coming to all sorts of conclusions. The earlier smiles have gone and they both now have a serious demeanour, but I find it hard to forget that they've obviously spent the afternoon together.

I'd love to know what they've been talking about.

And what else they've been doing.

At the time, we all seemed eager to get ourselves away as soon as possible from that epicentre of the pumice-storm – as if just staying there would validate the whole weird experience.

I take another gulp of lager.

'We don't specialize in the weather,' says Jake, 'apparently.'

The way he adds that last word immediately intrigues me. But the new beers arrive before I can question him.

'I have a few ideas, though,' continues Jake, after gulping half his pint in one go.

'About the weather?' I ask.

'No,' says TC quietly, 'about what happened last month.'

That must have been an in-depth conversation they had this afternoon if that was the subject.

Jake takes another swig of his drink, then nods affably to a group of card-players nearby, one of whom raises a hand in greeting, before turning back to the game.

'Do you mind if I put it into context?' Jake says. 'Those guys over there work as security guards at Eisencrick. And since you're local, you must have noticed them here before. But do you realize they're here every Wednesday night without fail? Look at them: Jon, Karl, Malcolm, Mark, Rick and Gags – they've been meeting here every Wednesday for years, to drink, have a chat, and play a game of cards. Know what that signifies?'

I shake my head.

'What it means is that over that time they've got to *know* each other so well that they must be able to anticipate exactly what response any comment of theirs will provoke. They now know each other's little mannerisms, each reaction, down to the last detail so that, to an outsider, it seems like they all know what the others are thinking. Which, in essence, is true.'

As we look on, one of them apparently makes a bad call, prompting a howl of derision.

'It's just a bunch of guys having a laugh,' I insist.

'Yep,' says Jake, 'but you are not viewing the situation objectively.'

I lose my smile.

'It's time to be blunt,' says Jake in a low voice, casting a look at TC, who nods back.

It's like he's just asked her permission – for what?

'A bunch of men playing cards,' Jake continues. 'As normal a thing as you'll ever see, Scott . . . *because* you see it all the time. What you *don't* register is that they're interacting subconsciously.'

I turn to glance at them again. To me, it still looks merely like some blokes having a good time.

Jake drains his glass and TC takes it from him for a refill. She gestures to Curtis, who starts pouring another pint. Jake pauses, as though collecting his thoughts, and he frowns. A few of the people near us keep glancing over, apparently interested in what he has to say. He waits until he gets his refill, however.

'Our brains give us the ability to deduce a staggering amount,' he says, 'but why should we be limited to making merely an educated *guess* about what someone else is thinking? Outside a few evolutionary anthropologists like myself, no one appears to be giving that much thought.'

As he drains at least a third of his second pint, I glance down at my own glass. I didn't think Americans were supposed to like our warm beer.

'So?' I ask.

'We hardly utilize our brains at all,' continues Jake. 'Yet the more we find out about what bit of it actually does what, the more questions arise.'

He taps the left-hand side of his head and he couldn't have grabbed my fervent interest more effectively.

That's exactly the spot where I feel those headaches after the universe-shifts!

I'm dumbfounded.

'Only this small part here is ever used for the initial recognition of words. You see, though many different parts of the brain are used to provide cognition of what lies on the printed page, only a little part of it is actually used for word identification.'

He continues tapping the same part of his head.

'Different cultures, different writing and different shapes – this one area of the brain reacts the same way to words. But we're not *born* with it in use for that purpose, Scott. How could we be? Evolutionarily speaking, reading and writing are only a recent invention. So to what purpose exactly was that small bit of the brain originally put?'

He spreads his hands as if expecting me to reply. People nearby start paying more overt attention to what he is saying. I give my CAMIC a little poke, but just receive some static hiss in my ear.

'It's a fascinating fact, but not many people care how they evolved,' he continues. 'Their brains do all this amazing stuff, but they don't care to know *why*. But *now* it has become very important to know this.'

He gives a pointed stare at the red ribbons some of the other customers are wearing.

'What if our brains possess powers contrary to what science considers possible? Could we be just so used to them that we don't even notice these?'

He shares yet another glance with TC, who quickly nods encouragement.

'Look at all the stories about sixth sense, telekinesis, telepathy – especially telepathy. Nobody has ever been able to *prove* any of that, but everybody the world over seems to think that it could be possible. Ask identical twins – they believe they can do it. And if we all possess an ability for extrasensory perception, is it something we've *always* possessed, or is it instead a more recent development? Three weeks ago, even three days ago, I would have readily dismissed either likelihood myself.'

He pauses, and I feel that upsurge of anxiety again. I know I won't like what he's about to say.

'I've discovered it's possible for a collection of animals to achieve group consciousness, a collective impulse born out of similarity . . . From this I have come to believe that the human race itself will achieve a similar consciousness, once its population reaches the optimum peak for self-sustaining synchronized telepathy. Furthermore, it will occur soon. In six days, to be precise.'

This last comment commands more than just casual attention from the customers standing near us. One or two even nod in agreement – as though Jake is expressing some long-held belief of theirs – though it's all news to me. He turns to focus on me again, and this time I have no doubt. He is actually addressing my CAMIC so as to reach as wide an audience as possible, and as quickly as possible.

'I have reached the conclusion that the human species has only a limited collective volume of intelligence yet to be achieved before it reaches a sort of nirvana level. The consequence of which – and last month was just a foretaste – is that we will be forced to . . . well, forced to deal with changes way beyond our current understanding.'

His voice has been rising, become more accented, till TC puts a restraining hand on his arm.

'We hurry to achieve it,' he adds, suddenly scowling and changing tack – as if he's confirming something to himself out loud. 'City upon city upon city: the same TV and the same ideas disseminated at the same time. The same lusts, the same mental cravings, the same self-interest. But never any worries about increasing the population of *similarity*. We're overpopulating our planet, while at the same time becoming unified in thought and action. The individual is becoming lost in a desire to be identical. We're heading for group consciousness and a shift in our universe. Yes, a *shift*.'

The little pub is now totally quiet – everybody listening hungrily to what Jake is saying. Then he stops and rolls his shoulders dramatically – having apparently now said what he wanted to say. Running a hand over his bald head, he frowns again on noticing the confusion on people's faces. But, before he can begin explaining himself in more depth, something really strange happens. Everybody in the room turns in unison to stare at the door. *Everyone*, including Jake and myself. And we wait, quiet . . . frozen into inaction. A moment later, the door opens, and in saunter four men. They look around at the silent crowd, glance at each other, then head towards the bar.

And now, everything suddenly goes dark for me. This is not another jump into some other world. Instead it is like an enactment of a recollection, some memory of those things recounted to me by my grandfather Roy. Except that – as has been the case with these experiences, ever since I was sixteen – I am actually *there*. Like the déjà vu, this is something that hasn't happened properly to me for days. It's like my own personal madness – the one I try not to tell others about. No wonder I'm an insomniac.

For suddenly I *am* Roy Anderson – the American paratrooper who was my grandfather. I do as he did – my actions are identical to what his were.

A voice shouts, 'Go! Go! Go!'

And, after twenty minutes of being hooked up to the static line, I am jumping out of the aircraft. The rest of the squad follows me out in a frantic surge.

My ankle gets wrenched as the leg-bag breaks its line, while simultaneously I am jerked backwards when the parachute opens.

I look down just as the shoreline passes beneath me, and I am now floating over water. I am parachuting straight into the sea.

I'm going to drown!

I start to prepare, fumbling to remove my reserve parachute since I'm too low to use it anyhow. I then change my mind and pull hard on the risers to fill the chute, to slow my descent. I manage to suck in a deep breath. I plunge into the sea.

So cold!

My feet touch the bottom. I am submerged well over my head. The motion of the waves above me pitches me up and down as I struggle with my equipment – all movements slowed to a cruel ecstasy.

So cold.

The reserve parachute is finally pushed away. Bellyband loose, leg straps unsnapped, same for chest buckle – and I let the harness drift away.

I need air, desperately.

I lean forward, push myself off the seabed and am lifted by the surge.

I break surface.

Air!

It is only an instant's relief, then back down into the dark and the cold. I remove as much equipment as I can: Musette bag, 30-calibre ammunition, Hawkins mine and gas mask.

I break surface again, and the waves carry me inland.

I wade ashore and collapse. Cold waves spend themselves on my back.

I am lying on sand, it is night, I am completely soaked through. Yet I am right in the midst of a cacophony of noise, so I readjust my grasp on the only weapon I have left: my combat knife. The jump-knife was lost in my frenzied struggle to remove my parachute. My rifle was in my leg-bag, and we came in so fast the thing was ripped from my leg the moment I hit the prop-blast.

I hold my breath for a split second, then I find I still have my grenades.

Good.

Away on my left, the sky is torn apart by anti-aircraft shell flashes, and is occasionally lit with red, green and white flares. A fan of tracer seeks out a stick of other paratroopers, helpless in their naked visibility. And then I know that this is D-Day; that I am part of the advance guard sent to land on the Cherbourg peninsula.

My breathing is rapid and ragged, until I force myself into taking slower, deeper breaths. I roll onto my side and look back towards the sea. The 82nd and 101st airborne has been scattered all over Normandy, so I am lucky. We over-flew the drop zone so I entered the sea in only about seven feet of water. Even so, I only just managed to make it to shore.

I look back on ink-black water, buckling with waves, shimmering with the reflection of the full moon and the flak explosions above, and I think about those men I have spent the last two years training with.

All gone to waste.

I was the first out of the plane – which means everyone else in the team has landed in water deeper than I did . . . and that while carrying over a hundred pounds of equipment.

I swear softly to myself, roll back onto my belly, and begin to wriggle further up the beach, gripping my knife as firmly as I can. I need to find a German and take his weapon from him.

As I creep up the shore, I pause behind a tank obstacle, for I'm suddenly feeling nauseous and have to be sick. But it isn't because of what I've just been through, or in fearful anticipation of what I am about to get into.

I *am* my grandfather, and I remember this most profound moment of his life just as *he* remembered it. The crucial moment that changed me too, when he told me of it years later.

I again find myself in the pub staring at the four louts standing at the pub door – the wave of nausea returning.

At that same moment, Roy had suddenly realized it was all going to be a waste of time, that this world would forever keep producing new versions of Hitler. The realization shocked him in its clarity. Even though Hitler himself might be removed by the efforts of people like himself, eventually an even worse monster was sure to come and plague us. And then others, in turn, would have to struggle against him.

That same night it emerged to Roy as a revelation, an absolute conviction. I figure it's him, therefore, I've inherited my gift of clairvoyance from. He was so certain of this insight, so positive that someone much worse than Hitler would arise in time. And as he crouched there – beside the metal struts that the assault troops would be using at daylight there on Utah beach, a few hours later – his premonition even gave him a name to put to his fears. At that same moment, it had simply sprung into his head: Pascal Toluene.

My grandfather told me all this just before he died from injury-induced pneumonia sustained after confronting Toluene's thuggish henchmen and being beaten up by them. He'd gone to London to confront Toluene at a public meeting, so convinced he was of his own forewarning. I was an impressionable sixteen then, and his conviction rubbed off on me. I saw myself becoming a weapon against the evil he predicted rising again. On the day he explained to me on his deathbed why he'd gone to London, he also instructed me to read his war diary and what it foretold. Comparing it with Toluene's recent political pronouncements, on arriving at Heathrow, it was as though my grandfather had genuinely seen the future. It was the same day when my episodes of déjà vu and my dreams involving World War II began. It was also the same day I started seeing ghosts – the most unsettling day of my life.

I don't care who thinks I'm mad. I just share my grandfather's conviction, and desperately wish to avenge him.

The four men entering the pub are all in their late thirties. They have close-cropped hair, have their shirts buttoned tightly up to the collar, despite the hot weather, and they are clearly spoiling for a fight.

As they notice the red ribbons, their blatant contempt indicates to me that they're Sonat.

One of them flicks a ribbon pinned on the arm of an old man standing near to us. 'Your days are numbered, granddad,' he sneers.

The boisterous noise throughout the pub has long subsided.

Then the soft noise of my CAMIC sounds bell-like in the quiet, and I glance down at the screen on the mobile link. It's suggesting tactics to me to cope with this situation.

Jake uses the distraction to take a quick step forward and place himself immediately in front of the thug. I can't see the expression on Jake's face, but from the reactions of the man's friends it must be something to behold. They actually step back from him.

'You're not welcome here,' growls Jake.

Has the leader a knife?

I begin to take a quick step forward myself, when the man begins to turn away. He pauses for a moment when he sees me.

'Let's go,' he says to the others, 'I don't like the smell in here.'

They step back outside, the leader pushing something metallic into the back of his jeans, and they shout a few general insults in our direction before heading for the car park. There is a collective sigh from the customers and the noise level shoots back up.

'I *knew* it,' TC says quietly. 'I *knew* it.'

She goes back to the bar, picks up her drink and uncharacteristically drains it in several gulps. She wipes her mouth with the back of her hand.

'I *knew* this was going to happen,' she says. 'This is what Jake is talking about, paranormal foresight.'

'Yep,' Jake confirms, turning to me. 'And it's going to get worse. Something's been triggered in all of us.'

He pulls out a piece of paper from his back pocket and hands it to me. I unfold it and recognize the writing as TC's.

Bastards at the pub. Possible fight. One will have a knife.

Even as I read it, I'm conscious of how, as I pushed open the pub door tonight, I felt a definite tension brewing and had the exact same apprehension.

Jake's right, it is *going to get more extreme.*

As I brood on the implications of Jake's earlier comments, I have a sudden image of Jenny in my head, and feel that she is nearby.

'Hello,' she says, coming to stand beside me.

As I turn to look at her, startled, all the panic building in me drains away. But I'm shocked at the change in her. She looks so pale, yet there is an excitement in her eyes that is difficult to gauge.

'What's the matter, Jenny?' I say.

Her voice is hoarse and low, but controlled.

'I saw the future,' she says.

'What?' I say, thinking she too is referring to what has just happened.

'Just now – at work. There was an anti-protester at the entrance to the car park. He was there with a bunch of louts laughing over all the dead birds caught in the pumice-storm. I suddenly had this perfect image in my head of what would occur. But before I could shout out a warning, it happened – a car, speeding down the road, knocked him over. He was killed, Scott. He's dead.'

She shakes her head. 'I *do* have the power to foresee things.'

I dare not remind her I've been experiencing the same for some years now.

Instead, I shake my head as well.

Everyone in this pub knew something was about to happen here.

A shout from outside startles her, and she puts an arm tightly around me.

What is *this change that's beginning to affect us all?*

I suddenly know that I have to get involved to help prevent it.

Marvel Speer gazes up at a young climber, dressed in gaudy skin-tight gear, who is negotiating the cream-coloured expanse of the Bighorn Mountain rock-face in North Wyoming, and he has to admit that it takes a certain level of courage to scale the sides of a mountain without any ropes, using only one's skill, strength and the emergency cleats inserted into fissures in the rock. It would take only one error to slip and tumble into the void.

Or a bullet fired into the hand at a crucial moment.

Marvel Speer sniffs, pinches his nose between his fingers for a second, then begins to unpack his rifle from the trunk of his car, glad that the climber does not possess a CAMIC to record the event that is about to unfold.

After he checks the workings of the weapon, he gazes around at the desolate landscape. While frequently insisting that the Lone Star State is the centre of God's own country, he'll fight anybody who doesn't concede that the whole of the rest of America also belongs to God's chosen ones. Wyoming, here, is okay too. It is perfectly empty, this wilderness he finds himself sharing with a man who will soon be dead, but he still takes the precaution of pushing a silencer onto the barrel – just in case there are any hikers about. He'll aim for the climber's hand instead of his head, because at first glance it will then look as though he caught it on a rock as he fell. Marvel Speer likes silencers because there is a strange sense of purpose to them, and Marvel Speer likes the certainty of that. He passionately believes that people need firm direction.

He takes pride in the fact that he can understand things with such clarity, and feels sure that was one of the first qualities Mr Toluene appreciated in him. And because he understands the workings of the world so instinctively, he knows that the services he performs for his boss put him in a position of power – even if it is one of danger. Both men became aware quite some time ago that Speer's activities might give him leverage over Pascal Toluene, therefore, and to safeguard against the day when Toluene might consider it prudent to 'remove' Speer from the scene, so as to prevent any embarrassing revelations, he now receives his instructions through third parties.

An eagle calls out. He usually finds that a heartening sound, but this time Marvel Speer does not turn to trace the bird. He is concentrating fully on getting the best shot. With only about seventy yards between him and his target, this will be no problem for a sharpshooter such as himself: the climber's hand he focuses on, through his telescopic sight, seems large and near.

Speer smiles to himself, confident that any unforeseen witness would have trouble in giving an accurate description of him to the police.

Marvel Speer, aged only thirty-three, has taught himself thoroughly the principles of disguise. At one time or another he has impersonated nearly every sort of American citizen possible. Except a black. Or a Jew. Or a queer. In Speer's eyes, such people don't deserve to be considered American. Nor do those immigrant lowlifes from Mexico, who take others' jobs.

Ruthless and without compassion, that's how he views Toluene's style of leadership; when Sonat finally takes the initiative it will be quick, it will be brutal, but it will also readily adapt to circumstances. Just as Nature herself dictates: rewarding the strongest, the quickest, the most able – that is life.

The young climber, having now reached the trickiest part of his ascent, is groping in the bag attached to his scarlet belt to retrieve an additional cleat to hammer into a convenient fissure. Speer takes careful aim at the other hand still clasping the rock face.

He finally squeezes the trigger and watches the young man fall – the climber's cry of terror echoing the screech from the eagle.

Marvel Speer smiles – this makes his fourth kill of ex-Springgreen pupils on his current Stateside mission. He'll celebrate it with a small beer or two at his hotel tonight. Tomorrow he is off to Europe, and specifically to Britain. He still has a lot of work to see to.

Then God commanded, 'Let the water be filled with many kinds of living beings, and let the air be filled with birds.' Evening passed and morning came – that was the fifth day.

Thursday
Day 5

Chapter Seven

Claire Beacon — English, thirty-four as of yesterday, a public-school French teacher who last night was rogered silly in her hotel room by Anthony Peter Manners, the music master — stands in the footwell of the coach beside the driver and tries to concentrate on her clipboard again. She's finding it difficult to make any sense of it.

In her head, she swears: Fuck, fuck, fuck, FUCK!

She purses her lips and glances up to check that she didn't say it aloud.

The trip has been going so well. Their four-day school excursion to France, during the last term of the school year, has ticked along beautifully. None of the girls has surprised them by giving birth in the hotel toilet, as happened two years before; no one has been mugged; no one has succumbed to a life-threatening illness; and the boys have not gone overboard in their under-age drinking (though the girls seem to have made up for that). She has since found that Mr Manners is indeed as well endowed as she'd imagined, and that it felt good to her to have acted such a whore, and such a delight to teach sexual etiquette to Mr Manners as he took her from behind.

Indeed, only a few minutes ago, Claire Beacon had felt

a curious well-being, despite a disquieting murmur of voices in her head coupled with a slight electric smell of forest thunderstorms. She had felt such calmness, as if taking stock of her life in a forgotten country church in Provence, with the sun streaming through tall windows to warm her face, with the smell of some local flower, sweet and golden, filling her nostrils with each deep breath she took, and a distant echo of an ancient hymn speaking to her directly from the corner of the chapel.

She peers at the clipboard yet again, and finally the names all make sense – except for one.

Who the fuck is Caroline Buster? *she asks herself.*

There, on the sheet of paper attached to the clipboard, are twenty names; the twenty adolescent charges that have been entrusted to her, courtesy of their parents. Twenty names, each with a tick beside them – except one: Caroline Buster.

Claire does a headcount of the teenagers. And then again.

Nineteen. She looks outside. No stragglers to be seen. The coach driver rolls back the cuff of his left shirtsleeve and makes an elaborate performance of checking the time by his watch.

'Where's Caroline?' Claire asks of the children.

For once, they fall totally quiet, sharing puzzled looks with each other.

'Where's Caroline?' she repeats.

'Who?' pipes up one of the kids.

Anthony Peter Manners gets up from his seat and goes to grab the clipboard from her, thinks better of that and asks for it politely instead. He glances down the list, then looks up. Frowning, he leans towards Claire and whispers in her ear. The simple act gives her a thrilling memory of last night, but his following words knot her gut.

'Who the fuck is Caroline Buster?' he asks.

INTERNET NEWS UPDATE by Janice Maclean
It's Thursday of the last week of Unit-C's Maxnet promotion contest, and the excitement mounts. We are now down to the last five contestants and our overnight news is that Tiff has dramatically fallen out of the top spot. The current running order is Natalie, Tiff, Scott, Jo and Mickey. Adi has had to go, alas, but I'm told that it was a very close thing between the bottom-ranking three contestants. My Unit-C contact begs me to persuade you to continue voting. As if they should worry: their market share continues to show a staggering rise.

'There's been a big response, Scott,' Gareth informs me.

'How could TC so closely predict what would happen last night, Gareth? Confident enough to write it down? How did we *all* anticipate it?'

'I don't know, Scott. Just go get some more votes.'

'Enjoy your wake-up coffee.'

'Try not to break a leg.'

SCOTT'S WEB-BOX COMMENTARY
Just when are the different FBI departments going to start talking to each other? I reckon this particular memo should be ringing serious alarm bells, and the information it contains should be emblazoned in winking lights on the cover of the US President's Orders-of-the-Day folder.

UNITED STATES DEPARTMENT OF JUSTICE
FEDERAL BUREAU OF INVESTIGATION
San Francisco Office
RE: LANDICO INC.

LANDICO INC. has recently purchased over one ton of industrial-mining 'plastic' explosive. This report has been initiated by the growing quantity of such explosives thus acquired by LANDICO, and by the fact that this recently formed company is a subsidiary of a larger corporation of which the far-right activist PASCAL TOLUENE has secured a majority control. Since this product has been registered for export to the company office in REYK-JAVIK, Iceland, I strongly advise that the Icelandic government be formally notified immediately.

It's only six-thirty, and now the day is getting started. I'm over halfway through a morning jog along the bridleway, and Jenny is with me this time. I can't even remember if I invited her, or if she just invited herself along. Whatever we said after those final few drinks last night, when I emerged from the house twenty minutes ago, I found her waiting for me. I was curious why she had not come and knocked at the door, then assumed it was because she did not want to waken my parents. We still haven't said more than a word to each other – just concentrated on loosening up with a gentle jog, then increased our speed until running at a steady pace. But I haven't yet got rid of the unsettling impression that for some reason she did not want to chance a meeting with my parents.

At first appearances, Jenny seems to have completely recovered from yesterday's traumatic experience. There is a confident focus to her running: a calm, composed, bouncing stride, so that she seems to carry a new kind of detachment with her.

I finally break the silence. 'How's it going?'

She glances sideways at me – taking a couple of seconds before answering. As she does so, for a moment the sun refracts off her eyes in that same colourful sheen that I'd noticed the other day.

'I'll race you, if that's what you want,' she suggests.

'I didn't mean the running.'

'I know.'

We continue in silence for another few minutes.

'So,' I say, trying again, 'how are you feeling?'

'Looking at myself in a different light.'

I stumble. She's had a shocking premonition of violent death that proved correct, and she's okay with the idea?

'Oh,' I say, 'you really believe we can possess that sort of power?'

She jogs on a few more steps, then stops abruptly. I continue a little further, then halt myself, turn around and walk back to her.

'You're kidding?' I say. 'Please tell me you don't really think that.'

'I'm *sure* of it,' says Jenny. There is a resolute look in her eye – momentarily hidden behind that refractive lustre. 'And I'm sorry I had to have it confirmed in such a way.'

'Oh, Jenny.'

She cocks her head to one side, and then I suddenly realize I'm absolutely misjudging her. This isn't something subtle – she's changed *completely* at some level and . . . become more assured, become *mysterious*.

I take half a step back.

'Want me to prove it?' she asks. 'Isn't it what you yourself have always wanted to show people?'

I hesitate, then move closer again and reach out my hand. Surprisingly there is no reaction from her as she lets me grip her shoulder cautiously – just a knowing half-smile.

'Jenny,' I say, 'we're all up against the same pressure, the same dread of what could happen next. I don't think I've slept a full hour in the past week. I daren't sleep. The déjà vu I keep experiencing is unreal, my dreams about my grandfathers have returned in force, and I'm still seeing ghosts. And I don't care how admitting all that makes me look. As Jake said last night, we're all beginning to go through a change. I know *I'm* experiencing something extraordinary.'

'Exactly. And for that reason, you should think seriously about what you may have ahead of you. *And* what you say. You're upsetting people, *dangerous* people.'

She suddenly snakes out a hand and strokes my cheek. Her smile confuses me again, and I catch myself wondering *exactly* what sort of person she has become.

'Bet you can't beat me,' she says.

And she turns and starts running further along the track. As I reluctantly begin to pursue her, she yells back, without looking at me, 'We *all* can have it, Scott! This power is now available to all of us! I've always said it was in *you!* You know I've never laughed at what you claim you've been seeing all these years!'

I again slow to a stop. After she turns a bend in the track up ahead, all I hear of her is her trainers slapping on the dirt.

I start running again – she's getting away from me, and I can't stand losing. Even if it is to some strange person who is scaring me with her new-found certainties.

I sense this is going to be a long day.

Then my CAMIC starts bleeping.

I allow it to automatically activate both retina Webvis cam-screen and voice-read.

CENTRAL INTELLIGENCE AGENCY

TOP SECRET
Langley
RE: GEN-FORK

Part transcript of internal memo from a EUROPEAN Biological Research facility.

'There are many ways in which a GEN-FORK virus aimed at ethnic groups could be distributed. One of the more sophisticated proposals, to hinder detection and thus aid depth of spread, would be to infect the international emergency agencies which are forced to move from one catastrophe to another in quick succession. Such relief teams generally enjoy swifter access through countries' borders and would initially spread the contaminating spores at airport terminals, and later, by the nature of their

work, in areas of greatest current
crisis. So the virus could be spread
worldwide within days and become well
established long before any containment
procedures are initiated.'

It's now about ten in the morning, and I feel queasy
about the purpose of Maxnet sending me such
stuff about Gen-Fork. TC and I stand on a rise leading
down to The Level hoping – actually it's become an
intense craving – for at least a whiff of breeze to blow
away our hangovers. My run with Jenny earlier did
little to help me, except build up a thirst. My head
aches from both the hangover and from thinking
about Jenny. My CAMIC mobile issues low-level
bleeps practically constantly to let me know of
increased activity via Maxnet. It obviously considers,
as it is programmed to do so, that certain e-viewers
have important information that may be of interest to
me. I switch it to automatic log and filter. My guess is
the messages can only be about Jenny's assertions that
morning.

No doubt confirming them.

But we discover no trace of a breeze up here; nothing that even resembles a whisper of air. Instead, the
sun merely heats up the humidity, and haze takes
over the horizon and gives it a nauseating shimmer.
We are both sweating profusely in our fresh-on-this-
morning T-shirts. It is indeed strange weather.

But at least the air here – thick and cloying as it is
– is clean. I daren't think about what it must be like
now in any of the bigger towns and cities; the fumes
from all older vehicles not yet fitted with chip-link

emission control must be escalating the mugginess tenfold. Tension amongst the population is surely mounting, and little wonder there have been violent injuries and deaths reported. There was nearly a riot in Manchester yesterday, after the main water supply broke down temporarily and then the back-up supply had to be turned off because it had become polluted. The supermarkets are reduced to their last few bottles of mineral water, and in some towns even the pubs have been literally drunk dry. What an ideal environment of chaos for someone to release a Gen-Fork virus.

I try not to think about it, having other more immediate things on my mind.

Despite a lack of breeze, the fumes from TC's chain-smoking always seem to drift straight towards me somehow. It reminds me irritatingly of my mother's Gauloises addiction. I study my companion's face, but all I see in those mirror-shades is a reflection of myself.

Her long hair is tied up in a giant French plait today and I'm impressed that she found the energy to handle that.

Setting off towards the shore, we are greeted by an amazing sight. The crowd surrounding Largewater nuclear power station has quadrupled since yesterday.

'There must be a couple of thousand down there,' observes TC, in awe.

I shake my head. 'Maybe even more,' I say. I'm stunned at how many people are gathered here today. But I shouldn't be, since the Maxnet newscast this morning commented on the rapid increase of protest

movements targeting scientific research establishments all around the world. In Britain these days,
every nuclear power station has its own permanent
encampment of protesters.

The sound of a helicopter distracts me and I turn
to search it out. It is still about three miles away, but
heading straight for Largewater.

'And here come the police,' observes TC.

I had already noticed how the police presence in
the area has gone up proportionally and dramatically
with the increasing numbers of protesters. If this is
true all across Britain, the famous 'thin blue line' must
be near to breaking point.

All the police in view are wearing basic riot gear,
together with security CAMICs as standard headgear,
while to one side an officer controls an aerial version,
steering it extremely close to the protesters' heads.

'It's going to get ugly, sometime soon,' I comment.

'Bring it on,' murmurs TC. 'Bring it *on*.'

I look at her, slightly stunned at this unusual vehemence.

'Do you want to know something?' continues TC.
'I feel like joining them.'

I have this sudden rush of déjà vu – and so, it
would appear, does TC. We share a brief, quizzical
look. After a moment's thought, I shrug. TC has said
something similar to this already, perhaps only the
other day, but I can't remember who she was then
talking to.

'Don't *you* think science has a lot to answer for?'
TC asks me suddenly, after several quick puffs on her
cigarette. 'And what about the present obsession this
government has with protecting us from ourselves?'

I shrug again, both as an answer and as an attempt at shaking off the bad feeling.

'Where do you stop, once you start on that track?' I say. 'I mean, yeah, scientists gave us the bomb, ever more efficient ways of killing ourselves, non-stick frying pans, chip-link ID cards for everyone's security . . . but that's not exactly what they're protesting about down there, is it? It's not *really* about the scientists themselves, but that they don't ever ask the question: what are the consequences of scientific development going to be? Who would've thought that eradicating smallpox would leave the world wide open to terrorist attack using the same virus?'

I think again about Gen-Fork, and it seems Maxnet got it right after all. That it *is* something I should be interested in.

TC wraps her arms around herself, as if somehow she is cold even in this cloying heat.

'Biology gives me the creeps,' she mutters.

'But isn't that what your friend does?' I resist a smirk.

TC turns and stares at me.

'Yes, sort of,' she says. 'But his work *could* prove a benefit to everyone. We'll just have to wait . . . but not for long.'

She finishes her cigarette and pitches it to the ground, then grinds it out.

'It looks like he'll find the results we need,' she adds quietly. 'That's what compensates.'

'And is he provided with lots of money to complete it?' I gesture down towards the crowds. 'Someone on my web-cast yesterday claimed that science is too intimate with the money-men. We're experiencing an escalation of science, he said, primarily because they want to make even *more* money. But if the driving force is making money, then it's inevitable that risky short-cuts will be taken.'

'Not always.' TC fingers her red ribbon. 'Not always.'

I find myself sighing. It seems so contradictory: TC's apparent agreement with the protest happening below us and yet her clear involvement with Jake.

A cheer from the crowds announces the arrival of an assorted convoy of trucks and old buses. The helicopter swoops low for a closer inspection, and the cheers turn to jeers as it does so.

'Ah, fuck it,' I say. 'I want to know some answers.'

'I'd like that, too,' says TC, quietly.

I turn and smile at her. 'Let's get you moved back in.'

'Okay,' she says. 'I'm ready.'

She throws away a fresh cigarette she's just taken from the packet, before even lighting it, then we head back to the place where TC has been temporarily staying, to pick up her belongings . . . She's going home today: taking a step forward.

TC has been waiting for the builders to finish, and today is the day she returns to the family home.

As we walk along in silence, something strange occurs to me again – something I haven't addressed. *I have absolutely no memory of her father.*

Gary strides past him with his guard dog on the lead, making his first afternoon inspection tour of the grounds. Jake is just about to stub out his cigar, when he notices that his favourite smoking hideaway has acquired an ashtray, complete with health warning fixed atop a metal post. He glances up at the CAMIC . . . then suddenly pauses.

He senses something.

He 'hears' it in his head.

It comes stronger. And stronger still – like a tidal wave of thought.

He suddenly recognizes it is the group-mind of his cloned mice.

And the emotion they are transmitting is one of distress.

Jake drops the cigar and starts to run back to his lab. As he bursts back through the fire door, he practically collides with Edwina.

'Like the ashtray I provided, dear heart?' she asks.

But Jake ignores her and races off down the corridor. He hears Edwina's footsteps hurrying behind him.

After impatiently pressing the keypad numbers, Jake throws open the door to his laboratory. He heads directly to his main PC and begins to scroll through the multitude of cam-shots. Practically every one is now bordered in red. The mind-thought of the mice seems far more powerful now that he is closer to them.

What's causing this anxiety?

Edwina manages to reach the door just before it closes. 'God, Jake,' she pants. 'What's all the excitement?'

As Jake taps on the keyboard, the reason for the mice's distress becomes apparent: the software controlling their automatic feeding supply has become locked. A quick reboot and a few seconds later food begins filling the receptacle in each of their cages. The red borders begin to flicker off, as the sense of anxiety fades.

'What's up, Jake?' repeats Edwina.

He slowly turns to her. 'Do you really want to know?'

So he spends the next five minutes explaining about the synchronicity he has detected in the mice, and his theory about there being a human equivalent. She listens with professional detachment, her eyes shifting across the various screens.

When he finishes, Edwina turns back to him. 'That's incredible, Jake,' she says, 'but are you sure?'

'I'm still in the process of confirming it, but I *am* sure. I'm convinced the human race is heading for another major crisis in about five days' time – something that will make last month's trauma seem like a minor headache.'

'Have you told anyone else here?'

He shakes his head.

'You should, Jake. You should.'

'Not yet. And promise me *you* won't, either.'

'Of course, if you say so.'

He gives a brief smile. 'Ed, I'm sorry to be blunt, but I need—'

'I'm dismissed?' she says, smiling as she leaves him.

He couldn't have been less unprepared for what happens next.

As soon as the door swings shut on her, the world around him changes, flickers, twists, rushes away in juddering leaps and sounds, and Jake finds himself elsewhere.

Click, click . . . *click!*

He only has an instant to recover before the dragon rearing up in front belches a noxious stream of fire towards him. Jake barely manages to step aside, as the heat sears the side of his helmet. Intuitively, he glances down at the ground through the choking fumes, and notices that some sort of molten poison the dragon emitted is dissolving the very stones. As the dragon turns to snort flame again, Jake realizes he is confronting a peril that far exceeds any previous incident. He starts to duck and weave under the onslaught, waiting for an opportunity to retaliate. He cannot afford to make a mistake. He must not lose, for humanity's sake.

The universe shifts again.

Click, click . . . *click!*

Standing by the door to his lab, Jake turns around to lean his back against it.

That's it. I must not lose. I have five days . . . or even less.

There is a thin film of sweat on my forehead, but the intense afternoon heat does not cause it. It's a result of the fear I feel about where I'm now standing. It's because this area has *history*.

'So where are we this afternoon?' asks Gareth. He sounds more formal than usual, because he's on air as I do my web-cast.

'Well, Gareth, I'm at New Delight Covert in Suffolk,' I explain.

'That's a nature reserve, I believe?'

He knows it is, as I told him earlier.

'Yes,' I agree. 'It's particularly significant for housing all types of rare wildlife.'

'Did your Jenny friend tell you that?'

Bastard.

'Yes, Gareth, I believe she did.'

'Scott, you know we've been getting a lot of viewers commenting that they think Jenny really suits you.'

Double bastard.

'Really? Well, thanks for that information, Gareth.'

I hear the slight sound as he switches in the software that cuts out his next comment from the outside world.

'Oh, get you.'

I hear the faint sound again.

'So, Scott, we're here at . . . New Delight Covert. What exactly is a covert, then?'

'It's a wood, Gareth.'

'It looks a nice spot.'

I glance around at the silver birch and ferns, trying to appreciate the quiet scene, as it deserves. I loathe these web-cast sessions, because Gareth seems to take a perverse pleasure in putting on people with a knack for irritating me.

'Okay, Scott, if you're ready, we have Sandra from Coventry waiting on the line. Sandra?'

'Hi, Scott.'

'Hi, Sandra, what can I do for you?'

'Why have you come to this lonely place? What's so special about it?'

'Well, this is the exact spot where Joseph Kennedy Junior died.'

'Who?'

I breathe in deeply, sensing this could take some

time. There is a soft electronic sound and Gareth sniggers in my ear.

'Joseph Junior was John F. Kennedy's older brother,' I say. 'JFK was America's president in the early Sixties, Sandra. The one who was assass— he was shot.'

'Oh, I think I remember now. In that car procession?'

'That's right, Sandra. Now, his brother Joseph Junior got killed here in England, at this very spot, during World War II.'

'By the Germans?'

'No. You see, he had volunteered for an experimental mission. The Americans had taken some old bomber aircraft and put in a very primitive remote control and about ten tons of high explosive.'

'Wasn't that dangerous?' asks Sandra.

I have the urge to suggest that anybody with half a brain would realize that fact, but I resist.

'Joe Kennedy was supposed to get that heavily laden aircraft into the air and fly a complex test-flight pattern, while the remote controls were checked by technicians flying alongside in another aircraft. And then Joe, with his co-pilot, would initiate the procedure to arm the explosives, bail themselves out, and the technicians in the other aircraft would then take over. They'd then be flying what was essentially a remote-controlled flying bomb, intending to crash it into the German Vee-three super-gun site at Mimoyecqes. But there was a fault with the arming mechanism and the plane blew up – just above where I'm now standing.'

'Was he killed?'

'The aircraft was carrying ten tons of high explosive. Of course he was bloody well—'

'Well, thank you, Sandra, for your interesting questions. And thank *you*, Scott.'

And for a moment, I think that I am alone once more, then I remember Maxnet and think about switching it off. Instead, I look up to the skies as suddenly that familiar shimmy of fear, familiar since my adolescence, crawls around my neck – and the ghosts arrive, as I knew they would. They are not as clear as the Hurricane and Stuka were, but the fainter transparency of these aircraft lends more poignancy to what I know is about to happen.

I force myself to remain motionless.

I remain as still as I can. As still as the two men who stand watching me from along the lane. Those two silent phantoms in American air-force uniforms, their faces indistinct and expressionless, just watching me.

I glance up again to see the big Liberator bomber coming towards me, escorted by a phalanx of other aircraft: the mother aircraft itself (a navy Ventura reconnaissance-bomber that carries the technicians detailed to take control of the Liberator), together with a B-17 Flying Fortress fitted with cameras to monitor the process, two Mosquitoes – one of them actually flown by the US President's son, Colonel Elliott Roosevelt – and further away a group of Mustang fighters which are shadowing the flight. It is an amazing sight – and sound. I picture Joseph Jnr now holding that over-laden bomber on course, as one of the technicians gets himself used to the heavy controls he is directing from the mother plane. Joe Kennedy is perhaps feeling pleased that he managed to get the massive thing off the ground in the first place, perhaps sharing a joke with his co-pilot Lieutenant Wilford 'Bud' Willy. The mother plane calls in, announcing it is about to finalize the procedure for arming the firing circuits – but will only fully arm the explosives after the two men have parachuted to safety.

The flight is nearly upon me, now.

I don't know if I can look at what is about to happen.

A stream of smoke appears from the belly of the aircraft. It has hardly begun before there erupts a brilliant vortex of light, and the plane becomes a myriad of fragments surrounding an expanding sphere of red and yellow. I watch this concussion wave shoot outwards, forming an even bigger, rapidly moving sphere, and see it blast away the ghosts of the trees that had covered the ground at the time, see it race up and toss the other planes around like wisps of paper. I hear a muted echo of the tremendous thunderclap it caused, and I watch as fiery fragments strike the ground like meteorites.

As these ghosts fade from sight, all I can think of is those last terrible seconds as the two men inside that Liberator smelt the burning wires and realized what was about to happen to them. Because they weren't the first mission to try, and fail, the pair knew just how dangerous it could prove to be.

I look back along the lane. There's no one there, now.

I turn for home . . . and start to run.

I have just feverishly resumed my writing about various aspects of the war, when I hear the phone start to ring. A moment later my mother calls up to me.

'Scott? It's Toni for you.'

I save my work in progress, check that my CAMIC mobile link is still active and charged up, then make my way downstairs to find my mother still holding the phone out to me.

I take the receiver and watch her turn away and head back to do whatever she was doing. I notice that she has that specific *mother* look in her eye, the one that tells me she's got some scheme in mind.

You can't hide anything from your own mother – especially mine.

'Hi, Scott,' says TC.

'Hi-ya.'

'Is ten tons of explosive really dangerous, then?'

'Oh, go take a jump. Anyway, how's things with you?'

I suspect she is finding it hard being at home alone. When, late this morning, I finally helped her move back in, she'd refused my offer to stay with her for a while.

'You sorted now?' I ask.

'Yep, I had some help.'

Jake? Jake helped her. Fuck.

'Jenny popped in. And then your mother.'

The jigsaw piece that was my mother's smile falls into place with a thud.

'Uh-huh?' I say, knowing that anything more intelligible would be the wrong thing to say.

TC, Jenny and my mother all together in the same room?

I lean a hand against the wall and close my eyes.

'Yes,' says TC. 'They were great – just what I needed.'

'Uh-huh.'

'And once we were done, we had lunch out in the garden.'

'Uh-huh.'

'And we got talking.'

Oh, fuck.

'Oh, yeah?'

'Your mum seems to think it's about time you and Jenny went out on a date.'

'Well, thank you for that news, TC.'

There's a long pause – an extremely long one – and I'm damned if I'm going to be the one to break it.

I suddenly begin to read between the lines – the hidden subtext of what TC is up to. Her voice is a little too bright, a little too fragile.

'TC, are you okay?' I say.

There is no reply at first. Just the faint sound of breathing.

'Of course I am. Why shouldn't I be?'

I can think of at least half a dozen reasons for her to be climbing the walls, but I decide to just dive in – try being brutal to be kind.

'This Jenny stuff you're on about is just crap, TC. So *what's* the matter?'

I hear the click of her cigarette lighter, then exhalation of smoke.

'Could you come over, Scott?'

'Fifteen minutes?'

'See you soon.'

I slap down the phone, shout 'Cheerio' to my

mother, grab the chip-link card for my car and run to the front door. TC *needs* me.

I begin to wonder how much of this madness I can take. The self-assured and vibrant girl that I have grown up alongside has been transformed into a chain-smoking, shaking wreck. I realize, as I see her standing at her front door, that she must have lost at least a stone over the last month. And there is this look of fear in her eyes. I have seen it in others, too, but only momentarily, and now, as I enter TC's house and turn to her after she has closed the door behind me, I sense there is a danger that her barely disguised terror may become frozen in place.

She puts a finger to my lips and holds up the palm of her other hand as if to halt me from even moving.

'Follow me,' she whispers.

And TC then bites her lip, backs away, and turns to begin climbing the stairs. As she does so, she takes out a cigarette and lights it. I go after her, my mind filled with a hornet's nest of possibilities about what she wants me to see.

She halts at the top of the stairs, folding the free arm about her body.

'In there,' she points. 'In *there*.'

I look over at an open bedroom door, then glance back at her.

'What is it?' I ask.

'Just go in,' she answers.

I frown and march into the bedroom, determined to face down whatever monster she has waiting there for me. I stop and look around, puzzled. There is no dead body with a knife sticking from its back; no Dr

Jake Crux hanging from the ceiling with a noose around his neck; and no Gareth from Unit-C with another little box of surprises. All I can see is an ordinary bedroom containing a double bed, twin bedside cabinets, two double wardrobes, a vase of wilted flowers on a table by the window, and several pictures on the walls. In fact, it is everything that is ordinary about another person's bedroom. There is nothing that I can see there that could possibly warrant those haunted eyes of hers.

'Well?' I say.

She pauses, before asking, 'Who used to sleep here?'

It's such a bewildering question that it takes me about five seconds to answer.

'Your mother, TC,' I finally say, probably a little too patronizingly, wondering if I need to fetch a doctor for her.

'It's your mother's bedroom,' I repeat.

'Yes, it is,' she says, and steps closer to me. 'But who else's?'

And she points to one of the bedside cabinets. It's so conspicuous that it still takes me some time to register: a double bed with matching cabinets and separate wardrobes. Her mother might have treated herself to a big bed, but why bother doubling up on bedroom furniture? Why the need for two *double* wardrobes? TC slowly walks over to the nearest bedside cabinet, then stops before it, reaches down and picks up a framed photograph. She holds it with one hand against her chest, stubs out her cigarette in an ashtray and turns to face me.

'Scott,' she says, 'tell me, who's my father?'

I practically reel at such an incredible question. TC comes over and places herself right in front of me.

'Who is my father?' she repeats. 'I can't remember him, Scott. I can't remember *anything* about him.' She hands me the photograph. 'But look.'

I summon up the courage to take it, feeling light-headed as I do so. I stare at the picture, which appears to be a holiday snap, especially enlarged. It shows seven people, grouped together like two family units. TC stands with her mother, while an unfamiliar man has his arms around both of them. Jenny is there, too, with her parents, and also a young man who bears a passing resemblance to her. This looks like a fairly recent photograph.

'That was taken early last May,' says TC. 'Remember, we went on holiday to France. But who is that man with mum and me? Who *is* he?'

There is now an absolute panic in her eyes. She reaches out suddenly and touches me, as if I might suddenly run away.

'The rescue team found mum belted into the passenger seat of her crashed car, Scott. In the *passenger* seat.'

Even as I understand the implications, a voice screams at me that this must be impossible, that there must be some mistake.

'I've been wanting to ask someone else about that for weeks,' says TC, 'but I've been too frightened, as it just seemed so stupid. It's finding this photograph, Scott . . . and I'm going insane, I'm going crazy. Scott, who was driving? *Who?*'

I stare down at the photograph, down at the images of Jenny with her broad smile and the laughter captured in her eyes; down at her parents standing behind her, both looking proud and shy at having their picture taken; then at the young man in glasses right beside her, with one hand raised and fingers parted as Mister Spock habitually does in *Star Trek*; and then at the image of TC herself, caught as she glances up smiling – as her mother does – at the tall man confidently staring into the camera lens.

I feel cold inside, very cold indeed.

INTERNET NEWS UPDATE by Janice Maclean
I've just been alerted through my Maxnet connection to something fascinating for anyone following *Total Cover*. Go back and look at the history files, then tell me who that young man is, the one who was always hanging around with Scott. Their records say he's Benjamin Archer, an old school mate, but is there anyone out there who can actually remember him? Because I'm sure I can't. Is this some ruse by Unit-C to mess with the viewers' minds? I think we should be told.

It is late at the Eisencrick Institute – getting on to ten o'clock – and dusk is falling outside. A few high clouds swirl red and purple against the dark blue, then melt away. Halogen lights begin to warm up and soon the Institute is highlighted against the darkness. Ten blackbirds or more are bickering with each other in a silent squabble on the main expanse of lawn, till four foxes trot past them abreast in a line, their ears lying flat against their skulls, and their teeth bared.

Inside his lab, Jake sits at his workbench, slowly drumming the fingers of his left hand on its surface. On the screens in front of him a red border surrounds practically every cam-shot, and they have been in this condition for the past two minutes. This is definitely the longest period of synchronized activity that he has noted, and he is curious to see how long the mice will maintain it. He doesn't even bother to flick through all the other screens, as he has now written a short program providing a bar-indicator to one side of his main screen, which denotes the percentage of mice acting as one.

It currently stands at about ninety-five per cent.

Jake has been aware of their high level of group-mind activity for the entire duration of their current link-up – a powerful comprehension, one that he is unable to interpret. It is a fascinating phenomenon, yet vaguely deadly in its attraction.

Three minutes.

And the bar suddenly jumps from ninety-five to one hundred per cent. Jake stops drumming his fingers, sits up straight and pulls his chair closer. He frowns, his first thought being that something has gone wrong with his program. But then he experiences a tremor of excitement as he realizes that he now has evidence that they *are* all acting as one.

He pauses, frowning again.

He then starts to sequence the screens, and soon notices that those cages without a red border contain no mouse to monitor. Jake taps a request into his PC. Out of the initial two thousand cages, forty-two have been quarantined by his previous tests, so were registered blank and not taken into account by his program and thus should leave nineteen hundred and fifty-eight in use. But, according to his screen, he has eighteen hundred and sixty-nine cages containing mice, plus another eighty-nine which are empty and therefore no longer monitored by his new program. Jake does a quick mental percentage calculation – eighteen hundred and sixty-nine divided by nineteen hundred and fifty-eight – and comes to a figure of about ninety-five per cent. The same figure his program had been indicating only moments before.

He sits back into his seat and goes through the various screens again, pausing now and then to study the empty cages.

Four minutes.

The red borders begin to waver and flicker off.

The bar had been registering ninety-five per cent, then leapt up to a hundred.

Jake's experiment is now missing eighty-nine mice from the nineteen hundred and fifty-eight the experiment had been monitoring. What happened to them?

It seems logical to postulate that there were eighty-nine mice not acting in synchrony with the rest, and that they are now no longer there – even though Jake can't remember them being included in his calculations anyway.

He has absolutely no idea how such a thing could occur. But he knows that whatever caused it, it is important to find out.

The borders turn red again.

And the bar rises straight to one hundred per cent.

So God made the two larger lights, the Sun to rule over the day and the Moon to rule over the night; He also made the stars. Evening passed and morning came – that was the fourth day.

Friday
Day 4

Chapter Eight

Christina Belleto – Italian, twenty-two, wild-girl-rich-kid-queen-bitch, secretly desperate for someone to stand up to her and tell her no – checks the altimeter and then the compass, for the fifth time within a minute, to confirm that she is at the right height and on the right heading. She touches her new CAMIC for a moment, then looks down on Monte Cassino from the old Cessna 152 aeroplane in which she is taking flying lessons, and finds herself dealing with a rush of conflicting emotions.

Her family had once lived in the town she is now soaring above.

That was before the war, but her great-grandparents informed Christina Belleto about all the dramatic things that had happened below.

The destruction wrought during the Second World War by the Allied bombing of this mountaintop Benedictine monastery had been mirrored in the slaughter of countless ground troops fighting and dying for the rock of Cassino itself – fighting and dying to seize a better position, fighting and dying for an ideal. Christina catches herself even thinking she can hear their shrill laments at all those chances at life and love they relinquished during those bloody weeks of early 1944. She imagines she can even smell the smoke from their guns.

But then she spots the beautiful white and blue ribbon that is the river Rapido moving fast and sure below, and she licks her lips guiltily at an intense relief in being young and alive, of being Christina Belleto.

She smiles and turns to make some comment to her instructor.

The other seat is empty.

Christina chokes back her words and the aeroplane bucks. She is jolted upright, and she struggles to correct her error. Her concentration on this takes half a minute's distraction. When she sneaks another glance, the other seat is still empty. She even peers around behind her – as though her instructor can have hidden himself somewhere else in the cramped cockpit. Just then, the CAMIC starts bleeping.

'Holy Mary,' she whispers, taking one hand from the control column to cross herself.

This is only her third time up in a light aircraft.

Where is the pilot? There must have been one. How else could I have taken off?

She can remember the plane accelerating down the runway, and she can remember the exhilaration of lifting into the sky, but she cannot recall (however hard she struggles to) any person seated beside her at the controls.

But that all becomes incidental, since it is she who now has control of the aeroplane.

Christina Belleto wants to throw up.

Crossing herself once more, she forces back the nausea. Although she cannot work out how she has come to be airborne all by herself, she instinctively knows it will take a novel type of self-discipline to get her safely back down on the ground. She surprises herself by feeling sure she possesses such a degree of skill.

She reaches for the radio to commence a Mayday call.

INTERNET NEWS UPDATE by Janice Maclean
The pace as *Total Cover* draws to a close is now more intense than ever. After Mickey's dramatic eviction, amid vehement accusations of vote-rigging, we are now down to the last four contestants: Nat, Scott, Jo and then poor old Tiff, in that order.

'What's happened to those FBI reports I was receiving, Gareth? I find I'm blocked whenever I try to access the updates.'

'You've been a bit of a naughty boy, there. An injunction has been placed on releasing them to you – or to the viewers.'

'Oh, why?'

'We're currently investigating. You'll probably find them available next time you check.'

SCOTT'S WEB-BOX COMMENTARY
This is downloaded from the Lone Smoking Rifle website.

'Want to cause some mayhem? Then blow up a glacier! That's right, I've had reliable reports that someone plans to create more space for building holiday accommodation in picturesque Iceland by destroying an inconvenient glacier. Don't we have international environment regulations any more? Given that it's in the same area as a major volcano blow-up a few years back, I would have thought there'd be warning bells about triggering another explosion locally.'

'Anyway, why destroy the very landmark that the tourists come to admire?'

Just back from my usual early-morning run, I am now bench-pressing weights – the heaviest I own. I need to work off the tension that has kept me awake again for most of the night, and I'm getting to feel punch-drunk without proper sleep.

It doesn't take a genius to link the purchase of large amounts of explosive by Landico with a conspiracy website's warning about glaciers being destroyed. But what possible motive would there be for Toluene's mob to release so much fresh water into the ocean? I find it hugely disturbing and I've posted some questions to let Maxnet sort it out. Someone out there may have a suggestion that agrees with my hunch.

And amongst all I now have to worry about is the realization that people I apparently once knew have vanished without trace. Pushing weights has become the only thing I can think of to give me focus in this mad environment of alternative realities.

My thoughts eventually return to Joe Junior. At Harvard, Joseph Patrick Kennedy Jnr had become involved with an organization opposed to American intervention in the European war. He apparently thought an 'accommodation' with Germany made more sense than going to the aid of the side still expected to lose. Then he surprised everyone by ditching his final year of college and signing up with the Naval Air Force. His wealthy father probably used political weight to ensure his oldest son spent the first part of this service in flying anti-submarine patrols, but Joe Jnr insisted on moving on. Friends said that he seemed determined to get himself exposed to exactly the same level of risk as everyone else. Even after his official tour ended, he persuaded his crew to fly another ten missions. Then he heard news of a 'special', for which he volunteered. That was how he came to be flying *Zootsuit Black*, which was packed with nitroglycerine-based Torpex. So packed that it even had its armament removed to accommodate more explosives – so filled with explosives that there were crates of it stored on the flight deck.

There had been six previous failures, in successive operations, and both he and his co-pilot were repeatedly advised that they could decline this mission with no smear on their records.

I push hard at the weights, that strange aggression surging through me.

They knew the risks, yet they went ahead. They got that flying bomb off the ground and into the air, its big engines screaming under the massive load. It must have taken a while to gain height, before they began the testing on *Zootsuit Black*.

The barbell is getting too heavy.

Thirty-six. Just another one.

Suffolk stretching out beneath them: the Blythburgh valley and its mudflats reflecting the August sky with a thin sheen of surface water.

Thirty-seven. And another one.

Thirty-eight.

Taking another look at the countryside below. Then giving the call sign that the tests were complete.

'Spade Flash,' I say aloud to myself.

Thirty-nine.

Oblivion.

Probably the biggest airborne explosion Britain has ever experienced.

I really struggle with my fortieth lift.

Yes!

I grit my teeth and do five more.

And then five more again.

Oblivion.

Zootsuit Black – a metaphor for what lies ahead?

It's late morning and I have the parapets of Orford Castle all to myself. I head over to each one of its three sets of railings, to gaze out over the surrounding countryside. From this high up, the view is extensive. Below me, and beyond the car park, lies the old village of Orford itself – red-tiled and small-windowed, brickwork and timber – while stretching out beyond it are wide fields and narrow dykes that gradually merge into the green woodland and hazy distance that comprise the rest of Suffolk. When I move to the railing immediately overlooking the main entrance, I can see the river Ore, with a long spit of vegetated shingle which is Orford Ness, and further out lies the sea itself.

Along with all the other little mind-messing things I have recently been made aware of, I rediscover something else about myself: I've never been comfortable with heights.

After a spasm of vertigo, I swallow hard and force myself to look, but all I can think about is the narrow railing.

What if I got crazy and climbed over it? Who'd be there to stop me?

As the thumping of my heart begins to ease, I grip the metal bars and pull myself up on the narrow ledge to get an unbridled view of the surroundings. The vista, in all directions, is truly exhilarating.

This is the minor stuff compared to some of the worries besetting others. The universally shared sense of waiting for some imminent disaster is inevitably causing cracks in people's personalities. Judging from the proliferation of websites, almost everyone is absorbed in worries about something less tangible, some terrible futuristic Grendel that is stalking the human race. And all coinciding with Jake's timetable?

I myself constantly feel as though there is someone following just behind me – and not just all the other cameras. It's like having somebody stalking me whose breath I have yet to feel on my neck. This sense of unease has been compounded by what happened at TC's house. I have really no idea who that man in the photograph was, any more than she does, but we both suspect it was her father. If so, where has he gone – and *why* do we have no memory of him?

I offered to stay there with her, but TC insisted she was okay, that she had just wanted to have it confirmed she wasn't going crazy all on her own. As I was approaching the front door on my way out, she had already picked up her mobile. I wondered if Jake's number was programmed into it.

When I reached home, I tried an experiment of my own. First I sought out our family photo albums, the most recent one starting from the beginning of last year. In it I found four pictures of myself with other athletes – guys I clearly knew then, by the way we were laughing together, but whom I no longer recognized.

As I closed the book, I found my mouth had gone dry. I didn't feel ready to involve my parents.

Last night, I think again I slept only for an hour, maybe less, and, *now* I remember, even that small amount of time was plagued by vicious little nightmares. I still don't think I have completely dispersed the fear tightening my stomach, which stopped me from eating breakfast. In fact, I *know* I haven't.

This *thing*, this event towards which we are heading, is all about fear.

And I sense that I have to address these shifts affecting me in the next day or so. I tell myself again that it's why I'm here: coming to this place means I can challenge their accumulated terror. It's also another exposed place where I'll be vulnerable to attack from Sonat thugs. The pressures weigh heavy.

I contact Gareth and tell him that I'm ready for my regular web-cast. That makes me feel better, because it means I'm confronting my problem, not allowing myself to be a mere passenger to events.

Gareth begins by reminding me that we're down to the last four contestants. And then he informs me how much money the winner is likely to get and it is astronomical.

I reach up to touch my CAMIC. 'This thing is only a camera and mike watching and listening to everything I do. They're everywhere these days anyway, so it's not as though I'll feel I've particularly earned all that if I win.'

'You can give it to charity, Scott, if it upsets you so much.'

'I'll make my own mind up on that, thanks.'

There's a pause, then, 'I notice we're quite high up, Scott.'

Has he somehow been listening in to my thoughts?

'About four storeys,' I say, 'raised on an earthen mound.'

'What is this place?'

'It's a twelfth-century castle built by King Henry the Second. Basically it comprises a tall, circular keep with three rectangular towers positioned at regular intervals along its sides. They contain the stairwells giving access to each floor.'

He switches on the software that eliminates his voice from the ongoing broadcast.

'And where have you hidden your guidebook, Scott?'

I smile, peering over the parapet. 'As you can see,' I try to read the information from the Webvis web page now illuminated as a pale floating image before me, 'the outer curtain wall has long been demolished, and only the earthworks defences remain.'

I turn and head into one of the small rooms atop the nearest tower, removing myself from the view of the sheer drop to the ground. When I speak again, my voice echoes.

'It's a rabbit warren of passageways in here . . . a perfect example of fortification of its time.'

I switch off the Maxnet image as I choke in the close heat, and find I have to go quickly back outside. My potted guided tour is over, so I can now get to the real reason for my being here in the first place.

'But why here, Scott? You said only the other day you were primarily interested in World War II sites.'

'Yes, those wartime sites offer something more

important to me than this medieval castle does, and I'll be heading off to visit some of them soon. But today is not about this actual place itself. I just thought it would be interesting to get myself up somewhere high so I can show you *these*.'

I point towards Orford Ness. There in the distance, practically indistinct on the horizon, loom two strange buildings, incongruous because of the bleak and empty strip of shoreline they are built on. At first glance, they might resemble white marble Greek temples – similar in size, but stripped of their inner core. For they have no external walls, only a succession of pillars supporting a roof constructed of tiered blocks of concrete that taper in size towards the top.

'Good God, they look like giant pagodas,' comments Gareth.

'That's what the locals call them, but to me those buildings seem even more ominous than Largewater. Those so-called pagodas are one of the few sites around the world where science and weapons of war have become intrinsically intimate. They represent to me the embodiment of techno-fear.'

He responds so fervently, he has apparently forgotten he's on air.

'But what on earth are they for?' insists Gareth.

'You're looking at the Cold War over there. Those two buildings are Labs Four and Five of the Atomic Weapons Research Establishment based at Orford. That is the same site where they tested the firing mechanisms for nuclear bombs.'

'They tested the bomb *here*?'

'No, Gareth, only the trigger mechanism. But since the trigger mechanism itself involved a considerable

amount of explosive, in case of an accident those
buildings you see were designed to direct a blast outwards rather than upwards. That was a fail-safe and,
before you ask, the reason for directing the blast outwards was because any contamination would spread
out over the beach and the empty shingle, rather than
upwards to be carried away on the wind. Mind you,
that does beg the question why, if there wasn't any
fissile material there, they would need to worry about
any contaminated material being blown into the air –
but there you go. You have no idea of the amount of
research that went on over there, do you? The Ministry
of Defence used the place for decades, experimenting
on quite a few innovations subsequently used in warfare. Want to find the best aerodynamic shape for a
bomb? Drop it on Orford Ness. It doesn't matter
whether they're small World War I bomblets or a huge
World War II twenty-two-thousand-pound Grand
Slam monster, just drop it here, and study how it flies
through the air. A Grand Slam bomb didn't fall to
earth, either, Gareth, as it practically *flew* to its target.
Munitions? Blow them up too and see how they
behave. And radar? Some of the first tests were done
here before they moved down the coast to Bawdsey.'

I stop there. If ever anyone wants to get a feeling
for how alien science can seem, they need only to
come here and look at these pagodas.

*That stuff will get me votes from the anti-science
brigade – which will keep me in the show. This is showing
them their fear in physical form. And I am well aware I'm
being ruthless in manipulating them.*

It feels so apt to be standing here, on the rooftop of
a castle that is *centuries* old. It must have presented a

terrifying spectacle when first erected – at the very forefront then of warfare technology. Somewhere back in the mists of history there were men that looked up at this very structure and felt much the same way as I do about those now-disused research establishments over on the horizon: a stark reminder of how men continue conspiring to kill one another. I look around at this castle and am impressed by the awesome sense of history it contains, but somehow I can't envisage someone from the future ever seeing those research pagodas as representing something noble, something symbolic of our heritage. They look cold, and they must surely have ghosts, but I don't ever intend investigating them, as they're bound to be grotesque.

'Gareth, if you like you could travel down here, buy a ticket for the boat at the quay and go across there for a sightseeing trip. They must be quite a sight, close up.'

There is silence to that.

I keep staring over at the distant structures. I remember when I was fifteen, some of our school class decided to go there for a day out. I refused to join them and kept visualizing some sort of catastrophe befalling them as I sat apart – inert and incapable of rational thought. They all returned safely, talking excitedly about what they'd seen there, but I always suspected that those high spirits were a front. I *knew* they must have sensed the ghosts that lurk there.

The slight static noise in my ears switches off with a soft click. Gareth must want some time to reflect on what I've said. At least that means I won't have to deal with any of our e-viewers for the moment. That definitely seems a bonus.

I suddenly hear the sound of a familiar vehicle and I glance down to the car park below.

Ah, fuck.

It is Crux in his Landrover, with TC sitting beside him. In the open rear seat, I spot a small wicker basket.

Double fuck.

They're obviously here to enjoy a picnic lunch on the grassy bank overlooking the yachts and fishing boats. Suppressing my fear of vertigo, I clutch the guard rail and watch as Jake swings his Landrover into a parking space and turns off the engine.

When does he ever find time to do his precious research?

He jumps out of the vehicle with a nimbleness I would not credit in a man of his bulk, retrieves the basket, and turns to join TC, who has paused to light a cigarette. Jake puts the basket down and reaches into his pocket. There is a flash of reflected sunlight as he flips open his silver cigar case. He removes one and, lighting it from TC's cigarette, they both head into the castle's grounds.

Watching these small actors playing out such an everyday scene from my lofty perch, I feel curiously robbed. I've only recently started to imagine possibilities between TC and myself, and it looks like I've missed out by not seizing my opportunities when I should have. I allow myself a few minutes of driving myself crazy with imagining it was Jake that TC was phoning as I left her house yesterday. I even start to doubt she stayed in her own home last night.

Jake stretches himself out on the grass while TC

inspects the contents of the wicker basket. The pair of them seem to swim in and out of my focus.

I tell myself it is because of the height. My head aches. I close my eyes to the pain.

I reopen my eyes to look down at them again. Instead all I see is another reality – a dark place.

What?

I look around desperately and, as I do, the 'pagodas' snap back into view again, then just as rapidly blink away.

Once again, the world before me judders like a faulty film.

Click, click . . . *click*!

I have to stop myself from throwing up.

I start to shake. This is not just because I am frightened – even though I'm startled by this new universe-shift – but because I find I am being physically jolted around. Peering around through the surrounding gloom, I try to discern any recognizable features. I am intensely curious to discover where this place is – or *what* it is.

As my eyes gradually adjust, I find myself crouching in the cramped and darkened fuselage of an aircraft (a single dim red bulb its only illumination). One hand is gripping a rail above my head, to steady myself, and my ears recoil from the deafening roar of engines. I am positioned immediately behind the same dark-haired Czech from our assault course earlier, but he is now dressed in thicker clothing and wearing a parachute as he intently peers down into a black circular opening at his feet. Now the trembling in my muscles *is* caused by fear. With my free hand, I reach up behind my back and discover I too have a parachute.

This is a joke! I can't do this!

I am aware now how much I most *definitely* don't like heights, yet I am obviously being expected to throw myself from this aeroplane. At night, at God knows what altitude – and God knows where.

Make it stop. I can't do this. Give me a chance to think. Czechoslovakia?

It comes to me suddenly: Project Anthropoid. If this particular shift follows on from the others I have already experienced, then in all likelihood I am set to parachute into Czechoslovakia in late December of 1941, in the first stage of the SOE-sanctioned plan to assassinate Reinhard Heydrich.

But by parachute!

Talk about having your worst fears thrust into your face.

I look behind me, to see other men sitting along narrow benches, smiling up at me. I turn back to face the void I'm expected to jump into. Before I have time to think further, the same English officer as before gestures as the red bulb beside him turns off, and another one lights up with a faint green glow.

'First two, go! Good luck! Go!'

The man in front of me glances back and says, 'Watch your butter-feet,' then steps onto the rim of the hatch, and drops from view – pitching slightly forward to stop himself from clipping the rim itself with the back of his head.

This is the real test, this is the—

'Go! Go!'

I compel myself to follow the previous man.

Stepping onto the hatch rim, I take a small jump with my feet held together, my head dipping forward as the guy before me did. It is only as I start to drop into the void, disappearing into the blackness, that I realize I don't know even how to operate a parachute.

The blast of the props and the turbulence of the slipstream take my breath away – as does the absolute cold that snares at my face. As I frantically feel around on my chest, haphazardly seeking some sort of rip-cord, the unexpected happens and it feels like someone has kicked me simultaneously in the stomach and groin. I am flung backwards for a second, my head ricochets forward, then it is jerked right back so that I can see above and behind me. The black wings of the Halifax rush away from me, and in that moment, my parachute billows out into a classic mushroom canopy. I laugh as I realize that I'd been attached to a static line, and all I'd had to do was jump. Gravity will now do the rest.

I reach up and clasp what I think are called the risers. I haven't a clue how to steer myself, but they give me something to hang on to.

I gradually look down. And wish I hadn't.

I could admire the beauty of it if I had the time: the utter blackness of the sky on the horizon, the myriad stars scattered like some astronomer's wet dream, the virgin white of the snow-covered fields below me, the black-stalked copses, the distant farm buildings. But the speed at which this winter scene is approaching me is worrying. Our pilot must have given us the green light at a very low altitude. Five hundred feet? That's barely the height of a normal block of flats. The ground still rushes straight at me, big, white and . . .

Before I can think further, I hit the ground, my legs buckling instantly. My left knee takes the brunt of the impact, as I continue to shoot forward, ramming my face into the snow.

Twisting my head, I splutter snow from my mouth, the half-collapsed canopy tugging at the straps on my back and I realize I have just performed something I never thought possible.

Then this world of snow and icy wind and hard-frozen earth begins to flicker and jump.

I did it . . . just like my grandfather Roy did back in the war.

I tell myself that I still loathe heights, however brave I now feel.

Click, click . . . *click*!

Reality stutters and alternates quickly, then slows to a stop, and I am back where I was before. The warmth of the sun envelops me again, its brightness dazzling me.

Turning away from my vantage point, I limp over to the head of the stairwell. My kneecap feels as if a hot knife is being probed underneath it, while in my boot my ankle is rapidly swelling.

For a strange few moments, as I negotiate the stairs with both hands held out to each side to support myself against the walls, I sense the presence of Jenny beside me. I have no idea where this thought has come from, but I envisage her helping me carefully down the steps, ensuring that I don't trip.

By the time I reach ground level, I've decided to give her a phone call to see if she's available to go out with me this afternoon.

The spontaneous thought surprises me.

I head over to my car, making sure I avoid the other two.

Jake watches as TC stares up at the sky for a moment, before turning her attention to their small picnic basket. She lifts out crusty rolls, a box of fresh Camembert, seedless red grapes, strawberries and a bottle of Chablis chilling in an ice-filled plastic container. She then stretches out on the grassy knoll overlooking the estuary, and he sees how her face relaxes. As Jake joins her there, they begin to reflect on their encounter of the previous night. TC had then badly needed to talk: to confess things she had done, to expunge the memory of her nightmares and the fear she experiences of her reality shifts. She had finally exhausted her outpourings at about three in the morning, and promptly fell asleep on the couch. Jake noticed how she slept with a frown, as though perplexed by her dreams.

It is a novelty for Jake to find a woman so interested in him – and he realizes that TC is much more versed in the ploys of romance than he is. This lunch today provides as complete a distraction as they could wish for, but both know it must end soon. It is just a welcome interlude before he must continue his research.

Her account of her father's mysterious disappearance has stupendous implications for his experiment. TC believes Jake's findings could prove more persuasive with the general population if he could provide further firm evidence of the paranormal activity undoubtedly happening all around the world. Jake senses she is genuinely frightened by it all, but feels the burden will be easier when shared.

Back in his office, Jake deftly tears the completed cryptic crossword out of the paper, picks up a pen and prints '7 mins 52 seconds' just above its list of clues. He stands up, rips down his previous record from the wall, and attaches this new achievement in its place. He then stares at it for a moment, tapping his fingers on the adjoining brickwork.

Heading back to his leather chair, he drops into it, and leans back with his eyes closed. TC's discovery of that family photograph has prompted further speculations about what else could be happening out there.

Other people are *vanishing – and there are reports on this appearing from all over via Maxnet – but is it just a beginning?*

He himself has a similar mystery to contend with. How could it be that he has simply 'lost' eighty-nine mice? The answer occurs to him as quickly as he poses himself the question, and he realizes how to check. If any of his experimental mice have indeed 'disappeared', there will be recorded evidence to prove it. Jake opens his eyes, lines up his keyboard . . . then pauses.

I'm getting ahead of myself. First check the initial proposition.

He calculates that this procedure will take him just over two and a quarter hours.

Instead of resorting to the maze, Jake uses three boxes from a separate experiment, which used different symbols to embellish the opening into each. He first tests several of the mice by putting the food prize in the box with a black circle painted around its opening – fumigating the box after each attempt so as to eliminate any scent remaining. Even when he changes its position with respect to the other boxes, the mice very quickly learn which box to choose for their reward. As previously, he then returns the mice to the quarantined section to join all the others. At the next experiment, following a five-minute interval, the fresh batch of mice he tests heads straight for the box with the circle.

Jake then fixes a blob of plastic to the top of one box, shifts it to yet another position within the test area, and switches off the light. The mice take longer now, but they get to learn where it is from touch this time, and in turn appear to pass on that knowledge to the rest of the group. Jake switches the light back on, slides in additional boxes without any separate markings or additions, except for digital counters clicking at different speeds. Yet again the mice, after learning the trick of it – the counter changing fastest indicating the food – somehow pass on this information to the rest.

They have the power to reason. This is intelligence at work.

The sudden noise of a klaxon going off perplexes Jake. As it screams in a succession of different tones, he quickly realizes it is not the fire alarm. Jake instantly begins to consider the possibility of a biological alert.

'This is not a fire drill,' a voice sounds over the tannoy. 'I repeat, this is not a fire drill.'

Jake pauses at the door, calculating his options for

escape if this emergency should arise from some organism getting loose inside the building.

The disembodied voice continues: 'We have intruders present on site, and are currently taking all the necessary security precautions. Do not worry, as the situation is under control.'

As soon as he hears the words 'Do not worry', Jake leaps forward to open the door – just before the electronic bolt is remotely activated. He steps into the corridor, letting the door bang futilely against the now-extended bolt. The aerial CAMIC still inside taps against the door in its repeated attempts to exit the room and follow him.

'No way,' he mutters, taking off at a run down the corridor. The siren is still shrieking as he passes a series of doors from behind which come the muffled sounds of people banging and swearing. Reaching the fire door, he finally pauses, wondering if that too will have been locked. But the door opens unhindered and Jake steps outside.

'Dr Crux?' voices another tannoy positioned near the door. 'Dr Crux, please return to your own laboratory.'

Jake ignores it and begins to jog around towards the front side of the main building. There is a fair amount of noise audible from that direction.

As he comes within sight of the gatehouse, he comprehends the reason for the security alert. There seems to be a small riot in progress, as an unusually large group of security guards grapples with intruders who have infiltrated the Institute grounds. There must have been some sort of diversion caused that enabled some protesters to scale the perimeter fence.

Jake can see ladders propped against the fence itself, with sacking draped over the razor wire that crowns it. As he watches, it seems uncertain to him whether the extra police that have just arrived can hope to restore order.

Amongst the scattered groups of screaming and shouting people and barking guard dogs, Jake sees a man in his early twenties break free from the grip of the policeman who has tackled him. The intruder now races directly towards Jake, who for a moment feels confused; the man's expression of hatred seems directed at him personally. Then Jake notices the stick, just as the man is about three metres away.

Raising it above his head, he screams, 'You fucking, *baaaaastard*!'

Jake drops to a crouch, then launches himself up and under the man's guard to tackle him by the waist. They both crash to the ground, but Jake pushes himself rapidly upright. Jamming a knee over the assailant's outstretched arm, he pulls the stick from his grip and throws it away, then punches him hard on the jaw. He feels the young man's resistance drain away as he passes into unconsciousness.

Jake stares down at him, scarcely believing what he's just done. He seems capable of using a fury he's never before allowed himself to unleash, like the one that manifests when he finds himself fighting dragons. Before he can think further, the policeman rushes up and goes to swing his truncheon at the intruder's head.

Jake quickly raises his hand. 'Stop!' he yells. 'He's out cold.'

The policeman looks disappointed and reaches for

his handcuffs instead. He rolls the unconscious man over, pulls his arms back and clips on the handcuffs with a practised flourish. He looks up at Jake, who has risen to his feet.

'You all right, sir?' the policeman asks.

Jake inspects his knuckles. 'Yep,' he says, 'I'm okay.'

He glances over towards the Institute entrance. Order is slowly beginning to be restored, with both the police and the security guards seemingly using extreme force. Jake glances down at his attacker, and reflects on the sheer violence of the man's attack on him.

As he continues striding towards the main doors, as an afterthought he adds to the policeman, 'Have a nice day, now.'

The man's office is devoid of any personal mementos. Instead, to one side, stands an illuminated glass cabinet containing varieties of antique scientific glassware, while on the opposite wall are fitted several wall-to-ceiling mirrors. On the glass-topped desk stand two slim PC screens, along with a laptop and two telephones – one currently off the hook. Even here, in this inner sanctuary, an ubiquitous CAMIC is monitoring events from up in one corner.

As Jake opens the door, without knocking, and strides in, Oscar Brightwell is just returning to sit at his desk. From the way the glass is becoming opaque in the windows, Jake assumes Oscar has just been watching what is going on outside – and probably saw him heading this way – before switching on the reactor-light blinds again. As always Oscar's face betrays no emotion.

Seizing the initiative, Jake takes several large steps and manages to reach Oscar's desk before his boss can say anything. Oscar slowly swings his chair around, and picks up the telephone as if Jake were not even there.

'Yes,' he speaks into it, 'that's being dealt with. It was right for you to call. We'll talk later.'

He puts the phone down in its cradle, then glances at a computer screen.

Jake gives a quick smile and tries out several conversational gambits in his head before speaking. He notes how Oscar did not express any surprise at seeing him.

What did you think of me hitting that man outside? Jake settles for a blunt opening gambit.

'Is it legal for the Institute to forcibly incarcerate its staff even for security reasons? Is that permitted by conditions of the fire certificate issued by the Fire Brigade in this country? It certainly isn't in America.' Jake leans forward, placing his hands on the near edge of Brightwell's desk.

Oscar leans forward in turn, as if intending to push away Jake's intruding fingers. Jake backs away at the last second, stands up straight and folds his arms.

'Well, is it?' he asks again.

Oscar dabs the area where Jake had touched his polished desk surface. 'How are your tests progressing?' he demands.

Jake frowns. 'I know you heard my question.'

Oscar leans back into his chair, and rests the tip of

each index finger on the near edge of his desk, as though to steady it.

'The situation demanded it,' he says. 'Now, what about your research?'

'*Situation?*' Jake snorts. 'That was a small-scale riot.'

Oscar lifts the two fingers from the desk, and turns aside to tap out a fast rhythm on the keyboard of his laptop.

'Jake, we're intending to allocate more money to your project,' he says. For the first time since Jake has burst into the room, Oscar shows some small emotion by venturing a little smile. It looks so forced that Jake wants to laugh.

The smile quickly fades. 'The board is extremely pleased to see that you are producing results,' Oscar continues. 'And they're particularly interested in your most recent discoveries.'

Oscar turns the laptop around and slides it towards Jake. Jake glances down at the screen and what he sees there surprises him. His budget has been increased by a factor of ten, and it seems three major laboratories will be freed up for whatever purposes he decides upon. Also, extra staff will be made available to assist him.

Jake looks up at Oscar, wanting to ask the director how he got to know about his results and why he bothered asking about them in the first place.

He wants me *to be aware that* he *knows.*

Jake wonders who exactly has been spying on him. *Tightened security? And for how long?*

He smiles to himself as he considers all the months of work now behind him. He has some appreciation of what it feels like to be Scott, constantly being watched during some reality e-show.

Or even what it must be like to be one of his own mice.

They both just stare at each other, with Jake inwardly cursing that the very interference from the Institute that he was trying to forestall is now being demonstrated here in pixel form. With the large amounts of money being proposed, Jake knows that there will be more emphasis on rapid results.

Oscar Brightwell's face remains inscrutable.

And Jake wants to punch him – which is another concern. *Where is all this anger in me coming from?*

Jake smiles at Brightwell, nods and turns to leave. But he knows his boss isn't fooled for one instant.

'Don't forget to shut the door after you,' says Oscar.

Jake doesn't look back, and he slams it with just enough force to make the frame rattle.

He is beginning to hate Oscar. And he knows if he allows that to continue it will blur his thinking.

After all, Jake needs to stay focused.

Chapter Nine

Jeff Koplasky – American, thirty-five, small in build for a prison officer, moustached and Charlie Brown to his very core (everyone else thinks he has a short-man-in-big-trousers complex) – is painfully aware that he has to change his job. He has assisted with five state executions and, instead of it becoming easier, as the rest of the team claimed, Koplasky now realizes they have been lying to him, and that they are as sick as he is of the whole messy business. It's the ones who aren't closely involved in the process, the ones who don't feel the trembling in a condemned man's arms as he is escorted to the execution room to be strapped down, who vaunt its worth as a deterrent beneficial to society.

The authorities may have ensured that the process be as clinical as possible (a quick injection performed with medical efficiency), but for Jeff Koplasky it is still all about a group of men escorting another man to a small room containing only a table, some straps, a needle and a viewing window for the witnesses. It means securing the doomed man to the table, the needle being inserted, opening the curtains of the window, then standing by in an adjoining room to watch on a video monitor as the death sentence is carried out. He has noticed, on each occasion, the victim twisting his head to stare at the people staring in at him, as if somehow they might change their minds, smash the bulletproof glass and rescue him. Jeff Koplasky has yet to imagine anything else more macabre.

He marches down the corridor, copy of the order of sentence in hand, staying well away from the bars of cells containing future recipients of a similar document. And he tries to ignore the din – as if the whole prison is making its case for life – so all Jeff Koplasky can hear is a low murmur of voices in his own head. Now that he has made his mind up that this must be the last time he performs this filthy task, he is overcome with a wonderful sense of doing the right thing, and even the whispers in his mind fade away under the euphoria.

He stops at the cell door and coughs politely after he sees what is happening inside. Down on his hands and knees, on the floor inside, the prison chaplain is peering under the single bunk. He abandons his search and gazes up at Koplasky.

'Wasn't I here with someone a moment ago?' The chaplain looks confused. He pauses. 'Why am I in here, Jeff?'

Jeff Koplasky looks around. He realizes what is wrong; apart from the chaplain, the cell is empty.

Jeff checks the name and cell number typed on his sheet of paper after the words come back into focus, then looks into the cells on either side.

Who the hell is Rick Albertain?

And, more to the point, where is he?

The afternoon sun shining through my bedroom window makes my weight-lifting efforts seem even more strenuous. I am covered in sweat, the metal bar slippery in my hands, and I can't believe I'm enduring this challenge a second time in one day.

Forty . . . eight.

Pushing up again, I grunt an expletive that makes me feel marginally better, then feel the muscles in my arms begin to quiver as I desperately struggle to lock my elbows.

Forty . . . nine. Come on, one more, one more.

I slowly, carefully, ease the bar back down to my chest. I grunt and again push up, urging myself to complete the fifty repetitions I'd planned.

Come on!

My arms lock at the top of the final push.

'Fifty!' I call out. 'Yes! *Yes!*'

I ease the bar back onto the rests of the bench-press and let my aching arms fall to my sides. I lie here a while, to get my breath back, letting the pressure ease from my head. I feel the constriction in my neck begin to fade.

I let a minute pass, then I sit up very slowly, shaking my head at my own folly. I shouldn't be lifting this level of weights without someone behind me – it's too easy to overdo it and have the bar drop onto your neck, killing you.

As I stand up, my knee gives a little twinge. I look down at it questioningly, knowing it was the result of an excursion into another reality. I pause to analyse it all.

Deep down, the new force is driving me – yet, for all my confusion, there is a clarity to it.

I shake my head to banish such thoughts.

I had an idea back at Orford regarding a place I want to check. And maybe give the Sonat guys yet another opportunity to confront me. They must jump to take the bait sometime.

I had decided then to call up Jenny and see if she would come with me to the Sutton Hoo museum. It contains some of the best Anglo-Saxon artefacts ever found in Britain, all of them discovered locally. The mound where they were uncovered is believed to have been the grave of Raedwald – a seventh-century king of the East Angle tribes that dominated this area. It gave me a thrill to visit it as a child, shortly after we arrived back in England, and it is the place where my deep interest in history began. Situated on a sandy plateau overlooking the town of Woodbridge and the river Deben, I then found the loneliness of the area exhilarating. There, under the sweltering sun of 1939, local men helped the archaeologists uncover treasure such as little boys dream of. Only days after they'd finished their excavation, both the archaeologists and their labourers had to face up to the fact that their country was now at war with Germany. Such is the special poignancy I always feel about Sutton Hoo.

The prospect of returning there disturbs me strangely . . . but it has to be done.

And, for a moment, a sudden shiver covers my arms in goose-bumps. I pass my mother on the landing, about to head downstairs. She reaches out and lightly touches my shoulder. When I turn to look at her, she says nothing, but simply smiles, then carries on downstairs, shaking another cigarette from its carton.

I feel a little embarrassed at her small gesture of affection.

Jenny has picked me up in her work's Landrover, and we're heading over to Sutton Hoo. She keeps glancing at me enquiringly, but I rebuff any direct questioning with a cautious 'Wait and see'.

So instead she starts telling me how we're all separated by just six people – that if you name any two people on this planet, you will be able to find a link between them involving just six others or fewer. Jenny insists that shows how close we really are to each other. I ignore that, and also her pagan stuff about us all being linked with the universe, knowing I myself am now regularly connected to about five million people and the furious bleeping from my CAMIC mobile seems to confirm this.

As we finally pull into the car park, I nod with grim satisfaction. As I thought it would be, the place is deserted. The time and the place would indeed be ripe for Sonat. And indeed ripe for me . . . there are weapons in here and I'm pumped with aggression. It would be a very bad move on their part, for I'd stand a very good chance of surviving. I feel strangely excited.

'Where is everyone?' Jenny leans over the steering wheel to peer around. 'Surely this place should be packed on a day like this.'

'Anywhere will do.' I gesture towards all the empty parking spaces and smile at her.

She turns slowly to scrutinize me, her eyes again momentarily glinting with that strange, wonderful colour, then she manoeuvres the Landrover up to the main building.

'So?' she asks, switching off the ignition.

I gesture for her to follow me, and CCTV cameras track our movements. I give my CAMIC a good shot of the notice board – I want Sonat to be absolutely clear about where we are.

Nearby stands a half-scale replica of the same burial-boat the archaeological team dug up in the summer of 1939. I spend a few minutes circling it, giving anyone who may have been following us on the road time to catch up; I then lead Jenny towards the exhibition area.

Inside the main building are real items or copies of the treasure itself. This is the treasure of fantasy: there is gold, there is gold and garnet, exquisite intricately fashioned buckles and belt fittings; there is silver, an ornate shield, a long sword to rival Excalibur; there is also the helmet adorned with the face that would become the symbol of all that represents an Anglo-Saxon warrior.

'Do you understand now why there are no other visitors?' I ask.

She turns and stares at me. 'What do you mean?'

I launch into the speech I'd already prepared in my head.

'Centuries ago,' I continue, 'a dead man was laid to rest here, along with this staggering array of grave goods, to symbolize the respect in which he had been held. He was the man they depended on to lead them in times of trouble, and a sense of their appreciation has been handed down to us all. It is like the legend of King Arthur sleeping until his country again needs him. Back in that summer of thirty-nine when he was discovered, I'm sure that there were many who recognized him as the sort of leader they needed then, too. Someone to stand up to Hitler – a true bulwark against our invaders.'

As I say this, I am suddenly overcome with intense trepidation. It quickly passes, and I continue. 'There is a tangible power to the history represented here. Is it the warrior ethic? Simple camaraderie? It's why this place is deserted today. You see, not many people want to face up to the evidence that we each have to draw our own strength from somewhere within us. History tells us who we once were, and therefore points out who we are now.'

She points to one of the gold shoulder-clasps, with its intricate decoration of inlaid garnet and glass, and looks back at me.

'You'd be hard pushed to make something like that *today*,' she comments. 'But just imagine, this was made *centuries* ago. You're right to think that we need to pull together, Scott. Even though we're all individuals, we have to act together, but why is it always necessary for violence to become the answer?' She gestures again at the nearby exhibits. 'What about the people who are left to remember? Where are *those* individuals, Scott? Where are the people who lived here?'

She pauses by a particular display, which contains one of the 'sand men'. King Raedwald's isn't the only grave that archaeologists have unearthed here over the years – the whole place was an ancient burial ground. But the soil is so acid hereabouts that any corpse quickly erodes, leaving only a different colour to the sand.

'Isn't that the saddest thing?' Jenny says. 'To have a dark shadow in the sand as the only thing people know about you? You're right, this place is filled with ghosts, Scott – ghosts of those who left their mark on history merely as shadows, with sand for a coffin.'

Jenny cocks her head to one side. 'Do you know that whenever I experienced *my* shifts, I realized I was on trial?'

It takes me a second to adjust to this change of tack.

'On *trial*?' I probe . . . and then I pause.

'Yes,' she says, apparently grateful that I've understood. She frowns in concentration as she remembers the details. 'It seemed to be sometime in the late seventeenth century and I found myself standing tied to a stake in a town square, protesting up to the last minute against that bastard the Witchfinder General. Matthew Hopkins he was called, and on every occasion I had to try a different argument. And all around me, there were dozens of people watching . . . watching with *eagerness* in their eyes. They *wanted* to burn me, Scott. They wanted to see me burned alive. But I won my case each time. And in the last incident, they had to let me go . . . I'm positive I won't have to experience any more.'

She looks at me with furious agitation in her eyes, then she suddenly turns on her heels and heads for the exit.

'And as you suspected, it's *changed* me, Scott,' she says over her shoulder. 'It was *me* that put the thought into your head to invite me to come here with you. Because I wanted you to understand what's possible now.'

But before I can ask her more, Jenny is already at the door.

'It's funny,' she says, pausing. 'I won my case, but it seems they were right. I *do* possess powers that they're afraid of . . . I even know what happens in *your* experiences, Scott. Do you think you'll get close enough to kill that bastard Heydrich? And I didn't get *that* from any Maxnet file either.'

After about ten seconds' pause, I hurry after her, my plans to tempt Toluene out into the open momentarily forgotten.

Marvel Speer makes himself as comfortable as he can in the back of the London taxicab. He has been in the oppressive and sticky capital for less than two hours, and is now on his way to Docklands to pick up a rifle. He is extremely disgruntled at the prospect.

A few years ago and he could have safely sent on ahead his own weapon, hidden in some sea-going cargo, but now he has to use Pascal's intermediaries. He just wants to ensure the transaction will take place as quickly as possible.

As a professional he knows it shouldn't matter what weapon he uses, but he always feels easier with his favoured type of gun. He just hopes that his contact has clearly understood he would not settle for anything less than a perfect equivalent. Speer doesn't want a repetition of his trip to Liverpool last year, when he had to use a nail gun on the courier to express his displeasure.

Marvel Speer stares back into the cabby's eyes reflected in the rear-view mirror – until the man stops studying him and concentrates on his driving.

As Speer opens the window, the heat of the day drifts in. The weather here, he finds, is almost as hot as being back home. He glances at the people on the streets in their sunglasses and short-sleeved shirts, but all he is really aware of is the pervasive stench of stale sweat. It makes him want to puke and pull the window back up.

'Don't these guys even have air conditioning, yet?' he mutters.

As Jake prowls the corridor outside his lab, the door to Otis' laboratory opens. Otis himself appears to be leaving for home – he has put on his Blues Brothers' hat and sunglasses, even though it is now getting dark outside.

'Still here?' Otis closes his door quickly behind him and tests to ensure the lock is engaged.

'Evidently,' says Jake, as he increases his own fast pace.

Otis gives a quick wave of his hand as in dismissal.

Late at night though it is, Jake has just received a phone call summoning him to the boardroom for an emergency meeting and he is so frustrated by the interruption, he feels like kicking a wall.

A couple of minutes later, Jake pauses at the door to the boardroom. He counts to ten, then walks straight in without knocking.

He is immediately surprised. Instead of just Oscar and a couple of other managers, there appears to be a full session.

At this late hour?

At least twenty people are sitting around the long, glass and chrome table, and near the top of the table, to one side of Oscar himself, is Professor Edwina Byfoot.

You're devious, aren't you . . . dear heart?

Edwina's face is blankly non-committal as she adjusts her glasses.

254

Jake treats her to a quick smile.

Are we going to have a little talk soon?

'Ah, Jake,' Oscar says. 'Please take a seat.'

Jake sits down at the foot of the table, near the door, and looks round at each of the other attendees there in turn. He hardly recognizes any of them, and most return his gaze with apparent ambivalence, though a few stare back aggressively.

'Thanks for coming in at such short notice,' continues Oscar.

He glances round at the table, where some nod as if in agreement.

Or consent? Who's really in charge here?

'The board has decided that we want you to move on in your experiments.'

So that's why you promised me more facilities and money.

But actually, Oscar could not have surprised him, because Jake has a sudden intuition about Oscar's thinking and indeed everyone else's in the room.

They're so goddam scared. They're absolutely bloody terrified.

Oscar continues. 'We now want you to try to duplicate your recent results with human beings.'

Jake blinks rapidly, being tempted to ask Brightwell to repeat what he has just said. But Jake also instinctively realizes he has been thrown into the midst of some bizarre power game where he'll just have to discover the rules as he goes along.

'To what end?' he says finally.

Two or three of the people seated at the table cough in response, and another couple stare fixedly at him.

He also notices Brightwell do another quick visual confirmation with the others.

Who are these idiots that seem to have got Oscar by the balls?

Brightwell gestures towards Edwina. 'You've already been given an informal chat about what we do here, Jake.'

Oh yes, Edwina . . . crowd-control? I wish I'd known.

'You were employed here because of your proven intelligence and your innovative approach to your area of expertise, Jake. Your field of endeavour largely coincides with our own.' Oscar leans slightly forward, trying to smile again. 'Tell me, what do you think might be the consequences of sensing what someone is thinking?'

More than you'll ever imagine.

Jake doesn't answer yet.

What if we could develop telepathy? Then forget CCTV, forget chip-link ID cards, forget DNA registration. I think they're only just beginning to comprehend what we have here.

Jake then decides to play Oscar's game, but on *his* own terms.

'It would become the ultimate in eyes-and-ears monitoring.' Jake pauses. 'Especially if you could find a way of being in control of it.'

Oscar smirks. 'We're on the same page, Jake. That's really good.'

'You'd make millions,' says Jake.

This is going too fast – way too fast.

Jake sits in his leather chair, swivelling from side to side, and clenches and unclenches his fists. He is familiar with the phrase 'panic in the boardroom', but had never experienced it. Jake is now certain that events are escalating, and that practically everyone else in that room has undoubtedly begun to experience shifts like his own – a transference to an altered state, another reality – yet he also is convinced that that is not what primarily was worrying them. Back now in his lab as the time heads towards midnight, he asks himself the question: *exactly* what *have I got myself into?*

Whatever the Eisencrick Institute's reasons for wanting to exert control over such large groups of people, Jake does find the prospect of extending his own experiment exciting.

To establish once and for all that the human race is capable of extrasensory perception? And I'm sure I'm actually able to prove it.

But he needs to prove that it is possible within just three days, or else . . .

Or else what?

Maxnet remains the only forum that makes sense, with tens of thousands joining the system every day. Surely by that means he *can* get the message across.

A beep and sequence of flashes alert him that something is happening.

He studies the partitioned cam-screens on his PCs as their borders all turn red together. The bar that indicates percentage synchronicity is showing one hundred per cent.

Jake leans back in his seat and suddenly decides he now hates his experiment. He knows he was naive to believe that he was being employed to do pure research for the sake of science – and today he has had his innocence shoved back in his face. Jake knows he cannot blame the animals but, studying their synchronized activity, he now finds that he detests them – hating the group-mind that they have developed over the last few days.

The bar suddenly plummets to zero, and the red borders switch off.

Jake stares at the screens. Every cage is empty.

In his ears there seems to be a distant echo, as of a huge crowd of people talking, singing, crying – a mournful lament that disappears as soon as he begins to notice it. He also feels the sudden stab of a headache.

Something is wrong, but he can't work out what.

Why am I staring at rows of empty cages? Shouldn't there be something inside them?

Jake *knows* he has just witnessed something crucial, but he can't work out exactly what. And then, even though he has no actual recollection of them, Jake remembers something about an experiment involving mice.

But, if so, where did they go?

He named the land 'Earth' and the water which had come together He named 'Sea'. Evening passed and morning came – that was the third day.

Saturday
Day 3

Chapter Ten

Juan Costola – nineteen, Brazilian left-wing student, great at arguments that involve hyperbole, slow with common sense, fascinated by fashion and good at roller-blade street hockey, much to his parents' consternation for a multitude of gender reasons – runs down a corridor of the Tanistan Embassy in the Venezuelan capital Caracas, repeatedly trying to pull back the breech mechanism of his stolen police Heckler-Kock 9mm in order to load the first round.

Although panicking at his clumsiness, he is also laughing. He finds it all amazing. Up until this moment, he had thought sex with Yvette was the ultimate buzz, preferably after a good riot to rub the capitalist pig-dog-mother-fuckers' corporate noses in their own fascist bullshit, but now, as he races towards the state reception hall of the embassy, with five of his revolutionary comrades, the sheer adrenaline delight fills him with waves of happiness that are nigh orgasmic.

As the group reaches the doors of the hall, the blood is crashing so loudly in his ears that he can imagine he is back in glorious carnival time in his native city of Rio de Janeiro. He feels just like a child again, dressed up in sequinned cape and three-quarter-length satin pants, swinging to the beat, dancing his part with one of the samba schools. In front of him, Christof, their leader, kicks the doors open instead of using the handle, and they all rush into the huge room, exulting in their excitement mixed with fear.

That is before it all goes wrong, when the four embassy bodyguards start shooting to kill. Juan just has time to see the Venezuelan Foreign Minister half-rise from his seat with a puzzled look. The man is staring at an empty chair opposite him and at a broken coffee cup lying on the floor, its contents seeping into the carpet. As Juan Costola hesitates, now wondering who on earth he and his companions had intended to kill there, the first bullet punches him in the shoulder and he is suddenly aware that he is going to die.

He thinks about Yvette, about the parents who love him, and he struggles to remember why he has wasted his life so cheaply.

INTERNET NEWS UPDATE by Janice Maclean

The clock is counting down fast and cannot now be stopped. The chief news is that Tiff has quit. The sudden return of ex-boyfriend Tony has caused her too many emotional problems she claims.

So, we now have Scott in the lead, with Jo following close behind him, and Natalie falling away fast. That means only three are left now.

SCOTT'S WEB-BOX COMMENTARY

The latest report I have about Sonat, the fast-emerging American right-wing political group, is that they have topped two million new online registrations for the twenty-four-hour period since yesterday. Impartial observers, however, point out that, despite an increase, this figure actually refers to the number of hits recorded on Sonat's website and is thus purely propaganda. My impression is that all these people supposedly signing up to Sonat are desperately seeking any political party that seems to offer what they believe is a new direction – a comfort zone for their fears. Pascal Toluene himself dismisses such claims, saying, 'They'll learn to respect our truth.'

Today, Saturday morning, there is no one else about. It's just an empty country track and me – but I am not happy.

The air seems as thick as syrup and I felt prompted to carry an extra-large water bottle. I've already drunk half of it, so I may have to turn back soon. I'm sweating as if I've been running for hours and the pain in my leg, from my last universe-shift, doesn't help in this heat. The weather seems permanently mutated into tropical rainforest, but surely it will have to break sometime soon. I heard on the early-morning radio that there has been no rain anywhere across Europe for the last three weeks, which only reaffirms my conviction that something catastrophic is about to happen.

And many others are beginning to take notice and to voice their opinions.

It will be the next Ice Age, claims one news report this morning. The ice sheets surrounding Greenland are melting faster, while the Siberian permafrost is releasing many extra thousand tons of fresh water into the Arctic. The consequent reduction in the saline content of the North Atlantic means the Gulf Stream Thermohaline Current is in imminent danger of 'switching off' and, if that continues, we are warned that within five to ten years we'll have icebergs floating in the English Channel.

Yet Pascal Toluene seems set on causing a major disruption to the North Atlantic conveyor current, by releasing millions of tons of fresh water into the ocean off Iceland. The number of people there becoming casualties of the immediate aftermath would trigger an influx of international rescue teams – but would Toluene exploit the ensuing chaos to make his move and use the Gen-Fork option?

I know now that I'll have to kill you, Toluene, if I ever have the chance.

That must be why the weather seems so extraordinary – it's caused by the climate being on such a knife-edge that it is about to topple.

For the last ten minutes of jogging along this track, I have heard no sound other than my breathing and the slap of my trainers on the sandy soil. It is the eeriest feeling.

I keep looking over my shoulder, and to each side, and glancing up at the sky. There are absolutely no birds to be seen, or any sound heard of the other small creatures scurrying into the undergrowth as I pass. Nature is silent and *absent*.

I suddenly realize that, despite the sweat running down my face, there are no annoying little flies swarming around me.

There are no insects? Surely the pumice-storm didn't kill off everything around here?

I suddenly *do* hear a noise. It is someone running behind me.

At last! They're coming!

They are gaining on me, and I have no weapon to

defend myself. I hasten my step, and start looking over my shoulder repeatedly – to be ready when one of Toluene's thugs gets close to me.

It's finally going to happen!

I adjust the fitting of my CAMIC. If I see they have guns, I may still surprise them.

If I'm quick.

I look around again, involuntarily clenching my fists. A shadow flits past a bush to one side and someone disappears behind the trees encroaching on the bridleway. When the figure re-emerges into the sunlight, I laugh out loud. It's Jenny, red in the face with the effort of catching me up. I breathe in deeply, smile to myself, and continue running – more slowly this time, and Jenny soon falls in alongside me. We exchange a silent look. For a moment, sheer relief that it's not one of Pascal's goons makes me happy.

But then I suddenly can't help wondering bizarrely if it is Jenny who has brought the deadening quiet with her. After her outburst yesterday, I am tempted to think she could be a harbinger of almost anything.

We jog on in silence.

Until we startle a blackbird.

It rises in front of us and flaps away into the cover of the woods. Without uttering a sound.

Jenny and I stop running.

A few feet away to our right, another blackbird does exactly the same.

'That's too fucking weird,' I say.

'I've been seeing them like that since I got up,' says Jenny. 'And other birds, as well. There was no dawn chorus today.'

I look at her. 'But *why*?' I ask.

She shrugs her shoulders. 'Search me.'

She looks so bright-eyed and innocent that I burst out laughing.

'Come on,' I say. 'Let's go.'

We carry on jogging, and fall into a rhythm. I find myself occasionally glancing across at her, and thus I catch her eye. We grin at each other, then try to concentrate on our running and not on the silence that envelops us. Every now and then, however, her arm brushes against mine – the contact of skin against skin. I've heard of someone's touch feeling like a surge of electricity, and each momentary caress does indeed send a jolt through my body.

It's incredibly erotic. And confusing.

I can imagine this easily and tantalizingly happening with TC, but Jenny's reason for contact is different. It is deliberate, yes, undoubtedly erotic, but I can't help wondering if it involves subtle manipulation of my emotions that I don't fully recognize. After yesterday's conversation at Sutton Hoo, about how she has apparently found a solution, a conclusion, to her shifts in reality, I find myself being forced to re-evaluate everything that I have ever thought about Jenny. There is that mystery about her . . . and then there's that occasional rainbow sheen I notice in her eyes when the light hits them right. For all I know, she could be sending me other signals that I am yet unable to interpret. And I gradually, but finally, comprehend exactly how much she cares for me.

Her arm continues to brush against mine and I don't move away. These little jolts of electricity are addictive.

I try to think of something else.

My wish for a distraction is unexpectedly granted.

Reality freezes. Reality jumps and leaps and stutters. Reality alters.

I brace myself mentally for the next shift. Then I am transported.

Click, click . . . *click*!

I find myself standing in a narrow cobbled street by a T-junction. There is a musty smell. The architecture that surrounds me looks slightly Gothic, a hint of the medieval. It is some old European city of whitewashed walls and red-tiled roofs. I glance up and see billowing cumulus in a cobalt-blue sky, a brief whiff of spring in the air. I smile. At least there is something to be cheerful about, I feel ready and willing to undertake whatever business is required.

I run my hand through my short hair, adjust my collar, and approach the corner to look up and down the street beyond. There are a number of people about: men in rough jackets and wide trousers, women with headscarves and heels, one of them pushing an old-fashioned pram. I am clearly in WWII again, and of course, there is a good chance that I am in Prague. I look down at myself – I too am in civilian wear – and I begin to walk along the street, but after a couple of steps I turn and head the other way.

There is no reasoning for this change of direction but, though unfamiliar with the layout of the city, I feel a compunction to follow my instincts.

This is what I have to do.

I know I am being drawn towards something, despite an intense sensation of dread.

After half an hour of tracking through side roads,

I cross the Vltava river over the famous Charles Bridge with its medieval towers (which I *do* recognize). The utter beauty of the city jars oddly with my sense of nervousness – then I come to a halt at another junction. There is a large building looming ahead of me – one that I also recognize.

I am face to face with the source of my discomfort. It is the Peãeh Palace. The Gestapo headquarters here in Prague. A swastika banner hangs over the main entrance – an emblem that makes me choke with disgust. As I stare at the flag, unruffled by any breeze, there comes the sound of heavy vehicles, and I turn to look.

A convoy of two Jeep-like *Kabelwagens* and a canvas-covered lorry is driving up the road. As the three vehicles pull up at the entrance, an officer in black uniform comes out to start issuing orders. Within moments, the tailgate of the lorry has been lowered, and men in civilian clothes are ushered from it and into the Gestapo HQ. Before returning inside, the officer glances at me for a moment.

I turn away, feeling very alone. And very angry.

Reality freezes. Reality jumps and leaps and stutters. Reality returns.

Click, click . . . *click*!

And, as always, no time has passed.

I'm still jogging along with Jenny, and her arm continues to brush regularly against mine.

As I look at her, I think: *It's okay for her – she says she's finished with these 'excursions'.*

What about the rest of us poor sods?

I try to relax and begin to think ahead to the rest of the day.

I don't need to ask if she got an early phone call this morning. TC rang to inform me that we're all going to see Jake later. Perhaps *he* may have an explanation for this unusual silence amongst the wildlife.

Jenny and I stand at the door to Jake's house, having both changed out of our running gear.

I've always suspected that some ex-naval bod built the house where Jake lives. It has Twenties' Art Deco curves that vaguely resemble the bridge of a ship – the front rooms upstairs have a sweep of windows all currently wide open, and, positioned on the crest of a small rise, must have an absolutely superb panoramic view over the marsh and the sea. The lawn looks as though it receives some occasional attention, but the rest of the garden has been left to run riot. My father would suffer paroxysms of confusion over it, before getting stuck in to force it back into some sort of order.

'Hi,' says TC, who must have practically crept up on us. Her long hair is tied back in a huge ponytail, draped over a white T-shirt. She's wearing a brand-new Maxnet CAMIC and our mobiles bleep in synchrony, as though they are swapping data.

'Hi,' says Jenny, and they give each other a hug. They do that female thing of looking at each other as though speaking without talking. I get the impression it is to do with me, but I merely shrug my shoulders.

Jake hears them outside, but pauses to collect his thoughts before going down to greet them. He takes another look around the chessboards laid out on their respective tables, studying the various pieces engaged in mortal combat, then he assesses the empty spaces where the cameras used to be that monitored the progress of these games.

A little over an hour ago, just after he'd returned from the Institute, three security staff from Eisencrick had turned up on his doorstep to claim the cameras back. One of these had been Gary, and Jake was amazed to note he had even brought along his dog.

'How can I help?' he said, looking at each man in turn.

'I'm sorry, Dr Crux,' Gary said, 'really sorry, but we've been instructed to recover the camera equipment you removed from the Institute premises.'

Jake was now looking down at the animal, which apparently didn't like such attention, because it started growling. Jake quickly glanced back up. He had had no idea that his movements were being *so* closely monitored.

'Sure,' said Jake. 'Come on in.'

As the three men moved towards the door, Jake suddenly pointed to the dog. 'That stays here.'

Jake tells himself now, as he looks again at where the cameras once were positioned, that he should not have taken such pleasure in seeing the hurt in Gary's face.

These activities by the Eisencrick Institute board were beginning to seem transparently threatening. He had already become extremely conscious of being watched as he sat at his desk in the early hours of the morning, struggling with both the evidence of the total disappearance of his mice and with understanding the records of their activities. It was plain that something fundamental had occurred in some experiment he had conducted, and reacquiring that information was of utmost importance. Because he was being monitored, he suspected that this sense of confusion may have spread meanwhile to the other board members and that Edwina had probably also been forced to go over her secret duplicate recordings of the experiment.

It was a race between them.

But while Edwina undoubtedly was being assisted, so too was Jake.

TC had begun research via her newly acquired Unit-C Maxnet CAMIC, and the reports on paranormal activity she received from around the world made interesting reading.

He now hears her call out his name from downstairs. He answers, but not verbally: *You didn't need to do that, did you?*

There is a momentary pause before he hears her reply in his head.

'I suppose not.'

Jake smiles to himself, and then feels extremely dizzy – light on his feet – not because of his lack of sleep, but from knowing that he has just achieved something remarkable. He can't wait to try it on the others.

'But you'll have to ease them into it, Jake. Don't hurry them.'

'You're right, but we don't have much time.'

We all follow TC as she walks into Jake's house. The downstairs area is open-plan, with the kitchen merging into a giant living room. Someone has put a lot of effort into this room: the floor seems to have been relaid with new floorboards, and is furnished with three luxurious sofas, bookshelves and a writing bureau. But the most striking thing is the number of plants arranged around it. I feel like I've walked into a botanist's conservatory. Climbing towards the ceiling are a group of fountain palms, their thin stems bursting into a clump of fronds at the top; there is also a variety of exotic ferns, those variegated broadleaf evergreens that I seem to remember my father calling Ficus, and different types of lily – mostly now in flower. And in contrast to most of his garden outside, it would seem that they are all well cared for.

As Jake comes downstairs, I can immediately sense that there is a change in him. Noticing this makes me re-evaluate everyone else present. We've all changed: all seem to have grown prematurely older. I don't know how it has happened, but we seem to have lost a degree of our innocence. He mutters hello, and TC goes over and kisses him.

'Here,' says Jake, 'let's all sit down. I know I need to.'

TC raises her eyebrows, but he waves her away and gestures to the sofas. Jake settles himself on one and TC quickly joins him. Jenny guides me to one of the others and sits down beside me.

TC suddenly jumps up again and brings over a small table with an ashtray.

Jake leans forward conspiratorially. 'I've just had a successful attempt at telekinesis.'

TC takes a couple of quick puffs on her cigarette, Jenny shifts forward to the edge of the sofa, and I wonder what I've let myself in for.

Why can't TC recognize this guy isn't stable?

'You did *what*?' I say.

'I tried it on one of those dragon chess figures that I play with,' he replies. He treats me to his peculiar micro-smile.

I glance around the room again. He obviously senses my disbelief and it is the look he now gives me, like a big jungle cat waiting for its prey's wrong move, that suddenly convinces me that Dr Jake Crux, TC's presumed lover, and my rival, does his thinking on a different plane to mine. The strength of his intellect intimidates me and makes me feel small.

'I kept staring at one piece,' he explains. 'Till I saw it move.'

He pauses, and waves a hand in the air as though dismissing the thought.

'Okay, I can't prove I did it, I didn't record it,' he says, narrowing his eyes. 'Just yet, that is . . . But managing to do it has physically affected me, too . . . there's been a reaction. You should maybe try it for yourselves.'

I stare at him.

'I know,' he says. 'I wouldn't believe myself either. It's beginning to fade, but I felt it so – . . .'

He frowns, closes his eyes for a long moment.

'It was . . . *mystic*,' he finishes, then looks momentarily embarrassed and laughs out loud.

'The viewers voting for you, Scott,' he continues, 'would they care that you're running around with some guy who sounds like he's losing it?'

I shrug.

'I've known *these* idiots here for years,' I say. 'One more loony doesn't make much difference. Besides, we're *all* losing it these days,' I say.

Jake holds up a finger to make a point. 'Ah, but

look what we could *discover*.' He turns to TC. 'Could you help me demonstrate?' She holds his look. 'Okay,' she says. 'It's time you showed them.'

She gestures towards me and I instinctively check the CAMIC as TC is addressing the e-viewers, not just us here in the room. She then switches her own off. Jake stands up and goes over to his writing bureau, returning with a post-it pad and a pen. After passing these to TC, he goes back and sits down at the desk, so he is facing away from us. TC stubs out her cigarette, and leans across to hand me the pen and pad. She then sits back again, bringing her feet right up so she can wrap her arms around her ankles, and rests her chin on her knees.

'Telekinesis a bit too much for you at the moment?' she jibes. 'How about starting with telepathy? Remember from the friary, the guessing game with the cigar? Well, go on . . . write down a word, anything you like, then pass it back to me. Make sure you're satisfied that Jake can't see it.'

I stare at her, unable to react. It's not that I think writing down a word makes me seem stupid or gullible, it's that I'm just plain scared about the consequences.

Jenny nudges me. 'Go on,' she urges quietly.

I get the very real impression that she already knew this was what had been planned.

But there isn't any colourful refraction in Jake's eyes right now. Nor in TC's. They haven't completely joined her . . . yet.

I stare down at the blank pad.

Then I write the word 'intrigue' on the post-it slip, peel it off the pack and pass it to Jenny, who reaches over and gives it to TC. She reads it, screws it up, and then turns back towards me. I'm certain that Jake cannot have seen any expression on her face that might give the game away, because he's still looking firmly the other way. In fact, he has his head bowed slightly, an elbow on the desk so that one hand is obscuring his eyes.

TC continues to stare at me. The silence continues.

'Intrigue,' says Jake, suddenly.

'Pardon?' I ask.

'Intrigue,' says Jake again.

A noise in my CAMIC suggests that Gareth is about to say something to me. There is another brief sound as he changes his mind. I find myself wishing he *would* say something to break the silence.

TC smiles and holds out her hand. 'Next,' she says.

I look at Jake, then at Jenny. I think for a moment, and then I write down 'Blitzkrieg'. I again peel off the page and pass it to Jenny, who glances down at it this time before passing it to TC. She, in turn, reads it and then glances up with a slight look of disapproval in her eyes.

Jake smiles. He says: 'Blitzkrieg.'

Two out of two.

I stare at the others. Jenny nods, urging me to write more.

I scribble 'compassion' and then 'Heydrich'.

This provokes an even greater look of agitation from TC as she reads what I've written.

'Ha!' says Jake. 'You think "Heydrich" and "compassion" are words that go together naturally?'

'Here,' I say, 'let me *really* test you.'

I begin to scribble words on several post-it slips in turn. After a few seconds I hand the entire pad to TC.

'Try these, then,' I say.

TC flicks through each slip, reading them to herself. She then sits up and stares at me, expressionless.

Jake turns in his chair, eyes us in turn, and counts the written items off on his fingers.

'Maxnet,' he begins. 'Unit-C. Landrover. Harley-Davidson. *Le Mans*. Morocco. Ayatollah. Molasses. Nightmares. Freedom. *And* you've even done a thumbnail sketch of the Statue of Liberty.'

TC holds up the pad to show Jenny my hurried attempt at the famous New York landmark.

Jake moves over to the sofa and sits down with TC. As she turns her CAMIC connection back on, it occurs to me that Maxnet can now see this performance in stereo.

'It's connected with my work,' he explains, and leans forward. He looks at me. 'I think there are only three days left for us.'

I find myself nodding.

'Okay,' he says, 'I've been conducting an experiment designed to study nature versa nurture in a group of cloned mice. But that's not really the major point any more. I set it up carefully so that they were subject to exactly identical conditions, and then I monitored them.'

He stops speaking, and I realize he's pausing for effect. I also comprehend that Jake is well aware we all know why he's doing it. 'And they all vanished.'

Even though no one immediately responds, it appears to me instantly quieter than before.

'How exactly do you mean, *vanished*?' I say, at last.

'Just that,' he says. 'They disappeared – evaporated into nothing.'

He gives that quick smile again. 'They simply ceased to exist in this present universe. And I recorded the event. I have recordings that show nearly two thousand mice just vanishing. And the really interesting thing is that I myself have no memory of them. Sound familiar?'

He absentmindedly plays with the post-it pad he has taken from TC. I realize that he's doing this deliberately – to emphasize what he is saying now by referring back to his telepathic display of a few minutes earlier.

'They achieved a group consciousness,' he continues. 'They were acting as one entity, as one interconnected neural network. And I suspect that either I myself caused them to disappear in a fit of pique, using some power I didn't know I possessed ... or they did it themselves.'

I think of TC's vanished father, and think of my old friends in that photograph album.

'What?' I still try to cling on to reality. 'You mean a group suicide?'

'No,' says Jake, 'group *elimination*. They had formed a hierarchy of synchronicity and *difference* was not tolerated. But even with cloned mice, there will always be slight differences. They annihilated themselves in an orgy of self-interest. Out of fear of competition.'

He looks around at each of us in turn.

'And if a collection of identical creatures of comparatively small brain size can manage that, what does it mean for higher life-forms such as ourselves? It seems we are currently causing *people* to disappear.'

In spite of the day's heat, I feel chilled. I feel certain that if I were to breathe out, the air from my lungs would form a visible cloud. But I think if I tried that, it would only add to this madness.

I feel Jenny touch my arm, and I don't pull away. She is trying to calm my trembling.

Chapter Eleven

'Tap' Cassidy – Australian, thirty-six, slicked-back-hair-sheila-killer, so cool he's forgotten his first name, but now spending more time than he wants to on maintaining his blond-haired tousle because of the damned bald spot and widow's peak he's recently developing – rides the swell above the Great Barrier Reef and thinks that life can't get any better.

Sod what's happening elsewhere in the world.

Tap is being paid a large amount of money to help crew The Inspired, which has been sent over from the Woods Hole Oceanographic Institute in America. As he's been diving since he was twelve, he thinks he could do the job blindfolded with two – no, three – women giving him very personal and preferably naked attention. Tap claims that sort of attitude shows commitment to his work: currently winch-man and compressor operator of the deep-sea diving apparatus that Woods Hole are employing to investigate the recent changes in ocean currents and temperature.

But now it's time to bring the diver up.

Tap looks out at the ocean – he enjoys the incredible blues and greens of the water, the flash of a shoal of fish uniformly banking over the bright coral, a turtle coming up for air. He loves looking at that July sky, so big and open and clear, breathing in the apparent new-made smell of the Pacific that promises adventure, and listening to the sounds of the waves lapping against the hull like a girl's laughter.

He sticks out his tongue. The salt that forms when the occasional spray splashes his lips, and then begins to dry, makes him think of licking tears of enjoyment from some girl's cheek. His bald spot suddenly seems such a dingbat worry. He could stay out here forever.

There is a boil of bubbles and the diver emerges.

Tap immediately stands up straighter.

But the diving suit hangs limp. There's something wrong. Tap flicks the controls and swings the diver aboard, some of the crew rushing forward to assist. Just as the heavy diving boots are about to touch the deck, Tap stops the winch — he has realized what some of the others have just noticed. The diving suit is empty. There is no one inside it. Tap can see no split in the suit fabric, the helmet is still in place; everything about the equipment is as it should be, except where it looks as though it has somehow melted and wilted. It is as if it were still hanging in storage, waiting to be used.

Tap reaches for his cigarettes. He lights one up with his disposable and takes a fierce drag.

'Hot shit,' he says, reaching up to stroke his bald spot, and then he starts laughing.

It distracts him from thinking about what may have happened to the man inside the diving suit. Because Tap can't remember him. And neither, it seems, can anyone else.

Jake has ridden over to the Institute on his motorbike, after receiving a telephone call from his boss, Brightwell, just five minutes after discussing his Eisencrick experiment on e-air. Meanwhile, Jenny, TC and I are heading over to the WWII airfield of Fersfield, in Jake's Landrover with TC driving.

I'm not happy, for the place we're now going to has associations that I want to explain to everyone following me via the CAMIC. Uneasy memories of those constant teenage panics of mine are not helped by the way TC is driving. I've been in a car with her at the steering wheel before – but the change in her driving today is staggering. And nerve-racking.

Jenny and I sit in the back and hold on to the sides, and occasionally each other. It's an incredible journey as TC drives as fast as she can.

I am still getting shimmers of anxiety about what Jake said: people unconsciously causing others to disappear; removing the memory of them in the minds of people who knew them. That chill of apprehension is running through me again. Yet I'm perversely feeling exhilarated.

TC keeps talking all the way, like some sort of tour guide, occasionally pointing out highlights of the countryside – alarmingly taking a hand off the steering wheel to do so. She even tries to light herself a cigarette, until Jenny insists on doing it for her. And, all the while, we are bounced and jolted around as she hastens along country lanes at reckless speed.

We've had four near-misses so far, and not solely because of TC. The other cars involved – older vehicles without chip-link safety over-ride – seem to be driven equally dangerously, one even careering up a bank on *our* side of the road. More evidence of the general agitation amongst the population.

Close to a small modern industrial complex, a few derelict buildings spring into view, and I recognize the ivy-covered red-brick and concrete ruins of the old airfield. We are finally here.

'Stop!' I shout, and TC jams on the brakes.

We come to a dust-clouded halt near the end of a road joining the perimeter road accessing the disused runways in the distance. They stretch away into the open fields and I slowly take in every part of the infrastructure's dereliction. No obvious attempt has been made to maintain or even refurbish the old buildings. The whole area appears to have been used just for whatever has proved useful – the rest of it simply neglected. The air of melancholy is profound. My old fears rush at me with whispers and cold fingers, and I choke back a cough to cover my extreme reaction.

As TC leaves the engine to tick over, I reluctantly clamber out of the Landrover and take a few steps towards the huge building that first attracted my attention. I glance back at the others and clear my throat.

'That's one of the old hangars,' I manage to voice, knowing what is about to happen next. 'It's been used as a makeshift barn, or something.'

And, as I turn back to look, I am suddenly gripped by a sense of intense foreboding . . . and I see them.

They are standing – some in small groups, others by themselves – silently looking towards me. Most are dressed in the uniforms of American aircrew – pilots, gunners – but there are also a number in RAF garb. The nearest, standing just a few paces away from me, is a British officer. His face is pale, expressionless; he's seemingly unaware that his chest is a mass of blood.

I then realize that there are others with wounds that are more grievous.

The few more modern buildings fade away, and the open space is slowly peopled with ghosts in uniform – less distinct than the stationary ones – who are engaged in various activities. A semi-transparent squad marches past me, an air-fuel bowser trundles the other way. There is even a metallic clank from some workshop. It was what I knew would happen. It was what I was frightened of. I start to shiver. A faint echoing throb of aircraft engines quickly builds to a roar, and a spectral Liberator bomber passes low overhead as it comes in to land.

Jenny comes and stands beside me. As I try to suppress my trembling, I'm surprised by what she says.

'I can see them too,' she whispers, reaching out to take my hand. '*You've* done this, Scott. This is *your* power.'

The stationary, silent men continue to do nothing as their own world continues around them. They do nothing except stare in our direction.

TC switches off the ignition to the Landrover before she comes over to join us.

'It's like watching an old film,' she says, glancing around her.

We're all *seeing this.*

'Scott, what's causing this? Where have these men come from? *Are* you responsible for this?'

I ignore Gareth's interruption and study both of my friends in turn. It is difficult to understand how they can be now witnessing something I thought was peculiar to me.

How have I achieved this? Is it telepathy given visible form?

We all instinctively duck, as another plane swoops low over our heads, one of its propeller props being feathered. Then, as quickly as they came, the ghosts become indistinct, the stationary men disappearing last as they melt into the air. Once more, we are confronted with a few dilapidated buildings and the newer industrial complex.

We remain silent. My head aches.

But somehow I find this experience less disturbing than the spectral Hurricane. Why? Is it because I'm discovering an affinity with Joe Jnr's last trip in *Zootsuit Black*?

'How did you make that happen?' whispers TC.

'I can't explain it,' I confess. 'This sort of thing has been happening to me for years. It seems I'm meant to witness such stuff. But now you can too. I think somehow I've managed to project it.'

She looks slightly scared of me.

Both our CAMIC mobiles bleep urgently.

'This is the airfield where Joseph Kennedy Junior was based,' I continue. 'He flew out from here on Operation Anvil.'

'You mean that guy that was blown up?' says Jenny, stepping in as if to cover TC's extreme disquiet.

'Yeah.' There is a short silence before I turn back to see how TC is coping. 'My grandfather, Eric, once met Joe Junior.'

TC blinks rapidly. 'Joe Kennedy?' she finally asks.

'Yeah, like Joe, Eric was a pilot. He flew on the famous raid over Hamburg.'

TC nods sadly. And then it happens again.

There is no juddering of reality this time. But this is not the shifting world where I am gradually pursuing Heydrich – here I am recollecting a wartime incident from my grandfather Eric's life. I have become the young pilot that he was, at the controls of a Stirling heavy bomber. It is night and we are approaching our target – judging from an intense light on the horizon, it is Hamburg.

I smell a whiff of oil, grease, fuel and sweat which alternates between being reassuring and then filling me with nausea. I lick my dry lips, conscious that we are a crew all acting as one. Though I may be the skipper, if the other half-dozen men with me – Nav, Radio, Flight and gunners – don't all do their job, then I won't last much longer.

I pull down my facemask for a moment so I can scratch my nose. Then I clip the mask back on and wriggle in my seat to get myself as comfortable as possible. I smile to myself at a pleasure in flying that refuses to be diminished. There is the continuous familiar tremor in the control column under my hands that gives me a confidence I find hard to explain to others. I am doing *my* part simply by being part of that plane. I understand her idiosyncrasies, I know how to make her respond. Eyeing the conflagration on the horizon, I check the air temperature thermometer fixed on the cockpit roof.

'Sweet blessed Mary,' I say aloud, to myself.

From behind me comes the voice of Henry, the new Nav who has joined the crew.

'Nearly there, Skip.'

'I know, do you want to look?'

'No thanks. The view's all yours.'

Ahead looms a fake dawn of red and yellow, one that perpetually pulses and grows. Silhouettes of other bombers – Lancasters and Halifaxes higher up with greater power, the lucky bastards – all with glowing undersides, begin to open their bomb-bay doors, and I can see their loads cascading in clumps and bundles into the inferno below. Just ahead, another Stirling from my flight, P-Popsy, begins her run, and I get ready to follow.

I have seen other cities on fire – all with sudden white-and-yellow expanding domes that result from bombs exploding – appearing and then vanishing in instants, but the blaze they produced were as nothing to this one.

I think of my new wife Rosie and am acutely aware of my possible fate. If we get shot down, it would be like falling into a thousand furnaces. The inferno is awesome: I cannot even look at it without squinting. The aircraft becomes increasingly difficult to control and I realize that we now have such a tailwind, generated by the influx of air sucked in to feed the firestorm, that we are getting dangerously close to stalling. Simple aerodynamics demand that the air must flow the other way for the wings to function.

I reach up to my throat mike. 'Gentlemen, I believe we have the target up ahead.'

Charlie, the bomb-aimer, replies instantly with a laugh. 'At least I won't need to aim carefully, Skip.'

He'll have already seen what I can see.

'Somewhere in the middle of that lot there will do us fine,' I suggest. 'Opening the bomb-bay doors,' and I flick the switches that are partially hidden behind the throttle-control levers. 'Let's hope the heat doesn't set the bombs off while they're still in the bloody aeroplane,' I mutter. 'And you others, keep your eyes open. We don't want to get bounced by night fighters. It would be a bit of a tricky landing down there.'

The plane begins to buck more violently, then a surge of flame, far higher than the rest somehow, reaches up thousands of feet and temporarily engulfs P-Popsy, which is still ahead of us. I pull our own nose up a bit – I don't want to try heading through that. As the flame dies down, another aircraft suddenly appears in silhouette. It is long and thin, with huge antennae protruding from its nose and wings. Cannons slant upwards from the nose itself – angled so it can fly in an enemy craft's blind spot, behind and below it. This is a German night-fighter and before I have time to shout a warning to my crew, it rises back up into the blackness, still illuminated but moving away fast. It must have fired its weapon.

'She's hit, Skip,' says a voice. 'Popsy's taken one.'

His voice echoes and re-echoes.

'She's hit . . . Popsy's . . . hit.'

The dream fades away and I wince at the harsh sunlight over Fersfield. I am immersed in sweat as the fear continues to whisper, daring me to stay in this spot.

'What happened to you?' TC is peering at me. 'You just went blank there for a couple of minutes?'

'Come on,' interrupts Jenny. 'You said you wanted to explore this place.'

I stare at her, knowing that, unlike TC, she somehow knows what I have just experienced. Jenny turns away, and TC goes with her, wearing a slightly confused expression as though she suspects she has just missed something. I stumble after them.

A few minutes later and we get to a road junction, but still within the confines of the airfield. To one side stands a copse and, engulfed within it, partially hidden from view, are the remains of rows of living accommodation for the men who flew out of Fersfield.

They are long, red-brick, single-storey constructions, and most are finally beginning to lose their roofs. Ivy and horses' tail, sycamore and birch climb around them, and, in some cases, grow inside them. Moss is everywhere. One building looks like it was once used as a chicken coop, but even that is so broken down it could have been used as such only during the Sixties. There is a strong smell of rotten wood, and amongst the various greens are the bright orange and red tints of rust.

I don't think I've ever seen anything exuding such a sad aura of neglect. I feel an incredible yearning to step back in time and see them how they were when still in use. It's as if they wish they could speak, and the fear inside me whispers that I can see ghosts . . . if I want to.

I resist – I concentrate on controlling other anxieties.

I'm just adjusting to this sudden rush of melancholy and summoning up the courage to peer inside one of the dwellings, when Jenny speaks.

'I had a brother,' she announces.

'What?' I turn to face her.

'I had a brother.' She looks through a broken window for a moment, then turns to me again. 'The birth certificate says his name was Benjamin. But don't worry, *I* don't remember him, either. Though I'm beginning to get hints of memories. Perhaps I'll remember it all sometime.'

She makes this statement calmly, with no hint of distress. I look towards TC, recalling from that photograph the young man who was standing next to Jenny.

Jenny touches my arm. 'My parents and I suddenly realized that there was all this *other* stuff. That's when my father accessed Unit-C's Maxnet history files on you – and us – and we found the photographs. It was my mother who then discovered the birth certificate.'

In frustration, I kick out at the door of one of the abandoned buildings. And then I hear something I haven't heard for ages: the pitter-patter of raindrops in the upper reaches of the trees.

'Finally!' I sigh, looking up. 'It's starting to rain.'

These few seconds of relief disappear when one of the raindrops bounces, wet and slimy, off my hand. It appears to be green.

'Yurgh!' yells TC.

'What the fuck—?' says Jenny.

I can't believe my eyes.

I look down at the ground. Then up at the sky again – in a panic.

'Into the hut!' I shout.

We pile through the doorway into the comparative protection of the musty interior and immediately turn around to discover exactly what it is that's falling from the sky.

It is certainly not rain.

Tumbling all around us, in a huge green cloud, are hundreds – no, *thousands* – of tiny, baby frogs. Each is so small, one could fit comfortably on a fingernail. They can only just have transformed from tadpoles and begun to crawl from a pond.

They land on the higher leaves, then slide again to the ground. The open spaces are soon covered with them, as they crawl and squirm and make little investigative hops.

I shake my head as the heavens deposit even more froglets onto the ground. The little green creatures tumble in a heavy rain outside and onto the roof, but in diminishing numbers.

And then it all becomes too much.

I leave the girls and just begin to walk away through the long grass outside, the last few tiny frogs bouncing off my shoulders.

Jenny calls out to me, but I don't respond. I think to myself how within a few days our world might possibly come to an end. I think of my increasing sense that I must accomplish a task in some alternate universe before this one crashes to its climax. I think that I might also die at the hands of thugs who have come to hate me. And how those same thugs could move in to take over our world by means of some terrible bio-weapon. And now this . . .

I pat the wall of one of the huts as I pass it, daring it to reveal its secrets.

And then I start laughing at myself – at the ludicrousness of it all.

Jake has his hand already on the handle of Oscar's door, ready to enter, when he pauses. Yet again he has been summoned to see his boss, and he is calculating the reason.

This has to be more bad news, and he can hardly have liked what I announced publicly via Scott's CAMIC.

As soon as he thinks that, he finds he is elsewhere – this time with a rapidity that makes him laugh.

The world flickers, jams for an instant, then stutters into something else.

Click, click . . . *click*!

Jake finds himself again in his fantasy world, and he is panting with exhaustion. A lindorm – a giant snake-like dragon with two legs positioned near its head – lies dead. He clutches its hot heart in one of his hands, while in the other he still clasps the great sword that cut it out. Standing before him is an ugly midget swathed in too many clothes and carrying too much fat. The apparition is jigging from one foot to the other, rubbing its hands together, and sweating profusely. A drop of blood that, during the fray, had splattered through Jake's helm and onto his lips stings him sharply, but Jake senses that it nevertheless is working some kind of magic. He can hear the birds in the trees conversing – in a language he can understand: they are talking amongst themselves of the planned betrayal by the little man with the evil intent. As Jake looks down into the smaller man's eyes, the midget stops dancing, and his jaw drops as he realizes Jake has somehow discovered his intended treachery. Jake drops the dragon's heart, yelling his anger to the winds, raises his sword and beheads the little traitor where he stands.

A flicker . . . a juddering pulse.

Click, click . . . *click*!

Jake is back where he was – hand resting on door handle.

The calculation is getting easier: these shifts are related to thought.

That's got me in the right mood.

Jake enters Oscar's office, annoyed with himself because he can't instantly discern Oscar's intentions. But he doesn't have to wait long to find out. As he approaches his boss's desk, the man himself looks up and speaks.

'I'd like you to clear out your desk,' says Oscar.

'What?' Jake is stopped in his tracks.

'Security will then escort you out. We treat theft extremely seriously, here at Eisencrick.'

Jake bursts out laughing, which causes Oscar to stiffen visibly.

'Horse-shit!' says Jake. 'You're seriously using the fact that I borrowed a few cameras to get rid of me?'

Oscar relaxes. 'Theft is theft,' he says. 'Now go and clear your personal effects.'

Jake steps over and places his hands flat on the desk surface. He leans forward so that his face is as near to Oscar's as he can reach.

'You want that badly to take over my experiment?' Jake asks.

Oscar coughs. 'You have just one hour. You don't have much to remove, do you?'

Jake chooses his words carefully. 'You *pathetic* little man.'

Oscar pulls his chair slightly away from the desk.

'More of that and I'll have to call security immediately.'

'You'll need more than security to help you,' says Jake, who then turns and heads for the door. 'You *all* will,' he adds. 'And you know I'm right.'

Oscar starts to say something, but it is lost to Jake as he shuts the door behind him.

They will. They all will.

Including me.

We go on to spend the better part of the evening getting drunk in the pub, which seems a sensible place to be after the events and revelations of the day.

By the time we decide to leave, TC, Jenny and I are swearing eternal friendship. On the way home we decide to revisit the abandoned school where this momentous friendship began.

It is not exactly sensible, but we have the urge to do something silly, something stupid, some high jinks that will prove we haven't grown *that* old too soon. Fortunately TC is still wise enough to suggest we both switch off our CAMICs. We then wend our way unsteadily along the dark roads to Springgreen Open.

Creeping up the path we find an unsecured downstairs window. With appropriate shhhhing noises, TC reaches to open it, and we climb in.

Even with all the weirdness happening recently, the experience of setting foot in this deserted place stands out as peculiar. The school appears to have been abandoned like the *Marie-Celeste*. On the staff common-room table there are a yellowing newspaper and a couple of cups containing mould. There is even a forgotten coat hanging on a peg near the door. It takes us about a minute to get our bearings, and then we go exploring.

We seek out our favourite classrooms – all in the same dusty, frozen state – and drunkenly vie to relate exploits we can remember from our school days.

Then it gets a little fuzzy. Some time passes.

I find myself in the principal's office, with TC sitting in the principal's chair, demanding I take dictation. Lying on the principal's desk, surrounded by dust, Jenny burbles approval.

I look around for some paper, and a pen. And then notice the filing cabinet in the corner. It is altogether too tempting – I have an urge for a good rummage. The top drawer finally opens after TC gives it a good thump. Most of the contents have gone, but I still find some correspondence that has slipped down between the empty folders. It takes me some time to realize what I am looking at. I read the papers again, and what makes them shocking is that they are so revealing. They include a copy of a budget request made out to the Eisencrick Institute. And details of various payments to the parents of the children.

I have to read that again, several times.

Springgreen Open School had been receiving money from the Eisencrick Institute, and for some reason it was *paying* the parents of its pupils.

As I pass the documents to TC for her to read, I have suddenly sobered up enough to want to get out of this building fast. Jenny slowly sits up, and asks us what's happening. I begin to fear that the school has not been so much abandoned as mothballed. It probably still has a silent burglar-alarm link to Eisencrick, and probably hidden CAMICs as well.

We stumble and stagger out into the night, like a bunch of teenage kids knowing they've overstepped the mark. I don't know about my companions but, as I run, I am rapidly filled with a terrible rage. It now seems to me that one aspect of my childhood has been tainted, that what I had thought was as perfect as you could get has somehow been made false. And I have an outlet for my fury: my parents. I run harder, planning to have a good old-fashioned shouting match with them – a good ol' drunken son's righteous outburst with Mum and Dad . . . who take the edge off my intended onslaught by me finding them up so late and fully dressed. They are in the living room conversing fervently and, from my mother's quick touching of my father's arm as I enter the room, I assume it must have been about me.

My mother smiles. 'Hello, Scott,' she says. 'We just had Gareth on the phone. He was very insistent that you turn your equipment back on.'

Even though I suspect that she is telling a half-truth – since Gareth probably *has* called – I am sure they've been kept up by a telephone call from the Eisencrick Institute. I nevertheless instinctively reach up to switch my CAMIC on. I turn my attention to my mother first.

'Why?' I say it as quietly as I can. 'Why did you send me there?'

My mother attempts a frown, as if she doesn't understand what I am talking about. My father simply glares at me.

'Springgreen,' I prompt my mother. 'Why did you send me to Springgreen?'

She exchanges a quick glance with my father, and I suddenly feel a fool. Once again, I've got it all wrong, and I can't believe how much of an idiot I have been. *He* was the one who organized it, not my mother as he'd always led me to believe. My father had been the one responsible for getting me enrolled at Spring-green School.

'I thought you *hated* the fact that I went there,' I challenge him. 'You *loathed* what it stood for – you've been telling me that for years.'

My father holds my stare and for the first time I really understand the power of the man. He isn't about to let himself be out-argued by a drunk.

'It was an experiment,' he says at last. 'An experiment I was glad to get involved in.'

My mother interrupts, the previous smile now gone, and the change is startling. 'The Institute could have demonstrated that the world needs direction or it falls apart. It becomes . . . contemptible.'

It takes a moment for that message to sink in.

I laugh bitterly. 'It must be a bit of an upset for your friends at the Institute to know that we've proved the very opposite and succeeded,' I say. '*Our* style of co-operation has worked out for the best.'

My father shakes his head. 'There was an error on our part, we recognize that now. Children such as yourself, from good families and with inherent leadership qualities beyond the norm, got included in the experiment, and you were bound to influence the results unconsciously. It should have been carried out in some kind of isolation, free from the contamination – the *dilution* by example – of children with higher skills from the average.'

'That was the mistake, Scott,' adds my mother. 'You should have been in a control group. Or elsewhere.'

I struggle with the implications of what they are saying, and I turn to my father.

'So, *you*, not Mum – it was *you* who sent me to that school, because you wanted me to be part of an educational experiment funded by a bunch of right-wing nutters so as to prove that, without order, without your interpretation of authority, children would simply run wild and become worthless members of society? And you were even prepared to take that risk with your own son's future? What did you feel when you realized that the experiment was failing?'

He continues staring at me. 'I rarely repeat myself, boy. It failed because it wasn't set up correctly. There was no risk to you and you've clearly absorbed the skills needed to flourish . . . under any circumstances.'

The enormity of what my parents have done suddenly finds form as I realize what he's just said . . . what he actually believes in.

'You played with the outcome of my childhood based on *that* philosophy?'

I tap my CAMIC. 'What do you think I'm fighting against?' I say. 'This threat from right-wing crap merchants needs to be resisted. Your own father came over from America to stand up to it during World War II. Mum's dad did the same on behalf of Britain. Whole *nations* stood up to it. Wasn't that the ethic that drove *you* in the army – to protect your own country?'

'Don't be so naive,' he growls.

I can see my father is angry – probably even angrier than he himself realizes. Or perhaps it's the prospect of what is impending in the next few days that is prompting him to be so open. He has just told me more than I ever wanted to know. More than I could ever have guessed.

'Have you *any* real idea what I was doing in Africa?' he says finally.

His change of direction surprises me. I try to follow his train of thought.

'Peace-keeping, supposedly,' I reply.

'That's what the army was paying me to do, but in reality I was using my position to give assistance to the rebels.'

When he smiles at me, he looks so normal. I suddenly picture him there at Wannsee, with Heydrich and the others.

My mother interrupts. 'That's how the world works, Scott, and you had better get used to it.'

My father continues to eyeball me. 'We're going to change this world, my colleagues and I.'

'But you were shot by the rebels?'

'Because I failed them. I couldn't prevent the arrest of their leader, so they handed out the punishment they thought I deserved.'

'It was appropriate,' interrupts my mother. 'That country could have moved itself forward years earlier than it has done, if your father had fulfilled his part satisfactorily back then.'

'We could have had use of their mineral wealth four or five years before we did,' my father interjects, 'so could have instigated our programme of improvement ages ago.'

Bizarrely, he smiles. 'After we'd discarded *them*, as well.'

What they have said keeps repeating in my head: *My colleagues and I. My colleagues and I.*

And then it comes to me. I remember that evening when I sat with my grandfather, Captain Roy Anderson, D-Day veteran, watching the news report that pictured his son – my father – being wheeled away on a stretcher. I remember noticing someone in the background, behind the attendant medics, who seemed particularly concerned about a camera recording the event. He had quickly turned away, but not before I glimpsed the satisfaction in his eyes.

Through all the intervening years, I'd subconsciously stored away the image of that face. It was Pascal Toluene.

My grandfather wasn't sitting there gulping whiskies because he was worried about his son; he was doing so because the premonition he had once experienced in Normandy was coming true. Roy too recognized the mystery figure on the television – it was the same man he had envisaged on D-Day; the monster destined to out-do Hitler. Such was the depth of my grandfather's conviction that, two years later, he went off to confront Toluene in person when the man himself arrived in Britain.

Pascal Toluene, the man responsible for the death of my father's own father – my parents have contacts with the man I so hate. The same man I've been deliberately provoking.

It suddenly occurs to me that if I don't succeed in eliminating Heydrich in one of my universe-shifts during the time Jake claims we have left, then Toluene will undoubtedly triumph. If I die going up against Heydrich, if I too disappear in this universe, then Toluene definitely wins.

Along with a massive surge of anger against both my father and my mother, I feel shame for the years I've been stumbling through a darkened tunnel of ignorance. Now I'm about to pass through a gate leading into the arena to where the combat must take place.

I just have to find myself the appropriate weapon.

Then God commanded, 'Let there be a dome to divide the water and keep it in two separate places.' He named the dome 'Sky'. Evening passed and morning came – that was the second day.

Sunday
Day 2

Chapter Twelve

Jeanie Swallia – twenty-seven, South African, ER nurse, dental fanatic to the extent of using disposable tooth-brushes, antique teddy-bear collector, a woman who can drink most men into a stupor while herself still belching the national anthem, but who has now had to quit because she's four months pregnant – sits astride the patient lying on the gurney as other members of the Emergency Room team hurtle them both from the ambulance towards the crash room. She is administering CPR.

'One, two, three, four, five,' she calls as she pushes down on the man's chest. As she says five, another nurse, running to keep level with the man's head, squeezes the air bladder covering the patient's nose and mouth.

'One, two, three, four, five.'

Squeeze.

'One, two, three, four, five.'

Squeeze.

Jeanie closes her eyes for a moment, trying to ignore the guilty realization that this is, in all probability, the position in which she conceived her child, given how her boyfriend likes having handcuffs used on him. The instant she starts to think such an outrageous thought, she relishes the surge of absolute completeness enveloping every cell of her body.

She is going to be a mother. *Jeanie Swallia has another life growing inside her. From being an efficient, no-nonsense, stereotype, work-hard, play-hard nurse, she has met and fallen in love with Michael, and she is going to have his child. She feels as though she's a goddess, and one that rightly needs to be worshipped. From Eve, to her, and on through her to every girl forever into the future extends one immense bond of sisterhood that recognizes the maternal urge.*

She is going to be a mother – one of the pregnant women lucky enough not to have miscarried on The Night.

Jeanie smiles. It seems to her that the current commotion in the ER room is like a choir proclaiming the Annunciation.

She opens her eyes as the gurney rattles to a stop.

Jeanie goes to begin counting again, pitches forward, and jars her arms against the hard, hot surface of the gurney. There are gasps from her colleagues as Jeanie sits there on her haunches. She looks around herself, then at her hands, which feel as though a mild irritant has been spilt on them, then down at the gurney. What is she doing here? Jeanie glances around again. The rest of the team seem as perplexed as she is. The nurse handling the air bladder is inspecting it as though it's something contagious. Jeanie struggles off the gurney with as much dignity as she can muster. The doctor helps her – a frown crossing her forehead.

'What the hell just happened?' Dr Novac asks.

Jeanie Swallia, four months a-mother-to-be, hurries back to the nurses' station, one hand on her stomach, as if trying to protect the life-force inside it.

INTERNET NEWS UPDATE by Janice Maclean
The competition is coming to its natural end. *Total Cover*
is now a contest between Scott and Jo. Who do *you*
think should win? Scott Anderson has persisted in questioning recent developments in world politics and has
put forward some startling accusations about attempts
to alter our climate, or even worse. His manipulation of
the CAMIC technology that produced those unusual
ghostly effects out at a disused airfield is now being
investigated by Unit-C. His ratings, though, also seem to
climb with each outrageous assertion and stunt.

Jo Kingwaverly on the other hand has, in the last few
days, thrown her hat in with global protests against
uncontrolled scientific development. Her argument that
science has taken us too far is part of a pervasive opinion sweeping across the world, so she is attracting
thousands of votes through her passionate outbursts. It
is now fantastically close between them, so Scott will
have to do something special if he wants to win.

The three of us stand on a mound of shingle at Bawdsey Point. It is eight in the morning and I am rubbing
my aching eyes as I look around, slowly panning the
CAMIC across the view, as I've become accustomed
to doing. To one side of us stretches the North Sea; to
the other, across the estuary of the river Deben, lies
Felixstowe Ferry. Two round Martello towers stand on
the opposite shore, their solid forms still guarding
England from Napoleon, while the hamlet itself consists of a short row of thirties' terrace houses and
some wooden homes constructed on metre-high stilts,
as protection against unusually high tides. On the spit
below, several men are attempting to move a yacht,

the *Sea Thrush*, which Maxnet tells me beached here some days ago. They have attached a towrope to a small tug and are excitedly shouting instructions to each other. There seems to be a lot of work involved for little result. I wipe my brow. Although it is still early, the humidity is incredible, and I'm surprised there is not even a slight breeze up here to cool us.

My head throbs and my eyes feel heavy. We all have horrible hangovers, and I, for one, haven't slept at all. Not even for an hour. I've now lost track of my sleepless nights, evidenced by the dark patches under my eyes, and I'm drained of coherent thought. As I stand here on the beach, squinting in the sunlight, I find I wish I could think more of the good time we had at the pub, and less about what we discovered in the early hours of the morning.

The rare sound of a passing ship's horn, as it heads for Felixstowe docks, brings me back to the events of today.

A few people gathered on the opposite shore see us, and begin waving and call out our names. A young bloke shouts that he wants to marry TC. I wave back briefly and then turn to study the large building that is Bawdsey manor house. That is what I've come here for.

The building is a hotchpotch of styles in red brick and every turret is capped with a small dome of verdigris copper, which nicely complements the weathered brickwork. Its two wings are linked by a building in Victorian Gothic, which possesses an open colonnade running along the front.

'There you go, that's the birthplace of radar,' I explain. 'Orford Ness was where it was conceived, but it was here that they brought it to life. Unfortunately, they took down the experimental masts years ago, so there's not much left to see from the outside.'

I stare at the building, waiting for its ghosts to materialize – but nothing happens. I decide I will probably need to get nearer to it.

'It's a kind of metaphor for you, isn't it, radar?' says Jenny. 'Seeing ahead? A clairvoyant nod to a sixth sense? . . . Premonitions?'

'It's what we're all experiencing now,' I mutter.

I must be saying the right thing, because Jenny has that knowing expression back in her eyes.

I continue this line of thought. 'Premonitions? You're right. We've all been experiencing premonitions of one sort or other, haven't we? Everyone seems to have had them, and that's what everyone's so upset about. We all somehow suspect that we're in danger. The proof is all around. People are *disappearing*. Oh, sure, we find evidence later that they've vanished, but as to actually remembering them – nothing.'

I spread my hands to indicate our surroundings.

'And what if it is accelerating, as Jake insists? What if there are more and more people disappearing before our eyes each day? We may not be noticing it, but are we *sensing* it happening? If that's the case, then what the *fuck* is going on? Being chosen is like some kind of international lottery.' I pause and frown to myself. 'Do you know what the oddest thing is about these premonitions? It's that everyone seems to think that *their* interpretation of the future is the correct one.'

I look over at Jenny. I am really beginning to lose my cool.

'What's with this other crap we're all going through?' I snap. 'I know, I damn well *know* that I'm somehow being flung into another world, some other weird fucking universe, always involving World War II. What madness is *that*?'

I point to Jenny. 'Jenny here was arguing for *her* life in some different world where people wanted to burn her as a witch,' I say. 'And now that she's succeeded, she seems to have morphed into some sort of bloody superhuman who lives in an extrasensory world.'

I pause and stare at her, then continue. 'You *know* what it is that's going to happen, don't you? You don't even have to guess, do you?'

Jenny looks at me hard. In my head, I hear a whisper, faint and indistinct, but I realize it is her speaking to me.

'Don't be angry with me, Scott. Please.'

She smiles briefly, and turns to TC. 'You can win too, TC.'

A look of panic instantly comes into TC's eyes. 'What are you talking about?' she says.

'In *your* other world,' Jenny answers. 'You *have* to win, TC.'

TC shakes her head and stares down to the shingle. 'I don't think I can,' she says. She kicks at the shingle and pebbles fly everywhere. I mournfully watch one splash into the sea.

I turn back and freeze.

I can see my ghosts – the ones that haunt Bawdsey.

A group of men stand some distance away, beside some old tank obstacles. Their eyes are fixed on me. I look away in disgust from the state they are in, and stare out at the sea instead. What I see there is worse.

In the surf are several bodies, semi-transparent but still discernible. They wear the remnants of German uniforms and their corpses are charred so badly that their hands are hooked like claws that reach out for a last consoling embrace. That's another secret the locals don't like to discuss around here. Nobody knows if these dead men really were German soldiers burnt alive while attempting a raid on our coast, or if they actually were British soldiers accidentally killed in an exercise.

I realize that TC and Jenny are not looking in the same direction as me. But my CAMIC is, and its mobile starts bleeping as the world also sees what I do. I have brought some ghosts to visible life again.

Then they fade back into history, and again the waves slip onto an empty beach. The other phantoms, still standing there, now turn about and fade as well.

As they do, there is a sudden shimmer.

So soon?

I close my eyes. My stomach's too fragile to witness the familiar judders as I take another leap. I wonder if Jenny has somehow initiated this one.

Click, click . . . *click*!

Opening my eyes again, I find I have indeed been transported again. But I know exactly where this is: it is the Prague suburb of Holešovice, and I am walking up the Rude Armady VII Kobylisky, ascending the hill from the Traja Bridge. I know this road from photographs. This is where it all must happen. Quickening my stride, instinctively knowing my direction, I suddenly pause to check if I'm carrying a weapon. I find I am not.

This shift must involve only a reconnaissance, one

carried out before attempting the killing of Heydrich. The road rises steeply to a sharp bend, and the tramcar that passes me has to struggle to negotiate the corner.

I stop moving and pause to watch. The tramcar halts to let a passenger off, then pulls away with a squeal. I can see how a vehicle would need to slow down considerably on such a tight bend – even it were conveying someone as important as the Reichsprotektor himself. That could provide an ideal opportunity for an ambush.

From the strength of the sun it feels like the beginning of summer, therefore I suspect that Himmler has already made his visit to Prague to ensure increased security around Heydrich, because of other attacks on German personnel throughout the occupied lands. But Heydrich, in turn, has disregarded such orders – such is his arrogance he feels it will 'undermine' his authority amongst the Czech people. I feel a shudder of excitement run down my back.

As if on cue, a *Kabelwagen* with a lone driver appears over the rise and heads down the road towards me. For a second I wonder what it will feel like to be waiting in the same position, with a Sten gun hidden under my coat.

As the *Kabelwagen* gets close to me and slows to take the bend, I gasp. The driver looks exactly like Jake. He has the same build, the same facial features – he even has Jake's deep frown.

Why is Jake . . .?

Then the vehicle passes and I am left feeling stupefied.

Why have things been twisted like this?

I turn to watch the car gathering speed, and for a moment even wonder if I am meant to kill Jake instead of Heydrich. My mouth is dry. I am plagued with an abiding panic.

What am I meant to learn by being here?

The world pauses, stutters and restarts.

Click, click . . . *click!*

I am standing on the shingle again – but still immersed in my panic.

Jenny also seems frightened. 'But that can't be right,' she murmurs.

'What can't?' says TC.

'Just an idea,' I say.

You're reading my mind, aren't you, Jenny? You went with me, saw what I saw. And you're also worried about seeing Jake driving that Kabelwagen, and whether that means he's someone we should be fighting.

And as I stand at Bawdsey Point, I feel pensive again.

Now there's Jake to worry about, too?

Maxnet bleeps.

Does it now know what I'm thinking?

UNITED STATES DEPARTMENT OF JUSTICE
FEDERAL BUREAU OF INVESTIGATION
New England Office
RE: PASCAL TOLUENE

Memo extracted from hard drive of TOLUENE'S PC during covert operation.

'With the closure of the SPRINGGREEN experiment, I had anticipated that most of the individuals involved could be assimilated easily back into society, and that the rule of authority would soon rectify any misconceptions they had developed about the world. However, ANDERSON's son, by his populist stance on Maxnet, is a constant slap in the face. In *my* face. This irritant has to be removed as soon as possible. With extreme prejudice.'

CENTRAL INTELLIGENCE AGENCY
TOP SECRET
Langley
RE: GEN-FORK; EISENCRICK INSTITUTE

Operative working with customs officials in ENGLAND reports that transportation of genetic-interference virus, GEN-FORK, from biological production site EISEN-CRICK INSTITUTE, SUFFOLK, ENGLAND, has proceeded. Operative is issuing high-status alert after deception discovery at HEATHROW. Consignment had been replaced. Location of genuine item unknown. The PRESIDENT has been notified.

I post this information back into the increasingly refined system that is Maxnet. I have achieved part of my objective: I have provoked Toluene into doing something about me. And I've also confirmed a link between him, the Gen-Fork virus and now the Eisencrick Institute. And therefore with Jake.

How to tell TC?

Marvel Speer turns off his laptop. A quick investigation of the *Total Cover* website has been most useful. He smiles to himself as he wishes all his intended victims would be so obliging as to partake in a reality show and thereby provide a constant update of their movements. He considers Scott Anderson a complete idiot for leaving himself so obviously vulnerable. But once Anderson is dealt with, he, Speer, can concentrate on eliminating all the other remaining ex-pupils of Springgreen Open who still live in Britain.

He knows that around the world there are other agents performing a similar task in removing such mistakes from the population.

Yes, the dead generally provide less trouble. He wonders how Anderson would feel if he knew the real truth about Joe Kennedy Jnr's death – how the traitor was deliberately blown up in that aircraft over East Anglia. Marvel Speer has good information – received from the grandson of the very man who sabotaged the remote-controlled Liberator – that Joe Jnr had been given a just reward for turning his back on his pre-war sympathies. It was no accident.

Yes, the dead are seldom a problem.

Marvel Speer knows how he is going to kill Anderson, he is reasonably certain about the place . . . and all he needs to do now is to work out exactly when.

However, he knows it must be soon.

Chapter Thirteen

Thomas Waverly — English, fifty-two, a sixteen-stone ball of frustration waiting for either a neurological abscess that will allow him to justify killing all these sour-faced travellers with their Unit-C CAMICs, or else a virulent exotic cancer that will also provide him with an excuse to wreak carnage on the London Underground — stands in the front carriage of the 10.30 Tube train on the Circle line, in a crush that is surprising for a Sunday morning. He keeps getting jolted left, right, left, right, and he wonders exactly when it was that he became so bitter.

But Thomas Waverly already knows the answer. As always, she springs into his mind as clear as any memory can be. He had been twenty-five then, she a year younger. She had seen straight through his bluff exterior, straight into his personality and, with a stroke of her fingers on his cheek, announced that she had found the man that she'd never known she needed.

And he blew it.

He was only twenty-five, the world was his for the taking, he had a gorgeous, wonderfully vital woman worshipping his entire being, and he blew it.

He just had to screw around with every girl he could seduce or impress.

And he had to throw it all in her face – the big-shot that he was.

The train rattles and rocks, rattles and rocks.

What a prat!

And now, suddenly, in the middle of his remembered misery, Thomas smiles to himself. It is the weirdest thing, but he knows, completely and with utter certainty, that she has forgiven him. Just like that.

Where did that thought come from?

And he knows there's more. He's now aware that, as she has got on with her own life, she's kept tabs on where he is and what he has been doing. She knows that he never married – she knows he lost himself in his business under the guilt of his folly. And she knows where his office is situated; the place he is heading for now, although it's Sunday, to alleviate his panic about what might happen tomorrow. She knows his destination.

Thomas Waverly is absolutely certain, as he stands here in this crush of people, that she is even now seeking out his office telephone number.

He looks around to see if the faces that were previously sour and bitter are now looking friendly and welcoming. But the crowds don't have smiles on their faces.

The train jars to a stop just as it enters Embankment.

The passengers are so tightly packed that no one is thrown far, because they all cushion each other. There are a number of screams. And a chorus of swearing.

Thomas forces himself over to the door and gets his fingers in the gap between the rubber seals. Another commuter helps him, and the door slides open.

Thomas jumps out onto the platform and moves quickly away from the carriage. He then sees another passenger standing at the front of the train, staring past him into the driver's compartment. Thomas turns to look for himself, thinking that the driver may have collapsed.

He's stunned by what he sees. There is no driver.

As the rest of the commuters stumble from the carriages, Thomas Waverly has to push his way to the exit. He hasn't a clue as to what has just happened, but he wants to reach his office before she telephones. It will be so good to hear her voice.

Fuck the future. I feel twenty-five again.

Jake cannot believe how easy this is. He and TC may now be walking into a situation that will complicate their lives more than they need, but they are acting so brazenly that nobody is thinking to stop them. They have passed at least four guards on their way in, all apparently accepting that Dr Jake Crux has authority to bring a female companion onto the Institute premises. They probably assumed their orders about excluding the doctor had been rescinded.

The pair now stand at the door to his laboratory. 'They'll have changed the door code,' Jake remarks.

TC stares at the keypad.

'It's nine-one-one-zero-one,' she declares.

Jake reaches out and quickly taps in this five-digit number. A green light comes on and the magnetic release mechanism hums. He nods to himself, gives the door a push and they walk in. TC glances up at him, a moment of doubt and indecision in her eyes. Tentatively she fondles the small bulge in her pocket which is her CAMIC, but resists switching it on. She thinks Scott's new-found suspicions about Jake are wrong, but the Institute is another matter.

Jake glances around the room. 'They haven't wasted any time, have they?'

All his pictures and posters have been removed. Also gone are his row of coffee mugs and his selection of coffee beans. Jake turns to TC and notices her attention is fixed on a corner of the ceiling. It is where the Institute's security CAMIC is located. Her eyes drop to meet his.

'We haven't much time,' he says.

He puts down on his desk the large plastic bottle he has been carrying, goes over to the PC and switches it on.

'If they've downloaded my results and records already, then we've had a wasted journey,' he warns.

The display starts flickering through its start-up routine. It sings out the opening bars of 'Thus Spake Zarathustra' by Richard Strauss, familiar to many as the music from the very beginning of *2001: A Space Odyssey*.

'Okay,' he says. 'They installed a particular security program.' He moves the mouse over the icons. 'It monitors exactly what files are copied onto CD. I was supposed to check daily whether there'd been any unauthorized use of my machine. But I used this program only twice. Ah!'

He rapidly runs a finger down the screen, checking off the folders and files in turn.

'Nope,' he says. 'Nope . . . Nope.'

'Hurry up,' urges TC, quietly.

'Nope . . . Nope . . . Good, they haven't copied anything. Okay, let's do it.'

TC picks up the bottle.

'Anywhere?' she asks.

'Anywhere and everywhere,' says Jake, as he begins to climb up onto a bench. As TC flicks the lid off, she cannot resist taking a sniff.

'It's not petrol,' she observes.

Jake is reaching up to the smoke alarm on the ceiling.

'Thinners,' he says. 'I use it to dilute the cellulose paint I use in painting my chess pieces.'

He unclips the cover to the smoke alarm and takes out the battery. He then jumps back to the floor, opens a desk drawer and removes a sheet of printer paper. TC has nearly finished sprinkling the thinners over his computer equipment.

'Okay, then,' says Jake. 'Let's go. That stuff evaporates really quickly.'

He takes the bottle from TC and pitches it up against the CAMIC. The lens shatters and the body inside falls from its charging unit and smashes to the floor.

'Nearly forgot, that thing has a fire-alarm failsafe. Flames will trigger a response if they are automatically detected on screen,' he says. 'But hopefully security hasn't been watching us too closely.'

TC opens the door, checks that the corridor is clear and steps out of the room. Jake is just about to follow, when he pauses.

'Hurry up,' she hisses.

'Just a moment,' he says, then picks up the brand-new chair that replaced his old leather one and hurls it against the window separating his office from his experiment lab. The large pane of glass explodes into fragments.

'That'll give the fire access to the rest of the lab.

Let's destroy the whole lot,' he murmurs. Then he takes out his lighter, puts a flame to the sheet of paper, contemplates it for a second as it begins to take hold, then tosses the burning paper towards the main PC. Quickly stepping out of the room, he shuts the door behind him. Less than three seconds later, there is a dull thump and an explosion rattles the door.

Jake looks down at his hand, still on the door handle, and suddenly thinks about the myth of Pandora's Box.

There are some things that people should never know about.

'You're right.'

Jake snaps a look at TC as he hears her voice in his head.

She merely smiles at him.

And as they begin to walk quickly – running might attract attention – along the corridor towards the exit, Jake realizes that he understands more about himself by doing what they have just done. The conflicts he has undertaken with the very real-seeming dragons in that other shifting universe are like the beasts that were let out of Pandora's Box. Once you open that box and peer inside, you never know what you might uncover.

That's what science is all about.

I am pushing my way through waist-high ferns in Bestleton Woods, with Jenny walking alongside me.

I am very hot – and still seething.

We were contacted just before two o'clock – it seemed more like a summons – and told to meet up with Jake and TC in The Walks. I am becoming more uncertain of him after seeing him in my last shift. I'm even contemplating the possibility that Dr Jake Crux may even *want* to help unleash this paranormal phenomenon he claims is happening to us all and which he, and the other two – but particularly Jenny with her strange serenity – seem capable of accessing. I feel surrounded by deceptions.

Jake's supposedly intelligent, so he must have known what the Eisencrick Institute was up to.

I swipe out at a large fern, I feel so righteously furious.

Jenny keeps casting looks back in my direction. I don't like the fact that she can apparently invade my private thoughts at will.

Jenny, I will not be dissuaded from what I have to do . . . But can I stop you from listening in?

As she glances back again, her look suggests I could if I tried.

I swipe another fern. I feel ready.

Let's see if I can get this over with. Now!

As always, I am surprised by its suddenness, even though I wanted it to happen now.

Click, click . . . *click*!

I am now standing by that same sharp, uphill bend at Rude Armady VII Kobylisky. I look around me. There are few people about, and I guess it is midmorning. After the excessive heat of my own world, I enjoy the sensation of the ordinary summer warmth in the air. Standing across the road, but further up the hill, is a man who holds my gaze for a second, then continues staring up the road beyond the bend. Glancing to either side, I realize I have no other accomplice immediately nearby – only my compatriot across the road, waiting to signal the approach of Heydrich's Mercedes. The lack of a third assassin worries me; I again remember that if small events in this world are different, then other things are possible . . .

I realize there is a chance it might be *me* who gets killed. Or it might be Jake I have to remove. I roll my shoulders to ease the sudden tension. I will succeed. I *have* to.

I move closer to the railings – the trees beyond obscuring my view up the road – and hope that the raincoat draped over my left arm completely conceals what I guess is underneath. I check in my left trouser pocket and feel a can-sized object which must be the explosive I'm carrying as a back-up. Under the left flap of my jacket is a simple holster containing a .32 Colt automatic.

But the primary weapon, concealed under my raincoat, is a ready-cocked Sten gun, with a magazine of thirty-two bullets. The bolt is not in the safety-notch, so it is ready to fire. The sub-machine gun suddenly feels very heavy, and I adjust my grip on it.

I can feel the selector above the trigger is set to automatic. Three one-second bursts will empty the magazine; but even if I have a replacement, I don't think I'll get time to reload. The most important question is screaming in my mind: *Can I pull the trigger? Can I kill him?*

I think of my target: Heydrich, the Butcher of Prague.

Urbane, sophisticated, but a psychopath – in a position of absolute and ultimate power. And I am here, albeit in a version of my own world, weighed down with weapons, waiting for the monster's car to appear.

I realize my heart is running in synch with my rapid thoughts. It is as if I am poised at the top of some extraordinary fairground ride – high in the air, and waiting for the drop. And, yet again, even as I know what the consequences will be of what I am here to do (the Gestapo will extract a terrible revenge), I ask myself again the main question: *Can I kill this monster?*

I blink as a shaft of light flashes across my eyes. It happens again and I look up the road. The man on the corner flashes his mirror one last time: Heydrich is on his way.

My hand checks the Sten once more.

Step up close, throw off the overcoat, point the gun and squeeze the trigger?

That's all I have to do. I can't run away from this.

The man on the hill begins to walk down towards me. I hear a car as it changes down a gear.

A tram squeals to a stop nearby. The sound makes me jump and I realize there will be innocent bystanders nearby. Then a black open-topped Mercedes springs into view and stops all thought. There is Heydrich himself, sitting in the front seat, alongside his hefty chauffeur, Klein.

It's not Jake!

Only twenty metres between the approaching vehicle and myself. Twelve. Five. It slows even further as it negotiates the bend.

Can I really do this?

I throw off the overcoat, bring the tubular butt of the Sten close in against my body, point the muzzle at

Heydrich, open-mouthed as he sees me, and squeeze the trigger.

Nothing.

I glance down at the sub-machine gun. I look up. Heydrich is now about to pass me. He stares at me. I try again.

Nothing.

The car glides past, then he shouts at Klein to stop. I curse: perhaps the magazine is not seated correctly. I feel myself frown, and catch a brief glimpse of some of the tram passengers gawking.

As the car stops, both Heydrich and Klein reach for their guns. And start to open their car doors. I throw the Sten to the ground and reach into my trouser pocket. I should have earlier transferred the bomb to my right-hand pocket, consequently I fumble. As he un-holsters his pistol, Heydrich continues to stare me down. For one strange moment, I think I recognize his eyes. He then leaps upright in the car, and raises his weapon. I now have the bomb in my left hand and I hurl it. Heydrich fires a shot at me. The bomb misses the vehicle's interior, as a bullet zips past my ear. The explosive strikes the outside of the car. There is a sudden flash, a bright red and yellow light, then a grey-purple-black cloud and a roar of sound. I stumble back under the blast-wave, a piece of shrapnel grazing my forehead. Through the booming after-effects of the explosion, I hear screams from people hit on the tram. I glance in their direction and see that the tram windows have been shattered. As I turn back, Heydrich rises through the smoke and starts firing again.

I find I cannot even reach for my Colt to return fire,

so I turn and run. All I can think of is being punched in the back with a bullet.

How much will it hurt?

Something deep within me causes me to hesitate. 'Fuck!' I shout.

I pause behind a lamp post, reaching in my jacket for the automatic. I turn, slide the breech back, snap the safety off, squeeze off two shots at Heydrich – before I realize that the German commander is leaning against the heavily damaged car, his pistol lying on the ground. He is clutching his right side. I can see blood.

I start to run hard towards my accomplice further up the hill. He is covering his own escape by shooting at Klein, and keeping him pinned down behind the car.

As I keep running, I wonder why there is no sense of triumph – no sense of relief in the strange exhilaration that boils my blood. Then I hear the wounded cries of the passengers on the tramcar – and remember. And I contemplate that, though I have completed *this* mission, there is still more to learn, more fighting to be done.

I will have to come back to this place.

Click, click . . . *click*!

We have gathered in The Walks. After my recent Heydrich episode, I am now suffering from a bout of intense dread – and the after-effects of shock – a trembling excitement. It is made worse by the semi-remoteness of where we are meeting.

This is a quiet place: the birds are still not singing. Myriad silver birches stand amid a lawn of ferns – the white bark of the slender trunks, and their pale leaves, contrast brilliantly with the dark mass of waist-high greenery surrounding them. A wickedly bright sun flashes through the canopy of birches beyond, turning the topmost leaves into thin wafers of polished brass. Finding a clearing of soft grass, under cool, rich-smelling shade, we stretch out, ready to listen to whatever Jake needs to tell us. I notice TC is not wearing her CAMIC, and to me it seems a betrayal. She was the one supposed to monitor Jake.

But I myself now feel I can take on anything – and keep seeing that look of surprise in Heydrich's eyes as he realized that someone actually had the audacity to attack him.

The merest hint of a breeze rustles through the airy space between the trees.

Suddenly I feel the ripple of a shiver down my neck.

The others all appear equally nervous. Jake and TC look rather flushed – perhaps because they both know what he is about to say.

He gives a quick cough and begins. 'I'm an evolutionary anthropologist by profession . . . Or I was until yesterday.'

I begin to think that's a strange thing to announce in such a formal way, considering where we are. Then I notice he is staring directly at me, and realize Jake is not talking to us so much as using me yet again to talk to the world via my CAMIC. I don't like this, and prepare to turn my equipment off.

'I made a discovery,' he continues. 'It is to do with The Night . . . I know what it means.'

He gives us his now-familiar flicker of a smile, his

gaze resting on each of us in turn, finally returning to me as I stroke the CAMIC off-switch.

'Let me begin with a warning . . .'

There is a firmer tone in his voice, and I sit up slightly. My CAMIC mobile is beginning to bleep. Clearly others on Maxnet are interested and they want to hear him, so I leave it on.

'The universe knows no emotion,' he goes on. 'There is a supreme coldness to its construction and development that every sentient living thing must accept.'

He shrugs his shoulders, as if to indicate that can't be helped, then gestures at the woodland surrounding us.

'The payback for us,' he says, 'the payback for *life*, is the sheer beauty and wonder of it.' He slowly raises his eyes towards me. 'And its diversity. But we've over-populated the world,' he continues. 'There are now too many people . . . too many *minds*. This is what I was talking about on Wednesday, before those four intruders interrupted us. Any anthropologist, any biologist, will tell you the same, that Mother Nature finds ways to curb over-population. That's a fact of life: if too many entities are trying to survive on too little available sustenance, then nature will make amends – using any means she can. And the thing that applies here is that *we're* going to do it for her. Not with nuclear war, not with a man-made plague, not even with imaginary satellites showering deadly rays of God-knows-what upon us all, but we *are* going to do it to ourselves.'

He leans forward, and I resist backing away from him – as I feel inclined. Obviously he is referring to

Gen-Fork and, given where he works, I suddenly wonder if he could be a carrier.

'Mankind is going to force this curb on itself in a unique way,' he says. 'We have nearly achieved a group consciousness, and already an unconscious collective group-mind is starting to eliminate those that are different.'

He suddenly laughs and I cringe – startled by this outburst.

'In order to save ourselves, we have to employ the hidden and overlooked abilities that we all possess,' he says.

He has my total attention now.

'We live in a multitude of universes, and they can somehow be altered, can be *shifted*, to accommodate Mind.'

With a gesture of his hand, Jake includes me in what he is about to say. 'Most of us are uncomfortable with change: we see it as unnecessary, even scary – because we don't know what that change may bring.'

He raises his eyebrows, as if seeking agreement.

'And, of course there are people about who will twist that uncertainty into fear. How they do it is to equate change with *difference*. That's what we've been taught as we evolved from camp, to village, to town, to city. We don't feel comfortable with the stranger in our midst. We don't like those who do not conform to what *we* perceive as normal. It's a vice that has grown from the practicality of living together, and there are those who would have us all carry our prejudices with pride. *They* declare that some people are better than the rest. I think, in a way, that's what Scott here has been going on about.'

I frown. Jake continues.

'The Nazis preyed on the fear of difference . . . however nonsensical. For understanding reduces the fear caused by ignorance. Across the whole of nature, co-operation remains the best survival technique.'

'But everyone tells us it's survival of the fittest,' I interrupt, thinking of my parents. 'Dog-eat-dog – that's all I ever hear.'

Jake winces. 'It's a myth perpetuated by those who want us to believe it. Yet the evidence has always been there to contradict it.'

Over the back of my head, a startled blackbird suddenly swoops past in silence.

Jake smiles. 'Birds, animals, plants, *every* living thing on this planet, they have *all* evolved to co-operate with other creatures in some way. The lion, being the archetypal jungle top dog, is a great example. It actually thrives because it is, in its own way, in co-operation with its prey.'

He nods – as if agreeing with himself.

'It *would* choose to devour the fittest, the strongest of the herd, if it could, because they surely would provide the better meat. Instead, it feeds on the weakest, the oldest, the *least* fit, because they're easier to catch. And so the herd itself evolves to become stronger, and fitter, until even the least of their number is stronger and fitter than its ancestors were. Which benefits the lion, because it is nourished more efficiently as it too evolves to counter its prey's advancement.'

He wipes his mouth.

'But *we* have stagnated,' he says. 'We've forgotten the hunter-gathering instincts that we had developed for *that* particular lifestyle. Skills that we possessed for thousands upon thousands of years – suppressed until now.'

He pauses. 'We evolved to possess paranormal abilities, which were once extremely useful to us. But, by making the change from hunter-gatherers to farmers, they fell into disuse. And they were even further suppressed when we learnt to read.'

He taps the left side of his head with a fingertip.

'The part of our brain that recognizes written or printed words has blocked the neural connections we once habitually used for our sixth sense. But now, because of imminent over-population, because of the approach of optimum level of our group consciousness, they are beginning to resurface through different pathways. We have to embrace them consciously, for they will save us.'

He stabs a finger at me.

'All you people watching this, you're beginning to find yourselves being tested in some way, aren't you? That's because the universe is shifting, adjusting to our unconscious wishes, and is throwing you into other worlds. You *have* to win those challenges, solve those problems, learn those lessons . . . you *have* to succeed. You're fighting against the unconscious paranoia of the farmer-in-the-city group-mind that dislikes you being different – which we *all* are. We're all part of something bigger . . . a sort of giant organism where new cells are added when a child is born, and where old cells are removed when any of us die. But this collective consciousness faces a problem: because of its current unconscious nature, it's turning in on itself. What is coming . . . what is coming is a sort of Armageddon, and those that fail will be cast into a void of our own making.'

He pauses. 'It's what religions all over the world have been foretelling for centuries.'

He pauses again, gives us that micro-smile, then gestures to Jenny.

'The prophets had an innate knowledge of what is going to happen, knowledge born out of their unique grasp of the sixth-sense abilities they were able to tap into. They knew that we would judge *ourselves*. And, understand this, it is not, somehow, God's punishment for unbelievers, it's just the way we ourselves have decided the universe works. But we've lost track of our connection with it. It's what these protests against science represent. It's been intuitively perceived that technology, our city-dwelling life, has taken us away from our birthright, which is total knowledge of the universe.'

He laughs again.

'Yes, the prophets understood this: they were in touch with *their* premonitions – which is why they gave us the commandments that you will find in all different religions. They knew what the solution is. It's just that over the centuries, like Chinese whispers, we have interpreted their teachings wrongly.'

He frowns. 'I have to emphasize how it is now imperative for all of mankind consciously to reacquire its paranormal abilities. That is the survival move it must make, seemingly a retro move, a step back in order to leap forward . . . and in doing so, save itself. Here, TC and I will demonstrate the inherent power we all possess.'

He gestures to her and she reaches into a rucksack.

And whatever they are intending to do, I am certain they will do it.

The fear he has engendered in me is making me shake.

I feel like running away, just to give me time to think.

As I panic, there is a blurring shimmer in the air. My reality jerks away – and jumps into another.

I was right, I haven't finished with these shifts. There is still more to lose . . . and possibly more to gain.

My fear now takes me away to my other world – the one where, Jake says, I am up against the unconscious selfishness of others.

Click, click . . . *click*!

I recognize the smell immediately: no hospital can ever obscure it. I am in a single-bed ward and the thin yellow acetate blinds to the windows are closed. I move towards the bed and see the man lying there is Heydrich. His breathing is shallow, intermittent. His face has the sheen of a polished doll. In the explosion, parts of the car – including some of the horsehair stuffing and broken springs from the rear seat were punched right into him by the force of the bomb and are still embedded in his body. All because his natural arrogance prevented him from installing armour on the outside of his Mercedes. And if he had had his infected spleen removed, where foreign bodies still lurked, and then been treated with the precious penicillin acquired from Allied medical teams taken prisoner, I know that there would still be a chance the monster could recover. Instead, his doctor has refused to operate, and is relying on an earlier sulphonamide. Consequently, Heydrich is dying of septicaemia.

I am the only other person in the room, though I can see through the round windows of the double doors, there are SS guards outside in the corridor. Perhaps I am meant to be the doctor checking up on him?

What I am supposed to do now? Or have I somehow already altered events by refusing to remove his spleen? Can I have done that without being aware of it? Have I been shifted to this hospital before, and not known it? Are these shifts sometimes unconscious occurrences? And what do I do now? Smother the monster?

Instead, I lean over the prone body and whisper harshly in the man's ear. 'I hope it hurts, you bastard.'

That provokes a reaction. He manages to open his eyes and we stare at each other. There is that odd sensation of recognition again. I smile at his look of hate. He blinks, then blinks again. The intervals while his eyes are closed become longer, until there comes a time when they do not open any more. There is a long exhalation, and it is over. The Butcher of Prague has breathed his last. I smile to myself. It is a wicked pleasure for me to know that I caused his death.

I stand up straight again and adjust my collar before taking a final look at the man in the hospital bed, prior to leaving. He has changed into Jake.

With a gasp, I step back, knocking over a chair. The door is pushed open and an SS officer rushes in.

'Is he dead?' he asks.

'Yes. Yes, he's dead.'

'Then the world has lost a great man.'

I look down at Jake's body. I am so terrified that I cannot say anything, even though I know the soldier expects it.

The world judders and I am hurried back to the

reality that is my true life – the one I am in danger of being permanently removed from.

Click, click . . . *click*!

I smell fern and moss – I am back in Bestleton Woods.

I try to recover myself. Jenny gives me a quick look and shakes her head.

'*I told you,*' she speaks empathetically in my mind, '*Jake is not a threat.*'

I try not to look at him. His significance in my vision-shifts has me very confused.

What's next? I find myself mind-asking Jenny.

'*They'll show you.*'

TC is reaching into her rucksack and takes out what at first appears to be a rectangle of thin wood. She unfolds it, doubling its width, and places it on the grass between Jake and herself. I now see it is a wooden chessboard and I assume it's of Jake's construction. TC picks out handfuls of chess pieces – slim, elegant creations – and begins to arrange them on the square. In less than a minute, the chessboard is set up ready to play.

I wait for Jake to make his first move. He appears to be concentrating extremely hard.

The breeze must have picked up, as the white pawn in front of his king seems to have wobbled.

It judders again – then slides two squares forward, and stops.

Jake sits back and relaxes. 'Away you go, hot-shot,' he says to TC.

She, too, appears to start concentrating.

I lean closer, my mouth half-open.

After a short while, her equivalent pawn slides

across the board, lightly knocking Jake's pawn, then settles down two squares in front of her own king.

Neither Jake nor TC has touched either piece.

They haven't even touched the board.

Jenny's fingers dig into my arm. I glance over and see the excitement in her eyes.

Jake's knight, the one next to his king, rises into the air and slowly drops down near his pawn which moved earlier.

TC's queen's pawn immediately moves one square forward.

Jake turns to us. He looks very pale – but pleased.

'We can all do that,' he says. 'We just have to free our minds. It will become the only way to protect ourselves. And I'm certain the faculty will improve once you succeed in your shifts.'

He stares at me. 'Just ask Jenny.'

'*He's right*,' she says in my mind.

TC just looks terrified at what she's done.

I try to seek normality. The sun shimmers through the birch leaves, which rustle as the wind picks up. I look up and see thin streaks of cloud racing across the sky.

The weather's changing. At last!

I look around at the others, to see if they've noticed, too.

For a moment, I feel as though something is different, as though there is a gap of silence and space that needs filling with a lost moan. It seems a repetition of the feeling of something being there, but just out of recognizable vision – a memory that cannot be recalled. Another quiver of fear makes me shiver, I don't know why.

I look around again, slowly.

Jake, Jenny and me.

Jenny, Jake. Me.

There is a smell of lightning and storms.

I notice the others seem momentarily as perplexed as I am.

In the left side of my head is that slight pain again, while echoing in my ears is the faint call of that crowd that ebbs and flows, rises and falls, that large mass of people talking amongst themselves a vast distance from me. I still cannot discern what it is they're saying – again, they could be chanting, they could be arguing. I still can't tell, but I am certain that there are thousands upon thousands of people. There could even be millions. I have the urge to run to them, if possible, and find out what it is they're saying. And then . . . and then I smell the grass, and the voices fade away.

I look at Jenny, and Jake.

I seem to be the only one shivering, lost in my own thoughts. It is as though something had has happened and I've somehow forgotten what.

I still cannot work out why I feel so perturbed.

It is as if I have misplaced something.

Or someone?

Then I remember Jake moving chess pieces without ever touching them, but can't recall if he had an opponent doing the same. I allow the various muscles in my face, arms, hands and legs to twitch and to tremble as much as they wish – I don't care if the other two notice.

I don't know who it was, but someone recently

amongst us has disappeared from this universe. Someone has lost the fight against unconscious hate.

Above me, the clouds begin to thicken.

Marvel Speer watches until they depart. The events he has witnessed have been remarkable – the trick with the chess pieces would indeed have been perplexing if it had been real and not fake. It was clever, though he can't remember which of the other two was actually helping the doctor perform it. He had been sure that damn blackbird he disturbed would give him away when it flew off, but for some reason it didn't make any noise. Speer has a sudden little shimmer of doubt about what he has to do. He has been so involved in his task that he has barely been conscious of what is happening elsewhere in the world, and he himself has indeed had some bad dreams, but the anxiety caused quickly disperses. He reckons that Dr Jake Crux's arguments are just so much crap, even when backed up by clever parlour tricks.

Marvel Speer sniffs the air and smells rain. Then he stands up and moves away from the clearing. Marvel Speer loves hunting.

Chapter Fourteen

INTERNET NEWS UPDATE by Janice Maclean

It is the mystery of the moment and everyone is talking about it. And I do mean *everyone*. Officials are trying to quell fears that, to add to our current uncertainties about what is happening around us, there is evidence that increasingly large numbers of people are simply vanishing. Incredible as it may seem, reports are pouring in from all over the world describing widespread incidents of people just disappearing. Governments are trying to lessen anxiety by claiming these reports are false, that it is simply a form of mass hysteria fed by the media. Others are more open.

'I wish it was Hallowe'en,' said an unnamed source in our own government. 'Then we could all have a good laugh at how we are scaring ourselves silly. The problem, though, is the abundant evidence, whatever my colleagues may be saying. Up until yesterday, records indicate there was a cabinet minister named John Tristan. He even featured on this afternoon's repeat of *Any Questions?* on radio, but no one can place him at the moment, nor can we find anyone who can actually *remember* him. It's totally bizarre.' Asked if the government really believes it has things under control, the same source said, 'You have to be joking. Have *you* any idea what's happening?'

Jake is sitting on his own on the dry grass, his back resting against a big silver birch at the edge of the woodland. He is looking across Dunwich Heath towards his home. The strengthening breeze rustles the leaves above him, and the early evening skies are filling with clouds. White streaks, at first, that then pulse with grey and black, then melt back to white again, as their numbers continually multiply and merge. But the longed-for breeze serves only to push the inherent mugginess around. Jake smokes one of his small cigars, savouring the taste of it, rolling his tongue around the end. As he waits, he tries to enjoy the moment.

Because they have a long night ahead, and are all hungry, Jenny and Scott have left him here alone while they head back to Jenny's to collect some provisions for a barbecue down on the beach.

He feels a great loss about someone, and she keeps drifting on the edge of his memory. He tries desperately to concentrate.

They are all aware that the police could easily track Jake down by simply identifying locations Scott is seeing via his CAMIC. Scott offered to switch if off, but as his contest is reaching a crucial stage, they felt the attention he is receiving would guarantee even more e-viewers for Jake, too. Jake has noticed how the idea of winning seems to have set Scott on edge, as though there were bigger implications at stake. It will be getting dark by the time they set up the barbecue, which will more easily give Jake the opportunity to join them.

Jake watches another police car pull up outside his home . . . so there are now four police vehicles and about eight officers surrounding his house. He wonders what they're finding so interesting that requires so many of them.

Clearly his former employers are out to apprehend him. He hadn't expected anything less, but had assumed the law might be more interested in coping with the building chaos in the towns, rather than chasing arsonists like himself.

It's probably more therefore to do with what I've been saying, and demonstrating.

He knows that public disorder is escalating, and at a speed they will soon be unable to contain.

It's been building for centuries, and now it is imminent. So they're going to need more than just a few police cars.

Jake laughs to himself at the thought, and takes another slow puff on his cigar. He decides that it is time to settle things, to prepare himself, so he closes his eyes. He can initiate this.

Jenny has resolved her conflict in her own other version of the universe, while he himself has begun to open his mind to those sixth-sense paranormal abilities he knows people are going to need to utilize over the next few hours. But he still hasn't won his conflict, nor has Scott . . . which could be a problem.

Jake concentrates hard. He has attuned his brain, embracing the rejuvenated neural pathways, and is now sensitive enough to detect the slight tremble of the ground. He feels reality jump and change.

Click, click . . . *click*!

And opens his eyes.

He vaguely recognizes where he is as his world refocuses. It is the main circular hall inside Orford Castle, but brightly coloured tapestries now hang on the walls. Standing in front of them, the same battered and bloodstained suits of armour that he has used in previous encounters are arranged on simple tailor's mannequins, together with the various weapons. A gigantic log fire blazes in the huge fireplace, the heat from it managing to remove the chill from the stone walls. The strong sweet smell of burning wood is mixed with the musk of candles and sulphur.

And what Jake is also painfully aware of this time is that he himself is a lindorm – and the woman standing before him, clothed in overlaying thin silk dresses, is someone he feels he should know.

Jake – now Jake, the lindorm – finds himself speaking.

'Take them off,' he hisses, snaking his head down to indicate the garments.

The woman cocks her head to one side, the long Pre-Raphaelite hair falling off her shoulders.

'Is that an order?' she asks, in a vaguely familiar voice.

'Just do it.'

She holds his stare. 'For every one of these . . .' she says, grasping the material of the topmost dress. 'For every one of these that I remove, you must shed a skin in turn, you must be prepared to strip yourself to the bone.'

There is no hesitation with Jake's response. 'I promise.'

She casually slips off the first layer – it flutters to

the floor – and Jake stretches his frame and cracks a line in his outer skin, shedding it as promised.

She smiles and pulls off another thin robe. And Jake sheds another skin.

Finally, the young woman reaches her last garment. She has never stopped looking straight at Jake, and now she slowly removes this dress with a look daring him to glance down at her naked form. Jake, as the lindorm, slides up to her, but she doesn't flinch. He envelops her in his coils, as the last of his own skins falls away. And, as it does so, he reveals to her that beneath all those layers of dragon skin is Jake himself – naked.

Jake, become man, embraces the woman, and they begin to caress one another gently.

He feels an ineffable sadness that perhaps he has left it too late. He wishes he could remember her name.

The world and the universe shimmer.

Click, click . . . *click*!

The scurrying clouds above him continue their build-up.

Jake glances over the heath towards the policemen coming and going from his house.

He smiles – he has succeeded.

He now has protection.

Having caught up with Jenny, he has become part of a new partnership, part of the new organism that humanity can evolve into – and now needs to continue convincing many others to do so, too.

His doubts have totally disappeared – like so many vanished people have done in actuality. He feels sad for them but, in a few hours' time, millions upon millions will follow them – unless he helps prevent it. Even though he has adapted, and has won his battles, he just wishes he knew whether he'll survive it himself. There may be other adversaries to confront, still waiting in the wings.

I'm not that certain of everything. At least there's still some mystery.

Dr Jake Crux is complete. He has grown, he has evolved: telepathy as one aspect of his development, telekinesis another. He is confident of using them wisely. He is awed by the potential for mankind. It is boundless.

It was always to be our destiny.

Jake now also has a link to humanity's past, to Cro-Magnon Man and those paintings on the cave walls in France – something he has always striven for in his work. Thousands of years ago, before they settled down to a life of farming – before they invented writing – men, women and children roamed the planet, using the same skills he now possesses.

He knows that must have been a totally different lifestyle to how humanity has lived in the last few thousand years. First it would have been tribal, a group probably averaging no more than one hundred and fifty – and they would have lived their lives completely in step with nature. True, as they colonized the world, they left their impact – unintentionally driving some other species to extinction – but if their paranormal abilities put them way ahead of any competition, there were still other balances naturally in place. The world constantly evolves, and the hunter-gathering man was just the new predator, so the Earth would have adjusted to keep this upright ape in check.

It would have been a natural Eden.

Jake briefly grimaces. He had been uncomfortable making the religious connections, but reckons it isn't time for lies any more.

God could be anything . . . It could even be us. If the human race is to survive, then it will need to be honest with itself. It will have to deal with the truth about what it means to be alive.

Jake smiles, scanning the heath and, in the distance, the sea.

He has also found that, with these reacquired abilities there comes an inner peace – a fantastic affinity with everything about him.

Everyone as God . . . everyone touching the universe.

The scientist part of him wants to experiment immediately, to see how far his telepathic capabilities will stretch. Likewise, he wants to know over what distance he will be able to move things. And what the maximum mass of a movable object would be, if there is one.

But those questions can wait. He now has to help stop the entire world unconsciously, unwittingly, turning in on itself. And he has just been given the courage to attempt this – by the act of confronting his own demons.

Fighting those dragons has given him both a new confidence and belief in himself that are beyond anything he has ever supposed was possible.

He just wishes that his vague awareness of the future could be more precise. Then, of course, he'd know the outcome. Foreseeing *exactly* what will occur was probably not a skill completely developed by Stone Age man. Perhaps that was how nature balanced things up. Mankind may never have turned to farming if it had possessed total precognition.

He carries on with his cigar, waiting for just the right time.

UNITED STATES DEPARTMENT OF JUSTICE
FEDERAL BUREAU OF INVESTIGATION
London Office, Britain
RE: EISENCRICK INSTITUTE
Internal Report passed to Special Agents of the Bureau.

Interim progress analysis of PROF. E. BYFOOT's investigations at the EISENCRICK INSTITUTE.

BYFOOT has assisted in making recent improvements in SOUND ENERGY CONTROL (SEC) and developments of AUTO-SUGGESTION GAS WEAPONS (ASGW). The EISENCRICK INSTITUTE has long been at the forefront of developing modern CROWD CONTROL, providing valuable data on various methods of maintaining order. Their psychology department is renowned for propagating new techniques in propaganda, while their biology and genetic research department has significantly advanced the development of a new enzyme to be used in perfect cloning. It is this department which CIA sources indicate as being primarily involved in the development of the virus known as GEN-FORK. Such biological and genetic investigations performed by the EISENCRICK INSTITUTE are the prime reason for the private funding it receives from a source in the USA.

The arson attack committed by DR J. CRUX on his

laboratory not only destroyed his office and all its contents, but did substantial damage to the adjoining research areas. Using computer back-ups via internal links that DR CRUX was unaware of, in conjunction with material already assembled by PROF. BYFOOT, who had been covertly monitoring DR CRUX's experiment, the EISENCRICK INSTITUTE has for some months been undertaking similar and associated experimentation both with mice and with humans, with impressive results. Over the last week, Drs O. MERIDIAN and M. KRISTEN have clearly established that chosen subjects can be prompted to perform telepathic acts and minor feats of telekinesis. It appears there was a quantum leap in progress after the event known as THE NIGHT.

DR CRUX's own experiment with mice was being replicated in the adjoining laboratories, and records now show that these particular cloned mice attained a 'group consciousness' three days before the so-called 'NIGHT' actually occurred.

They, too, soon rapidly vanished.

INTERNET NEWS UPDATE by Janice Maclean

It's getting nasty out there. Riots have broken out all around the world, as scientists themselves are being seen as legitimate targets for protesters. At least a hundred protesters were killed or injured by the army when they attempted to infiltrate the mysterious Area 51 in Nevada – the USA's hush-hush establishment that every conspiracy theorist has become well aware of. Meanwhile, at the Cape Canaveral launching site for NASA's space programme, a large number of research buildings were severely damaged when protesters broke in to conduct an orgy of vandalism.

The President of the USA has declared a state of emergency and martial law has been imposed in seven American states. The National Guard has orders to shoot on sight anyone suspected of rioting. Major incidents of violence are also reported in France, Germany, China, Brazil, Australia, Japan, Egypt and Italy. The total death toll worldwide has been variously estimated between six thousand and fifteen thousand. Police have advised the public to keep calm, but this reporter has to ask: what will it take to stop this chaos?

Chapter Fifteen

UNITED STATES DEPARTMENT OF JUSTICE
FEDERAL BUREAU OF INVESTIGATION
Jacksonville Office
RE: PASCAL TOLUENE

After spending nearly an hour securing the family residence with extra guards, for the protection of his wife and three children, TOLUENE has spent the last thirty-six hours at his business headquarters in JACKSONVILLE. Senior executives of his companies have been recalled from their offices in SAN FRANCISCO, DETROIT and NEW YORK.

It is our conclusion, based on these increased activities, that whatever he has planned is about to be put into effect.

The onshore early evening air carries the smell of seaweed and fresh crab meat on the breeze, and I can see the silent gulls and terns that are fighting down near the surge – tormenting each other as they skilfully ride above the breaking brown-dirt waves, which toss onto the shingle desirable morsels of food. As the herring and black-headed gulls wait for any opportunity to snatch another's prize, the terns fly low and parallel to the surf, then angle upwards over the breakers, before dropping down to continue working the line – low-high, low-high, banking and gliding all in one go. Again and again these patrols of delicate birds – storm-grey and brilliant white – flirt along the beach, sometimes dipping their heads to nip something from the sea.

Above them the pale clouds have finally joined together to become one darker mass that looms in the sky like a vivid, silent ghost.

I have nestled myself into the lower tier of the huge pebble dune that sometimes protects the village from the encroaching waves, and I watch as Jenny sets a fire using twigs and dried moss gathered from the copse we walked through to get here. Sitting on the pebbles – fidgeting from one position to another, cross-legged one moment, then buried into the bank the next – I watch as her carefully stacked pyramid of driftwood sizzles alight. Occasionally, kingfisher-blue and salmon-pink sparks snap amongst the yellow and red flames, before joining the twirling column of oyster-grey smoke.

I'm far too agitated to relax. I've made sure that Maxnet keeps highlighting the reports it has sent me, and I wonder how Jake feels about the duplicity of his employers – who seem to have duped everyone.

I get up and make myself busy by wrapping tiny potatoes in aluminium foil and carefully sticking them into the fire's heart. It's probably too early – as the heat is not yet regular, but I'm hungry. As I lick my burnt fingers, Jenny lovingly spears oversized Lincolnshire sausages on bicycle spokes driven into the shingle, then aims them inwards towards the blaze.

As she concentrates, Jenny sticks out her tongue to one side, and frowns.

She's contemplating the future, thinking about where we are heading.

I look up at the sky. It's not going to be properly night for some time, but it is getting darker. There's a big storm coming.

Stars would be good right now: to have the infinite to contemplate.

I wonder how many other beings there are on other planets looking up to their alien heavens.

And I find myself imagining what war may be like on other planets, in other systems. Under a sky lit by one giant yellow star, accompanied by two bright dwarves that circle its equator, ripping solar flames from the surface, lies a desert plain of silicon, scarred by typhoons of ether and butane, where two alien armies battle it out, grappling with an opponent that seems to be identical. And as they destroy each other, do *they* wonder at the waste?

How often does life destroy itself?

The flames of our fire flicker and shimmer.

The universe leaps, and I am instantly afraid.

I have not yet won.

Click, click . . . *click*!

I look down on a village, from a slight rise. I know it has to be a place called Lidice. It is a summer evening; the houses sit in a shallow valley, surrounded by open fields and a few trees. It would be an idyllic vision if not for the German troop lorries marked with black crosses. I stand hidden behind a tree, some distance from the nearest cordon, wanting to run but knowing I have to witness what is about to take place. Small groups of women and children are being forced onto the lorries, and I see the men of the village being bullied over to the side of a barn. As the lorries pull away, with the odd keening of a child old enough to realize what is about to happen, the first bursts of gunfire drift in on the summer breeze. As the women in the trucks hear it, their wailing and screaming echo to each tat-tat-tat, tat-tat-tat.

I stand immobile in my ineffable sadness – forced to watch, helpless, as grim history unfolds. I know that any attempt at intervention would be useless.

And it is now too late anyhow, as the guns fall silent and the trucks pull away.

I watch the remaining soldiers move around the empty village streets. They laugh as one shoots a frantic dog tied to a gatepost, the rest of them passing a bottle between them – and I wonder to myself how *any* of us are supposed to win.

The sun rises higher.

I claw at the trunk of the tree in my frustration.

An hour passes. No man from Lidice remains alive; no woman or child remains to witness the conflagration. After the Nazis set Lidice ablaze, the flames leap and burst and flower and send waves of heat rolling across the fields, yet all I can feel is an intense cold – one that emanates from my heart.

The universe changes.

Click, click . . . *click*!

I am back.

I have just spent an hour in another universe and, once again, as always, no time has passed here in this one. But I have learnt something about consequences.

Jenny rests on her haunches, nodding her head.

354

She turns to look at me as if she's made up her mind to tell me something.

'I have a confession,' she says, looking down at the fire for a moment, and taking a deep breath. I keep my gaze away from the fire: I have seen too many flames, heard too many screams, to look into its heart at the moment.

'I'm being paid by Gareth's team,' she says.

This throws me.

'What for?' I ask.

She smiles. '*I'm* supposed to be the agent provocateur, here just to stir things up for you.'

I burst out laughing. 'You've been worrying about *that*?'

In my ear, Gareth starts to comment, but I ignore him.

Jenny frowns. 'I thought you'd be upset. It *was* a kind of betrayal.'

'Bollocks, it's nothing,' I say. 'Just part of the sideshow. I assumed it was Jake.'

'I also have another confession,' she says.

Jenny reaches over to the fire, removes from its spoke a sausage that is beginning to char, and stands up.

'Do you know I have German blood?' she asks.

I say nothing.

'My grandmother came from Hamburg.'

I find myself staring at the flames of the fire again – all salmon-pink and kingfisher-blue.

'My great-grandmother,' she continues, 'worked in a high-class brothel in Berlin in the late thirties, early forties . . . My grandmother was the child of one of her clients.'

I want to help Jenny, but I figure it is something she has to say for herself. She stares down at me, forcing me to look at her.

'It was Heydrich,' she says. 'Your Obergruppen-führer Reinhard Heydrich. My mother is convinced he was her grandfather. She's never come to terms with it.'

The Butcher of Prague – I realize now how we give monsters labels to make them seem removed from common humanity.

'Do you think Jake could tell me?' asks Jenny.

'What?' I ask.

'If it's in any way inherited?'

I start to reach out to her, but she backs away. I say quietly, 'Jenny, you're wrong.'

But before I can say any more, she turns and begins to run. Kicking up the shingle, she heads up towards the woods. I sit down to watch the flames of our fire, hoping that somewhere in its heart is an answer for me.

I try not to think of what lies ahead. If my shifts to alternate worlds continue, then, even though they have occurred slightly differently to how historical events actually unfolded, it is highly possible, as I have always known, that I will get killed. Toluene will then win. From my research, I know that the men who completed that mission of assassination all those years ago did not survive. They were caught hiding in the crypt of a church, betrayed by one of their own to the Gestapo. I myself just want to last long enough to finish what I have started with Pascal Toluene, and my efforts so far must surely have brought him to the attention of those who can stop him, even if I can't.

I suddenly feel very tired, so completely exhausted that—

'Scott?' Gareth's voice makes me jump.

'Yeah?' I rouse myself from sleep and rub my eyes.

'Scott, it's now just after midnight.'

'Whoopee.'

Yawning, I glance up at a black and starless sky. It seems to be moving, undulating. I look back down in disgust, repelled. The fire is now just a soft glow, the sausages shrivelled shadows, the potatoes glowing like embers.

'The results are in.'

I sit up, and push the CAMIC further into my ear.

'And?'

He pauses.

And?

'You're our doomsday winner.'

The fire crackles.

'Did you hear me, Scott?'

I think about what Sonat has promised to do if I won.

'Yeah,' I say. 'I heard you.'

He laughs. 'Prepare for the media rush. They'll by hunting you down.'

I reach out for a burst and cindered sausage and bite into it. Its charred remains are still ferociously hot.

I ignore the pain as it burns my lips.

In the beginning, when God created the universe, the Earth was forlorn and desolate.

Monday
Last Day

Chapter Sixteen

01.02

What Jenny doesn't realize is that my grandfather Roy Anderson was acquainted with both her grandmother and great-grandmother. He met them during the war. My grandfather also told me how he was certain that there is no Hell – at least, not of God's invention – but there *are* such places which man has constructed. For Sergeant Roy Anderson believed he himself had witnessed the absolute worst of what humanity is capable of. After parachuting onto that beach in Normandy, armed only with a knife instead of the usual rifle, he had got himself a gun from a young German soldier, killing him with his bare hands after the boy tried to ambush him coming off the beach. The German was only fifteen years old, or younger, and I figured Roy had been forced to either break the lad's neck, or strangle him. But a far more harrowing experiénce was helping to liberate a concentration camp. That was the incident that started off my own nightmare during The Night.

And that camp was where he had met Jenny's great-grandmother and her young daughter. It was the silence that got to him as he made his way warily through the main gate.

Seeing all those prisoners in their striped pyjama uniforms, his first startled reaction was to laugh, then he quickened his pace. Along past rows of low huts, past wire fences strewn with corpses, until he came to a haystack of broken sticks that were not broken sticks at all. He called out to God, then began to cry.

And as he stood there, unsteadily, with the last vestiges of his faith deserting him, an emaciated woman shuffled up and embraced him.

'Thank you,' she whispered, in English.

He stared at that frail woman, at the child hovering beside her, saw in the little girl's eyes the absolute confusion and pain he felt himself.

Sometime after he had taken personal charge of getting this fragile couple proper attention, in their conversations the woman revealed something inside of her that kept the door slightly open for my grandfather to believe that the good in man can eventually conquer the evil.

And she told him her story, without shame, without embellishment. And comforted *him*.

She had originally come from a good family, had a good education, but her father was doing business with the Jews and his wealth was eventually confiscated. To survive financially, she ended up becoming a showgirl – enduring a basic wage in a Berlin nightclub in the late thirties, till she was forced to take work in a high-class brothel. It was there she had the honour of 'entertaining' the Nazi elite. And it was there she caught the eye of Heydrich, and so began a long-term, abusive association. She would not tell my grandfather exactly what Heydrich had done to her, but was convinced that he was the father of her child.

When the 'Butcher' was later assassinated in Prague, the recriminations were spreading far and wide, and to avoid any possible involvement, she returned to her native Hamburg.

She thought she and her child were safe – till the night of the firestorm.

As the inferno screamed its song of destruction, a terrible wind was brought into existence. Everything unsecured became airborne, even trees were uprooted. Flames soared to the heavens or roared along the streets, melting the tarmac.

As she struggled to get to the river, still desperately clutching her young child, a young man had suddenly reached out and grabbed hold of her. He had secured himself to a lamp post with his belt, and clasped her arm, pulling them both close to him. And for a long time they clung there, watching others being sucked into the surrounding inferno. If it had not been for his intervention, she and her child would have surely perished, too.

Ever since The Night, I have sensed that the young man who saved them was me. The man clasping the lamp post, rescuing the woman and child, was somehow me. I *have* affected the past – or at least been involved in it.

And, incredibly, I was also above them – saving them in another way.

That certainty comes from those of Eric's memories that I have experienced first-hand.

Once again, I smell the faint whiff of oil, grease,

fuel and human sweat. Ahead of me is a fake dawn that moves and pulses and grows. Just ahead, P-Popsy begins her run.

'Opening the bomb-bay doors,' I say, and I flick the switches.

The plane begins to buck even more violently. A flame, bigger than the rest, surges up and temporarily engulfs the aircraft in front.

A night-fighter shoots.

'She's hit, Skip,' says a voice. 'Popsy's taken one.'

A trail of flame is belching from the near-side port engine of the Stirling.

More flames leap up at me from below. I am shaken as my plane jolts and shudders in the turbulence. Behind me, Henry swears. I glance over to the bomb jettison switch.

'I'll let them go here, Skip?' says the bomb-aimer.

I don't know why, but I call out. 'Charlie! Hold it! Hold it!'

We fall silent, as the plane travels on. Through the engines' beat, I believe I can hear the crew silently asking themselves why I have chosen to override the bomb-aimer's decision.

I wait another moment. And another.

'Okay, Charlie, do it now,' I order.

The plane suddenly jerks upwards, becomes lighter, easier on both hands and feet. We gain height.

'Bombs gone,' I hear in my headphones.

I quickly flick the switch for the bomb-bay doors and get the plane into a nice steep bank to port. It feels a little heavy and I wonder if we've actually dropped all our bomb-load – it's happened before when the release mechanism gets stuck on some of them. I really hope not. I glance around again and peer over the leading edge of the starboard wing, through the gap between the engines. The plane ahead is now totally enveloped in flames from its engine fire, so that the only bits discernible are the nose and the wingtips. I see two men emerge and tumble into the vortex of fire below.

'What a choice,' I murmur to myself.

A voice comes in my ears. It's Charlie.

'Skip, it's getting a bit warm up here.'

'Quit your belly-aching,' I say. 'This heat's nothing.'

The aircraft ahead explodes, and the two falling men turn into flailing sparks.

I straighten up our plane. We have silence – no one has anything to say. Two or three more seconds and it could have been us. P-Popsy's luck ran out, but we still have ours.

'Let's go home,' I say, finally.

'That would be nice,' says someone, I don't know who.

Somehow, therefore, in some crazy, weird twist of the world and history and the universe, I caused my grandfather, RAF bomber-pilot Eric Edwards, to delay dropping his bombs. Bombs that would have surely fallen directly on a woman and child who were currently being saved by a man tied to a lamp post.

A man that was me.

Jake is right: the universe is being shifted, being radically changed. Many different versions of it are all around us, and we slip from one to another whenever we make choices, whenever we make decisions about a course of action. Somehow, I've got involved in places where these versions have touched, where there's been some interaction.

But did the fact that I caused that momentary delay in releasing the bombs cause the problems the crew subsequently suffered on the flight home?

It was only some time later, when returning to the English coast, that they caught a last bit of flak that damaged one undercarriage assembly, and Eric had his suspicions confirmed that they hadn't released their full complement of bombs. He was forced to make for the emergency landing strip at Woodbridge – five times normal width and thus providing plenty of scope for manoeuvre. All the while he kept frantically trying to dislodge the remaining bomb-load by throwing the aircraft around as violently as he dared. If he hadn't succeeded in this, just as they reached the coast – the bombs falling harmlessly into the water without exploding – they would all have had to bail out before reaching the base. Not an option to take lightly, but better than crash-landing with bombs still on board.

All these images are where my phobia of military places came from. A fear born of a premonition of what I would experience as an adult – in my nightmares. My life has been a full circle of interlocking universes.

The air shimmers, begins to judder as reality starts to snap away into something else. And with absolute certainty, I know this will be my last universe-shift. It must now reach a conclusion – one way or the other.

But I am ready.

Click, click . . . *click*!

And I look around in horror.

How can I ever win here?

Apart from the traitor who gave them up to the Gestapo, everyone else involved in the operation died in this place.

It is dank and wet. I am standing in a metre of swirling water, my legs numb with cold. The air is fogged with gun-smoke – the stench of it makes me choke. I slowly turn to the other three men with me – the black-haired man smiles back at me. They are my compatriots who formed the nucleus of Operation Anthropoid, and now we are all hiding in the depths of the Karel Boromejsky Church in Prague. That sound of running on the marble floor above us is the Nazis regrouping to attack us, and kill us. The rising water is gushing in from outside via a fire-hose rammed into a ventilation slot above our heads. Floating in it, at the bottom of the steps leading down to the crypt, are the corpses of two German soldiers – one with no face remaining.

More footsteps, more shouting.

There is no other conclusion but that this is the endgame to Anthropoid. It will all soon be over. All we can do is wait.

Over the sound of the water spurting through from the ventilation shaft, there comes a final yell as someone urges us to give ourselves up. The voice is not German but Czech, and one of my companions wades over closer to the entrance and shouts back, 'Fuck off, traitor!'

Except for the gushing of water, there follows silence. It is only a pause, till an order is bellowed. Then more shouting, but from different sources. I realize these are the shouts that men make to overcome their fear. Boots slap on the floor, echoing as they enter the crypt at the top of the stairs. Grenades spin out from the blackness and splash into the surrounding water. We duck, covering our faces, as the water explodes. Before the spray has time to settle, three German soldiers are charging down the steps, firing wildly. We raise our own Sten guns and let loose two short bursts each. The Germans stumble, cease firing, and collapse into the water. One is not yet dead, but is unable to pull himself back up to safety, so we watch him drown.

I check the magazine of my Sten; and find it is empty. As I look around at my companions, everyone is shaking his head. One by one, we drop our submachine guns into the rising water.

Consequences, consequences.

I have eliminated SS Obergruppenführer Reinhard Heydrich, and the Nazis have started to respond – and will respond further. A moral grotesque had been removed, but at a great cost. Those citizens who have hidden or helped the paratroopers of the Czech Brigade have been betrayed by others and are now dead – mostly tortured in obscene ways beforehand. Lidice has been obliterated, with the men of the village shot and buried in one of the pitiful mass graves that are fast littering Europe. Their women and children have been transported to the death camps, soon to be joined by many others as part of the Nazi reprisals for Heydrich's assassination. There will eventually be over three thousand deaths in consequence of the Nazi reaction to Operation Anthropoid.

As I stand in the water, I sense the blood of all those people on my hands. Like me, the others are now standing with their Colt automatics cocked, ready to fire. I try to answer the awful question that keeps whispering softly in my head: *Was it worth it?* But who knows for sure what the future might hold? Where would we be if Heydrich had survived to take Hitler's place?

And then I have the answer.

We, all the men in that crypt, smile at each other and together raise our guns to our heads.

It is an odd way to win a fight: committing suicide. But at least it takes away any satisfaction from the soldiers waiting above us. And any possibility of us being forced into betraying others.

As I squeeze the trigger of my Colt, I realize that I love these men, and that I feel proud.

The world shimmers. Reality shifts.

Click, click . . . *click*!

I find myself shaking at being still alive. I have undergone the ultimate ordeal in comradeship and survived.

I exhale in sheer relief. I know what each of those men was thinking: that the sacrifice to remove that monster was worth it. And following that thought is an instant realization that *all* who kill themselves for a cause must find a pure justification in some way. Even suicide bombers? The problem arises when you try to define who is evil and therefore needs to be removed to make the lives of others better. Comradeship is empowering – in both a good and bad way. Some things are worth fighting for. Some things are worth dying for.

Now I know for sure that I will somehow this day

meet Pascal Toluene, and am prepared to make that ultimate sacrifice.

I'll find a way to remove him from this world, even if it means I have to escort him on that lonely journey we all eventually have to make.

An image of Jenny comes to me suddenly, and I find myself imagining I can physically reach out and touch her. I don't know if these thoughts are about love, or are a surrogate lust for someone I can no longer attain, or even if they're just from a need for companionship.

I've been afraid of commitment: that's what *my* universe-shifts were all about. But that's what I've resolved. They've helped me to define myself. To make myself realize that I am stronger with others. And that we all have moral options. Heydrich was, in my mind, the ultimate in evil – it could never have been Jake, as I imagined towards the end of my universe-shifts. It is what Jake *believes* in that frightened me. That's why Jake occasionally replaced Heydrich, since these shifts were also about confronting fear.

I can fight alongside him now. And that's something we're all about to do.

I just hope I'm not too late.

UNITED STATES DEPARTMENT OF JUSTICE
FEDERAL BUREAU OF INVESTIGATION
New England Office
RE: SCOTT ANDERSON

FBI Text Intercept

I am getting near to SCOTT ANDERSON. He will be removed soon. At first light.

03.12

'Jake?'

I hear Jenny in my head. She is somewhere close by to where I am sitting on Dunwich beach. Her voice drowns out the building chorus of other voices I can hear.

Jake answers. 'Yes?'

'It's going to happen soon, isn't it?'

'Yes.'

'Jake, we must try to reach as many people as possible.'

'Scott?'

'Yes, Jake . . . I can hear you.'

'Let's meet.'

'Okay. Gareth says that the media are coming here in force.'

'That's good. So let's do it.'

I feel an immense shiver run down my back.

The New World beckons. But I am prepared to let it happen without me.

I must now take on Toluene.

Chapter Seventeen

INTERNET NEWS UPDATE by Janice Maclean
It's now official. As from 04.00 this morning, the government has imposed martial law. With at least one hundred and fifty people killed in overnight clashes with the police in London alone, and casualties in Manchester and Liverpool combined reaching a similar number of fatalities, it became inevitable that such action would be necessary. There are as yet unconfirmed reports of – apparently co-ordinated – explosions at scientific establishments around Britain, including the Sellafield reprocessing plant in Cumbria. There is now an exclusion zone of half a mile around all British nuclear facilities, and any intruders perceived to be involved in terrorist activities will be shot on sight.

Other essential installations and institutions will be guarded in a similar fashion. It is expected that later today the Home Secretary will announce restrictions on travel within the country, while all ports and airports will be closed by this evening. Trading on the stock exchange has meanwhile been suspended.

The Internet service providers have been instructed to close down all access to Maxnet links, while Unit-C has been ordered to recall all personal CAMICs.

Severe restrictions are being placed on the media, as all terrestrial television channels are to be subjected to centralized control and censorship, with satellite companies expected to follow shortly. It has been announced that the Prime Minister will address the nation at eleven o'clock this morning.

This is Janice Maclean wishing everyone good luck.

Marvel Speer looks over to the horizon and then glances at his watch. It will soon be dawn, and what it will bring in terms of weather, he has no idea, but he is certain that his boss's wishes will be fulfilled. Standing behind his hatchback in the car park, he studies the other vehicles pulling up – some of them are vans with aerials attached to their roofs. Speer smiles to himself. Toluene has organized things perfectly, as usual. Some of the TV companies have dispatched units to cover the announcement of Scott Anderson's win; others want more of Dr Crux and his views; but a good proportion have been 'instructed' simply to cover the result. Toluene wants Anderson's death to be extremely public.

Marvel Speer looks down to the beach and decides that the rows of wooden groynes reaching out into the sea every few metres along the shore will give excellent cover.

He turns away and reaches into the back of the small car to retrieve a long canvas bag.

04.52

Though it is now dawn, it's hard to tell, for the clouds are heavy and dark, flecked with tinges of yellow and purple. They even look tropical, as though a monsoon is gathering to transform the sky into a huge whirling torrent of rain. And the wind is building powerfully: it has the smell of smoke and seaweed in it. It makes me long for the previous humidity instead. The incoming waves roll in higher and more aggressively with each successive surge. They crash against the shore with a fierce rush and thump, so I half expect water-spouts to rise from their crests and swirl away with the foam.

Further back from the coast can be heard shouts from the crowds of protesters. Someone with a megaphone is telling them that they are breaking the law, that they have to move on. There is a loud echoing jeer in response. As the hubbub dies down, another voice takes over the megaphone to announce that martial law is now in effect, that the army is arriving shortly, and that the crowd must go home or get shot. The jeers redouble, along with shouts of anger. This tide of noise, and the fear underlying it, causes a great sense of foreboding in me – like that I felt when watching the destruction of Lidice.

They will shoot. I know it.

As the crowds begin to mass together, the lights in and around the complex are suddenly turned off so the reactor and its auxiliaries become dark silhouettes in the dawn's bleakness. Largewater is instantly turned into a Neo-Gothic icon. The protesters momentarily fall silent, then raise their voices with even greater intensity.

I watch the obscure shapes of both protesters and police moving around, like a nest of black ants against that ominous backdrop, and I wonder how many will survive through the next few hours.

As Jake approaches him from behind, he sees Scott visibly stiffen and supposes he has become subconsciously aware of Jake's presence.

All night long he has been dodging the police, while Jenny returned home and has been online most of the night – passing on Jake's urgent message about what needs to be done.

As he reaches Scott, Jake decides not to tell him about what Jenny has discovered from inspecting the records of the contest Scott has just won. It seems two close friends from his schooldays have already vanished, and there may have been others.

I hear a noise behind me, and I turn around to find Jake approaching. I'm relieved till I notice his eyes. Then I assume mine must be refracting the light in the same way now.

'Morning,' I say. 'Hey, wait there a minute.' And I reach up, intending to remove my CAMIC.

'That's okay.' Jake holds up a hand. 'I think I'll have enough time. It seems the authorities now have more to worry about, even though they've been chasing me most of the night. And I've just been listening to Jenny's Landrover radio.' Jake grimaces. 'There's been a massacre in Tokyo . . . and an explosion causing meltdown at an American power plant in New Mexico. Just before all the news reports were replaced by non-stop music, they read out a list of countries from which no news at all has been heard for several hours now.'

'Music?'

'Every station, and particularly Mozart. At least

someone has had the wit not to transmit the Requiem Mass.'

I'm just about to reply with a grim joke of my own, when we hear a woman's voice call out. 'Scott!'

Jake and I both turn and, through the dim, eerie light, we see a woman running towards us, waving. I assume she is a reporter, because a cameraman and a sound engineer, burdened with equipment, are trying to keep pace with her.

'Scott!' she yells again – even though it's obvious we've spotted her.

Jake raises his eyebrows. 'Seems like you're on,' he says.

'Let's do it,' I say.

I mustn't let myself get distracted.

Jake comes to stand by my side, and he puts a hand on my shoulder. 'Jenny has arranged for as many TV people to turn up as she could manage,' he explains. 'Or, anyway, as many as are prepared to challenge the government's D-notice.'

I turn my head towards him. 'Where is she?'

'She wanted to be with her parents.'

'That's good,' I nod.

We walk the last few steps to the top of the bluff, and wait there for the TV crew to join us. As the three of them reach us, Jake points over to the car park, where already other TV vans are disgorging similar groups to the one whose reporter is now jabbing her microphone at us. Soon at least four other teams of reporters and technicians are hurrying towards us.

The first reporter and her film crew finally get themselves together. She moves straight at me, shakes my hand, then glances over to her cameraman, who nods. She turns back to me.

'Scott Anderson,' she begins, taking a half-turn to the camera and adopting a sudden smile. 'You're the contest *winner*! So how do you feel?'

'Oh, terrific,' I say flatly. 'Just terrific.'

'Would you like to say a few words now to all our viewers who e-voted for you?' And then I hear her real thoughts. *'That's okay, young man, I've got you.'*

She's lying. The woman's an impostor.

She is not from a TV company at all.

A glimmer of fear appears in her eyes as comprehension dawns that I'm already on to her. She glances nervously over her shoulder at her team of two, then turns back to me. Before she can say more, the other crews are surrounding us. As I try to keep an eye on her, I have the distinct sensation of being stalked.

There are soon about twelve film crews and another dozen paparazzi photographers all trying to get my attention. Not only am I assailed with questions, but my head is getting filled with the thoughts that are currently in theirs. It is a cacophony of abstract ideas, and I wince before I finally manage to reduce the mental intrusion of their onslaught. I realize, with relief, that it's possible to control it. Meanwhile I keep trying to bring Jake to everyone's attention – even though some of the film crews are confused enough to think that I *am* Jake. As I find myself shouting to get heard, my voice is drowned out by sudden screaming.

All of us up on the bluff fall silent and, as one, look down towards the crowd of protesters. The change in the situation below has been sudden and drastic.

Whilst the media have been vying with each other to secure their stories from me and Jake, the army has arrived in force, using the lack of light to sneak in without being seen. From up here I can't believe the sight – apart from their troop lorries, they are bringing in three light tanks. As the TV crews immediately switch their attention to what is happening below, I use the respite to scan their thoughts individually to discover who else might be working for Pascal Toluene. All I get is a mishmash, and then we hear further screams.

'What's happening?' I ask the cameraman standing nearest to me.

Without taking his eye from his long-distance lens, he replies. 'The army are up to something bloody weird down there.'

A paparazzo joins in with a running commentary, the motor-drive of his camera racing.

'They've brought in some sort of specialized gear,' he observes, 'and those poor bastards are falling like flies. Looks like they're all holding the sides of their heads . . . Hey! What the fuck is *that*?'

Jake comes and stands closer beside me again.

'Professor Byfoot's down there,' he remarks. 'From the Institute.'

I myself can hardly make out anything in the darkness.

'*You've* got good eyesight,' I say, turning my head to face him.

One side of his mouth turns up sardonically as he taps the side of his head.

'Well, in that case, don't *use* your eyes.'

I suddenly understand what he is saying. And

quieten my thoughts. There is a world of opportunity ahead of us: ways in which we can explore, ways in which we can turn things to our advantage – all we have to do is use our minds. I have a single instant of fear at what I am about to attempt . . . and then I remember how I once just stood on the top diving-board of a swimming pool, looking down at the water.

This is nothing . . . I must get used to this.

So I concentrate. I *think* about being nearer, about getting a clearer view.

And then I am there – in spirit, if not in body. But my vision of the world has become smeared in the rush. The speed at which it has happened is startling.

Fuck.

I find I am 'walking' amongst the hundreds of prone bodies that writhe on the ground. As I look over to another spot, reality melts again and I am instantly transported there – both landscape and images slid-ing and stretching at fantastic speed. Concentrating again, I examine the fallen people more closely. They are in obvious pain, and I quickly move away before the killer-sound affects me. To one side are assembled a number of army vehicles with parabolic dishes mounted on their roofs. By one of them stands a middle-aged woman in a camouflage jacket several sizes too big for her. She is wearing a CAMIC and appears to be giving a running commentary.

'Byfoot,' mutters Jake.

It is a shock to realize that I am still aware of what is happening where I physically exist – the place where my body is. I 'come back', melting intervening space with the speed of my travel, and return to within myself, and look over at Jake.

It's incredible . . . mental transportation?

He nods.

I recover my breath, then remember the activities below us.

'What are they doing?' I ask him aloud.

'Just what it looks like,' Jake explains. 'They're using something that the Institute must have dreamed up. It's crowd control . . . except they're killing them.'

He turns and gives me his familiar micro-smile. I frown. Then I hear him in my head.

'Let's see what we can really *do, shall we?'*

And I understand: he's suggesting we use the new powers we have at our disposal to disrupt the situation.

I concentrate again. Reality smears as I hurtle down towards them.

I am down amongst them once more. I do not pause, but head to the nearest army vehicle. Inspect one of the antennae. Then get closer. Find wires running from the back of the parabolic dish. Follow them back down and into the rear of the small truck. Go into the unit they are attached to. Go inside the box. See all the electronic components and . . . imagine them on fire. I imagine them blowing up and showering the operator with bits and pieces.

'Shit!' shouts a photographer standing near Jake and myself. 'Look!'

I return from my mental flight of destruction, and witness the results of my actions.

One after another, every army lorry has men jumping from the rear, escaping as the instruments inside spontaneously ignite. To regain control an officer shouts orders, but is ignored. Lying on the ground, those civilians who are still alive remove their hands from their ears and gradually unstiffen their postures.

'There y'all go,' drawls Jake, addressing the media. 'Will that do for you?'

For a moment it is all quiet, then everyone starts clamouring questions, as the cameras dither between the action down below and following what Jake has to say. I move aside, he nods to me, and I nod back. We are now working as a team. But . . . now it is all up to him, as he holds the undivided attention of the media.

As Jake gathers his thoughts, he wishes it were some time in the future: the future he once imagined having with a woman whose face he can't remember. He sees himself travelling around Australia, with someone Maxnet's records suggest was called TC.

Jake fervently wishes that he had more time, being painfully aware that the world hangs on a precipice overlooking a vortex of unknown dimensions and that people are beginning to fall over it.

Our group-mind is forming, amalgamating . . . yet it's still distorted.

A drip of water splashes on my forehead. Before I even register it as rain, a bolt of lightning streaks above my head and then, almost simultaneously, a thunderclap explodes. More rain slams down onto me in a sudden deluge. As separate bolts of lightning fight for attention in the sky, several ferocious cracks of thunder send a primeval fear running through me. A few seconds later and I am totally soaked.

The camera crews bunch together, hastily covering

their equipment, while Jake seems to stand even taller as he starts to address them.

Wiping the rain from my eyes, I brace myself.

Marvel Speer maintains a crouching position beside the support post of the groyne. His left knee nudges the wet timber while his right foot is thrust firmly into the shingle. The rain trickles into his boot, but he ignores it. The stock of the rifle rests hard against his right shoulder, and he cradles the breech in his palm, his fingers curled up against the wet metal of the barrel. The fingers of his other hand hover near the trigger-guard. With part of his left shoulder shoved against the wooden post, his elbow pushing down against the top of the groyne, he has established as stable a firing position as if he had a tripod. He peers through the telescopic sight at the man standing on the bluff. And eases off the safety. And slides his index finger towards the trigger.

Marvel Speer feels comfortable. He feels the perfect hunter.

That shithead scientist was right. It's good to win.

Through the rain, increasing by the second, he watches as the man on the bluff gesticulates to the cameras. He takes aim at the centre of the man's bald head. Marvel Speer takes a slow breath, and holds it.

He begins to squeeze the trigger. And realizes something is wrong.

He pans the telescopic sight to the target's left, along past the reporters. Another face flashes into his line of sight – this one a bit nearer to him, one much clearer – and Marvel Speer brings his rifle back to bear on it.

Staring at him, his face also awash with rain, is his proper target: Scott Anderson.

That was fucking lucky.

Speer had nearly made a mistake, but his sharp instincts have saved him from the error. As he takes another slow breath and holds it, and begins to take up the slack in the trigger, he finds himself thinking about the primitive skills that Dr Jake Crux has been going on about. What if he could succeed in killing people just by using the power of his mind? With this thought he is suddenly aware of a vague feeling of something being terribly wrong.

He is right, because they are the last thoughts he will ever have.

I stare down at one of the groynes. Even though the rain blurs his shape, my sixth-sense abilities know that there is a man partially behind it with a gun. It is aimed straight at me. He is the one sent by Pascal Toluene.

I stare at him, wanting to scream out my anger.

I sense him begin to squeeze the trigger. And a solution jumps into my head. Knowledge of a defence that is available to me, one that gives me pleasure that is almost child-like.

I know something you don't.

From my exposed position on the bluff, I smile down at him.

I sense him frowning.

I slowly turn my gaze to his left, ten metres further up the beach.

He hesitates then follows my gaze.

I look down at a spot on the shingle. I stare down

at what is buried there – at what has been buried there for so many years.

It is a large World War II bomb, one from the tricky load my grandfather Eric finally managed to jettison over the coast. It has been there, covered by shingle, ever since.

I smile, because using this is so beautiful. My grandfather went to war to fight the Nazis, and I'm about to use a piece of his original ordnance to annihilate one of Toluene's henchmen.

The assassin frowns. He's beginning to sense what I know.

I visualize the rusted detonator on the nose cone, and I see how it can be made to function. I imagine hitting it as hard as I can, with the largest sledgehammer that I can swing. I put all my anger into the effort.

I make mental contact with the detonator. The result is staggering.

Before me, a dome of vivid white appears, grows and, as rapidly as it began, fades into transparency.

A brief pause. Then comes the rabbit-punch of the shock wave, just like I experienced in my nightmare last month – a fast-moving momentum of energy that shakes the ground beneath me.

Along with the torrential rain, we are now hit with pebbles and splinters of wood. The reporters scream or cower. Lightning flashes across the sky again as the last few pebbles and bits of shrapnel fall at our feet.

I feel no guilt.

Jake looks at me questioningly.

'Go on!' I yell at him, through the rain, with a fierce resolve matching the violence of the storm. 'Tell them!'

Lightning flashes, again and again. The thunder bellows.

And I recognize the sight and sound of it all: it is from my nightmare. But instead of involving flames and a dreadful heat, it is a deluge of tremendous intensity whipped along by a vicious hurricane-force wind. That earlier nightmare was obviously a preparation for this intense moment of crisis we are all about to experience. I find myself anticipating each bolt of lightning, each shattering thunderclap – I have been here before . . . in another nightmare.

'Go *on*!' I shout.

Jake nods, then nods again. Like the others, he is still reeling from the blast down on the beach, but the strength of Scott's passion galvanizes him.

'This is it!' he shouts, gesturing to the sky. 'This is Armageddon!'

He ignores the fear his certainty generates in the reporters' eyes.

'This is what every prophet who ever lived has predicted! Doomsday! This is the eschatology driving every theology! The prophets, the mystics, were warning us all of today! But their message has been twisted through the course of history. Those who originally heard the Messiahs, the prophets, *they* knew; it's just been distorted with the retelling. Man was once in tune with nature, with the universe, but with each leap forward in technology we gradually lost that affinity. In our selfishness, we became violent towards one another. We've all become angry!'

He turns slowly and fixes everyone with a stare from some cosmic void.

'At the end of this very day, you'll only still be here if you understand what I'm now saying to you.'

I look around, and most of his audience seem terrified. As the storm still continues to multiply, I begin to hear another sound – which I recognize as one I've heard before. Somewhere in my head I feel the beginning of a slight pain, while in my ears is the dull whisper of a crowd that ebbs and flows, rises and falls – a huge crowd of people talking to themselves a long, long way from me. They could be chanting, could be arguing, but I can't tell. There could be thousands, there could be millions and I want to reach out and physically catch what they're saying.

'It's gathering strength,' yells Jake. 'The human race is approaching a transitional cusp! We'll now either wipe ourselves out in a carnage of non-existence, or we'll move on . . . by moving back!'

He looks around at them all, feeling his face totally contorted. Scott seizes his attention with a steady gaze.

'To all of you out there who have already succeeded,' Jake continues, 'you have to help the rest of humanity! Help the person nearest to you! Help them fight our selfish unconscious group-mind hatred! Then persuade *them* to help others! And pass your knowledge on! Just pass it on!'

The volume of chanting in my head increases until it begins to change into a scream I have heard before. This is the sound that accompanied the Hamburg firestorm. It is a sound that has haunted humanity all through its supposedly civilized existence. It is our unconscious guilt at waging war.

A camera falls to the ground. The female reporter standing nearest to it glances down at it, then back up at Jake and me, her eyes wide open.

The cameraman who carried it must have fallen victim to his own personal challenge.

'Now!' bellows Jake. '*Nowwww!*'

As the pain in the side of my head intensifies, I make a decision.

It concerns Pascal Toluene . . . and Heydrich . . . and the War.

It is cold excitement: this moment is what my life has been intended for.

I thoroughly hate the man that Pascal Toluene is, I hate what he represents. I hate him so much that I know I can take responsibility for my actions without guilt and without remorse. After killing Heydrich, I know I am capable of destroying such a man.

But I hope I am not too late.

I shall fight him in *his* mental battle, even if it means the end for me myself.

I focus, I concentrate. I am Joe Jnr climbing into *Zootsuit Black*. All those years of competing in the decathlon have provided me with an edge, a pragmatism beyond simply lashing out.

As I did in my nightmare, mentally I rise and travel through the air. The ground appears laid out below me, as I begin to move upwards through the raging storm. But all in my mind, all in my own reality. Lightning spikes all around me, rain blinds me, but I accelerate towards my fate. The ground below smears and elongates. I rush over the land, speed across the ocean, hurtling towards America and Jacksonville. I think back to the preparation that went into the assassination of Heydrich; I recall pulling the trigger of my Sten gun, finding it jammed and how desperately angry I was with myself for failing; I think of throwing the bomb that did inflict those fatal wounds on that bastard. Thereby I can justify myself. I streak down past the Florida coastline, towards the offices of Pascal Toluene, and then suddenly I am there.

I am with *him*.

Pascal Toluene is on the telephone, giving the authorization to initiate his devastating plan. He pauses as he senses something amiss.

I slide into his mind.

I take pleasure in his momentary panic as he tries to perceive what exactly is wrong.

He has not yet won *his* own battle in his universe-shift, but his sixth sense does warn him that something dangerous is about to happen to him.

It is too late.

We confront each other at a distance of about a metre. A void of nothingness surrounds us – it is now just Pascal Toluene and I. It seems we are enclosed in a vortex of slowly rotating fog: a semi-opaque mist that is brightly illuminated from behind in all directions. And there is a peculiar smell to it of must, decay, sulphur and ash. We could easily be in the smoke of warfare.

I can see deep into his eyes. They are the exact same eyes that stared at me at Wannsee – when Heydrich came for me as I stood at the door. They are the same eyes that challenged me as Heydrich reached for his gun in Prague. The same eyes as in the hospital, on his deathbed. The very same.

Pascal shakes off his confusion. 'Mister Anderson?' he says.

'Toluene.'

He smiles. I don't react, and the smile fades. I can see that, for the first time in a long while, Pascal Toluene knows he is facing a real threat. He knows he is confronting a true adversary.

And I know I am, too.

Pascal Toluene may be in his late fifties, but he still looks very fit and strong. He also has his battle experience from the Vietnam War to rely on. But I cannot let him win.

He thinks the same about me.

We stand before each other, like two samurai in a purgatory of nothingness, as one of us composes himself, once again, to do what humans find most difficult to do face to face – however many Hitlers, Heydrichs, Pol Pots or Toluenes may try to convince the rest of us otherwise – that is, to kill another human being.

As I kick out at him suddenly, he jumps back and produces a flick-knife. I'm unprepared for this; an advantage that I didn't count on. He crouches down, his left hand out to protect himself from any similar lunges from me, while his right hand, holding the knife, is down at his side and held back in reserve. He clearly knows how to use a knife.

I have to distract him for an instant, so I take two quick steps to my right.

He follows me – left hand still stretched out, ready to parry any blows.

I change my stance. I begin bouncing on my toes as though about to start a race.

As soon as I notice his slight frown, I move in, aiming a kick to his knee.

But he is alert to the danger, and he steps in closer towards me. I'm nearly thrown off-balance trying to adjust. His left hand drops to deflect my kick, and his right arm jerks out, just as my foot connects with his knee, and the blade of the knife makes electrifying contact with my stomach. I gasp and grunt at the pain of it, as he pulls the knife out and goes to stab me again. I jab my fingers straight into his eyes. I chop at his throat. He staggers back. I kick at a leg and he falls over, dropping the knife. I go to stamp on his face.

And I stop.

As Toluene looks up at me, his anger flashing as a cold hatred, I conceive the most original idea for a punishment that I could ever think of.

And, from his changing expression, I get the impression he doesn't like my smile of triumph.

Before he can react, I fall onto him and flip him over onto his front. I thrust a knee into his lower spine, lean forward and get my left arm around his throat, the hand reaching across to clasp my upper right arm. I ignore the sharp reaction in my gut and grip his jaw firmly with my right hand. He tenses and becomes very still beneath me: Toluene realizes I am now in a position to snap his neck.

He still manages a few words. 'You can't do it,' he grunts.

I whisper in his ear. 'I don't do dares.'

And I give his head a little twist.

'You'll bleed to death first,' he grunts.

I lean in even closer.

'That may be, but you'll be there before me.'

I lean closer still, till my lips touch his ear.

'I have a plan for you.'

I sense Toluene stiffen even more.

It is a wicked plan, and it came to me when I realized how identical his eyes were with Heydrich's.

I force all my new-found powers to become pure energy. Toluene begins to shake as I focus all my passion into the effort.

I'll do this . . . even if it kills me, too.

And then I cause Pascal Toluene to fade, to dissolve, shifting out of the universe we are currently in. Unleashing all the vehemence I can, I take him, cast him from the void we inhabit, back into history. This monster will not live in the present any more. I force the life essence that is Pascal Toluene – now screaming and struggling – back into another past, back into another person. One where I know the outcome. That will be a far better punishment than killing him here and now.

I take Pascal Toluene and coerce him into the entity that was Reinhard Heydrich, at a certain moment in time.

I take the soul, the *spirit* of Toluene, the creator and leader of Sonat, and project him into the body of Reinhard Heydrich, just as the future Butcher of Prague was shot down, in his fighter-plane flying over Russia in 1941. Instead of dying that day, Heydrich now lives. I exult my sense of pleasure into his ears as he wrestles with the controls of the aircraft. Now Pascal Toluene will live the last few months of his life inside the body of Reinhard Heydrich, knowing that it will be *me* coming for him, that it will be *me* throwing the bomb that kills him and sends him to hell. This will be a perfect torture – a natural justice for his crimes. Pascal Toluene will live only in the past where, whatever horrors he may commit as he tries to alter history, he *knows* in advance that he has an appointment with me on a Prague street corner, that his death will be painful and slow – not the quick and clean release of a plane crash as Heydrich's death undoubtedly would have been if I hadn't intervened.

It is done.

Somewhere in the past, the man that was Heydrich has been reborn with the personality that is Pascal Toluene. Living as Reinhard Heydrich, Toluene will still commit heinous deeds, many atrocious crimes. But history will stay the same, since you cannot change it, only influence it so that it still turns out the way the history books declare it happened. Heydrich was always present at Wannsee, of course, and if it had not been him orchestrating the Holocaust, someone else would have stepped in to do so. But *I* will kill Heydrich in the streets of Prague and therefore *I* will kill Pascal Toluene. He will never be able to murder the tens of millions that he has been targeting in *this* world. This time of mine will now become safe from him. Pascal Toluene has been consigned to the dusty records of history.

The universe has shifted.

UNITED STATES DEPARTMENT OF JUSTICE
FEDERAL BUREAU OF INVESTIGATION
New England Office
RE: ICELAND

The ICELANDIC police have arrested twelve men preparing to perpetrate an act of environmental terrorism in the VATNAJOKULL region, under cover of the current agitation sweeping through the world. It appears they were awaiting instructions to trigger a massive explosion that would have released millions of tons of ice into the North Atlantic, and which would also possibly cause volcanic eruptions leading to immense loss of life. There is some confusion about who exactly was the mastermind behind this conspiracy.

CENTRAL INTELLIGENCE AGENCY
TOP SECRET
Langley
RE: GEN-FORK; THE MISSING

Terrorists apprehended in ICELAND have been found to be carrying quantities of the genetic virus GEN-FORK. On arrival back in the USA, the one remaining terrorist (the other eleven are presumed to be amongst THE MISSING) was quarantined, questioned, and then 'disposed of'. GEN-FORK virus was removed for analysis. There is evidence of other terrorists planning to commit similar acts of destruction in INDIA, AFRICA, CHINA and MEXICO, but these are also considered to be among THE MISSING.

Following disclosures on the source of
the GEN-FORK virus, the UK government
has taken over the EISENCRICK INSTITUTE
and sealed it off until further investigations can be initiated.

05.31

Pascal Toluene has been defeated.

I sit down to wait. It shall not be long now. We're
entering the final moments as the shift begins to peak.
The rain stings my eyes, but I ignore it. The lightning
and thunder play with each other in the skies, and I
ignore that, too. All the recent weather anomalies
have been Nature's prelude to what is happening
now. Jake Crux comes and joins me. I feel my side,
where blood seeps out hot and viscous.

'I don't think we can do any more,' he says. 'I
helped rescue about a hundred. Hopefully they'll
have done the same with others. And so on, and so
on.'

He looks as though he has aged.

For some reason I think of how a river's shape
changes over time: how it erodes one bank while
building up another – always on the move, always
becoming something different. Nothing is ever constant.

'Look,' says Jake.

Down by the power station, the remaining crowd
of protesters are staring around, as though they've
lost something. I can still see the army vehicles and
police cars, but little sign of uniformed personnel. I
assume they, too, are now amongst The Missing.

I again feel as though something is different, as

though there is a gap of silence and space that needs filling – an awareness of something just outside recognizable vision, a memory that cannot be recalled.

The chanting that was ringing in my ears earlier now fades away.

I let my shoulders sag, and hear Jake let out a long sigh.

'It's over,' he says.

I notice that the rain, too, has stopped.

My CAMIC mobile quietly bleeps, indicating that Maxnet is still up and running.

But who'll be needing it now?

UNITED STATES DEPARTMENT OF JUSTICE
FEDERAL BUREAU OF INVESTIGATION
Washington Office
RE: THE SHIFT; DR JAKE CRUX

It is now calculated that between fifteen to twenty per cent of the world's population disappeared during THE SHIFT. Communities unable to receive DR JAKE CRUX'S broadcasts suffered the worst, though the Western world did not escape completely. Whole sections of humanity seem to have gone.

The majority of such SHIFTS throughout the world population occurred within a brief two-minute window, and those who survived through this period of peak activity attribute it mostly to receiving some form of psychic help from others more in tune with dealing with THE SHIFT. These fortunate ones then went on to help others.

Initially, about seventy per cent of the remaining population reported finding themselves unable to read but, aware of rediscovered ESP skills that helped them through, experiments are in progress to ascertain the range and diversity of man's reacquired capabilities. These powers come with a tremendous responsibility and a need for proper education in their use.

There is still a strong public desire to place restrictions on scientific and technological development, some perceiving them as a bar to the inner-personal development humanity has garnered from surviving THE SHIFT. The debate continues, but the consensus seems to be that mankind has been granted a gift. Like the discovery of fire, the benefits will depend on how we use it.

The world is now a changed place.

So is the entire universe.

Jake looks down at the blood pooling under his friend's fingertips.

Hey, Scott, you still don't really understand exactly what you've won, do you?

He reaches down and places his hand over Scott's midriff. He visualizes undamaged flesh; he imagines no pain.

He smiles as Scott frowns and tentatively removes his hand from his stomach and lifts his T-shirt. Beneath the blood is now a fresh scar. He looks up at Jake with a grin.

'Brave New World, Jake?' His voice sounds in Jake's head. *'We've evolved . . . but into what exactly?'* Scott then pats his newly healed stomach. *'This is terrifying – what will we do with it?'*

Jake sits down beside him. 'I don't know,' he says aloud.

Thoughts of Jenny crash into my mind and I stand up. I can just about hear her voice calling for me through the echoes of other people's thinking. For all my new-found abilities, I still don't know if it's our destiny to be together. It could mean a new adventure, a new journey. But I look forward to it.

The sky is rapidly clearing as the sun breaks through the clouds.

Somewhere in the distance, away over near the woods, I can hear a blackbird singing.

It sounds beautiful.

Don't rejoice in his defeat, you men. For though the world stood up and stopped the bastard, the bitch that bore him is in heat again.

Bertolt Brecht,
German playwright;
from his 1941 allegorical play about Hitler:
The Resistible Rise of Arturo Ui

The Team

Visit **www.panmacmillan.com** to read more about all our books and to buy them. You will also find features, author interviews and news of any author events, and you can sign up for e-newsletters so that you're always first to hear about our new releases.